# Osorkon

## Ruin of Sekhmet

Ryan Pope

Visit the author at www.ryanpopebooks.com

*Also available as an eBook.*

ISBN-13: 9798661231475

For my family who have supported me since I first put words to paper, and for my friends and beta readers who helped me get this book to where it needed to be. I could not have done it without you.

# Prologue

THE GOLDSMITH'S WORKSHOP was hot and smoky as the master and his apprentice stoked the forge fires to the sound of crackling coals and bubbling metal. The master looked up as a shadow crossed the doorway to his workshop, a tight smile tugging at the corner of his wrinkled mouth. Wordlessly, he passed the bellows to his apprentice and disappeared behind a curtain to the back room.

He returned with a cube of stone, little longer than his hand from fingertip to wrist, and set it on his workbench as the patron crossed the threshold to join him.

With chisel and mallet, the goldsmith cracked open the mould, careful not to scratch the precious work within. The cast fractured and crumbled, chips of stone tumbling from the workbench to the floor by the artisan's feet, before he took up a brush and gently cleaned the metal. The artisan set down his tools and held up his handiwork for his patron to inspect.

The gold heart was exquisite, tiny veins tracing the surface and fat arteries leading from the central chambers as they did in life. The goldsmith held it out to his patron who took it reverently in his hands, admiring the detail that had gone into the mould. The metal shone in the sunlight spilling through the window and the patron nodded in approval at the satisfying weight.

It was perfect in every way, a replica to replace one that was lost.

Osorkon handed the heart back to the goldsmith who wrapped it in a linen shroud and stowed it away in a nondescript crate. The master barked at his apprentice who scurried to the back room and brought forth three more crates of similar dimensions.

'Lungs, liver and intestines,' said the artisan. 'Made to your specifications.'

Osorkon nodded and opened the crates one by one to inspect their contents, ignoring the goldsmith's sniff of displeasure.

'You have done fine work, artisan. May Anubis think the same,' said Osorkon, directing his companions to collect the crates.

'Anubis will pass it. The demoness Ammit will go hungry this day.' The goldsmith coughed lightly and Osorkon smiled thinly, gesturing for his men to bring the artisan's payment. One of the companions returned with a hippopotamus tusk the length of a man's leg and set it on the goldsmith's workbench.

The goldsmith ran his hands over the ivory, searching for cracks or flaws but found none.

'I trust this is sufficient?' asked Osorkon.

'As agreed, my prince,' replied the goldsmith, with a shallow bow.

'The House of Herakleopolis thanks you for your service,' said Osorkon by way of goodbye before he turned and stepped out into the light.

'We supplied the gold. His price was too steep,' grumbled the man who had brought the tusk inside. Behind him, four more companions fanned out behind the pair.

'There are few in this land with his skill and dedication, Akhetep,' replied Osorkon. 'It is a small price to pay for Tibekh's resurrection.'

'As you say,' said Akhetep, unwilling to risk his friend's recent temper. 'Where are we going?'

'To the House of Purification. The proper consecrations must be in place if Anubis is to allow my cousin to pass beyond the scales.'

'Ah.'

'Those with good intentions have nothing to fear,' said Osorkon, his gaze fixed ahead.

The House of Purification for the loftiest nobility was at the edge of the temple district, a part of, but also apart from, the holy houses of the gods. Here were the servants of death, the embalming priests who worked among the neither here nor there. It was they who ensured the deceased's body would be preserved for eternity and so allow the spirit to be regenerated anew. Here the magic and rituals gave dead flesh life again, beckoning the elements of the spirit back home to receive the strength needed to face the myriad tests required to reached eternal life in the Field of Reeds.

It was not a place the living often went willingly.

The path from the goldsmith's workshop was through an affluent district of Herakleopolis, where the tutors, scribes, master craftsmen and minor nobility lived and worked in quiet, peaceful prosperity.

'It is as silent as the tomb valleys,' muttered Akhetep, suppressing a shiver even in the noon heat. The death of the nomarch's last surviving son had hit the city hard, but not as hard as the fear of the nomarch's vengeance against those he decided were lax in their grief. Curtains were pulled shut over windows and doors were closed to every house they passed by. The absence of playing children or the sound of social occasions likewise seemed plain wrong.

'The period of mourning is only halfway done,' said Osorkon with a grimace. 'Nothing can be decided and nothing done until it is over.'

Akhetep caught the expression and lowered his voice to a whisper.

'What is on your mind? You have been avoiding the Crag.'

Osorkon glanced sideways at his friend but said nothing, the crate with the golden heart clutched tightly to his chest.

'It has been weeks and this now is the most I have heard from you. Speak to me as a friend, I beg you,' said Akhetep, catching Osorkon's arm and pulling him to stand face to face.

Osorkon glowered, glancing sideways at the four charioteers following them. Each man watched their prince and commander unblinking.

'It is nothing,' Osorkon said finally. He pulled his arm free and set off down the street.

Akhetep let him go, ignoring the pitied looks from his men as the prince walked alone into the temple square.

Like the district through which they had passed, the temple quarter was almost deserted, though the temporal needs of the gods forbid it from being silent completely. Small groups of priests regarded their passing with curiosity, some offering a bow or nod of greeting as they recognised the Crown Prince. Others just watched the grim procession with fascination as the Thebans left the main square for the path to the House of Purification.

Akhetep was not to be denied. 'You think of Karoadjet? You fear she will change her mind,' he said, watching the barb strike home.

'That is for her to decide,' snapped Osorkon. 'Now, be silent. The Keepers of Death approach.'

Ahead, the House of Purification stood alone, the smell of brine and natron salt wafting down the street in the low breeze. The street parted around this temple of death, providing a ring of distance between the natron salt baths and the houses and workshops of the living.

A lone embalmer stood at the building's entrance, pale and shrouded in linen and animal pelts. He bowed at the waist as the Thebans approached, gesturing with thin fingers to follow him inside.

Osorkon nodded in return and stepped through the portal, the sandstone arch carved with spells and scenes of devotion and divine offering. Here the powers of Anubis and Osiris were at their greatest, the guardian jackal and the resurrected lord of the underworld watching on in patient judgement.

Without the ministrations of the embalmers, Egyptian society would cease to function, and yet Osorkon could not entirely help his fear and distaste at the services of the house. The stagnant air felt stale and thick and the smell of dead flesh seemed to cling to his skin, overpowering the perfumed oils he was accustomed to.

His cousin's body was not the only one entrusted to the care of the house, and within the building's chambers and courtyards, Osorkon could see the bodies of men, women, and children undergoing the various stages of the mummification process.

Several corpses lay naked on stone slabs, kept under a linen canopy in the outside air in the neighbouring Place of Purification. Each of them was covered in layers of natron salt for forty days to prevent rot setting in, but there were others still that had been freshly brought to the house. Osorkon turned away as he spied the embalmers attending to the corpse of a child, no more than two or three years of age. With dispassionate service, the embalmers made a deep incision into the child's right side and with practised precision, cut and then pulled out the bulk of the child's viscera onto the slab beside him.

The rear of the house was reserved for services afforded to the richest and most powerful and it was there that Osorkon found the house hierarchs. They turned as one as the Thebans entered the chamber, and Osorkon caught a glimpse of a desiccated corpse on the stone slab behind them.

'Honoured priests, I have come with offerings to Anubis, may he smile upon the nomarch's son,' said Osorkon, setting his crate on an empty table and bidding the charioteers to do the same.

The chief embalmer was pallid and thin, his long life spent among corpses and the magic of the land in-between worlds. He plucked the golden heart from the crate and held it to the torchlight. Fire shone from the burnished metal and the old man nodded in satisfaction.

'This will be sufficient,' he said, his voice reed thin.

'May I see him?'

The old man regarded the Theban prince for a moment before he slowly nodded and returned to his work. After six weeks, Tibekh's body had been freshly exhumed from the layers of natron salt. In that time the salt had stolen the moisture from his flesh and made his earthly body hard and unyielding. Tibekh's features had taken on the waxen and stretched texture of mummification and his body was wasted and shrunken, even more so than he had been in life.

He looks like a child, Osorkon thought, taken long before his time by the mindless fury of a bull hippopotamus. Osorkon tore his gaze from his cousin's face to the wound that had killed him.

Artisans of dead flesh, the embalmers had repaired the gaping hole in Tibekh's chest with thick stitching as best they could, but the deep tear ran like a ridge from his collarbones to his navel. Osorkon watched as embalmers cut the stitching, pulling the wound open once more as they retrieved the linen wadding and salt from inside Tibekh's chest cavity.

The chief embalmer waited until Tibekh's chest was hollow before he slipped his hand through the sleeve of dried flesh, setting the golden heart in place where the organ of life had once been.

'The others organs will be buried separately,' said the old man. 'Your service is at an end.'

Osorkon bowed in gratitude and lingered a moment more before he followed his men back the way they came. Most, including Akhetep, tried not to run back into the light and open air.

Osorkon breathed deep of the fresh air and closed his eyes as the sun warmed his skin. He felt no different than before, the hollow ache in his chest stubborn in its persistence. He turned to his second-in-command as the charioteers made to follow him.

'Set a guard, Akhetep. I entrust the house's protection to you until Tibekh's burial. Those golden organs are worth a pharaoh's ransom.'

Akhetep frowned. 'Who in their right mind would break into an embalming house?'

'Very few,' conceded Osorkon, 'but the land is no longer in its right mind. See to it that none disturb my cousin's rest.'

Akhetep watched as Osorkon took his leave, heading back alone towards the nomarch's palace and the home of his grieving uncle. The nomarch himself had ordered the bulk of the army of Thebes to head north for the inevitable clash against Shoshenq of Tanis, citing the logistical demands on his city. Unwilling to displease his brother more than his royal requisition of Herakleopolis already had, Pharaoh had been compelled to obey. The departure had left the presence of Theban soldiers in the city uncomfortably light, but even so there should have been a hundred others that could have been assigned such a laborious and drudging guard duty.

Akhetep shrugged in apology as he rejoined the four charioteers to form a perimeter around the house's entrance. Despite the prince's warning, not a single soul disturbed the silence of the city streets.

'It is a dark day when the most life to be found is in the Temple of Death,' he grumbled.

# Chapter One

THE LIGHT OF day shone on the people of Thebes, but Harsiese went to the Vizier's Palace with a dull ache in his heart. Borne aloft in his carrying chair, his gaze roamed freely over the heads of the crowd, but he noticed none of the hundreds of faces streamed past him with respectful awe, his thoughts too dark and disturbed to appreciate the respect due him.

His four litter-bearers moved with perfect rhythm, surrounded by a unit of his household guard, who pushed and bludgeoned aside those too slow to recognise the High Priest of Amun. Behind him, six more guards followed in his wake, a veritable show of force in the nobles' quarter and a reminder of his divine authority.

And such a reminder was needed, now more than ever.

Behind the façade of routine, an undercurrent of tension ran through the City of Priests. Life in Thebes had become tumultuous and unbalanced in the year since Takelot's coup against the former vizier Nakhtefmut. Where once there was order, now there was confusion as though the social pyramid was crumbling under its own weight.

The Priesthood of Amun was no longer of one mind and division and internal strife threatened to undo their hegemony if it was not soon contained. Even within his own administration he knew there were those that plotted against him.

Try as he might to rationalise away what he had seen he knew in his heart the poison they whispered when they thought themselves hidden away. The guilt of Senmut, Tasenhor and the others was no longer in question, and he knew the time was fast approaching when they would dare to take their treason into the open. That he was still alive meant they either still considered him useful or did not yet have the strength to depose him, but Harsiese was not fool enough to hope the status quo would last much longer. Soon, he would be forced to upset the temple's order by striking first and therein lay the problem. The rot was there, but how far did it spread? Could the wound be cleaned or was it safer to remove the limb?

Harsiese's concentration was broken as a bearer stumbled over a loose rock, unbalancing the chair and threatening to spill the High Priest onto the road. Like a horseman spurring on his mount, Harsiese reached down and whipped the offending bearer across the ear with his walking staff, satisfied at the man's sharp gasp of pain. The man glanced back at his master, but Harsiese's attention had already drifted.

The traffic began to thin as Harsiese entered the plaza outside the palace, a wide, open space that only a year before had been the site of a bloody siege. The Crown Prince Osorkon had taken the palace by force, deposing the old order to free his father from the executioner's sword. Despite the odds stacked against him, Osorkon's gambit had succeeded, spawning a new dynasty that was still finding its feet for good or ill.

The influence of this new dynasty on the politics of Karnak was still being revealed, and only through prayer and careful deliberation would the right path forward come to light. Until then, Harsiese was content to be patient under Amun's wisdom, trusting in the god to reveal the proper action at the opportune time.

He had their names, he knew them, but he had precious little proof. Without evidence, he risked instigating a battle of words that would ultimately lead to blanket sanctions against the temple. All would suffer for the actions of the few. Something had to happen. Before the few became the many.

Sarasesh was young and naïve, prone to fall in with the energetic rhetoric and religious fervour of revolution. Others, like Naroleth and Tasenhor, had served the temples for many years and held many important posts. In their case, ignorance was no excuse.

And behind it all was Senmut, he who Harsiese had once called friend. He who had led the priesthood astray. Men he had served beside for a lifetime had thrown their support behind this traitor, taken up by his honeyed promises of wealth and power. Slowly but surely, Senmut was tipping the numbers in his favour. Harsiese had felt their eyes on him for weeks, watching where he went and with whom he met, just as he was certain they tracked his passage now.

For an unexpected moment, Harsiese felt a touch of envy for those who eked out their existence in the mud brick hovels on the river shore. Their existence would go on unimpeded, no matter who sat on the throne or tended to the will of the gods. Not for them the gilded shackles of wealth and power, but the freedom and safety of poverty.

His musing was again broken as the captain of his guard called the column to a halt and the bearers lowered Harsiese's chair to the street. He climbed the palace steps two at a time, eager to be away from the masses and within the relative sanctuary of the palace walls.

His guards followed him to the entrance of the audience chamber, escorting him past the long line of petitioners who regarded the hierarch with sullen looks. Harsiese straightened the vestments of his office, a white shendyt and linen robe with an antelope skin draped across his shoulders, and went through the great doorway alone.

The scale of the audience chamber never failed to impress Harsiese. The hall was long and narrow, giving the seated ruler time to gauge each supplicant as they approached. Immense stone pillars flanked the walkway, supporting a cavernous ceiling marred with soot and smoke. Between the pillars, burning braziers gave the chamber a low-lit glow that compensated for the little daylight that filtered through the hall's high windows.

Beyond the pillars, the walls of the hall were decorated with scenes of Egypt's military might, vistas of subjugated peoples from distant lands crushed under the heel of the Vizier and his generals. Such was the chamber's grandeur, Harsiese didn't notice the cringing creature kneeling before the dais until he had nearly stepped on him.

Prostrate and trembling, the man knelt with his forehead against the ground as he awaited whatever judgement faced him. The palace guards stood on the lower steps of the dais with their spears held at attention. Further up, scribes sat on the stone steps, taking note of the vizier's decisions. Behind the throne, a gaggle of court advisors and councillors watched on with undisguised contempt.

At the centre of the gathering, the young vizier contemplated his decision. Hory, son of Nakhtefmut, drummed his fingers on the arm of his chair, offering Harsiese a weak smile as the High Priest joined them.

The garish throne that Hory's father had once ruled from had been replaced with a simpler and more austere chair, Harsiese noted with approval. But he was not alone. Where once there had been one chair, now there were two. Its twin sat to the vizier's left, occupied by Hory's wife, the Princess Isetweret. The daughter of Takelot and Karomama nodded an almost imperceptible greeting to the High Priest before she turned her gaze back to the trembling man. The man was clad in a tattered shendyt that barely covered his dignity and his face was purple with bruising. He cowered before the assembled dignitaries, searching for a sympathetic face but finding none.

'You have this one chance, Heret. Do you deny the accusations?' asked Hory. The vizier leaned forward in his chair, his face a mask of concern.

'Mercy, lord. Please, mercy,' said Heret, and he began to cry.

'That is as good as an admission of guilt,' said Hory, leaning back with a sigh. He stared down at the sobbing captive, letting the moment drag out.

Isetweret's hand brushed her husband's arm and his mouth set firm.

'Take him outside and cut off his nose and hands,' said Hory, looking over the head of the sentenced to the door beyond.

Heret paled and tried to rise, panic lending him strength. He managed just one step before a guard stepped forward and floored him with a single punch. Two more hauled the man's unconscious form away.

Hory waved the other guards back and bid Harsiese to approach the throne.

'A thief caught in the tomb valley,' said Hory, by way of explanation. 'Rest assured his punishment is a light one.'

Light indeed, thought Harsiese. Your father would have skinned him alive.

'It is good of you to come, my lord,' said Hory. 'We have not had the pleasure of your presence in some time.'

'To live in service of the temples is not an idle life,' said Harsiese, with a forced smile.

'The temples are well?'

'They are, Lord Vizier,' said Harsiese. He bowed a fraction at the waist, his hands clasped together in front of him. 'How may I serve?'

'To business then. I asked you to come because of this,' said Hory, gesturing for one of the scribes. The scribe bowed low and pressed a papyrus scroll into the High Priest's hand.

'I have received a requisition order from Third Prophet Senmut that is… unusual,' continued Hory as Harsiese read. 'Is it correct?'

Harsiese did not catch the frown before it crossed his face as he read and re-read the scroll. It was marked with the seal of the prophets and appeared to be authentic, but the order was magnitudes larger than anything he would ever have approved himself.

'I hope I have not offended you. I would have sent a man to Karnak, but I hear the temples are not so fond of outside interference,' said Hory, mistaking the source of Harsiese's discomfort.

Harsiese smiled thinly as he met the young vizier's gaze. Hory's features were that of his father twenty years before, but where Nakhtefmut's had been carved of stone, unyielding in their scrutiny, Hory's were soft and open, a clear mirror of his thoughts. Without his father's influence to curb it, Hory's natural honesty shone forth without restraint.

Harsiese would have to correct that himself, sooner rather than later.

'No offence is taken, I assure you. It is good to leave the precinct once in a while. Too long among the incense makes even me lightheaded,' he said, smiling as Hory laughed.

'Such a large request for temple-quality frankincense and myrrh is going to be expensive. What is it for?'

What are you planning, Senmut? Harsiese wondered, almost laughing at Hory's understatement. The order was enough to sustain the precinct of Amun for six months or more, discounting the stores already secure within the Karnak warehouses.

Harsiese recovered quickly. 'In times such as these, the proper food offerings are difficult to source, but the gods understand that our country is in need. We can compensate with additional gifts for the time being. They smile upon your rule and the prosperity of Thebes.'

Hory smiled again, but Isetweret was unmoved.

'I am pleased to hear it, but the precincts usually take care of their own supply do they not?' said Hory.

'They do.'

'And the shipment is not destined for Thebes, but Asyut, Qena and a number of smaller temples. Surely it is safer within the precinct walls before distributing it to those in need?'

'Were the people to become aware of such wealth flowing into the temples, they might begin to ask why we cannot afford to feed them. You understand that we could not risk the city's stability by bringing it in all at once.'

'Very astute, High Priest. Karnak is safe in your hands. To transport such riches from Punt will not be easy. The security detail alone will be expensive.'

Harsiese nodded thoughtfully as though he was considering the wisdom in the young Vizier's words. After a moment he smiled, coming to a decision. 'You are correct, Lord Vizier. It seems my prophets have been overzealous in their devotions. I will amend it. One-eighth of this amount will be sufficient for the remainder of the season. It would also be best if the shipment came directly to the palace stores. Please send for me personally upon arrival and I will oversee the transfer to Karnak.'

Seemingly satisfied, Hory bid the scribes to make note of his approval.

'All is well then, my Lord Harsiese?' asked Isetweret.

Harsiese looked up at her, almost surprised. She had not spoken the entire time he had been here. She had barely moved at all. 'It is. Senmut works with my complete confidence and trust, but sometimes even the prophets need a guiding hand.'

'Then I shall see to it,' said Hory, his radiant smile a contrast with Isetweret's scrutiny.

In his mid-twenties, Hory had nothing to his name but the ancestral blood in his veins. He had won no military victories, nor did he hold any of the religious offices a noble's son might be expected to have. But for the dubious fortune of being Nakhtefmut's only son and heir, he might have been content in another life as a tanner or baker.

Takelot's favour had granted Hory another chance, an offer of amnesty to the son of the man who had wished him dead. Few, including Hory himself likely, were under the illusion that he was anything more than a puppet vizier under Takelot's authority.

But Takelot was no longer here.

Eager to change the subject, Harsiese smiled up at the ruling couple again. 'How fares Pharaoh's campaign against Tanis and the usurper? Has there been word from Herakleopolis?'

'My cousin Tibekh was killed in a hunting accident,' said Isetweret. 'Other than that, there has been little of note.'

Momentarily wrongfooted, Harsiese's smile fell. 'My heart grieves at the news. If there is anything your family needs?'

Isetweret dipped her head in acknowledgement but said nothing more.

'Your brothers are well, I trust?'

'I have not heard,' replied Isetweret, watching him watch her.

She was every inch her mother's daughter, closed and reserved where her brothers were fire and passion. She would have made a valuable ally, thought Harsiese with a tinge of regret.

NAROLETH PACED BACK and forth in the office, pausing momentarily to shoot an accusatory glare at the Third Prophet. He stopped at the window, peering out at the life in Karnak, before he resumed his pacing. 'Harsiese knows,' he hissed, shaking his head. He glanced down at the central table where a stack of reports from

Senmut's agents in the south lay discarded. Almost at once, the wealth they had been accumulating in the name of the temple had dried up, their requisition orders cut or redirected entirely. Missives from suppliers seeking confirmation came almost daily. The last of them, a hastily drawn note written by a sympathetic palace scribe scant hours ago, had seen their order of incense cut to a fraction of what it was. There was only one man still in Thebes with the power and the will to do so.

'You worry like an old woman, Naroleth. Sit down and take a drink,' said Senmut, pouring himself another cup of wine. The room was small, even with just four of them. On the edge of the precinct of Amun, the office block was well out of the way of prying eyes or so the conspirators hoped.

Tasenhor held his wine steadily, watching the exchange with hooded eyes. Sarasesh sat in the corner, the young priest glaring at Naroleth as he drummed his fingers on the desk.

'How are you all so calm?' demanded Naroleth. He took another peek through the window before a cup was pressed into his hand.

'Hysterics gets us nowhere,' said Tasenhor, sitting back down. 'Harsiese is ignorant, but he is not a fool. It was stupid to think that an entire baggage train full of incense would not raise questions, even to that idiot boy vizier.'

'And when Harsiese finds out what we have done he will have us all killed. And if not him, then Takelot will do so,' said Naroleth. The priest began pacing again. When no one else spoke, he drained his cup in one gulp and slammed it onto the table. 'The plan was simple. By the grace of the gods, you somehow convinced a group of bickering tribes in Nubia to fight for us. That incense was going to pass through their territory with all the haste of an arthritic oxen, protected by a few dozen guards against three thousand tribesmen. That incense was enough to buy them outright. Enough to silence their greed and competition until Takelot is dead. Now Harsiese has changed it to what? A few scant crates?'

'Which is still valuable and will still be travelling the same road. When the Nubians reach Egypt, they will see just how much food and beer they can trade with it,' said Senmut. 'You disappoint me, all of you. This is a setback but a welcome one. Tell me how.'

The three conspirators turned to Senmut, frowning in confusion. He sighed and reached for the wine jug, taking his time to fill it entirely before he began to speak.

'As you said, Harsiese is not a fool but he is alone. Tell me, who in Thebes right now can Harsiese call upon as a friend? A true friend?' Senmut let the silence linger. 'I cannot give you even one name,' he said.

'So, your plan is to do what? Wait for him to expose us to the vizier?' asked Tasenhor.

'And risk losing face to the boy and Takelot's daughter? Harsiese would not dare. No, he will try to handle it himself, believing he has the initiative, but by then it will be too late. We keep his attention directed elsewhere, searching for conspiracy in the warehouses or the temple supply while the true threat to him remains hidden. He will join us or be cast out. I truly do not care which.'

'Which might work but for the fact your bloody Nubians can't march north without killing each other,' snapped Naroleth. 'What are we to do without an army? Preach Takelot to death?'

'Keep your voice down,' snapped Senmut, his previous humour gone. 'We are not finished yet.'

Tasenhor shook his head. 'The tribes stand together while they are paid to stand together. As soon as it runs dry, they will fall back to squabbling among themselves. None of them will follow a rival chief and even to get them to muster seems impossible without blood being spilled. Order hangs on the edge of a blade. You read the reports yourself.'

Senmut smiled. 'Do you have so little faith in me, my friends? Have I not foreseen every challenge to our plans and adjusted accordingly?'

'You have, Third Prophet,' said Sarasesh.

'Did you think me idle? None of you could have achieved what I have. None of you has vision, true vision. I have seen the way. There is one who will solve our inter-fighting.'

Senmut got to his feet and poured out a measure of wine for each member. This time Naroleth took it without argument.

'Off the shores of Punt, there is a terror that haunts the Red Sea. We have lost some of our own shipping to him in the past, but to the towns of that coastline he is a scourge of nightmares. A pirate lord of fearsome reputation with a fleet to match.'

Tasenhor chuckled as he swirled the contents of his cup. 'Your answer is pirates? Will they carry their vessels across the desert and into the river?'

Senmut shook his head. 'They will not need ships, not to sack cities.'

'As you say,' said Tasenhor. 'But what is special about this pirate lord? Why him of all men?'

'I have heard it said that even the chiefs of that region, the land of Bagrawiyah, fear this pirate. If he can keep a band of pirates together for ten years and escape capture by the King of Nubia while doing so, he can lead a band of unruly tribes. He was once a prince of Punt before his excesses led him to banishment,' said Senmut.

'How do you know this?'

'I am not so blinded by these walls as you all seem to be. The world is vast and opportunity lies everywhere if you know where to look.'

Tasenhor looked nonplussed. 'Who is he?'

'Malkesh.'

Tasenhor shrugged and grunted. 'The name means nothing to me. How did you track him down? Pirates generally do not like being found.'

'I sent a number of messengers searching for him.'

Tasenhor grunted. 'How many did you lose?'

'Enough,' said Senmut.

'And we knew nothing of any of this,' snapped Naroleth. 'How do you propose to bring a bloodthirsty pirate lord to heel?'

'Pirates love gold. We will compensate him with more than enough.'

'That may not be possible, Third Prophet,' said Sarasesh. 'The gold that Osorkon found under the Meshwesh fortress is almost gone and we will have to replace it before Pharaoh returns.'

'Ah yes, the gold Takelot had us swear to secrecy. No matter, we don't need it. Harsiese was generous enough to wait before he undercut our business. Incense, grain and precious stones are as useful to a pirate as gold. We have enough to begin.'

'You have made great strides without us, Senmut. How much more have you done without our knowledge?' asked Tasenhor.

Senmut smiled again. 'Nothing else, brother. Do not pout.' He turned to address the others. 'My friends, the fewer of us that know, the greater our chance of success. I trust you all, but an overheard word could spell our doom. Leave the particulars to me, but know I still have need of you.

'How?' asked Naroleth.

'A trusted representative of the priesthood with a suitable gift will make contact with Malkesh. He is hungry, but yet to bite the hook. One of us must buy his loyalty in person.'

Tasenhor's eyes narrowed, as Senmut turned to smile at Sarasesh.

'Sarasesh, I entrust this special mission to you,' said Senmut, turning to the youngest member of their gathering. 'You will go beyond Abu Simbel and bring this Malkesh to the muster. Lead him back to Thebes at the head of the Nubian army and we will have to power to bring Thebes to the true path, free of squabbling pharaohs and ruled by the priests as it was in days past. Should you fail, I fear our cause is lost.'

Sarasesh's eyes widened. 'Me?' he whispered. Senmut indulged him with a nod and the young priest knelt, ignoring Tasenhor's grunt of amusement. 'I will not fail.'

Naroleth bowed his head. 'Forgive me, Third Prophet. I should not have doubted you.'

'No, you should not have but you are forgiven,' said Senmut.

'And if anyone asks where Sarasesh has gone?' asked Tasenhor.

'They will not. We have Takelot to thank for that. What is one more missionary on the road? Tell them, "Sarasesh has departed for Punt to bring light to the darkness" or something like that. It is true, in a manner of speaking.'

'I am honoured beyond words with your trust,' said Sarasesh, his eyes fixed on the dirt in front of him.

Yes, I am sure you are, thought Senmut.

HIGH PRIEST HARSIESE was hiding something. That much was clear.

Isetweret paced down the palace corridor, ignoring the hasty bows and muttered greetings of the servants she passed. She resisted the urge to run. She would not have long before her absence in the palace was noted and she had no desire to be subjected to her husband's barrage of questions, however well-intentioned they might be.

The afternoon had passed in dreary boredom as a seemingly endless line of petitioners sought her husband's support to enforce debts owed to them or beg for leniency in their taxes and farming quotas.

She had barely registered any of it.

Harsiese's guarded words were etched into her mind as she searched for the meaning beyond the platitudes. There was something ill happening in Karnak and she resolved to find out what it was.

The palace was vast but she had endeavoured, upon her betrothal to Hory three years earlier, to learn every one of its secrets. It had only been through his knowledge of the palace's hidden pathways that her now-exiled father-in-law Nakhtefmut had evaded death at the hands of her brothers. Isetweret knew that the time may come when her own survival hinged on that knowledge. The safety and surety she had known as a child was fading a little bit more with each new day.

She stopped in the middle of a vast hallway that led to the palace's north wing and drew her shawl up and over her head. Her dress was plain, as she preferred, and she had removed much of the ostentatious jewellery that was expected of her office. Simple bronze bracelets banded her wrists and a leather cord with a silver image of Taweret hung at her throat, a recent addition to the icons of Mut she usually wore.

Content that she was alone for the moment, she slipped down a side corridor and through a doorway leading to the servants' passageways. The walls here were rough and unadorned. At this hour before dusk, most of the servants would be engaged in the kitchen or dining areas and the silence emboldened her further.

As the middle child she had grown up left to her own devices, with none of the pressures placed on the eldest, nor the coddling nurture imposed on the youngest. She was not destined to be a general or a prophet and in truth, service in the temples as a singer or divine adoratrice had never held much appeal to her. Her potential lay in her bloodline and her marriage to the vizier's son had secured that until Nakhtefmut had betrayed her family.

Now she would keep what she had won for herself, opening up the secrets of Karnak herself if she had to. The priests there led a blinkered existence, wilfully blind to the true order of the land. Her brothers would charge in with swords and spear, her father too, come to think of it. She loved them all, but they possessed none of the subtleties her mother had taught her. Her father had claimed the throne, but it was her mother that helped him keep it.

Isetweret shut the door behind her and crept down the stairs to a cellar that was long out of use. Cobwebs and empty crates concealed a reinforced timber gate, leading to a tunnel that emerged in an abandoned warehouse beside the Karnak precincts.

The trapdoor in the warehouse floor was surprisingly agreeable and she dusted herself off before she slipped through a side door and joined the evening traffic in the temple precinct. She found a quiet place to wait and watched the end of the Avenue of Rams at the outermost portal of the Precinct of Amun.

She watched the people pass by as she waited, the hubbub a stirring change to the lonesome silence that often filled the palace. None of those that passed her gave her more than a cursory glance and she felt a quiet thrill at being among the people unchaperoned.

Her quarry emerged from the temple gateway portal only after the sun had set completely and Isetweret rose to follow. Most of the priests walked with their heads down, exhausted after hours of prayer service or scribe work. With their shaved heads and plain shendyts, they all looked alike. Even so, it would only take one to recognise her for her plan to be undone. Had her husband known where she was, he would confine her to the palace in his naivety.

Sweet Hory with his idle dreams of greatness. He had a good heart and she was very fond of him, but his kindness was his only strength and one of his many weaknesses.

The pair of robed figures she followed forged ahead, their priestly garb ensuring they were given a respectful berth. Her common clothing gave her no such advantage and twice she lost them among the crowd before she spied them turning towards the nobles' quarter. Here the traffic was less dense and she caught up the distance easily, stopping at a cloth vendor when the pair paused to speak in the middle of the street.

After a moment they continued and she muttered her thanks to the merchant before she followed. She frowned as the pair made an abrupt turn down a side street and Isetweret jogged to keep up, pausing at the corner. The alley was dark and Isetweret strained to listen for footsteps over the sound of nearby taverns. She took a hesitant step forward and a metallic flash lashed out at her as she was thrown back hard against the wall.

Her head cracked against the bricks and she blinked away stars, suddenly aware of a sharp pinprick at her belly. One hand went to the point of the blade, desperately warding it off, while the other went to her throat, clutching the silver pendant of Taweret.

'Who are you and why are you following me?' hissed a voice.

'Pedubast,' gasped Isetweret, showing her empty palms to the priest.

Pedubast's eyes widened in recognition and he stepped back, dragging Isetweret further into the darkened alleyway. 'Princess, forgive me,' he said, slotting the dagger back into a sheath at his hip. He took off his cloak and draped it around Isetweret as the princess began to tremble in shock. The second figure emerged from the shadows and Isetweret managed a nod of greeting to Pedubast's brother, Iuput.

'One can never be too careful in times such as these,' said Pedubast, guiding her to sit on a step. His voice was low and melodious and she felt herself relax in his presence.

Isetweret slipped the shawl from her head. Her hair was cropped short and she ran her fingers through it as she collected herself.

'That is why I have sought you out,' she replied.

Pedubast glanced back down the alley, but the evening traffic passed by oblivious to the royalty in their midst. The priest took Isetweret by the arm and led her further into the alley.

'We should talk somewhere safer. Why are you here?'

Isetweret looked between the brothers. There was no going back now.

'I need your help,' she said.

# Chapter Two

IN HIS TWENTY-THREE years, Sarasesh had rarely set foot beyond the walls of Thebes. The villages and lands beyond the city boundaries were untamed and uncivilised and hardly worth the attention of a son of nobility raised in the City of the Gods. The token inspection of his father's holdings every flood season was an uncomfortable enough obligation that he had learned to endure.

In truth, there was little beyond the limits of the city that had ever interested Sarasesh, for his ambitions lay solely within the temples and the comforts of home. What was there of value that could not already be found within the troves of wisdom housed in the temple libraries? What luxury was not already available in the market squares and what sense of wonder could ever be stoked after witnessing the luminous vistas of the Great Hypostyle Hall?

The intimate trust of the Third Prophet, soon to be the new High Priest of Amun, had skewed those perceptions almost overnight. Thebes was the heart of the world, but he had been naïve to believe it existed elevated from the fabric of the world. Power and wealth now lay within his grasp if he had but the courage and faith to reach out and take it. Perhaps he would even rule as Senmut's right hand when the time came to throw off the shackles of royal rule.

Only the truly chosen would be blessed with such a chance at glory.

Sarasesh had dwelled on these thoughts for five days as he sailed south to the Aswan Cataract and beyond. The *Sobek is Content* was a small ship of twenty crew with a hold laden with gifts and supplies.

Richest of all was much of the remaining treasure that Prince Osorkon had wrested from the Meshwesh when he had struck down Great Chief Harelothis. Hidden behind a false wall in the ship's hull was secreted half a dozen chests of gold, iron and precious stones a substantial sum of what was left after Takelot had finished buying the loyalty of Hermopolis and Herakleopolis. Senmut had gambled it would be enough to buy Malkesh's trust, for they had no choice in the matter.

Using the prince's spoils to help unseat his father had been a source of delicious irony to Senmut, and Sarasesh considered that at least some of his rare generosity came purely from spite. Knowledge of the treasure under his aegis left him with a constant sense of unease on what was otherwise a gentle voyage, at least in mariner's terms.

The motion of the ship left him unsteady and his head swam as he tried to sleep each night, but it was a small price to pay to ensure Karnak's freedom. He would lead Malkesh back to Thebes and beyond, crushing the heretic king Takelot and paving the way for the rightful rule of his city under the Priesthood of Amun.

'We'll be coming up to Hesehem later this afternoon, my lord,' said the ship's captain, hauling on the tiller to follow the river's course.

'There is a sense of destiny in the air, Neptef. Can you feel it?'

'As you say, lord,' said Neptef.

Sarasesh grunted and returned to his watch. The captain was a dour man, dull and unimaginative as was usual among the common people, but he worked with purpose and had delivered Sarasesh up the river in good time.

Now that he was out here, Sarasesh found himself enjoying the sense of adventure. Behind him, the captain coughed and spat over the side, much to the priest's disgust. Sarasesh turned to rebuke him when Neptef forestalled him, sniffing at the air.

'Do you smell that?'

Sarasesh shook his head. All he could smell was the earthy stink of the river and the wretched odour of the silt mud crusted on the banks.

'What is it?' he asked.

Neptef frowned and sniffed again.

'Smoke,' said the captain, securing the tiller with rope and running across the deck past his bewildered sailors to the ship's hold. He emerged a moment later confused and ordered his men to find the source of the smell.

Sarasesh ignored them all, until the faint smell of ash reached him and he stepped down onto the main deck heading towards the ship's bow. Neptef joined him and the pair regarded the orange and black vista before them.

On the southern horizon a dust storm had been rolling in since sunrise, but as Neptef stared at it with dawning recognition, Sarasesh realised that it had never moved. The first kernel of doubt wormed its way into Sarasesh's gut for he possessed a secret known only to Senmut and himself.

Malkesh did not need to be bought. He already was. The allure of wealth drew him from the sea but a real reward was required to keep him on dry land.

The temple's order for months' worth of frankincense would never arrive. Its loss would be blamed on the Kingdom of Punt and restitution demanded at the point of a sword. Not even the boy vizier Hory could ignore an insult such as that.

It was brilliant and Sarasesh's admiration for Senmut grew daily.

The fact that this Malkesh had already agreed to fight for them made his plan guaranteed to succeed and his glory as the forerunner of their salvation assured. 'Go to Hesehem and find Malkesh. I have promised him more gold than is in a pharaoh's tomb. Gold we do not yet have. You must stall him until Takelot is destroyed. We will buy his peace then,' Senmut had told him. The omission with their conspirators sat ill with him, but Senmut assured him it was necessary and so Sarasesh had departed with a hopeful heart, trusting that Naroleth and Tasenhor would understand when the truth inevitably came to light. How could they not understand when they realised the honour and victory he would bring to the priesthood of Amun?

'Slowly now. Half sail and keep it steady,' called Neptef, his eyes fixed on the distant haze. The sailor on the tiller nodded his acquiescence once and then the ship went quiet. The hours went by slowly as the *Sobek is Content* sailed towards its destination. As the ship came closer to shore there could be no mistake that something terrible had happened to the people of Hesehem.

'Steady, men. Keep your arms close and watch the shoreline,' said Neptef as the *Sobek* sailed sedately fifty metres from shore. The ship's crew looked upon the scene with horrified fascination.

Hesehem was no more. Huts had been burned to cinders and charred frames. The people had fared no better. Sarasesh could see the shapes of torn bodies left where they had fallen.

'Set's arse,' breathed Sarasesh, holding a linen kerchief over his nose and mouth.

'This is the agreed upon place, lord,' said Neptef gently.

'Are you sure?'

'Yes.'

Sarasesh swallowed. 'By Apophis, what has happened here?'

'Perhaps you can ask the man you are seeking,' Neptef muttered in reply.

The captain ordered the ship in close. Any non-essential sailor watched the land with an arrow nocked to his bow.

Neptef's voice dropped to a whisper. 'Priest, what of the chests below?'

The thought of Malkesh's men killing him out of hand suddenly occurred to Sarasesh and he shook his head. The treasure in the hold might be a bargaining chip he could not afford to lose. 'I will take the smallest with me and make contact first if I can. I will return for the rest later.' His voice was steady, which surprised him. The priest eyed the rope ladder uncertainly as a sailor tossed it over the side. 'Will you wait for my return?'

The captain glanced at the smoke, clearly uncomfortable with tarrying, but unwilling to abandon his charge so readily.

'Until sunset. Then we anchor well offshore. You have four hours, my lord.'

SARASESH PICKED HIS way through the smoking ruins of the town, keeping his eyes ahead and trying to ignore the smouldering corpses that lay in his path. Many were burned beyond recognition and bile rose in his throat at the sight of smaller bodies lying beside the larger.

Hesehem had been at the frontier of the Egyptian empire, far beyond the notice of Thebes, on the border of Kush. Sarasesh had known little about the place before now, but the scale of destruction suggested that hundreds of people had lived here.

Had this been part of Senmut's plan? No, that was why he was here. To bring the savage Kushites to heel and lead them in righteous cause. He carried with him a small chest, no larger than a loaf of bread. Within the chest were ingots of silver and uncut stones of lapis lazuli, amethyst and emeralds. Though it was a pittance to the wealth of the temples, Sarasesh hoped it was enough to impress the savages and stoke their greed.

He flinched as the remains of a wall crumbled behind him, disturbing the crows that scavenged between the ruins. The carrion birds returned quickly and the priest watched as two crows fought for control of a corpse, though it was but one of many slumped in the street. The larger one pecked at its competition, plucking a feather from the other's wing and driving it away. Sarasesh brought his kerchief back to his mouth and looked away as the crow squawked in triumph, tearing a morsel away to reveal a glint of white among the blackened flesh.

He heard the sound of guttural speech ahead and through the gloom he saw two tribesmen sifting through the ruins of a house. They were swathed in loose robes stained black and brown with ash, and each wore a headscarf that covered their faces. The skin around their eyes was covered with ash and blood. Sarasesh could not understand their words but they seemed to be arguing.

Before they could come to blows, Sarasesh stepped out from behind the wall and called to them. At Senmut's advice he had removed the gold bands around his wrists and throat before he came ashore. He was glad for the decision.

'Hail, men.'

The tribesmen jumped in fright, perhaps convinced that a restless spirit had appeared before them. He took a step closer and the tribesmen charged with their spears raised, hollering a wordless war cry.

Sarasesh threw up his free hand to ward off the blow. 'Malkesh,' he said, his voice coming out high-pitched and quivering. 'Take me to Malkesh.' Invoking the pirate warlord's name had an instantaneous effect. The tribesmen froze and shared a sideways glance and lowered their weapons. One of them took a hesitant step towards Sarasesh. The spear butt lashed out and rapped against the priest's leg. Sarasesh flinched and recoiled, but the tribesmen visibly relaxed at his reaction.

'Malkesh,' repeated Sarasesh and the tribesmen chattered between themselves before turning and heading deeper into the ruins. Assuming he was meant to follow, Sarasesh trotted after them, cradling the chest in his arms.

The smoke was thinner here, the devastation less saturating and the corpses fewer in number. Clearly the town's inhabitants had tried to flee for the safety of the water and been cut down clustered together at the shore.

The tribesmen led him to the outskirts of the town, where they stopped to speak to another of their number. They immediately deferred to this newcomer, and Sarasesh guessed that he might be one of Malkesh's crew, one of the fearsome pirates of the Red Sea.

At first glance, the pirate and the tribesmen appeared similar but as Sarasesh watched their animated discussion, he began to distinguish between them. All had the same dusky skin of Nubia and the people of Punt, though the tribesmen deferred to the pirate with obvious fear. Where the tribesmen wore robes from neck to ankle, the pirate wore a shendyt in the Egyptian style and a loose cloak that was open at the front and left his arms free. The pirate possessed much finer weapons, a curved sword and gilded dagger, and as he walked over to Sarasesh there was a swagger in his step. The tribesmen followed him gesticulating at the waiting priest, but the pirate ignored them.

'I am Sarasesh, Honoured Priest of Amun in Thebes and representative of the Karnak Brotherhood, on behalf of the revered Third Prophet Senmut, Blessings upon his name.'

The pirate simply stared at him. The tribesmen spoke again and the pirate snapped and rounded on them, sending them retreating into the ruins with their eyes lowered.

'Do you speak Egyptian? Do you understand my words?' asked Sarasesh.

The pirate grunted at him and turned away, beckoning for him to follow.

Sarasesh was led out of town and across a valley to a vast city of nomadic tents and dwellings that had been set up in the shadow of the ridge above. The ridge was a natural barrier, a divide between the fertile river valley and the sprawling desert to the east. It was large enough that this mobile army of thousands was entirely concealed within its shadow. Sarasesh was led within and after the openness of the valley, the close press of humanity was almost overwhelming. Here and there, the iconography of different tribes and peoples blended into a riot of colour. Many had come. That was good.

Many of the tribesmen he passed stared at the chest with undisguised fascination and Sarasesh clutched it tighter as he picked his way through their tents.

In the centre of it all was a grand tent that would not have been out of place when Pharaoh himself took to the battlefield. The pirate leading him gestured towards the opening and shouted a few words to the guards standing outside. Without waiting for a reply, he turned away and went back towards the ruins of Hesehem.

Taking a moment to compose himself and straighten his shendyt, Sarasesh waited for the guards at the tent's entrance to admit him. The spearmen glanced at him but made no move to block his passage nor announce his arrival.

'Ignorant savages,' Sarasesh muttered under his breath and push aside the tent doors himself. The interior of the tent was quite cool though it was filled with people. Retainers, servants and warriors filled the space to the buzz of conversation, and Sarasesh was forced to push his way through the crowd. He spied a cluster of Nubian chiefs speaking quietly together off to one side, swathed in robes the colour of the desert, embroidered with colourful trims of blue and green. Their hair was twisted in thick braids and strung with beads, and bands of gold adorned their wrists and ankles. Each of them regarded the others with impassive expressions that showed nothing of the thoughts within. For a fractious coalition, they were tight-knit enough now.

'Priest, you are late.'

Sarasesh's attention was drawn to the towering figure seated on the throne at the end of the tent. More pirates lounged by the throne, drinking and laughing as they regaled each other with tales of the slaughter of Hesehem.

Malkesh was big, a head taller than Sarasesh and almost twice as broad. His skin was tanned dark and his body hair allowed to grow unchecked, the priest noted with distaste. His hair hung lank around his shoulders and his face was lined with scars. His robe was open at the chest, revealing a torso thick with corded muscle and knotted scar tissue.

'You are Malkesh? I demand to know what has happened here. You were to meet here with the tribes, not butcher the town!'

Malkesh was unmoved, but a thin smile graced his lips. 'Is this not what your prophet wanted? Is that not why we are here?'

'Not here. Not now.'

Malkesh chuckled, a low throaty laugh. 'I had to see if these tribes of the land possessed mettle. I am pleased.'

Sarasesh risked a glance at the tribal chiefs. There were four when there should have been six. He knew them by name and reputation alone and had to deduce which of their tribal styles was absent.

'Where are Nessesar and Prektef?'

'They fell in battle,' shrugged Malkesh.

Two chiefs already dead, in a fight against barely armed peasants, thought Sarasesh. You have overreached yourself already, Malkesh the Pirate.

'That is dire news,' said Sarasesh instead.

'Do not fear, priest. Their men follow me now. You will have your army.'

Sarasesh's gaze wandered to crates nestled at the foot of the throne.

'You have found our gift to you?' he asked.

Malkesh rose from his throne and stooped to pick up one of the crates, reaching in to pick up a handful of its contents. 'Fragrant rocks,' said Malkesh, letting a handful of the resin fall to the ground. 'What need have I of this?'

'It is valuable. Worth its weight in gold,' said Sarasesh.

'Not to me.'

Because you are an uncultured savage, thought Sarasesh. 'They are worth gold to the priesthoods. They will pay well for a stable supply. Consider it an investment.'

Malkesh smirked. 'Why trade for something I can just take?'

Sarasesh's mouth fell open.

'You cannot plunder the priesthoods,' he said, his voice shrill. 'That is blasphemy of the highest order.'

'Not to me,' said Malkesh again, his beard splitting into a toothy grin. He laughed again. 'Relax, priest. Your temples are safe. For now.'

The pirates at Malkesh's feet laughed with him and Sarasesh realised he was being toyed with. Before Sarasesh could form an excuse to leave, Malkesh noticed the chest in his arms and stepped forward.

'You have brought me something else. I like you priests,' he said, waiting for Sarasesh to surrender the riches, almost challenging the priest to try keeping it for himself.

'I bring you this gift, in honour of the accord between yourself and the Priesthood of Amun,' said Sarasesh.

With this offering, Senmut was all but promising the impoverishment of the priesthood of Amun, but his gamble would pay off. It had to. This man was violence personified. With Malkesh as the hammer to Shoshenq's anvil, Takelot would be swept away.

Malkesh looked down at the gemstones before he passed off the chest to a pirate who secured it with the wealth of frankincense. The pirate lord went to return to his throne, when a thought stopped him.

'Did you bring anything else with you? My men are hungry and this town was poor pickings,' he asked.

'No, I only brought one small ship with me,' said Sarasesh, his thoughts already returning to the safety of his cabin aboard the ship.

Malkesh grinned. 'Then that will have to do.'

SLEEP CAME UNEASILY to Isetweret. Since her meeting with the priest Pedubast and his brother Iuput, she spent many of her nights staring up at the canopy of her bed. When she could not bear to lie still any longer, she sat at her vanity and reading under the light of a small oil lamp. When sleep did come, it was shallow, threatening to break at the slightest sound or disturbance. She did not dream, not as such, but in the quietness of her bedroom with the lamps extinguished and the servants sent away, a feeling of dread settled over her that she could not erase.

By the time she had returned to the palace after her escapade, Hory had been on verge of sending out the palace guard to look for her. With all her charm she had soothed his fears, assuring him she had been at the Temple of Hathor to seek some quiet reflection and to pray for her mother in these difficult times.

Being apart from her family was difficult to bear, she had said, and in that her husband understood. Content and relieved beyond measure, Hory pried no further and led her to their chambers. She had pretended to be unaware of the extra guard at their door that night.

As near as Pedubast had been able to tell, a schism had formed between the prophets, led seemingly by Harsiese on the one side and Senmut on the other. A political divide he had said, nothing more than an ideological rift. The sanctity of the temples was intact, an internal disagreement that was embarrassing but that should be left to the priests themselves.

She had known she had been right in seeking out the priests of Amun, but she felt little better for their counsel. Pedubast could not explain the source of the conflict but could not deny it was there.

Despite his assurances, she could not bring herself to believe Pedubast any more than she had trusted Harsiese. The priests of Karnak had always been a close-knit brotherhood, made even more inclined to their secretive and esoteric ways by the freedoms granted by her great-grandfather, Pharaoh Osorkon II. They would not give up their secrets easily, never admit weakness or discord and were loath to even be questioned by an outside force.

The hours of audiences spent by her husband's side passed in a blur as she mentally sifted through each petitioner's words, searching for some connection or meaning, but she found nothing concrete. She often wondered if her mother would have broken open the brotherhood's secrets already and considered writing to her more than once, but the words dried up as soon as she laid out the papyrus, and each day, she put off writing until the next.

She looked up from her bed as Hory entered the vizier's chambers, his posture slumped and his expression weary. She bit her tongue as he tossed his cloak over the back of the chair at her vanity table and picked at the untouched grapes laid out for her lunch.

'What are you reading?' he asked as he crossed the room. Hory dipped his hands in the washbasin and sighed with pleasure as he splashed the cool water over his face.

'The Ode of the Lotus,' she said, tossing the papyrus onto a nearby table.

'I met with more than a hundred petitioners today and there is dinner tonight with the Nomarch of Nekhen to discuss the disturbance in shipping off the coast,' he said, drying himself off and coming to sit on the edge of the bed beside her. 'Tell me your day was better than that.'

'Boring,' she muttered. 'No word from Herakleopolis. There is nothing to do but sit and wait.'

'I can think of something we could do,' he said, his hand caressing her leg.

'Not now,' she said and pushed his hand away. He reached for her again, and though she let him touch her, she made no effort to return his affections.

'What's wrong?' said Hory, his tone immediately marked with concern.

'We are at war, Hory,' she said. 'Everything is wrong.'

Hory wrapped his arms around her and pulled her in close and this time she relented, burying her face in the crook of his neck.

'The war is a long way from here,' he said. She stiffened in his embrace and he pulled back to look down at her. 'Your father will triumph and Egypt will be at peace once more. All will be well. Have faith.'

'Shoshenq will not back down from this and he matches my father in military might. If you hope for an early victory then you are a fool,' she snapped.

Hory's eyes narrowed but he bit back the retort forming on his lips.

Isetweret clutched the pendant around her neck. 'I should be in Herakleopolis with them. I should be fighting beside my family. And yet I am here, doing nothing of importance and watching over an ungrateful city.'

'You are too harsh on yourself. I am only trying to help,' he protested.

'Well don't,' she snapped.

Hory recoiled and held her at arm's length. The hurt in his expression melted through her anger and she reached for him.

'I feel so alone,' she said.

'You have me.'

Isetweret said nothing. After a long moment, Hory pulled away and stood.

'Your family deposed mine,' he said quietly. There was no anger in his voice. 'My father is gone. I do not know if he still lives. I don't know if my mother, brother and sister still live. Were it not for our marriage, I might have been killed at your brothers' hands. Instead, I was simply left behind by virtue of not being with them when your brothers tried to kill them. They are gone and I remain.'

Too late she realised the depth of hurt she had opened. She crawled across the bed to reach him but he was already at the chamber door.

'I'm sorry,' she said, but Hory did not look back.

She should have gone after him. She should have chased him down. But as she saw him leave, she felt nothing but her own turmoil.

# Chapter Three

CAPTAIN NEPTEF CHEWED on a piece of dried fish and considered the problem before him. The sun was setting rapidly and he had to choose whether to make good on his promise to the priest to wait or to anchor further downriver and return to Thebes without him in the morning.

Though Neptef had never met the priest before, the temple had chosen him for this voyage, so he was clearly a figure of some importance. The temple had paid Neptef handsomely to bring this Sarasesh beyond the First Cataract, but had said nothing of a return trip nor had payment been promised to bring him safely back to Thebes. Once an hour the captain had gone below out of sight of his crew and checked the false wall in the hold, content that barrels of beer and crates of linens and grain kept it secret and unlikely to be found by anything less than tearing the vessel apart back down to its keel.

The checks kept his thoughts occupied, but not for long.

As far as the captain was concerned, his task was done and new ventures beckoned him, yet he felt a lingering sense of responsibility for the priest.

The town was utterly destroyed and it was likely whoever had brought it to ruin was still close by. His charge was not a warrior, that much was clear, and he possessed the fleshy idleness common to priests and scribes.

At the same time, it was not Neptef's problem to care for another's suicidal stupidity.

'Any sign of him?' he called to the sailor manning the helm.

'None, sir,' said the sailor.

Neptef sighed and returned to his watch. 'Come on, you bastard. Where are you?' he muttered to himself. The shore was no more than a few metres away but the smoke rising from the smouldering ruins obscured sight of all but the first few buildings of the town. Who knew where the priest had gone or what he was doing?

His task from the Third Prophet had been vague and discretionary. 'Take the priest to Hesehem,' he had been told. Had he not done that? At the same time, his payment had been more than generous and it seemed unlike the learned priesthood to pay him for a lost cause. Perhaps the priest's safety was implied in the bargain.

It was unwise to disappoint any priest, let alone a prophet, and the consequences of doing so would follow him into the next life, no matter how he was sent to it.

The captain looked over his shoulder towards the west. The sun was already sinking low in the sky and the blue overhead was quickly taking on the orange and purple glow of dusk.

Darkness would fall within the hour and he had warned the priest of the consequences of being late. Neptef consoled himself with the knowledge that if the priest wasn't already dead then he must have found safety.

He drew breath to shout for the anchor to be raised when a startled cry stopped him. From the rigging above, a sailor pointed towards the town. Then Neptef heard it. The pounding rhythm and a rising cry that chilled him to the bone.

'Men! To arms! Fight!' he roared, going for the recurve bow tucked against the railing. Neptef nocked his first arrow and his heart sank as he saw the number against them. 'Belay that! Spears, get us away,' he shouted to the sailor at the helm as those sailors not armed with bows dropped their spears and went for the ropes. From the smoky mist, the tribesmen of Kush threw themselves into the water and made straight for his ship.

Neptef snarled as he missed his first shot. His eyes were getting old and the light was getting poorer with each passing minute as he aimed for the bobbing heads coming towards his ship. His second shot was true, punching through his target's face and marking the water around him a dull crimson.

Neptef muttered a prayer to the Sobek to intervene, to feed on the spilled blood and grant them deliverance in whatever violent way the Lord of Crocodiles saw fit.

The *Sobek is Content* was edging away but slowly, far too slowly. The first tribesmen reached his ship with a thud as they dug their daggers into the hull to find purchase.

Behind him, the sailor at the helm let out a strangled shout as a dark figure cut him down, slashing him open from groin to shoulder.

Neptef lashed out with the bow as a bearded face came up the railing, puncturing the man's eye and sending him crashing back into the water. He drew the short sword from his belt as more attackers clambered up and over the railings. Around the deck, battle was joined as the tribesmen outnumbered and overwhelmed the ship's crew. Neptef dashed for the helm, but found his path blocked.

'It'll take more than that,' he snarled, charging at the nearest man and stabbing him in the belly. His return stroke took the hand off another warrior. He darted past the howling tribesmen when a shape loomed above him.

The man was huge and it was on subconscious reflex that Neptef raised his sword to ward off the crushing blow. He cried out as his shoulder was jarred almost from its socket, feeling his fingers go numb and almost dropping his sword. In desperation he lunged, the point of his blade angled low at his enemy's belly.

His stab was neatly deflected and as he looked into the face of his enemy, a meaty fist slammed into the side of his head, smashing him down to the deck. His vision blurred. Around him, he could hear the screams of his crew wounded and dying.

Through groggy eyes, Neptef saw the giant's sword raised high. The pommel cracked into the side of his head and all went dark.

SARASESH STARTED AS the captain's eyes flickered open. He had hoped Neptef was already dead. A clean death in battle would have been kinder than whatever fate Malkesh had in store for the captain of the *Sobek is Content*.

Sarasesh stood on the ship's deck beside his newfound allies, his skin crawling as the bodies of the crew were hauled overboard to feed for the crocodiles. He supposed, in a grim sort of way, that Sobek would be content, but it was a damnable way to go for an Egyptian.

Without an intact body, they would never reach the afterlife, and Sarasesh offered a prayer to Amun to deliver their souls wherever they may be.

Perhaps Amun was testing him. Had his faith in the father of the gods been lacking of late? No, else Senmut would not have placed his trust in him so readily. He would find a way to tame Malkesh and lead the army that Thebes so sorely needed.

The *Sobek* was tied to the shore and the deck leaned as the keel hit sand. Neptef drooled through his gag, his head hanging limp from where he was tied to the mast. A low groan escaped his lips and the gathered warriors chattered excitedly.

Pirates and tribal warriors both watched their lord as he paced around the deck, running his hands over the rigging and testing the sturdiness of the railings and timbers. He closed his eyes and smiled at his assembled throng.

'Too long without getting on a ship is not good for a man,' he said to raucous laughter. Below deck, more pirates looted the ship's hold, carrying armfuls of bread and beer over the side and back to camp. Some had even rifled through Sarasesh's belongings, sharing his jewellery, cosmetics and clothes among themselves. He did not have the courage to protest.

Sarasesh turned as he felt eyes upon him. Under his lank mop of hair, Neptef glared at him with eyes that lusted for his death. Sarasesh looked away, unable to meet the captain's hateful gaze.

The priest flinched as the pirate lord came up behind him and looked down at Neptef. The captain tried to speak but the gag turned his protests into muffled groans.

'Have you ever killed a man, priest?' asked Malkesh, watching the captain struggle like a trussed gazelle.

Sarasesh blanched. 'No, never!' he cried.

'But you don't mind us doing it for you?' Malkesh said. His voice was the rumbling of thunder over a stormy sea and he fixed Sarasesh with his deep ocean eyes. 'I don't mind. I enjoy killing. I am good at killing. I have spilled enough blood to give the Red Sea its name.'

Malkesh drew a dagger from his belt and ran a finger across its edge. He showed Sarasesh the red line scored across his fingertip and let a drop fall to the deck. 'There is nothing to fear from blood.' The pirate lord reversed the dagger and thrust the handle into Sarasesh's hand.

'Do it.'

Sarasesh paled as he met Neptef's pleading eyes. The captain strained against his bonds but the men who tied him were sailors of the open seas and their knotwork kept him immobile.

'Cut his throat,' said Malkesh as he circled behind Sarasesh to the rasping sound of an unsheathed sword.

Sarasesh hesitated and felt a pinprick in his back.

'Or I run this through your heart. Your people believe the heart and soul are one, don't they? What happens if you lose yours?' asked Malkesh.

Sarasesh felt himself paralysed with fear. The handle of the dagger was slick with sweat.

'Forgive me.'

The captain's eyes widened and he struggled against his bonds as Sarasesh slashed the dagger's edge across his throat.

Sarasesh's trembling hand missed the main arteries, slicing instead through the captain's windpipe. The captain's eyes bulged, his breath coming in a wheeze through the hole in his throat and he coughed and writhed against the rope as he choked on his own blood. Sarasesh dropped the dagger in horror, unable to tear his gaze away from Neptef's final moments.

Malkesh stepped forward and watched the captain buck and twitch against his bonds.

Slowly, too slowly, Neptef's spasms weakened and the blood at his feet pooled into a crimson puddle. As Neptef's last breath rattled from his chest, Malkesh began to laugh. The warriors on deck laughed too, a final mockery of a life lived true.

Sarasesh was nearly knocked from his feet when Malkesh clapped him on the back. 'That was well done, priest. To draw out the suffering like that. We will make a warrior of you yet.'

'I am a priest of Amun,' said Sarasesh, trying and failing to conceal the tremor in his voice. 'And I demand your respect.'

Malkesh laughed again but it was a hollow sound bereft of anything good. 'When I lead these men into your lands, even your gods will be powerless to stop me. Now come on, priest. I will show you how men fight. Take us to your war.'

'YOU SPOKE TO the Lady Isetweret?'

Pedubast looked up from his work, blinking away the afterimages of supply figures and correspondence with the other temples of the nome. The oil lamp was running low and as he set his reed pen down, he glanced up at the window set high in the wall. The stars had moved from where he remembered them being. He massaged the palm of his hand as a deep ache began to set in the bones.

'You are here late,' he replied, as his unexpected guest stepped into the room.

'You did not answer my question.'

'Because it did not sound like one. But yes, with her knife at my throat, I spoke with her,' replied Pedubast, closing the ink stopper and shuffling the papers into one pile.

Senmut pulled up a chair, his eyes darting to the sheaf of papyrus on the desk between them. 'What did she want?'

'Reassurance.'

'No riddles, Pedubast. Tell me what the princess wanted of you.'

'Very well,' said Pedubast. 'It seems your plots are not as subtle as you think they are. Something has piqued the princess's... curiosity. She came to me with her concerns. Naturally, I assured her that the temples were in perfect harmony, though there was discontent with Harsiese's ineffectiveness as leader. Internal politics and nothing more. She seemed content enough when we parted ways.'

'And why would she come to you? Why you of all people?'

'This feud is between you and Harsiese. Even the novices have noticed. I can only imagine something the High Priest has said has set her on this trail,' said Pedubast, ignoring the other man's questions.

Senmut glared at him. 'I find your closeness with Takelot's family disturbing, Pedubast. I think it is time you cut ties with them.'

'Do not presume to order me, Senmut. I am not one of your underlings, and it is through my efforts that we are given as much liberty as we are.' Pedubast grunted as he stood and shuffled over to a shelf where he retrieved and lit a second lamp. He filled the vessel with oil and the flame banished the shadows that had begun to surround him.

'What time is it?' he asked as he set the lamp down in the corner.

'An hour before midnight,' replied Senmut. The Third Prophet sniffed and sat back, looking up at the window. 'She cannot discover what we are about. Not until the proper time,' he said.

'No, she cannot,' agreed Pedubast. 'On that we are of one mind. Wine?'

Senmut nodded and Pedubast brought them two cups. Senmut took a sip and chuckled as he set the cup back on the table.

'One of Harsiese's? Are you trying to goad me?'

'Perhaps,' smiled Pedubast. 'For all his faults, our High Priest is a fine vintner. It will almost be a shame when the time comes.'

'We will remove the man, not his vineyards,' said Senmut. 'It is necessary. I had hoped he would see reason, but I no longer think it is wise to try. He is too tied to Takelot and Osorkon to risk betraying them now.'

'Takelot's ambition has set Egypt ablaze. I would rather that Thebes remains untouched, as do you,' said Pedubast, watching the prophet over the rim of his cup.

'The chaos of Apophis follows Takelot wherever he treads. All is not well in Herakleopolis, where our beloved pharaoh now resides.'

'I have heard,' replied Pedubast. 'Do I sense your influence in that city somewhere?'

'Not this time,' said Senmut, truthfully. 'Still, the events of Herakleopolis only make me more assured that we are on the right path. Tell me, does your price remain the same?'

'It does. A prophethood would suit me well enough. Naturally, you would supplant Harsiese as High Priest. You will need a Second Prophet to keep the administration and courts out of temple affairs. A return to the days of Nimlot, gods keep him.'

Senmut laughed, though the sound was forced. 'You think I trust you?'

'I think I am the only one you have any trust in at all,' replied Pedubast, sitting back down and leaning back in his chair. 'Who else do you have? Your legions of loyal followers? Tell me, is Sarasesh even still alive?'

Pedubast smiled as he saw the smirk slide from Senmut's face.

'When you take control of the priesthood, and I believe you will, you will name me your second, your advisor. Your equal,' said Pedubast.

'And if I don't?'

Pedubast shrugged. 'Then you will not be High Priest for very long.'

Senmut's expression darkened. 'Is that a threat?'

'I don't make threats, Senmut. Nor is it a promise. It is a prediction. You surround yourself with sycophants, but few are willing to tell you what you need to hear. Weak men follow, they do not lead. Takelot thought he could control Thebes by installing a puppet vizier and look how that is faring.' Pedubast watched Senmut over steepled fingers. 'You will need a new vizier too and I will help with the choosing. A strong man and competent commander who is utterly devout to the temples.'

'You would set up another rival?' asked Senmut, his cup halfway to his mouth.

'It is a lesser risk. Would you truly risk another weak man like Hory being manipulated by your enemies? Harsiese, Takelot and now you, all seek to bind him one way or the other. He will break. It is only a matter of time,' said Pedubast.

Isetweret's willingness to go behind her husband's back was proof enough of that. She knew him better than anyone, and if she had doubts...

Pedubast took another sip and watched Senmut's thoughts play across his face. 'My advice, if you elect to take it, is to keep your secrets even closer than before. People are beginning to notice that all is not in balance,' said Pedubast. 'You are a man of vision, Senmut. I would hate for that to go to waste.'

'Remember who is the senior here,' snapped Senmut, slamming his cup down on the desk with a sharp crack. Wine spilled over his hand and onto the desk and he blinked, as though the outburst had surprised, and now, embarrassed him.

'We are partners in this, not master and servant,' replied Pedubast, pouring himself another measure and leaving the carafe within the other man's reach. 'I will not ply you with platitudes, Senmut. That is how you can be sure that I am serious in my intentions.'

Senmut ran a finger around the rim of his cup, appearing deep in thought. It was a nervous habit that Pedubast had long since noted.

'Suppose I do name you Second Prophet, the second of equals. What of your brother? What will he desire out of all this?'

Pedubast shrugged. 'Iuput is a gentle creature. He has no design for power. He will do as I ask and he is under my protection. My spoils will be shared with him. Agreed?'

'Agreed,' said Senmut, all but bouncing to his feet. 'Thank you for the wine,' he said as he turned to leave.

'And what of your other allies? What will become of them?' asked Pedubast, as the Third Prophet reached the door.

'Useful for now. Who knows? Sarasesh might still be alive,' said Senmut. Then he was gone.

Pedubast watched the Third Prophet depart and pinched the bridge of his nose as a sudden headache threatened to steal his focus. He slipped the sheaf of papyrus away in a drawer. He would get no more work done that night. He locked the drawer and slipped the necklace with its key over his head. His eyes ached and he drained his cup before he stoppered the decanter.

Takelot might have set the fire, but Senmut's ambition would keep it blazing.

# Chapter Four

HARSIESE DIRECTED THE packing of his house with a stern eye, the sparseness of his accoutrements and furnishings giving him the feeling of having looted his own living quarters. The cart outside was nearly full of furniture, his favourite chairs and writing desk among the treasures he could not leave behind. Among the furniture, bulging sacks of grain, vegetables and dried meats made up much of his supplies, as well as spare clothing, writing supplies, perfumes, hidden caches of gold and silver, and all the other endless travel essentials of the nobility.

His servants silently swarmed through each room, ensuring their lord's journey would be comfortable and forgetting nothing of his needs and wants. Outside, his household guard waited patiently lounging beside the cart, ready nonetheless to sell their lives for their master's possessions. Dressed in travelling cloaks, they looked little different to desert mercenaries, with concealed swords on their hips and a bow and quiver strung over their shoulders.

The High Priest himself had removed the vestments of his office, secreting the leopard skin cloak beneath the robes in the cart. He wore now a simple shendyt that itched and rubbed at his skin. His chest and shoulders were bare and he had allowed the hair on his scalp to grow to a light shadow, an oversight usually unthinkable in temple service. The road to his estates was not without peril, especially in times such as these, and he had no intention of needlessly trading one danger for another.

Chaos would engulf Thebes with or without him here. The princess's interest in temple affairs would not abate and it was only a matter of time until Senmut noticed enough to take swift and decisive action. It would be prudent to establish himself elsewhere before the swords started swinging. Neither side would count him as their ally, not truly. His father's actions had sealed his fate as an outcast, his reputation forever the son of a usurping and power-hungry Heretic King, no matter how much he achieved for himself.

He owed them nothing. Not the priests or prophets, nor even the self-proclaimed royal family. If Isetweret wished to move against Senmut and drag them both down, then all the better. Both sides would have dismissed him as an irrelevance, but Harsiese vowed he would return to sort through the ashes.

Harsiese slotted the dagger home in his belt, feeling reassured by the well-worn grip of the ivory hilt. It was one of the few possessions of his father's that he had been allowed to keep as a young boy. Everything else had been entombed beside his father's sarcophagus, to be forgotten beneath the desert sands.

'My lord, someone here to see you.'

Harsiese looked over his shoulder. The captain of his household guard bowed low and gestured outside. Harsiese followed him out onto the street where a cohort of the palace guard stood to attention. His own guard watched them warily, but Harsiese gave them the order to stand down as the palace guard parted and the princess Isetweret stepped forward.

'Lord Harsiese, do you have a moment?' She spoke as though making a polite request of a friend, not with the implicit threat present in her entourage's presence.

Harsiese was transfixed, not by her beauty but that she should be here at all. Why have you come? he wondered. Do you not know what you are risking being seen here with me?

'I always have a moment for the daughter of Takelot. Please come in,' he said, with a deep bow. He ordered all but two of his guards to remain outside, a gesture of trust he hoped she would reciprocate, but as he led her inside, he became conscious of the palace guards filling out his dining room. His servants paled at the sight of so many unknown armed men. With a curt gesture, Harsiese banished them to the upper level to go over his bedroom one last time.

Harsiese gestured for her to sit on the bench and unstoppered a wine decanter, holding up a cup in offering.

'Thank you, but no. I won't stay long.'

'As you wish,' he replied, and poured a cup for himself. Harsiese sat on the other side of the table, mindful of the guards watching him and him alone. Whether they were solely loyal to her or reported to Hory, he would not risk a misunderstanding arising from misconstrued familiarity.

'Where are you going?' she asked, her eye lingering on the wagon that even now was being covered with a linen shroud to guard against the weather of travel. The pair of bullocks at the wagon's head were being watered and rubbed down. Beside them, Harsiese's horse was having its hoofs inspected and its saddle straps checked one last time. Five more minutes and he would have been away already and he sensed the princess knew it.

'For a tour of my estates,' he replied. 'The harvest season is here. Soon enough that too will be over and I must inspect the dykes and seed stores before the next flood. Such is the price of owning a famous vineyard and grain fields that feed this land,' he said, with a smile.

She nodded, tearing her gaze from the wagon.

'I have come to talk to you privately, if that is possible?' she said.

Harsiese raised an eyebrow and looked over at the palace guard standing to attention at each entrance of his house. After a moment, she took his meaning and with a wave of her hand, sent the guards to wait outside with Harsiese's men. Harsiese likewise dismissed the pair attending him. The captain of the palace cohort moved to stand beside the princess and Harsiese watched him carefully.

'Keptefankh is loyal to me. Pretend he is not here,' said Isetweret. She waited until the last of her guards was out on the street and the house was silent but for the murmur of traffic outside.

'You are holding out on us, my lord.'

'My lady?'

'There is a rift in Karnak and you are at its source. What is happening? The vizier needs to know.'

Harsiese's gaze ventured to the unblinking guard captain at her side. 'I am afraid I do not know what you are talking about. The temples are at peace and in balance, as always. Theological differences exist, certainly, but these are internal matters.'

'I have spoken to others in the priesthood who have confirmed that is not so. It is important that you tell me,' she pressed.

'Who have you spoken to?'

'They are in my confidence. Do you deny it?'

Harsiese rose and walked towards the front door, watching as the guard captain's hand tightened on the pommel of his sword.

'With respect, my lady, I do not believe the vizier has the strength or will to do what must be done. Nor for that matter, do you. For your own wellbeing, stay out of this. Amun's blessings upon you,' he said.

'What has come between you and Senmut?' she called after him.

Harsiese's smile tightened. 'Does the vizier know you are here?' he asked, watching as the question struck home.

'Of course, he does,' she replied.

'Then I will speak to him about this on my return. Until then, I must insist that you leave my house. Unless you are choosing to detain me illegally?' he said.

Isetweret stiffened and rose from her seat, nodding formally to her captain as she led him back out onto the street.

'I will not keep you any longer. Have a safe journey, my lord Harsiese,' she said, climbing back into her carrying chair.

Harsiese watched the palace guard form up on either side of their lady. He waited until she was out of sight before he called his servants back downstairs. Harsiese took his time finishing his wine as he considered the frustration in her words. The challenge would be irresistible to any of Takelot's children, but to Isetweret it would become an obsession.

One he was happy to leave her to.

Satisfied, he tossed his empty cup to a waiting servant and called his column to order.

One servant knelt beside his horse and Harsiese used him as a step to climb into the saddle. He nudged his horse into a canter, half-expecting another column of soldiers from the palace to block his exit but none presented themselves.

Within minutes he was on the main road leading to the city gate. Within the hour he was outside the city walls. A sense of freedom and peace washed over him as the press of humanity and the worries of the politics of Karnak receded from his mind.

Harsiese could not risk open confrontation with Senmut, but perhaps he would no longer have to. With one conversation, he had placed a huntress on their scent and idly, he wondered at the courage and stupidity of her contact within the temples, whoever he was. Such a leak could be dealt with in time, but it did not harm to let Isetweret risk the first strike.

THE MERCHANT SHOOK the bloodstained sack before his face and cast it down at the foot of the dais steps. The fabric was ripped and frayed, the blood a dark crimson brown, dried with age. As one, the guards on the step glanced down at the sackcloth, then back to the increasingly agitated petitioner. Two of them went to step forward, but a curt word from the top of the dais stilled them before they could.

Isetweret watched the display with distaste. Her stomach turned at the sight of the sackcloth and her surprise and irritation at her own squeamishness only made it worse.

Beside her, Hory leaned forward in his chair, peering down at the evidence of murder. At Hory's shoulder, the newly appointed Chancellor Pereftep snapped out another order and the guards stood back to attention. The chancellor had been a senior scribe in his exiled father's administration and an old friend and confidante of Hory's for many years. It was clear now that their relationship went deeper than simply a teacher and favoured student to one resembling father and son. Though it rankled her to have Hory look elsewhere for counsel, Isetweret did not have the heart to deny him and so the office of chancellor had been formed without her knowledge or agreement. She looked away as the chancellor's eyes fell upon her and glanced back at the merchant instead.

'Trading with Nubia has become fraught with danger. I might as well cast my grain into the river for all the profit sending it to Punt will bring. What is to be done about this?' asked the merchant.

'Master Hopen, might I remind you that you are in the presence of the Vizier of Thebes,' said Chancellor Pereftep. 'You will conduct yourself accordingly.'

Hopen went on. 'My caravans refuse to go. No amount of gold in Egypt will compel them to try. It is certain death, they say. The desert guides have disappeared and the desert police have refused to answer my concerns. Something needs to change, quickly. Respectfully, of course, Lord Vizier,' he said, catching himself.

The border with Nubia was controlled by Egypt alone. Only through the diligence of the towns at the First Cataract was Upper Egypt kept safe and now it seemed they were failing in that task. War in the north and unrest in the south. The security of Thebes was rapidly becoming in jeopardy. The thought sent another wave of nausea coursing through her.

'You are not the first to speak of such things, Master Hopen,' said Hory.

'Then that is more reason to be concerned!' cried Hopen, momentarily forgetting himself. The palace guards turned from their vigil to stare at the petitioner. Hopen swallowed noisily and bowed his head in contrition. 'I have spoken with the grain farmers' guild, Lord Vizier. I am not the only one who has lost an investment in this unrest. It cannot be allowed to continue.'

'I understand your concerns, Hopen, but this unrest is beyond our nome.'

'But not Upper Egypt,' replied Hopen. 'Are you not charged with the defence of the south? With trade to the north impossible, we must open new markets if we are to prosper. The merchants of Thebes will not stand for this any longer.'

Hory's eyes narrowed with irritation, but it was Isetweret that spoke first.

'Speak out of turn again and we will have you flogged,' snapped Isetweret. 'And that will be a kindness compared to how your insolence should be rewarded.'

Hopen blanched and took a step back, but Hory rounded on her with fire in his eyes.

'Forgive Lady Isetweret, her tongue runs away with her,' snapped Hory, holding up his hand to silence her next protest. He turned his attention back to the merchant. 'I will send word to the nomarch of Ta-Seti for clarification. Until then, there is little I can do for you.'

Hopen bowed his head low and turned away. He risked a single glance over his shoulder, then all but fled the audience chamber.

Chancellor Pereftep walked down the stairs and retrieved the merchant's abandoned cloth. He brought it up to Hory who examined it closely. The fibres were neatly cut, and the bloodstain too large to be anything but a non-lethal wound.

'To think that someone died against this,' said Hory.

'The merchant was too forward, but he was right,' said the chancellor. 'The situation is getting out of hand. We must respond before our enemies multiply.'

'Perhaps we could offer the merchants and farmers compensation from the state stores until this crisis is resolved,' said Hory.

'A benevolent action, my lord, but perhaps an option for another time. Reward the clamour now and it will only get louder,' said the chancellor. He glanced over the vizier's shoulder at Isetweret. 'But neither should we antagonise the situation needlessly.'

'Then what do you suggest?' asked the vizier.

'Standing up for yourself would be a start,' said Isetweret.

'You spoke out of turn,' Hory replied, but Isetweret cut him off.

'You are the vizier,' she hissed. 'Why do you allow them to speak to you so? Put them in their place. The next man that dares speak to my husband that way I will flog myself if I have to. Twenty lashes on the soles of their feet should remind them to treat us with respect.'

'You heard Pereftep. We should not make this situation any worse than it already is. We do not want this unrest to spread to the streets.'

Isetweret scoffed. 'And you think this will all magically go away if you sit in here and ignore the world out there?'

Hory's mouth pressed into a thin line. 'It is easy for you to say, watching from the outside. It is another thing to be entirely responsible for this city, the homes of the gods themselves. There are tens of thousands of people within these walls, Iset.'

'Mobilise the police and city guard. We must make a show of force.'

'Like your father has?' Hory snapped. He caught himself and his jaw set. Takelot has my respect and gratitude, but his show of force has dragged the whole country into a civil war. I will not bring ruin upon them because you feel left out.'

'Left out?'

'Your family is winning glory in the north and you are stuck here with me. I am sorry that the life you lead does not content you, but I will treat my people fairly according to Ma'at. I am not my father. Or yours,' he replied, stony-faced.

'No, they both would have made an example of that fool and saved themselves the trouble of more crowing merchants,' she said.

Hory looked away. 'And for my father's actions your brothers tried to kill him. We have been through this before.'

'My brothers are on your side.'

'Are they? Then why do I feel like you are no longer on my side, my love?' Hory turned to face her, but there was no love in his eyes.

Isetweret felt tears prickle at her eyes. 'How can you say that?' she said.

'You are distant and combative lately. What does it take to keep you happy? I am the vizier here, Iset. Not you, not your father or brothers. Me.'

The merchant Hopen was gone and another petitioner stood at the chamber threshold waiting to be invited further. Isetweret was on her feet in a moment and brushed away his grasping hand, fuming as she walked away.

Hory let her go.

'BROTHER, I HAVE a question.'

Pedubast opened his eyes from where he lay on the couch and looked across to where Iuput was sitting at their dining table, surrounded by a fortress of scrolls and papyrus texts. Outside, the streets were alive with preparations for the Festival of the Harvest, the bustling world beyond an ever-present yet soothing hum. For a brief moment in time, the people of this city could forget that there was a war on.

'Ask away,' he said.

'Why haven't you taken a wife?'

Pedubast chuckled and sat up. He set down his own scroll, a fascinating treatise on desert poisons, and stifled a groan as he rose to his feet. He shuffled over to the bench beside the fireplace and picked at the bread and salted fish that had made up their lunch. Brushing away a handful of herbal leaves that had fallen from his drying racks, he picked through the food, settling on a handful of dried fruit to finish as he sat beside Iuput at the table.

'Why do you ask?'

Iuput shrugged. 'It seems like something people do. Most of the priests have families.'

'I am content with the current arrangement. If I were to be married, she would live here and you would have to move out.'

Iuput frowned. 'Could we not all live together?'

'The roof is barely large enough for both of us now, brother. You wouldn't like my hypothetical bride up there too. Trust me,' said Pedubast, with a grin.

Iuput nodded and returned to his reading. He was kind and good-natured, but all too easily led.

'Why did we come to Thebes?'

'Bubastis was too small for us. We will serve with distinction here.'

Pedubast's eyes roamed over the assortment of papyrus, some of which would not have looked out of place on a vizier's or prophet's table. His gaze settled on scroll in Iuput's hands. The penmanship bore a passing resemblance to Egyptian hieratic, but very few of the words were familiar to him. Iuput seemed to read it with ease.

'Is that Nubian?' asked Pedubast.

'Yes, Nerymut of the brotherhood of Mut lent it to me. It is quite interesting.'

Pedubast chuckled and shook his head. 'You never cease to amaze, brother.'

Iuput nodded, accepting his brother's praise but unsure what to do with it. When he wasn't reading the sacred texts aloud in the temple service, he was found in the libraries or here at home, absorbing texts just as the river banks drank deep of the life-giving floods.

'It's not so hard,' said Iuput, turning the scroll around to show his brother. 'The symbols are borrowed from ours with a slight variance here and there. This one represents the 't' sound.'

'I'll leave you to it,' said Pedubast, but in truth he was glad of Iuput's good cheer. His brother was prone to long periods of despondency that only time could draw him out of. Iuput had always been withdrawn, living within himself, and even their parents, Amun rest their souls, had nearly given up on the sullen and silent younger son. Bullied and mocked by the older boys, Iuput had retreated into words and stories. At least, until Pedubast had sought his revenge and left scorpions in their beds and piss in their wine. Iuput had been left to his own devices after that.

'The princess is pretty.'

Pedubast raised an eyebrow. 'Yes, she is, and with a temper to rival her father. But listen, you must not say things like that around others. That is how scandals begin.'

'I don't understand.'

Pedubast smiled again. 'You have a voracious mind, Iuput, but in the realm of people, leave it to me.'

'As you say,' shrugged Iuput and returned to his studies. 'Will we see her again?'

'Perhaps,' said Pedubast. He rose to his feet, plucking another morsel of bread from the platter. 'I must return to the temple. There is something I must see to. Sunset is not for another three hours, so meet me at the temple entrance thirty minutes before. Do not get distracted this time.'

'Her necklace was in the image of Taweret,' said Iuput. 'Did you notice it?'

Pedubast frowned. 'Who? Isetweret?'

Iuput nodded. 'A silver pedant with the hippopotamus mother.'

Between nearly cutting her throat and then placating her paranoia, however well-found it might have been, that seemingly insignificant detail had eluded him. Not Iuput, though. If his brother could memorise whole texts without effort, this detail would be a trifle to remember.

'Her patron goddess is Mut,' said Pedubast. 'This changes things.'

# RUIN OF SEKHMET

# Chapter Five

'BROTHERS, WHY THE grim expressions?' Senmut smiled, as Tasenhor and Naroleth shot apart like misbehaving schoolchildren. Tasenhor's hand hovered over the platter shared between them and Naroleth's cup hovered an inch from the table. Around the hall, other priests of the Amun precinct talked and ate, the chorus of conversation smothering any individual words. The presence of a prophet in their midst, however, turned heads. Senmut gestured for Tasenhor and Naroleth to follow him outside.

'Has there been word from Sarasesh?' asked Naroleth, stepping out into the daylight. Senmut led them around the corner of the hall, well out of earshot, before he spoke.

'None.'

Tasenhor grunted. 'Are you expecting word from him?'

Senmut smiled back at them. 'Of course.'

'I admit, I would have told you to go to the underworld one step at a time if it was me you had asked to go,' said Tasenhor.

'I would have forbidden it. Sarasesh has a much more agreeable disposition than you do,' replied Senmut.

'Are we all so disposable to you, Senmut?' sighed Tasenhor.

For a moment, Senmut almost looked offended, but his smile returned quickly. 'No, I need you both. Follow me.'

'I am sure you told Sarasesh the same thing,' Tasenhor muttered.

The trio fell silent as another group of priests passed them on the way to the eating hall. Senmut murmured a blessing over them in greeting as Tasenhor and Naroleth made holy signs with their hands.

When they were alone again, Senmut nodded towards an office by the warehouses. Of late, the non-descript, little square building had become one of their newer safe houses. With the temples consolidating their ever-shrinking holdings, the civil strife in the north, and Takelot's exile of those with connections to Nakhtefmut, more and more of the precinct's buildings were falling into disuse.

'Speak truthfully, Senmut,' said Tasenhor, as soon as the door was closed behind them. 'Has there truly been no word from Aswan?'

'Not directly no.'

'Meaning?'

Senmut gestured for them to sit at the central table. 'Meaning that Malkesh seems to have succeeded in uniting the tribes. The towns of the First Cataract burn. They march north as we speak.'

'They are supposed to destroy Takelot,' hissed Naroleth.

'And they will,' said Senmut, raising a placating hand. 'They just needed to be blooded.'

'You said they were pirates and tribesmen of Nubia,' snapped Tasenhor. 'They are blooded enough already. You also said you had need of us. Why should we still believe you? It seems your use for Sarasesh was singular.'

'I did need him. I still do. It is up to the will of the gods to ensure his survival now.'

'Then what do you need from us?' asked Naroleth.

'Your roles are just as vital as that of Sarasesh but much... safer,' smiled Senmut. 'Tasenhor, we are low on funds and in need of refilling the coffers. The last of Osorkon's treasures will not go far if we need to buy others. Ask for donations from the people. If that is not enough, bribe the most corruptible scribes with whatever we have left to skim some taxes to recover our losses.'

Tasenhor frowned. 'That is high treason, Senmut.'

Senmut rolled his eyes. 'That ship has already sailed, so to speak. What we do, we do for the good of the people and the preservation of Karnak,' he said. 'Do not tell me your fervour has dimmed now that we come to the crux of it all? Have I cause to doubt your piety, Tasenhor?'

'You are not a god, so my belief in you is not a matter of piety, brother,' said Tasenhor, emphasising the final word. 'I will follow you in this, but many will not. What of the priesthoods of Mut and Khonsu? Will High Priests Merenmut and Nebneteru support us? It must be all of us.'

'I have considered that,' said Senmut, turning to the other priest before Tasenhor could protest further. 'Naroleth, it is time we started sharing our beliefs. Choose carefully who you trust or we will all be undone. Speak to the other priesthoods as well as our own. Let them take this message to their families, who will spread it to their friends. When the time is right, the people will be crying out for change.'

Senmut watched his companions as they shared another look. He smiled thinly and raised his open palm. 'Now go, with Amun's blessing. May the light of the Theban Triad, father Amun, mother Mut and the moon child Khonsu, be with you.'

As one, Tasenhor and Naroleth rose from the table and slipped through the open door, parting ways immediately. Senmut watched them go, his smile dissolving into a sneer. He had seen them in the hall, seen them both when they had thought they were alone. The look of guilt on their faces when he had approached had been unmistakable.

Perhaps their usefulness would soon run its course after all.

ISETWERET VOMITED INTO her chamber pot, tears streaming down her face as yellow bile drooled from the corner of her mouth. Her handmaidens held her by the shoulders, holding her hair back and rubbing her shoulders as the spasms wracked her body again.

'Let it out. You will feel better,' crooned her lady-in-waiting, Neferet.

The angry retort died on Isetweret's lips as she gritted her teeth together, falling on her backside a moment later and breathing hard.

'Where is the doctor?' she hissed.

'Not coming. No need,' said Neferet, holding up her hands as Isetweret rounded on her angrily. 'There is no denying it any longer. When was the last time you bled?'

Isetweret shrugged. 'The akhet festival? Maybe before?'

'That was six weeks ago, my lady,' replied Neferet. She shared a look with the other handmaidens who all bore a knowing smile. 'Mother Taweret has smiled upon you.'

The handmaidens giggled as the princess paled.

'Bring me wine,' she growled, heaving herself up onto the edge of the bed.

'Watered down for the baby's health,' insisted Neferet, after the retreating girl.

The handmaiden bowed and withdrew, heading for the palace kitchens. Among the servants, the news would be the talk of the palace by day's end, Isetweret knew.

'How long does this last?' she asked.

'It depends on the mother goddess. For some it passes quickly, others until birth. Even after,' replied Neferet.

'Gods below,' she groaned. 'Osiris, take me now.'

The handmaiden returned with her wine before too long and Isetweret sipped at it gingerly, sighing as the spices went some way to alleviating the tremor in her belly and cleansed her mouth of the foul taste of bile. She had finished the first cup when another voice called out to her.

'Iset, what is wrong?' Hory stood at the chamber door, frozen at the sight of half a dozen women clustered around a chamber pot on the floor.

Isetweret looked up and Hory paled at the sight of her. Her hair was dishevelled, her dress stained and her eyes sunken and rimmed with tiredness.

'What has happened? Why are you all smiling?' he demanded.

The handmaidens shared a grin and looked him up and down. Isetweret could not help but laugh too as she saw Hory flush a shade of crimson at their scrutiny.

He came to her but her coterie shooed him back as they fussed about her. Within minutes her face was clean, she wore a new dress and her complexion was darkened to a healthier tone with a brush of ochre cosmetic. When they were satisfied, the handmaidens went about the task of keeping the vizier's bedchambers, and Isetweret noticed, trying not to look too obvious in their eavesdropping.

'I am sorry for my outburst,' Isetweret began, coming across the floor and taking Hory's hands in her own. 'You were right. You are the vizier. I should respect your decisions. I have not been well lately, in body or mind.'

'What do you mean? What is going on?' he asked.

Isetweret took his hand and placed it on her belly. For a moment, confusion creased Hory's features before realisation came to him. Hory's eyes lit up and he took a step back as he stared at her. His shock gave way to laughter and he swept her up, eliciting a squeal that brought the handmaidens running. Isetweret waved them away and they scattered, knowing better than to risk their lady's ire.

'I am sorry too. I should not have been so dismissive of you,' said Hory, as he put her down and led her to sit on the bed. His voice dropped to a whisper so that even Isetweret's servants could not hear him. 'This pressure is too much some days. We have enough to worry about without adding more ourselves. After all this is over, we will take a trip to the estates and be away from it all for a while. Would you like that?'

Isetweret nestled into his shoulder, her hand wrapped around the image of Taweret hanging around her neck. 'I would.'

Hory pulled away and faced her. 'I have news for you too. I will not stand idly by while our people suffer. Your father secures the north but it is up to us to secure the south. More so now for the future of our house and our family,' he said.

'I have sent word to all the towns between Asyut and Hierakonpolis and mobilised the Theban reserve cohorts. This unrest in the south cannot be allowed to continue. We will fight.'

The nausea hit her again and she rushed back to the chamber pot. Hory knelt beside her and held her close to him, but this time she smiled through the pain.

# Chapter Six

HARSIESE WATCHED THE gentle swaying of the golden wheat that filled the fields of his estate. Like windswept water, the thick stalks and fat kernels undulated in a rippling wave that brought at once a sense of peace and pleasure. The bent-backed slaves harvesting it worked with renewed fervour as they recognised their master passing them by. Many of them had been a gift from Osorkon, the spoils of war after the prince had crushed the Meshwesh horde at the Dakhla Oasis.

The road on which he travelled ran along a high ridge overlooking the fertile flood plains below. The manse itself was built on a rise on the ridge, like a watchtower. Closer to the house, long lines of grape vines grew up and down the slope, the fruit ripe and fat with juice. Harsiese watched more slaves move through each row, cutting down bulging bunches of grapes and placing them with care in the wicker baskets at their feet. A year from now, the juice from those same grapes would be a rich and deep red wine, stored in heavy amphorae and ready to be transported to every corner of the Two Lands that could afford it, gods willing.

The deed to the land was worth all the gold of a royal tomb and its loss twenty years before had crushed a young boy's ambitions and condemned him to a lifetime of penury, at least compared to the luxury to which he had become accustomed.

Raised in a modest household, he had long held the dream of recovering his birthright and of finding the lost tomb of his father. The former had been recouped piece by piece through sycophancy and flaunting a disinterest in the machinations of power. His hopes for the latter had only become reality when Takelot had claimed to a throne in Thebes and appointed Harsiese as the High Priest of Amun in his stead. Now with the war so very far away and uncertain, his fortunes were once more in flux, tied to a man who held the same ambitions that had destroyed his father.

The High Priest of Amun settled into a canter, close enough to the safety of his estate that he felt comfortable leaving behind his guard and retainers to escort the baggage train. Word of his coming had sent the household into a flurry of activity. His manse was prepared and his staff turned out to greet their master. He should not have been surprised. His own eyes and ears went far enough. It was only reasonable to assume they had word of his unannounced coming.

His head slave waited patiently, if not calmly, at the front gate. Hekhenfer had sold himself into Harsiese's service some years before, unable to pay off his substantial debts at a time when Harsiese's fortune was but a shadow of his current condition.

The merchant's gambling problems had seen him lose everything; his wife, his warehouse and all the stock his family had painstakingly accumulated. In his ruin, Harsiese had seen a kindred spirit and offered him a place as his household chamberlain for a period of ten years.

Gratefully, Hekhenfer had accepted, not least for the protection Harsiese's house offered against the loan sharks that sought to feed him in pieces to the beasts of the river.

'Hail Hekhenfer, how are you?'

'All the better for seeing you, my Lord Harsiese. We did not expect you until the end of harvest tally,' said Hekhenfer, his eyes respectfully fixed on the dirt beneath the hooves of his master's mount. The turnout and pristine maintenance of the estate put the lie to his words, but Harsiese was content to play along.

'As intended, I assure you,' he said.

Behind the head slave, the servants of the household knelt in the dust, their heads bowed low and their palms turned upward in symbolic offering.

'Rise, all of you. I come with glad tidings. But first, help my men unload the carts. I bring fare from Thebes. Tonight, we all feast.'

His household all but rushed the carts, falling upon the supplies with childlike excitement. The wine and venison would never see the servants' table, but the beer, dried fish and fresh bread would be a veritable banquet for the serfs and a reminder that their own fortunes were tied to the destiny of Lord Harsiese of Thebes.

Harsiese gestured to his head slave. 'Come, help me down.'

Hekhenfer did as he was bid, and the two embraced as old friends. Some barriers could be broken in the moment, though other bonds of friendship would only be renewed away from prying eyes.

Walking side-by-side with his master, Hekhenfer glanced nervously at Harsiese.

'So, nothing is wrong, my lord?'

'Everything is fine, my old friend. I have need of your expertise though. Tell me, do you still have a way of contacting any of your old captains? One with a fast vessel and a still tongue?'

'It has been a great many years, my lord. But yes, I think so. I can think of one or two that may help. They may not be pleased to see me.'

'They will not touch you. You are still under my protection and you will walk with my personal seal. Tell them their debts will be settled if they do this thing for me.'

Hekhenfer's eyes narrowed. 'With all respect, lord, you are making me nervous with such talk.'

'See that your part is done flawlessly and you need never worry again,' said Harsiese, keeping his voice low as several of his servants ran past them back to the house, hefting sacks of grain and pots of beer.

Hekhenfer forced a smile, a convincing image of a relieved servant greeting his master. 'And what, may I ask, is this job?'

'I need to get a message to Herakleopolis, and I need it done without being seen.'

That night, the dining room of Harsiese's manse was dark and quiet, illuminated by thin candles that gave off a wan, but warm glow. Shadows danced on the walls as the two diners ate and drank.

But for the murmurs of appreciation at the fare and the quiet conversation, all else was silent and still.

'Even as a gambling man, I say you are taking a great risk. You have just won it all back. Why would you throw it away so readily?' Hekhenfer set down his goblet, his meat knife clattering to the table.

Harsiese sat across from his chamberlain. The other slaves had been dismissed and Harsiese poured them both a measure more of wine. 'The war is coming whether we do something or not. I intend to profit from it,' he said.

'And you tell me this Senmut has already betrayed Takelot?'

Harsiese nodded. 'Him, and several others plan to.'

Hekhenfer continued. 'And that an army from Nubia will march upon the Crag of Amun and beyond to Herakleopolis to catch Takelot and Osorkon engaged against Shoshenq?'

'A fine tactic, don't you think?' said Harsiese over the rim of his goblet.

'Very fine,' agreed Hekhenfer. 'And you wish to throw yourself in the middle of it all? My lord, with the greatest respect, that is the stupidest thing I've ever heard.'

'That's hardly respectful, Hekhenfer, but the point remains. Takelot does not trust me. He thinks I am bound to him by virtue of being gifted back my own birthright. Senmut and my own gods-cursed priesthood do not trust me and think me bound to them by their collective standing. Let them all burn,' replied Harsiese.

Hekhenfer watched his master for a moment, toying with a piece of venison on his place. 'You are playing a dangerous game, my lord. I do not know of which side to be more afraid.'

'Neither do I. Senmut is a gullible fool. Takelot will not dare go against me after returning my estates. Both of them fear being made to look weak. In that they become predictable.'

Hekhenfer swirled the contents of his wine cup around as he watched his master's anger burn. 'And what comes after?'

'Ashes and the redemption of my house.'

Hekhenfer nodded slowly. 'You have many steps to reach it. You trust Pharaoh?'

'Not at all. My problems would be solved much swifter with a knife through Takelot's heart. One for the Crown Prince too, come to think of it. It is not a possibility I am discounting, in truth. Osorkon returned my lands to me with a damned flourish of his pen. He knows he can unmake me just as quickly.'

Hekhenfer chuckled darkly. 'You were my friend even before you became my master and if this is your will then I will follow you for good or ill. What would you have me do?'

'Warn Osorkon.' Harsiese smiled, his lips thin and stained red with wine. 'I will send you to the Crag with a letter explaining Senmut's treachery and that I have had to flee the city or risk being caught up in the betrayal. You will see that it reaches Osorkon's hand and his alone. Not Akhetep's, not Bakenptah, none who claim to speak for him. It must come to the Crown Prince only, understand?'

'I understand, my lord.'

Harsiese's smile faded quickly. 'You are a truly loyal friend, Hekhenfer and I am glad that the gods brought you to my service. Bring me ink and papyrus and then eat and drink your fill. You leave at first light.'

HERAKLEOPOLIS WAS IN mourning at the death of the nomarch's last son. Vendors shut up shop and merchants kept their warehouses securely closed for none could be certain whether Tibekh's passing would cause the fractious relationship between the nomarch and Pharaoh to descend into violence.

Nobles fretted in their homes, their opulence doing nothing to assuage their fears, for unless the unstable Nomarch Khonsefankh took a new wife, his line was at an end. If the rumours had any truth to them, their independence would be absorbed by Pharaoh Takelot's ambitions, the glorious hegemony of Middle Egypt to be ruled by a puppet nomarch in their lord's stead. Under Takelot's orders, Khonsefankh had been kept under sedation since his son's death, adding fuel to the rumours of a takeover. Access to the grieving ruler had been severely restricted and many a hopeful noble, seeking to garner his favour with expensive gifts, had been turned away.

Osorkon watched the city from the palace roof, the silence of a tomb descending on the city streets. Here and there, lone figures darted between buildings, but all else was quiet as the city held its breath.

'I was starting to think you had forgotten about me.'

Osorkon startled, his reverie broken by a soft voice from the rooftop stairway. 'You speak of the impossible, Karoadjet. Thank you for meeting me here.'

'Of course, husband-to-be,' she said, stepping out into the sunshine, her kohl-rimmed eyes sparkling with mischief. She approached the edge of the roof, peering down at the drop and she closed her eyes as the wind caught her hair.

'The city is quiet,' said Osorkon. 'Your people hide in their homes, but mud brick walls will not save them.'

'From the storm you bring with you?'

Osorkon's eyes flashed, but Karoadjet smiled sweetly.

'People always fear change,' she said.

'And you? What do you fear?'

Karoadjet smiled, twirling the end of her hair around a finger glittering with gold rings. 'A great many things,' she said finally.

She sat beside him, her back to the wall, and watched him carefully. The dark circles under his eyes revealed the truth of long and restless nights. Karoadjet had taken a leaf out of her future mother-in-law's book and made it her business to know what occurred within the nomarch's palace in these trying days. Candles burning until dawn, the cries of recurring nightmares that stirred the palace servants, and the frictions of a family held together by a ragged will had all reached her ears.

'You have not returned to the Crag to your men. Nor do you participate in the administration of this city with your parents.'

'My uncle does not wish to even lay eyes on me. The army is already marching north and I am forbidden to join them until after my cousin's interment. There is little to do in the meantime.'

Karoadjet sniffed lightly. 'Surely it is not me that keeps you here for I have not seen you in two weeks.' The stir in the prince's despondency revealed she had hit her mark.

'Truly, my family could not have picked a more inquisitive woman to be my wife,' he sighed, and looked back out over the city.

Karoadjet's smile faded and she went to rise. 'I am sure there a hundred women down there that would that would kill for the chance to marry a prince. Shall I go find one for you?'

Osorkon held up an apologetic hand and Karoadjet's sudden fury faded as quickly as it had appeared. 'Forgive me, I spoke out of turn. I did not mean it.'

'Speak then, and earn my forgiveness.' Such was the imperiousness of her command and the strain on his own mind that to Osorkon, in that moment, nothing could have been funnier. He laughed, a laugh that broke the dam in his mind. The usurper of his great-grandfather's throne was coming to kill them, he was responsible for his cousin's death and the end of his father and uncle's brotherhood, and the city they were using as a forward base was in a state of terrified self-curfew. Yet for all that, what wrong-footed him the most was an interrogation by the beauty he was to marry in a few short days.

Karoadjet's eyes narrowed. 'Do I amuse you?'

'Yes,' said Osorkon, honestly. 'But probably not in the way you think. Listen then, Karoadjet of Herakleopolis, and see if you still wish to marry me.'

The prince sobered, and he picked at a loose thread on his shendyt as he shared with her all that had happened. Nimlot's death and the vizier's betrayal. The trial of his father and his failure in capturing Nakhtefmut. The night with Chief Pediese and the snake out in the desert. With each tale, he became more animated, frequently speaking in tangents before Karoadjet gently guided him back.

By the end of it, his mouth was dry and a new weariness had taken hold, but his eyes were alight with life and the fervour of a man rekindling his purpose. Sometime during his telling her hand had found his and the feeling of her fingers between his stirred him deeply, a feeling of needing to be near her.

'I could have saved him. I should have saved him,' said Osorkon.

'You killed the beast. That is a worthy feat in itself.'

'Perhaps, but I have killed a great many things. Rarely do I relish it.'

'You cannot change the past. Why do you linger in it?' asked Karoadjet.

Osorkon considered the question carefully. 'Penitence.'

'And who does that serve? You are suffering. The nomarch is suffering. You parents are suffering. Your men are leaderless and the gods remain unserved. What does this self-pity achieve beyond giving our enemies more time to mass against us?'

Osorkon shook his head and looked away. 'I am beset by fear and doubts.'

'As are all who wield power, but you were born to lead,' said Karoadjet, taking his chin in her hand and bringing his gaze back to hers. 'You do not have the luxury of inactivity. Let others around you carry the burden of fear and doubt and when it comes time to act, leave those burdens behind.'

'You are a strange woman, Karoadjet, but I have become very fond of you.'

'Fond? My prince, I had no idea you were so poetic.'

Osorkon's cheeks burned red and he hoped the sun hid the worst of it, but her smirk told him he hoped for too much. 'Must you tease me so?' he protested.

'Yes.'

He kissed her then, a long and lingering kiss that he had rehearsed in his mind a thousand times. For a moment, she was taken by surprise, and Osorkon was glad he had at least this over her. Then she kissed him back and the power was hers once more. They came apart and the powder on Karoadjet's cheeks was not enough to hide her blush.

'I walk a dangerous road, Karoadjet. You still have time. You can find a rich merchant to buy you all the jewels and dresses you could ever desire.'

'I have those already, enough to fill my tomb twice over,' said Karoadjet.

Osorkon was not dissuaded. 'I warn you now that there will be blood. I do not know where the war will be fought or for how long, but I do know what it will bring.'

'You are a prince and a general. Life and blood are yours to spend as you see fit. Make sure you spend them well.'

Osorkon shifted. 'You speak of it so plainly.'

'How else is there to speak of it?' asked Karoadjet. 'Unless you are going to overcome Shoshenq in a battle of poetry, which for you I do not recommend, you must look at things as they are, not as you would wish them to be.'

'There are some things that are as I wish them to be.' His stare made her blush again and she frowned at him, irritated at the betrayal of her own body.

She pulled away from him, though the smirk never left her face. 'Then you had better fight to keep them that way.'

The loss of her touch struck him deeper than he had ever thought it would as she made her way back to the staircase. Her black hair faded from view and the loss was complete. He stayed a moment longer, the scent of flowery oils from her skin lingering in the air.

THE ROYAL MARRIAGE celebrations took place three days hence. There was no formal ceremony of their union, simply an announcement of the intention to join houses and the heart-wrenching news to the bachelors of the city that Lady Karoadjet of the House of Herytep was a married woman. No vows were spoken but those the lovers spoke in private and no priest ratified their union. The coming together of man and wife was witnessed and maintained by the gods regardless of who the couple was or where they were.

On the day of the announcement, the families convened to witness the signing of the marriage contract. The papyrus was the length of a man's arm and filled from top to bottom with tiny hieroglyphic script, ready to be later transferred to stone on a commemorative stela. The wording spoke little of romantic devotion and almost nothing of the legal stipulations of the married couple.

Instead, it was dedicated almost entirely to the alliance between the two wealthy houses and the land deputations, trade statutes and political friendships that confirmed the union.

At the top of the papyrus, two names written in stylised cartouches formalised Karoadjet's joining of the Theban royal family, bequeathing her with the title of 'princess' and future Great

Royal Wife. In honour of her new mother-in-law, she had taken Karomama's epithet 'Beloved of Mut' as her own, a fitting accompaniment to her husband's station as High Priest of Amun.

Lord Herytep was the first to sign, before passing the pen to his new son-in-law.

Osorkon took the pen gently, meeting Karoadjet's gaze from where she stood beside her mother. Lady Neferadjet wept unashamed tears, the kohl around her eyes smearing at she dabbed at them with a linen kerchief. Osorkon's own mother was in a similar state, the tautness of her face giving some insight into her self-control.

The fathers too were overjoyed, wishing their children well as they turned their attention to the logistics of transporting Karoadjet's possessions from her family's manse to Osorkon's suite at the Crag of Amun, before talk quickly turned to the beginning of their business partnership.

The fifth guest at the signing did not share in their happiness.

Khonsefankh watched the gathering with hooded, listless eyes. The grief-stricken nomarch had been awakened from his stupor and fed a concoction of simulating herbs that flushed the sedatives from his body, but the medicines did little to ease his mind. His reclusive nature had only deepened in his depression. As nomarch, he witnessed the signing in sullen silence, refusing to speak and directing venomous glances between his brother and nephew.

For their part, no one paid him any mind. His presence was no more than that of a lifeless statue, his absence from feasts, administrative meetings and military planning making his presence now an uncomfortable obligation that he would end as soon as possible.

Without the influence of his sedatives keeping him still, Khonsefankh had begun a habit of disappearing for hours at a time. Even his own servants were often ignorant of his whereabouts and no one had yet bothered to find where he went, the demands of the war and of managing their southern kingdom were simply too great.

Osorkon, for his part, was relieved. Khonsefankh's spirit was already dead, even if his soul was still encased in living flesh. His will had blackened and his moods were bleak and he was no longer able to hold any of the responsibilities of nomarch.

The prince looked away from his despondent uncle and handed the reed pen back to his father-in-law. Lord Herytep held out the pen to his daughter and Karoadjet made her mark beside the prince's without hesitation.

With a final flourish, she set the pen down, and Herytep clapped his hands in delight. Nothing more was to be said and nothing more to be given for the wealthy Lord Herytep had refused the obligatory wedding gift, though it had been offered more than once. Even so, Takelot had seen to it that several jars of wine from the royal cellars had found their way to his house.

'What is more gold to the prospect of royal grandchildren?' Herytep had said, when Osorkon had asked what material price could be attached to so heavenly a bride. The prince had made a token gesture anyway, spending days and nights hand-crafting a crocodile skin dagger sheath for Herytep and a turquoise necklace inscribed with blessed hieroglyphs of warding for Lady Neferadjet.

Karoadjet moved into the Crag that afternoon. Osorkon had taken great pains to create a sense of comfort and sophistication in his surroundings, but they remained a far cry from the lavish suites to which Karoadjet was accustomed. Expensive rugs of fine linen cloth and furniture painted with exquisite pigments of blue and green filled his suite of rooms. The royal apartments were one of only a few entirely new buildings in the fortress. Constructed upon Osorkon's custodianship of the old fortress, renovation had begun as soon as Bakenptah had brought him the news of his engagement.

Karoadjet's perpetual amusement never left her as she glided into the rooms, already reimagining the decorations Osorkon had laboured over for weeks. Her train of handmaidens and servants, released from Herytep's employment into hers, immediately set to work, moving her furniture and furnishings in and rearranging the layout to follow mystical guidelines that would ensure an effective conception and a contented marriage.

Bewildered, Osorkon left them to their devices and sought out Akhetep elsewhere within the fortress. He found his friend working with the chariot engineers, reforging the metalwork for a machine that had suffered chassis damage in the last scouting expedition to the north. Shoshenq's army yet remained in Tanis, though for what reason they had not marched south none of the charioteers could say. No Tanite emissaries or scouts were detected and merchants coming south reported nothing of import that might divine Shoshenq's intent. The desert remained silent and barren, devoid of threat or friend, as though it held its breath for the bloodshed to come.

Akhetep looked up from where he was hammering nails into the axle joins as Osorkon entered the workshop. He handed the hammer to the forge assistant and wiped soot-stained sweat from his brow. He grinned at his friend, but the expression was strained.

'All settled in?'

'Not yet. If she starts redecorating the ramparts, you will let me know, won't you?' asked Osorkon.

'That is not a terrible idea. Perhaps a fine rug to kneel upon as we shoot Shoshenq's men?' said Akhetep.

Osorkon chuckled and knelt beside the mended chariot, inspecting the joins and metalwork. The reforged components were flawless, the reconstruction perfect, just as he had expected. Few men knew the workings and balance of a chariot like Akhetep.

Osorkon looked up at his friend. 'You didn't meet me in the city.'

A shadow passed over Akhetep's face. 'I have been inclined to solitude lately. I am sorry I missed the signing. The nomarch was there?'

'He was, but my uncle has not spoken since I took his son home. Our fathers made a toast to their new business partnership, and I am sure the city will find its own way to celebrate and come out of hiding to drink before they die. A fine start to a happy life together.'

Akhetep raised an eyebrow. 'Since when were you prone to thoughts of gloom?'

'The same time you became inclined to solitude.'

'Fair enough,' replied Akhetep, his smile returning. 'It is good to see you, my friend. Forgive me, I really am sorry I missed the occasion.'

Osorkon took Akhetep's wrist in a warrior grip. 'Say no more of it. We live in interesting times. We yet live and there is food to eat and beds to sleep in.'

Akhetep nodded slowly. 'I have not slept well of late. My dreams are disturbed,' he confessed after a moment.

'The hippopotamus?'

'I have never seen a beast of its like. Men, I understand, will travel far for war. But we were half a kilometre inland on a rise far beyond the flood plain. Only a beast of darkness goes against its own instincts like that. What kind of bloodlust would propel it so? What does it mean? What force of darkness sent it against us?'

'I do not know.'

Akhetep dismissed the forge attendants, taking the bellows for himself, and pumped fresh air into the coals. The forge roared with heat and the air rippled with haze. Akhetep pitched his voice low, so that even Osorkon had to lean in to hear. 'Speak plainly. What is our next move? Is your uncle expelling us from the city? Where is Shoshenq?'

'He has not yet left Tanis, though I cannot imagine for what purpose he remains there. Whatever it is, my father believes it will not be long now until we see dust over the northern horizon. We prepare as best we can. Nothing more.'

'Ill times, indeed,' muttered Akhetep. 'What of Tibekh's preparations?'

'Complete, or thereabouts. His body is ready, but his tomb needed work. The artisans are going as fast as they can to complete the necessary protective spells. The way he died… those spells are important.'

'Osiris keep him and judge him justly,' intoned Akhetep. He depressed the bellows again and the coals burned white hot with renewed heat. He took a rag from the work bench and dipped it in a barrel of water before wiping away the soot from around his eyes.

'What of the Crag?' asked Osorkon. 'Are the widows well cared for?' Three of the charioteers killed in the hippopotamus attack had left families behind. War was still leagues away, but already his people felt the cold ache of loss.

'Materially, yes, but the mood is sombre as expected and we can only do so much. We should send them back to the city. It would be safer and more comfortable there.'

'I will ask them, but I will not cast them out if they do not wish it. Many can take new husbands from among the company, if they wish. We can train the boys, and the girls can help in the temples. The community we have built here will endure so long as we do not break it up. True friendships are hard to come by.'

Akhetep tossed the filthy rag aside. 'You have your head on straight well enough for a married man. See that it remains so after you drag yourself from your marriage bed.'

With each passing day, Harsiese was further emboldened, confident in his decision to reach out to Osorkon. By day, he tended to his vineyard and supervised the fermenting of the season's grapes, breathing deep of the actinic tang of the tanks and relishing the peace and predictability of industrial processes. Ra had smiled upon his harvest and the sun god's beneficence would bring gold raining into his coffers.

His nights were tormented though, and he cried out from until the first light of dawn as terror and a sense of formless dread disturbed his sleep. He could not entirely ignore the furtive glances of his servants at breakfast each morning and he busied himself working to exhaustion as he waited for word from the north. With Amun's blessing, the ship bearing his servant Hekhenfer would reach the Crag of Amun in the next day or two. Harsiese estimated it would take Osorkon another week to marshal his forces and then a week again to reach Thebes.

Then the first whispers among his staff reached his ears. Just as wind flowed across the desert dunes, so too did rumour and hearsay drift through the common-born. With uncanny swiftness, tales of horror and bloodshed spread through his household and Harsiese was powerless to stop it.

A Nubian invasion, they said, whispering among themselves after nightfall when the fields were silent and the oil lamps sputtered their last. The towns around Aswan had already fallen, their sacred places sacked and their people butchered. The pillaging would continue all the way north. It was only a matter of time until the marauders reached them here. Only the cities could be truly safe.

Thebes, with its mighty walls, would stand, until the time that Apophis and Set tore them down too. Divine punishment had come for them at last. Displeased at the civil war, Amun had unleashed Sekhmet in her most wrathful form.

Harsiese heard it all, and he was afraid.

Time was against him. Without his authority, without his influence, the vizier would crumble beneath Senmut's will. Isetweret would wrap herself in schemes unaware of the viper in their midst, and the city itself would fall into peril. If this truly was Senmut's doing and he opened the gates of Thebes to his horde, the whole city would be sacked. Karnak would be put to the torch, its treasures looted and its sacred places defiled. And when vengeance came from the north, as it surely would, Osorkon would know that Harsiese himself had neglected Thebes in its hour of need. The prince would not look kindly on his desertion and all of his own ambition would be for nought. He would be stripped of his titles once more and his lands seized by the state to recoup the costs of rebuilding. Exile would be lenient and his dream to locate his father's tomb would remain forever out of reach.

Harsiese could do little from the comfort of his estate, nothing at all if he was being entirely truthful with himself. He yearned for the safety and security here in this place, but as more rumours reached him, his night terrors only worsened, searing his waking thoughts with fears of what was to come.

Seven days after he had dispatched Hekhenfer to deliver his message to the Crag of Amun, Harsiese called his household to order. Expectant faces waited for their lord to make his pronouncement, from his trusted body servants to the lowliest field slaves. With halting tones, he delivered it. Only a skeleton staff of slaves would remain behind to tend the crops and the livestock used to plough the fields. Everyone else was directed to prepare for the journey to Thebes.

Given twelve hours to prepare for the march south, the servants awaited their master's direction as to his own provisions for few among the staff needed scant more than minutes to assemble their worldly possessions. As night fell once more and no word was forthcoming, the household staff settled in for their final night on the estate.

On the eighth day, Harsiese ordered his household to move once more. Though the servants muttered it among themselves, not one of them questioned out loud why Harsiese was leaving behind everything of value and comfort.

# Chapter Seven

IN THE FAR north of the country, on the waters of the Great Delta, the sun shone down upon a fallen king's final journey. The afternoon light was soft and the wind came gently across the water as the flotilla sailed through the tributaries surrounding Tanis. The division of the country and the shift of the capital from Memphis to Tanis had necessitated new tomb valleys to be constructed for royalty and the select rich who could afford to be interred among a pantheon of living gods. The tomb lands, nestled in the foothills of a select few Delta islands, were only accessible by boat, an additional security measure not enjoyed by their cousins in the south, and one for which Shoshenq had become increasingly grateful for.

The flotilla was modest for a royal procession, though it still numbered some thirty boats, each of them bearing a contingent of soldiers armed with hunting spears and bows. Quivers, thick with arrows, were arranged at regular intervals on the gunwales and one in every three vessels had a lookout posted at the top of the mast. It might have been a fleet on the war footing but for the unmistakable outline of the royal funerary barge at the heart of the fleet, bearing the coffin of Pharaoh Osorkon II as he was conveyed to his resting place.

Professional mourners flung themselves to the barge's deck in practised anguish, tearing at their clothes and smearing long lines of ash down their faces as they worked themselves into a grief-stricken frenzy. Those that watched from neighbouring vessels, among the closest of Pharaoh's courtiers, longed to do the same, but decorum forbid them from expressing their grief in public at all. Nobles, merchants, allied dignitaries, and ministers of the Tanite government all sailed in silence in final escort of their king. Many of the Tanites following in the barge's wake had gifted a portion of their wealth so that the king might be even better prepared for the afterlife. If their rich offerings bought the favour of the dead king's successor then all the better.

Exquisitely crafted furniture and weapons, rich foodstuffs, and rare and powerful books of spells had all been donated to pharaoh's tomb to serve his spirit in the afterlife. Each offering had already been carefully transported and packed away, filling the tomb from floor to ceiling. Only a single thin passage remained, leading to the great stone sarcophagus. All was in readiness for the final addition, the king's body.

The finest embalmers in the country had taken almost three months to prepare Osorkon II's body for eternity by drying, wrapping and imbuing the dead flesh with reanimating magic. Amulets of metal and stone had been placed within his linen wrappings, infused with protective power by the most learned magicians and a death mask of gold and lapis lazuli shrouded his sunken, deathly visage.

His mortal remains now resided within his wooden coffin, destined to never again see daylight. The coffin was superbly crafted, covered in fine inscriptions that had been picked out in brilliant pigments. The blues were turquoise, the greens malachite, the reds a rich ochre, alongside sunny yellows and bright whites. Scenes from Pharaoh's life adorned every surface, bordered by bands of protective hieroglyphs.

The funerary barge was similarly warded, built to house the coffin just as the coffin had been built to house the royal remains.

Shoshenq watched the barge's passage from the throne of his own warship. He had never been formally adopted and no blood ties bound them, but Pharaoh had been his father all the same. Osorkon II had raised him, nurtured him, given him opportunity and now had given him his throne. The throne of Tanis should have made him one of the most powerful men in the world, but he had lost control of half the country the moment he had first sat upon it. He had fought the Assyrians for a decade, learning all there was to know of warfare, of pitched battles and sieges, supply lines and logistics. Now, he was forced to apply those same lessons against his own countrymen.

Shoshenq rubbed at his eyes, feeling the first signs of a headache pulsing behind them. Beside him, Ankherednefer, the Inspector of the Palace, stood with his hands clasped behind his back. His gaze was fixed on the surface of the water, searching for any sign of disturbance from below, just as it had been since they had cast off.

'I am tired, Ankherednefer.'

Ankherednefer nodded but kept his vigil. 'We are nearing our destination. The interment will not take long.'

'That is not what I meant.'

Ankherednefer glanced at the throne. The Inspector was responsible for the palace's defence, the safety of pharaoh's person and the myriad other duties involved in safeguarding his master's seat of power. In quieter moments, he was also pharaoh's confidant.

'The people loved my father,' Shoshenq sighed. 'Look at them now, look how many come. Will they follow me, do you think, when I lie upon that barge?'

'These are difficult times. The people know that war is upon them and everything may change. It is only natural they seek the comfort of a safe past.'

'I suppose you are right,' replied Shoshenq.

'Some of them owe their livelihoods to Pharaoh's programs. Many might not even be alive if not for his patronage. Continue your father's work, my lord.'

Ankherednefer did not look back as he spoke, so Shoshenq left him to his watch, his gaze drifting back to Pharaoh's coffin. Shoshenq's vessel matched the funerary barge for speed, taking its place as the primary naval escort.

The warship was large, almost embarrassingly so given the occasion, but neither Shoshenq nor Ankherednefer were willing to risk the king's journey for the sake of propriety. The fury of a rogue hippopotamus or a host of territorial crocodiles could spell disaster, however unlikely their presence this far north. That spoke nothing of the far more likely manmade threats.

Out of the corner of his eye, Shoshenq saw a spearman tense, lean further over the gunwales and then relax again. He glanced left and right, seeing Pharaoh's gaze upon him. The soldier bowed his head and Shoshenq nodded in reply, watching as the soldier turned back to his vigil. They were, all of them, on edge.

Since civil war had descended on the land, Shoshenq had taken great care to ensure his own cult image was as flawless as his predecessor. An incident on the river would be taken as a sign of Sobek's displeasure and his authority would crumble beneath the apparent condemnation of the crocodile god of pharaonic protection.

Shoshenq looked out over the water, seeing ahead an island crowned by a long ridge of sand and bare rock. The island was devoid of the blues and greens of the surrounding landscape, as though life itself gave this place a wide berth. He shivered, and noticed only then that even the mourners had fallen silent. Shoshenq had never visited the Valley of the Kings, but he wondered if that land felt as this one did.

One day far in the future, gods be good and the Theban usurpers defeated, Shoshenq would lie beside his father in rest here. There, surrounded by the life-giving river, they could rule side by side once more as gods for eternity.

The flotilla peeled away from the funerary barge as the vessel bearing the coffin landed at the dock. The tomb builders were already waiting for them. Silently, they secured the mooring lines and fastened the gangplanks to the dock to give the coffin bearers a surer footing. The professional mourners disembarked first and waited for the coffin to reach dry ground before they took up their wailing and lamentations once more. The other boats moored where they could, tying their vessels to those that had already landed to make a bridge to clamber ashore.

Shoshenq was one of the last ashore, but all present waited for him to lead the procession. The nobles and merchants said their final farewells here for only a very few were permitted to go further than the dock. Shoshenq waited for all who wished to speak to do so before he turned and led the coffin bearers up the slope. The ridge was deceptively high. Sweat beaded his forehead and his breathing became laboured, a taxing walk even for one of his militaristic fitness. For the coffin bearers it must have been torturous, but they did their job well for there was no other choice. To drop a dead pharaoh and damage his gilded coffin would be a death sentence.

The view of the valley was breathtaking, one of desolation masking something greater. Shoshenq's time learning the temple arts had attuned his senses and opened up feelings beyond those of the purely physical. Great power lay buried here beneath the sands. Beside the dust and the heat, one could almost taste the powerful magic that warded this most sacred place.

As Shoshenq descended into the valley, he saw others were already here. Tomb guards stood watch over the entrance to the burial site, all of them sworn to uphold the valley's secrets. A unit of spearmen guarded the door, while archers crouched in groups of two or three, taking cover in the ridges and outcrops above. The great gaping maw of the king's tomb opened up before Shoshenq all too soon, the laborious walk taking no time at all now that it had come to an end. Shoshenq followed the coffin carriers inside, descending the steep stairs into the main burial chamber. The treasure of a king's lifetime was arrayed in the adjacent rooms, everything the king could ever need in the next life.

The coffin bearers lowered the wooden coffin into the stone sarcophagus, the system of ropes and pulleys setting it down inside as gently as a leaf falling to the ground. Like the coffin, the sarcophagus was adorned with all manner of spells and wards to safeguard the king's physical remains. It was a solid block of granite and Shoshenq reminded himself to gift the engineers generously for their devotion in moving it over land and water. Within moments, the stone lid was lifted into place with a final boom of stone settling.

'Farewell, father,' said Shoshenq, allowing himself that minor transgression in his regal stoicism. Though not of direct blood relation, the king had raised a young Senneker up when his noble father had died in battle against the Assyrians and his mother had succumbed to illness shortly after. To lose his birth parents as an infant had been tragic. To lose the man that had lifted him up like a god was heartbreaking.

Shoshenq lingered a while longer, his eyes roaming over the incantations and wards until he was satisfied no damage would impede the glyphs' function.

'Very well. There is nothing left to do. Seal the tomb,' he said finally, turning to follow the waiting tomb guard back to the surface.

None, save perhaps the wisest magicians and high priests, knew the entirety of what happened when a tomb was sealed. The disparate elements of the deceased's soul would reunite with the body, but what effect that would have on the physical world or those that remained too long, none could say for sure. Shoshenq stepped back into the light, feeling oddly cold, and watched the final step. The tomb guards wrapped thick corded rope around the door handles and pressed a seal of sanctified mud onto the knot. Shoshenq inspected their handiwork, but like all else they had done it was flawless.

'Bury it,' he said. 'Let our lord go to the underworld with no worries in his heart.'

The artisans, engineers and tomb guard alike stooped to shovel sand back against the entrance, building up the shape of the cut rock to look as natural as it had been found. By nightfall, it would look untouched once more.

Shoshenq followed the coffin bearers back down to the ships, the walk passing in just a few minutes now that they were free of their burden. None of the assembled nobility had left yet, perhaps hoping to show Shoshenq the depth of their devotion.

'He went well?' asked Ankherednefer, who had remained with the noble and merchant mourners outside the valley proper.

'As well as any of them. We can only hope the same for ourselves one day,' he said.

'Later rather than sooner, I hope,' replied Ankherednefer.

'That is not for us to decide,' said Shoshenq, with a sigh. He felt weary and soul sick, but content that his father would find his way through the trials to come. Ankherednefer followed him back to the warship, content to let his new king speak first.

'The mourning period has been observed. We are free to act, though our hearts remain leaden,' said Shoshenq, finally.

'And what is your will, sire?'

Shoshenq stepped onto the boat's deck, taking Ankherednefer's wrist and helping him on board. Together the pair reclined as the mooring lines were pulled in and the vessel drifted away from the landing. The oar slaves took up the stroke as soon as distance allowed, pushing the ship against the headwind on the way back to Tanis. The boat was well away from the docks before Shoshenq spoke again.

'The Thebans challenge me at Herakleopolis. I have given them my answer as decreed by Pharaoh and they have refused to heed it. I cannot let such a challenge go unpunished.'

'And the Assyrians?'

'We don't have the men to take back what Shalmaneser has stolen. We can hold the line, but this stalemate will last years. All the longer now that Shalmaneser is facing the same problems as we. It seems the Crown Prince of Assyria is as frustrated with the stagnation as we are. There is a coup against the Assyrian king.'

'Sometimes I think we are but players in a game that the gods laugh over.'

'Only sometimes?' said Shoshenq, with a thin smile.

Ankherednefer grunted. 'You have already made up your mind then? If you are trying to rationalise it to me, save your breath.'

'Only a fool makes a decision without consulting the ones he trusts most,' said Shoshenq.

'The decision is simple. Executing that decision is rather more difficult.'

'Give the order then, Lord Ankherednefer. Put the army on the war footing. If Takelot has not conceded to our demands by the time the army reaches Herakleopolis we will besiege the city and drive him out. We sail at dawn.'

Ankherednefer looked back at the sand dunes and wiped away a single tear for the man he had loved as a friend and mentor.

Shoshenq followed his gaze. 'I am glad our king did not live to see his own family turn against him like this. It would have broken his heart to see them die for their ambition.'

'Let us hope it doesn't come to that.'

'It will,' replied Shoshenq. 'It always does.'

THE LAMPS HAD burned low, the last drops of oil drawn up greedily into the burning wick, casting a pale orange glow and stuttering, shuddering shadows along every wall. Darkness had fallen hours before, but for the two inside, the outside world was little more than a passing distraction. The room smelled of sweat and incense, the heat cloying and heavy and filled with the moans and gasps of a marriage newly consummated.

Between a mess of sweat-sodden sheets, Osorkon and Karoadjet lay naked and entwined. The frenetic passion of before had fallen into a comfortable contentment. Osorkon fell, spent, onto his back, fatigue rushing up on him and stealing away his strength in moments.

Karoadjet rolled onto her side, watching him with new energy. Her eyes were bright and the crimson flush on her neck and chest remained as vivid as before.

'That was lovely,' she purred, running her nails down his chest and leaving little red scratches. 'I think we are going to be very happy together.'

Karoadjet lay with her wig removed and her makeup wiped away. It was the first time Osorkon had seen her so, just as this was the first time that she had seen him without his finery. Part of him felt oddly exposed, but Karoadjet seemed to relish in it, as well as the effect she had upon him. The oils rubbed into their bodies mingled into one heady scent and he turned to face her, the effort bringing a low groan from his lips.

Her natural hair was cropped close to her scalp, a tangled and sweat-sodden mess. Soft pink lips that made him ache parted under fine cheekbones and green, almond-shaped eyes. Her breasts were taut, pale nipples erect as his rough hands caressed them, and the curves of her hips drew his gaze further down to the hairless lips between her legs.

They had retired to bed at sunset, but he felt the ache of desire suffuse his body again. 'If I died right now my heart would be so light that the scales of Anubis would never feel it,' he said.

'We have a poet after all,' she laughed. 'Perhaps I inspire you?'

'You do,' he replied, and she smiled at his sincerity. With monumental effort he freed himself from her embrace and padded across the room where food and drink sat untouched.

He poured two goblets of wine, a wedding gift from his father, and sat back on the bed. The linen sheets were from Karoadjet's supply and far more comfortable than the rough-spun soldiers' blankets Osorkon was used to.

'Perhaps we could just stay here. Forget about the war,' he said, passing Karoadjet one of the goblets. Crafted of a light brass alloy, they too were from Karoadjet's possession.

'I'd like that,' she replied.

Osorkon set the goblet aside and lay beside her. She shivered as his rough fingers ran up her leg. He traced his fingers down her chest, teasing her soft pink nipple, before moving down her ribs to her belly. Neither had been untouched until now, but both had discovered something new and exhilarating in the other.

'I love you, Karoadjet,' he said.

She smiled, triumphant despite herself that he had been the first to break.

'I love you too, *my* prince,' she replied, setting her own goblet aside and rising from the bed. She put her hands on his shoulders and pushed him back down, kissing him as he fell back onto the mattress.

A shout came from the yard below, muffled through the thick walls.

'You let Akhetep train them too hard,' she murmured. 'What will their wives think if they are too tired for love?' Karoadjet straddled his waist, her hand wandering behind her to wake him again, feeling him stiffen and his body tremble at her touch.

'For a man there is no such thing,' he growled. He held her hips as he arched his back, burying himself inside her and making her gasp. She let out a low moan as she raked her nails down his chest and moved her hips in a slow rhythm that matched his.

Another shout joined the first and Osorkon opened his eyes.

He tightened his grip on her hips, holding her still. She frowned, petulant in the face of his refusal, but Osorkon's attention was already elsewhere.

The soft pad of running footsteps sounded outside in the hall and Osorkon's hand went to the dagger secreted underneath his pillow as the door burst open.

Karoadjet shrieked and threw herself off him, pulling up the sheets to cover her nudity. Fury twisted her features, but the scathing accusation died on her lips as she saw the expression on the intruder's face.

Akhetep's eyes were wild, seeing but barely registering their nakedness. 'Get dressed. We have to go. Now.'

Osorkon straightened, throwing himself to his feet and casting off his fatigue like a cloak. Akhetep's tone brooked no hesitation and the prince went straight for his weapons, arrayed on the long table.

From the bed, Karoadjet looked between them. 'What is it? What is happening?'

'Herakleopolis burns.' The captain of the charioteers crossed the room, plucking Osorkon's shendyt off the floor and tossing it over his shoulder at the prince. He poured himself a measure of wine, gulping it down in one swallow and wiped his lips on the back of his hand. 'I'll be downstairs.' Without a backward glance, he was gone.

Osorkon could hear him bellowing orders even as he ran back down the hallway. Osorkon dressed himself and helped Karoadjet into a robe. Both of them shivered, and he held her for a long moment before he followed his friend out into the fortress courtyard. The charioteers worked quietly but quickly, putting their horses into their braces before checking and rechecking their weapons. Though the fortress was large enough to house hundreds of charioteers, Osorkon counted at a quick glance no more than one hundred horses readied for battle. Akhetep would have summoned only the most hardened veterans, those unflinching in their duty to the prince and to Thebes, even against their own countrymen.

The prized chariots sat abandoned, arrayed in ranks in their sheds. Ruinously effective on the open battlefield, they had been discarded in favour of the speed and manoeuvrability of horseback. Not a man among them felt complete leaving the chariots behind, but the horses were well-trained and accustomed to the noise and blood of battle. Without a clear picture of what they were facing in the narrow streets of Herakleopolis, the war machines were more hindrance than help where the wheel scythes would indiscriminately cut down all in their path.

The rest of the fortress was astir though the hour was late, or perhaps it had become early again. Osorkon did not know. Taking the steps two at a time, Osorkon joined the sentries on the ramparts. On a clear night, one could pick out the distant glow of Herakleopolis like a bright star on the distant horizon. At this hour, the glow should have dimmed almost to darkness, but it burned as brightly as it did the hour after nightfall. At first, the outline shimmered and wavered. As his vision adjusted to the darkness, Osorkon began to see a thin layer of smoke haze rise from the glow before disappearing into the inky blackness. Now that he was here, Osorkon could smell the smoke, the scent of wood fire and pitch.

Osorkon turned from the scene, coming face to face with the watch captain.

'Give the man who roused the alarm a week's ration of beer and grain,' he said, taking a precious moment to clasp the watch captain's arm in thanks. Osorkon stepped down into the courtyard and jogged across to his waiting mount.

Karoadjet stood at the base of the apartment's steps, her features pale and pinched. In that moment, he felt the overwhelming desire to carry her back upstairs, wrap her in blankets and soothe her to sleep. Instead he steeled himself for the bloodshed to come and hardened his heart against her pleading look, for he knew what would come.

'Stay here.'

'I am coming with you.'

'No,' said Osorkon, tying his sword and spear to the braces of his saddle and checking the halter and bit. As expected of his stableboys the straps were perfect, but the habit kept his hands occupied as the last few of his horsemen readied their own equipment.

'Why?' she scowled.

'Because it is dangerous.'

'I am not afraid of danger.'

'Then because I command it,' snapped Osorkon. She scowled again, her pout showing genuine hurt and he was immediately contrite. 'I will see that your family is safe and send for you when I know more. In the meantime, please. Barricade the gate and let no-one through, even if they claim to be Theban. No-one, understand?' He did not wait for a reply and pulled himself onto the saddle. 'Captain, lead us out.'

Akhetep nodded brusquely and dug in his heels, sending his horse into a gallop in just a few short strides. The cohort followed him out, each racing to be the next but careful not to collide with one another.

Osorkon was the last to leave. He gave Karoadjet one last backward glance.

'Wait for me,' he said, and then he was gone.

'Be careful,' she whispered, but the sound of his galloping was already fading. Then, feeling suddenly alone and in the dark, she began to cry.

NOT A WORD was spoken during the desert crossing, the only sounds the rough rhythm of galloping hooves and the grunts of the riders as they spurred their mounts on to fresh bursts of speed.

Within a few short minutes, Osorkon had reached Akhetep's side at the point of a spear tip formation that would cut through anyone foolish enough to stand in their path.

None of them knew what to expect when they entered the city and Osorkon was pleased to see that Akhetep had prepared the cohort well. Every third man carried a long rope with a bronze hook on the end, and all were armed with the short stabbing spear as well as the curved cavalry swords. The charioteers that had trained as archers kept their recurve bows, while those that were usually drivers favoured a short lance. As they had trained, the lance carriers moved to the centre of the spear-tip while the archers ghosted the perimeter, ready to fall back at the first sign of resistance and pepper the enemy flanks with shafts.

Osorkon checked his own equipment, unlimbering his bow with his left hand and nudging the quiver with his right foot to loosen the shafts. His night vision was still adjusting but neither silhouette nor shadow marked the land. The dull glow of the burning city grew with every minute though their progress was still painfully slow to Osorkon's mind. Faster and faster he urged his mount, pushing his beloved horse to its limits without blowing its wind. The mare's muzzle was thick with foaming saliva and Osorkon could feel the heavy beat of her heart through his left leg

'Come on, girl,' he said. 'Our people need us. I swear to all the gods that you shall eat from the royal granaries for a month if we see my family safe.'

The city of Herakleopolis was built on a slight rise, and around the base of the ridge, groves of date palms and acacia trees grew above clumps of tall grasses and thick bushes. Osorkon took note of the itch in the back of his mind, warning him of the groves' suitability for an ambush. He nocked an arrow and panned the tree-line, a primal part of him desperately wanting an enemy to hunt.

'The gates are closed!' called Akhetep from his right side. Osorkon had held a thin hope that whatever madness had descended on the city had not stopped a band of Thebans loyal to his father from opening the gate and sending for them. The dark shadow of the immense reinforced gates towered over them mockingly. Osorkon knew from personal inspection that nothing short of a suicidal ram would have any effect in breaching it. Above the gatehouse, silhouettes of archers stood watch and behind them, the fierce orange aura of a city on the brink of destruction.

The riders did not check their speed, veering away from the gatehouse and passing by the groves of trees at a steady gallop. The cohort fell back from the wedge into a column of four abreast in a manoeuvre that would have made the generals of Thebes weep with pride.

The cohort passed by under the shadow of the walls, keeping close and out of arrow shot. When they were far enough from the gatehouse, Osorkon called a halt and slid from the saddle.'

'Hobble the horses,' he commanded. 'Four together. We will come back for them. Take only what you can run with.'

If the charioteers were reluctant to leave their war machines before, the thought of abandoning their precious horses came as a harsh and shocking blow. For the charioteers, the character and idiosyncrasies of their horses were as familiar, if not more so, than their own wives and children. Osorkon gave them a few moments to whisper platitudes to their mounts before he ordered the assault with a silent gesture.

The walls of the city were short and squat compared to the towering fortifications of the Crag of Amun, shorter even than the defences of Thebes, but they still stood the height of four men with sides as smooth as hewn marble. Fine craftsmanship had built walls that had never been breached by force, but defences were only as good as the men defending them, and in this the Herakleopolitans had forgotten much.

Osorkon took the grappling hook and spun the head in long looping arcs before he sent it arching over the wall to land with a dull clank on the walkway above. Beside him, thirty other ropes were thrown and secured, and the first warriors of the Crag began to scale the walls. With no footholds, the going was tough and Osorkon's arms burned with fatigue as he hauled himself up over the lip. He landed hard on the other side instantly alert, his bow in his left hand while his right ventured to the quiver at his back, but this section of the wall was deserted.

He turned to help the next man over the wall, then a third, and then they were through. They descended to street level through the tower stairwells, spreading out into the back streets of Herakleopolis like a lengthening shadow. Osorkon and Akhetep led half of the cohort each, threading their way through blocks of darkened houses, heading inexorably for the nomarch's palace. If Shoshenq had launched a surprise attack then that is where the fighting would be thickest.

For a while, the Thebans saw nothing and no one, but for the ever-present glow of firelight and smell of wood smoke. A distant clamour sounded up ahead, too far and too muffled to make sense of. Osorkon increased their pace, hoping that he had judged their route correctly so that that the central thoroughfare was up ahead. He rounded a corner, spear held loosely, and nearly impaled a young woman as she stepped out from the shadows of her home.

'Sir, what is happ-.' She paled at the sight of Thebans. Their iconography was distinctive, even in the dark. Osorkon lowered his spear and stepped into the light where she could see his face. 'Go back inside and lock the door. Everything is under control,' he said. Terrified, she swiftly obeyed.

They reached the main square a few minutes later, and here the first signs of battle began to show. Bodies lay where they had fallen. Men in the livery of Thebes lay dead among the far more numerous corpses of plain-clothed civilians. The sounds of clanging metal and the angry shouts of men in combat filtered through from an adjacent street, and Osorkon directed his men to spread out and cover the width of the road leading up to the palace. From their position, the Thebans could see the back of an angry mob, the ripple of their bodies moving like a wave against a static object. In the darkness, he spied the flash of unsheathed metal as the mob jostled in combat against their unseen foe.

Osorkon stepped to within fifty paces of the group and shouted with the voice of a general on the battlefield. 'Hail! Cease this bloodshed in the name of Takelot!'

The people at the back turned at the sound, and Osorkon had the sudden feeling of being a lion surrounded by snapping hyenas. For a moment, no-one moved. Then those at the rear of the mob turned and ran at the Thebans, waving swords, cudgels, and knives and screaming obscenities at the newcomers.

'Orders, my prince,' said the charioteer next to him as the ranks spread out to face the oncoming mob.

'If they stand against us, they die. Spears,' Osorkon ordered.

Two ranks of spearmen fell to one knee, their spears braced against the road in the manner of defending against a cavalry charge. A further two ranks of archers stood behind them, arrows nocked and ready.

'Halt!' called Osorkon again, but the madness was upon the mob and if they heard his command, they gave no sign.

'Draw,' shouted Osorkon, pitching his voice as one final warning. 'Loose!'

The archers released as one, sending a withering volley into the mass of bodies. Twenty men or more were struck off their feet at once, the charge faltering as the first ranks were cut down without mercy. At twenty paces the archers fired again, cutting down another score of mindless civilians as those to the rear of the mob pushed forward.

The archers fell back, discarding their bows and drawing their knives as the spearmen rose to the attack. The first rank met the charge head on, rising at the last second and punching their spearheads forward through unarmoured flesh. The second rank rose a moment later, stabbing overhead at the faces of those caught behind the wounded and dying. The butchery lasted mere moments before the threat of imminent death cracked through the mob's madness and they broke in stark terror.

'Let them go,' ordered Osorkon, as he saw several of the archers reach to retrieve their bows.

The mob streamed away, filtering through the lanes and alleyways, leaving behind the harrowed survivors, who Osorkon now saw were similarly garbed in the armour and livery of Thebes. Perhaps twenty were still standing and in fighting condition, with that number again sprawled on the city streets. Osorkon saw many were seriously injured. Several were already dead.

'I am Prince Osorkon of Thebes,' he declared. 'Who is in charge here?'

'Captain Ashrafa,' saluted one of the soldiers, his edged armour picking him out as an officer. He looked dazed, his vision unfocused, and dried blood coated one side of his face. Osorkon could not tell whether it was his or someone else's.

'My men and I have just come from the Crag of Amun, captain. What has happened here?'

Ashrafa shrugged and looked around to the bewildered faces of his men. 'With all respect, Prince Osorkon, we have not a clue. They've gone mad, sir. I can't explain it.'

'You have done well to keep them here.'

Ashrafa shook his head. 'We won't for much longer. They come out of nowhere and they fight better than civilians should. Something's not right here, sir. Madness, just madness.'

'Then get your men to safety, captain. The barracks and armoury are not far from here. You will be safe there for the time being.'

Ashrafa frowned. 'My lord? You are not coming with us?'

Osorkon pointed towards another intersection where another public square opened up. Even from where they were standing, Osorkon could hear the mad screams and incoherent battle cries amid the chaos of mob rule. 'My family is in the palace. I need to get there.'

The captain laughed without humour. 'The road is that way, but it's tough going. We tried to reach the palace when this all started. When they pushed us back, we tried for the gates. You can see how far we got. With the army up north, there are few of us left.'

'We must reassert control of the city. Get your wounded to the barracks and reinforce yourselves there. We will need you before too long.'

Ashrafa straightened a little and glanced towards the palace. 'Amun keep you, Prince Osorkon.'

'And you, captain.' He clasped Ashrafa's wrist and gave the order to move. The men of the Crag kept to the side streets, crossing intersections in small groups and making detours when they found resistance. Osorkon had no wish to be bogged down and he pushed his men hard, stopping to catch their breath only as a shrieking mob passed by on the other side of a block of houses. There seemed no method to their madness other than an animalistic desire to kill anyone that was not with them. They fought like beasts with brute savagery, smashing down doors seemingly at random.

Osorkon saw a group of ten run down the street that joined the next intersection. One, who seemed to be their leader, called the group to a halt and pointed at the houses one after the after as though counting.

He settled on the sixth house and barked something that was lost in the howls of his mob. Another stepped forward with a burning brand in hand and tossed it through the house's window. The group roared as the flames took hold and an elderly man came stumbling out of the front door, coughing and waving his hands in front of his face.

The mob leader stepped forward and cut the man down with one blow of his sword, leaving the corpse twitching in the street. Osorkon felt a twinge in his gut as he saw that the mob here wielded military-issue swords and spears, of far finer craftsmanship than even a moderately successful merchant would own. If the armouries had fallen then the city was lost and he was already fighting a losing battle.

The Thebans pushed through, giving the spot fires a wide berth as they drew the rioters like insects. To Osorkon's relief, much of the city was still intact, but the areas that were aflame burned brightly. At the centre of it all was the nomarch's palace.

Fires spanned its roof, ringing the edges like a burning crown. Black smoke billowed high from its centre in a thick column like that of a funerary pyre. Nobles' houses around the palace perimeter also burned, the flames leaping from structure to structure as embers rained out over the city.

Osorkon could feel the heat on his skin from the road and the burning air scorched his lungs as he sucked in a deep lungful of smoke. He stopped to grab a passing civilian and demanded to know what was happening. The young nobleman, little older than himself, looked at Osorkon as though the prince was Anubis. His mouth flapped uselessly as he tried to form his panic into words. Osorkon pushed him away.

Though the wind had dropped, the ashen reek was carried to them in thick choking waves, casting the city in a blinding grey haze. Osorkon stepped out into the main street, seeing the palace under siege only when the Thebans he led were nearly on top of it. The stone steps leading up to the front façade were a mass of fighting men, the howling mob throwing themselves in heedless bloodlust at the thin line of defenders.

Halfway up the stairway, a makeshift barricade of broken wood had been hastily erected. Archers stood on the rise, shooting indiscriminately into the crowd while soldiers wielding sword and spear thrust against anything trying to scale the wall. The mob had a taste for blood and for every one of them that fell, three more were ready to scale the gap.

The rioters were well-armed and one of them thrust a spear up at a soldier behind the barricade. The spearhead threaded through the barricade, snagging on a piece of wreckage before another thrust tore it free. The second thrust changed the angle of attack, catching the soldier by surprise and punching deep beneath his collarbone. The soldier fell back with a cry and was immediately lost to sight.

Osorkon's features split into a vicious snarl. The shouts of anger from behind told him his men had noticed the same thing. Osorkon ordered his men into formation and silently they advanced on the rioting mob.

The raging mass at the barricade stood firm, the rioters at the back pushing forward, ignorant of the danger behind them. The defenders were not so oblivious and a lone figure risked climbing to the top of the barricade to wave at the arriving Thebans. The rioters turned as the Theban wall of spears descended on them from behind, screaming in rage and fear as their rear began to fall like threshed wheat.

Osorkon's sword wove a bloody dance through the rioters, cutting off sword hands and punching through bellies as his scale armour protected him from the worst of their ill-disciplined strikes. Even so, there was something familiar about their attack, the patterns and techniques familiar to him but lazily executed and easily turned aside. Dagger thrusts and short stabbing spears grazed him, but he never stopped moving, always pushing forward and never letting his momentum settle.

Beside him, Akhetep worked with spear and shield, smashing the rim of his shield into raving faces and sending blood and teeth to scatter across the stone steps. His spear punched out rhythmically, lancing through chests when they faced him and punching through backs when they turned to flee.

The carnage began to fade as the madness gripping the mob dissipate in the face of the uneven bloodshed. Osorkon suddenly found himself without an enemy. He looked up at the barricade, seeing a familiar face at the top of the wall.

Bakenptah directed the archer volleys with dispassionate coldness. The Thebans loosed arrow after arrow into the howling mob as they fled. Osorkon's brother himself fired steadily into the mob, cutting them down with brutal precision.

'Open the barricade,' Bakenptah called, as the mob faltered and then broke.

Osorkon shoved his way through. 'Brother, what has happened? Who attacks us?'

Bakenptah's expression was grim. 'The nomarch has lost his mind, Apophis take him. He has turned the city against us.'

'And mother and father?'

'In the throne room. They will want to see you,' said Bakenptah, as the barricade was reformed and new spears and fresh quivers of arrows were brought to the front.

Osorkon followed Bakenptah's scrutiny. The light of the burning palace gave the whole avenue an eerie glow, and from the cover of the houses across the street, the mob was already reforming. 'Very well, I will return to you soon and help drive back these madmen.'

'See that you do.' Bakenptah launched another shaft, watching with some satisfaction as it sank deep into a rioter's neck. The spray from the wound only seemed to galvanise the mob's anger. Osorkon shivered as he watched Bakenptah nock another shaft as though it were merely target practice.

Osorkon shook off his foreboding and ordered the bulk of his men to reinforce Bakenptah's position, taking only Akhetep and an honour guard of his warriors to meet his family.

The atrium at the palace's entrance had become a triage site. Sandstone floors were streaked with blood where the wounded lay propped against walls and pillars. The few men Bakenptah could spare knelt beside them, giving them water and fresh bandages to hold against their wounds. Many, Osorkon saw, would not live to see the dawn. Without proper medical supplies, even the superficially wounded risked fatal infection.

Osorkon passed them all, offering a nod or shallow words of comfort, but he never broke stride. The expressions of the men tending the wounded were filled with pity and anger, following the prince's progression. Osorkon had walked through the portal to the throne room dozens of times before, but this time felt entirely different. Even now, in this twilight of the city, members of his household guard stood to attention at the entrance to the chamber.

He stepped through and his heart broke.

Two figures sat huddled together halfway up the steps to the throne. Tears spilled unashamedly down his father's face. His mother sat one step higher with her arms around his shoulders. A bloody sword was clutched in his father's right hand, and at the foot of the dais was the bloodstained corpse of Nomarch Khonsefankh.

'Father?'

Takelot tore his bloodshot eyes from his brother's body. Even in his grief, his relief at the appearance of his eldest son was palpable. 'My son. I feared the worst. Come closer.'

Slowly, Osorkon crossed the chamber floor, leaving Akhetep and his honour guard to converse quietly with the household guard.

Even in death, the face of Nomarch Khonsefankh was a rictus of pain and anger. His eyes were wide and his pupils glassy and unseeing. Osorkon knelt beside his uncle and closed his vacant eyes, if only so that the living would not have the endure the sight. He turned away from where the nomarch's lips had peeled back from his teeth in the agony of his final moments. The front of his tunic was torn where a gaping wound to the heart had ended him. He had died quickly then. A mercy.

'Father?' said Osorkon again. 'What has happened here? What madness is this where brother turns against brother?'

Takelot met his gaze. 'I killed him. He turned against us, and I killed him.'

Karomama rubbed her husband's back gently. Her hands were covered in the nomarch's blood and it congealed and cracked with her movement. 'Khonsefankh betrayed us,' she said. 'The demand to send our army north, the anger at our allies in the Meshwesh, the refusal to commit men to the war, all of it was a ploy to send us to our destruction.'

'There is no army,' said Osorkon. 'Else we would have headed north weeks ago.'

'There is,' corrected Karomama. 'We were just too blind to see it.' She nodded at the sword belted around Osorkon's waist. He had not had a chance to clean it yet and blood oozed from where the hilt met the head of the scabbard. 'The men you fought to get here. Were they armed as peasants? No, they were soldiers. The Herakleopolitan army has been here the whole time, waiting for the right moment. Thank the gods for Khonsefankh's ineptitude or they would have continued their training and fought as a proper army.'

Osorkon knelt before his parents at the foot of the dais. 'How do you know this?' he asked. The sound of combat outside and the crackling of flames on the palace roof seemed to press down on him with this latest revelation. They would not have long.

'I never trusted your uncle, not fully. I had some of the servants intercept his messages. One of them found this,' said Karomama quietly. She produced a papyrus scroll no larger than her finger. She handed it to Osorkon who unfurled it and read.

'"The time is now. Alive if possible. Heryshef be with you",' he read. Osorkon passed the scroll back to his mother. 'Wishing the blessings of the fertility god on a man who just lost his last child? Who would do that? Shoshenq?'

'I do not know. We confronted him tonight, but all reason had left him. He had sent the signal to his men before we could stop him. I believe your match with Karoadjet snapped the final thread of his sanity. The last of his control was torn away,' said Karomama.

'So, he waited for us to find out? He wanted us to know before the end?'

Karomama sighed. 'I do not know,' she said again.

Somewhere high above a rumbling crash shook the throne room. Dust rained down from the ceiling. Osorkon rose and drew his sword. 'We have to leave. The palace is burning.'

'He said something to me before he died,' said Takelot, rising to his feet but his gaze never left the ragged hole in his brother's chest.

'What, father? What did he say?'

'He said we are betrayed.' The bronze sword clattered to the ground with chilling finality. 'Thebes has turned against us.'

# Chapter Eight

THE COMING OF dawn brought little relief to the horrors of civil strife. The eye of Ra came up with a vengeance, the morning heat a punishing weight upon Herakleopolis just hours after the death of its nomarch. Most of the fires were extinguished before dawn, but the first light of day only exposed the full extent of the damage. Whole swathes of the noble district had been reduced to sundered beams and piles of ashes, and the streets were littered with the dead of both sides. The roof of the palace's eastern wing was in danger of collapsing, and already, at Takelot's command, an army of engineers and labourers were at work assessing and reinforcing the damage. In a mark of divine perversity noticed by all within the palace walls, the flames had left the site of fratricide in the throne room completely untouched.

Smoke drifted high above the city, seen for miles around like an enormous funeral pyre, and as much a call for aid as the messengers that were sent to neighbouring villages and cities. With the ravaged city laid bare, Takelot had considered a total recall of the Theban army to assist with the rebuilding, but Karomama had persuaded him otherwise. The battalions under generals Ukhesh and Kaphiri were camped in the north, just east of the city of Lahun, as Nomarch Khonsefankh had commanded of Takelot when Pharaoh had taken up residence in his city. The march back to Herakleopolis would take mere days, but mobilising thousands of men even that short distance would be an undertaking that would span a week or more. Few were foolish enough to doubt that the reinforcement of

Lahun was still unknown to Shoshenq, and dire as circumstances were, the loss of the garrison would be taken as a sign of weakness the Thebans could ill afford.

Word from the palace spread quickly, fanned by the Thebans themselves, that Nomarch Khonsefankh was dead, executed by his own brother for the charge of treason and perfidy. The nomarch's advisors and councillors had been imprisoned and it was made known that Herakleopolis had been formally annexed into the Kingdom of Thebes. Any among the city's nobility who wished to object were free to come to the palace and do so.

Takelot let it be known that a hefty reward was offered for any information on his brother's activities and the identities of his conspirators, as well the names of the ringleaders of the rebellion from the night before. Whether there was any truth in the nomarch's final words was also yet to be determined for there had been little word from Thebes for many weeks. Before dawn, news reached the palace of escape attempts and suicides, and each name was meticulously recorded as another part of the nomarch's conspiracy. Doubtless, there were many more, and as an added security measure, a curfew was enforced from dusk until dawn. Anyone caught on the streets after nightfall was assumed to be complicit, and would face ten strokes of the cane to the soles of the feet for their temerity.

Only later did Osorkon learn the truth of it all. Several of the captured rioters admitted under persuasion to being part of the apparently absent army of Herakleopolis. Far from being disarmed, they had simply blended in with the local population, waiting for the signal to strike. Khonsefankh had been turned to Shoshenq's cause long before any soldier of Thebes had set foot in his city, but the death of his last son and heir and the marriage and integration of his brother's family into his own political arena had been too much for his grief-wracked mind. Of the Theban force of five hundred remaining in Herakleopolis, half had been killed or wounded by the calculated and sudden violence.

With a reverence owing to the political situation more than any lingering loyalty, the corpse of Khonsefankh had been conveyed to the mortuary temple to be prepared alongside that of Tibekh. Whether his heart was intact enough to be weighed on the scales of

Anubis was now his spirit's problem. As far as Osorkon was concerned, Khonsefankh could spend eternity as a restless ghost, watching the men he betrayed rebuild and live in his city.

Three days had seen little progress made in clearing away the devastation, but the Thebans worked with quiet diligence. The corpses in the streets had been taken away, but with each passing day, the Thebans came across more bodies that had died trapped in the fires. The flames had charred the victims beyond recognition, melting flesh and fat while the residual heat in the buried coals and the high daytime temperatures had started to putrefy them.

Osorkon himself led the recovery effort, as ash-streaked and grime-covered at the end of each day as any of his soldiers. On the fourth day, he came across the twisted and blackened claws of a dead Herakleopolitan, sticking out from the ruins of a house. Akhetep watched on grimly and handed his prince a thick linen shroud as a pair of Theban soldiers moved to dislodge the debris around the body. Osorkon knelt in the ruins and wrapped the shroud around his hands before he pulled on the blackened arms. He swore and stepped back as the melted flesh came off in his grip and the shoulders gave way with a wet pop. He spat a thick wad of saliva to clear the bile in his throat and calmly wrapped the stumps in the shroud. He heard a murmur behind him and turned to address the crowd that had gathered to watch the excavations. 'Do you see?' he said to the spectators. 'Do you see what you have done? They died for nothing. Do you hear me? Nothing!'

Akhetep moved up beside him, his presence as much a reminder to Osorkon as the crowd. Osorkon sagged where he stood, wishing once again for a return to that night in the Crag before the city had fallen into madness. Karoadjet had joined him the morning after the battle and the Crag was now maintained with a minimal garrison. His new bride's family was safe, their house far enough from the palace to escape the flames and violence. Many of their friends had not been so lucky, and Takelot and Lord Herytep took a roster of who had perished and what would become of their assets, while Karomama and Lady Neferadjet consoled the survivors, their friends and allies, promising them eternal assistance and friendship.

Osorkon went to lift the cluster of bricks pinning the corpse when a shout roused him. A commotion spread from the end of the street, a rising panic that culminated with the sight of Meshwesh cameleers scattering the milling crowd as they raced to the prince's position. The Theban soldiers went for their weapons, but Osorkon ordered them to stand down as he recognised the identity of their leader. Great Chief Pediese pulled up beside him, sliding from the saddle to land in front of the rubble. His expression was grim, his beard was ragged from fretful tugging and his eyes were dark and without sleep.

'Hail, Prince of Thebes. What a mess of this city you have made.'

Osorkon smiled without warmth. 'Great Chief, why does your expression tell me you're about to make a bad day worse?'

'Apologies, Prince Osorkon, but there is something I must ask of you,' said Pediese, and bowed. He had never done that before.

'Out with it then. It cannot be any worse than all of this.'

WITHIN THE HOUR, Osorkon had taken his leave of Herakleopolis, handing over control of the rebuilding to Akhetep and Bakenptah. The former protested at being left behind, while the latter accepted the task with sullen compliance.

Ignoring Osorkon's entreaties for information, Pediese led him through the western part of the city, taking the shortest path to the western gate. He led his own camel on foot, the snorting beast drawing wary stares from the press of soldiers and frightened civilians. The appearance of the Great Chief, with his colourful robes and beads in his beard, followed by Pharaoh's eldest son, was enough to clear a path through the tense city. Ten of the chief's warriors waited for them beyond the city limits with a spare camel that, Osorkon realised with dread, was intended for him.

'You come at a poor time, Chief Pediese. Perhaps you notice the city still smouldering?' said Osorkon, as they passed under the western gatehouse. The smell of smoke was still thick in his nose and an oily sheen of sweat and ash clung to his skin. His shendyt was stained with charcoal and the smudged kohl around his eyes only accentuated his exhaustion.

The Great Chief smiled thinly, looking past Osorkon into the city. 'We saw the smoke from almost a league away. We came as soon as we heard. I give thanks to Isis that you live. We feared the worst.' Pediese made the sign of his goddess, robes of bright colours bordering on garish swathing his strong, slender frame. Like the prince himself, he was long-legged and thin, a legacy of their shared Libyan heritage, and in the Great Chief's case, the result of a lifetime spent roaming the western deserts.

Osorkon spat a wad of black phlegm. 'Were the gods paying closer attention this could have all been avoided. We hold onto the city by a thread, the loyalty of the nome's army is in doubt, and my uncle is dead, slain by my father's hand.'

'In truth, my prince, I do not know whether my news will ease your grief or compound it, but you must see for yourself.' Pediese laid a hand on the camel's muzzle and the beast dropped obediently to its knees for him to mount.

Osorkon repeated the trick, surprised at its placidity for it was well-known among the Egyptians of the river cities that camels were temperamental beasts. Camels were less willing than horses to be broken, and with a tendency to spit and hiss even at their own riders, they were maintained as mounts by the desert police only. No respectable Egyptian would trust one, but Osorkon swung his leg over the saddle, following the Meshwesh lead and leaning far back as his mount regained its feet.

With a shout, Pediese set the pace.

Osorkon gripped the reins tightly, grunting as the beast's loping gait pulled at his aching muscles and battered flesh. The Meshwesh warriors fanned out into a broad scouting formation. Two raced ahead, becoming dots on the horizon, while the other eight went out singly to form a protective ring hundreds of metres around, leaving the prince and their chief alone.

Osorkon eyed them warily. 'I do not know what information you have received, Great Chief, but the war is much further north than here,' he called ahead.

Pediese half-turned in his saddle. 'And yet, your city burns.'

Osorkon glared at the chief's back, but Pediese had already urged his mount onward.

They rode for an hour, then two, in silence. The scouts led them due west, far beyond the green sanctuary of the river's banks, where the dunes gave way to flat sandy ground that stretched for leagues in every direction. In the distance, the smudge of a dust storm stained the line of the horizon.

Pediese's eyes fixed on it and he slowed to a canter, allowing Osorkon to catch him up.

'You will ride north with your father?' Pediese asked.

'I do not know,' said Osorkon. 'I wish to, of course. There will be great honour and glory in defeating Shoshenq, but my father is my king and I will fight when and where he wills.'

Pediese nodded and called his mount to a stop. He fixed the prince with eyes that had hunted the beasts of the desert.

'Will you win?' he asked.

Osorkon pulled up alongside him, noting that the scouts had all but disappeared, distant specks against the dust storm spreading inexorably across the horizon. 'Yes.'

'Then the call has not been in vain,' said Pediese. He kicked his heels and the camels raced towards the dust storm. Only now, could Osorkon see the falseness of it. The dust was too low, too thin and not moving fast enough to be one of the desert squalls that plagued the towns and cities of Egypt.

Even so, it was a marker visible from over an hour's ride away.

'Behold, the Meshwesh come,' shouted Pediese.

The train of humanity spread for kilometres, thousands of the Meshwesh coming across the land like an enormous viper winding its way through the sand dunes. Osorkon thrust the comparison from his mind as he looked upon his distant cousins. But for a quirk of fate and an ambitious ancestor, he too could have been born among the nomadic peoples of the west. Or, he considered, he would already be dead in one of the many wars they had fought against the river cities.

'Last time I saw that many of your kinsmen in one place, I was fighting them,' said Osorkon, coming to a stop at the edge of the cloud. Grit coated his eyes, nose and mouth and he gratefully accepted a head scarf from Pediese.

'The death of Harelothis is a debt the Meshwesh nation owes to you. Stories of his destruction have spread through our people like the wind over the sands. The mention of the Prince of Thebes has brought them all together, here and now. They fight for you.'

'How many?'

'Two thousand fighting men. Willing to fight Shoshenq in return for land at the river's edge. The agreement stands, yes?'

'Two thousand,' Osorkon whispered. 'An army to beat the pretender back into the sea beyond the Delta,' said Osorkon. 'It is a dangerous road we walk, my friend.'

'I know,' said Chief Pediese. 'But we pledged our swords and spears to you and so we have come. The Meshwesh nation asks for protection and succour from the great cities and peoples of the river.'

'Our stores will not last this long. We already have an army to feed.'

Pediese's camel honked and spat, sensing its master's mood. The Great Chief met Osorkon's eye and there was a hesitation there that the prince had never seen.

'Will you turn them away?' he asked. 'Will your father honour our bargain?'

'He is a man of his word. As am I. We will welcome you to the Great River, but I fear there will be scant lodgings in the cities for you. A temporary accommodation on the riverbank will be sufficient, I hope?'

'The river provides sustenance. There has been precious little of that in the desert of late,' said Pediese. 'By Isis and the spirits of the desert, the land has gone dry and even the spirit-sayers do not know why.'

Osorkon shook his head. 'You could have told me in Herakleopolis.'

'True, but what do facts and figures stand to the faces of frightened children, hopeful women and determined men. Would you have allowed them to come if I had told you eight thousand Meshwesh were coming to your city?' said Pediese.

Osorkon could hear his grin beneath the folds of the chief's headscarf. 'Gods above and below, you are making this difficult.'

Osorkon rubbed the grit from his eyes and looked back out over the horde. The train of Meshwesh tribes allied to Great Chief Pediese, and by extension Osorkon and Thebes, was in itself a coalition of nomads, come together for a singular purpose.

Most walked beside their camels, their beasts of burden laden with tents and other textiles, sacks of food and drinking water. Weapons were strapped beside sleeping mats, and great wagons pulled goods too heavy for pack beasts. Excitable children scurried between the legs of the camels and clambered over the wagons, the sounds of their mothers scolding them melding with the laughter of their fathers.

Osorkon saw horses too, fine-boned mounts, swift and agile, the pride of the Meshwesh people. Much faster than the camels, they were unparalleled in the raids that had brought Osorkon west to fight Harelothis all those years ago. Without the endurance of camels, they were seldom used unless a fight was all but certain.

Osorkon knew that certainty was increasing with each passing day.

'I will accept your people, all of them, under the following conditions. First, all men of fighting age come with us to Tanis. Once the war is won, my father will release them and they may live as free citizens with full rights and a land dispensation. Second, there will be no raiding or illegal hunting unless authorised by the nomarchs. We cannot deplete our own foodstuffs in times of such shortage. Third, they cannot all live in one place. The land will not support such a vast number. Keep them in family groups if you wish, but they must divide. Groups of five hundred, perhaps.'

Pediese followed his gaze. 'On behalf of the Meshwesh, I accept your offer.'

'Good.' Osorkon turned his camel to look back east. 'I must warn my father. There will be panic if you show up unannounced. Grain must be re-rationed, pickets drawn, and the tomb quarries will have to redivert their supplies of building stone to Herakleopolis.'

'You can keep your houses of stone,' said Pediese. 'We have brought our own shelters.'

'As you like.'

Osorkon's mind was awhirl, already turning to the logistical challenge of accommodating thousands of nomads, but it was a worthwhile exchange for certain victory. Despite it, he felt no joy, only a deep unease that even the contentment of his distant people could not entirely erase. He felt the Great Chief's scrutiny and shifted.

'You are troubled. And by more than the horde I bring with me,' said Pediese.

'It is nothing. Just a feeling.'

Pediese's eyes narrowed. 'What is it?'

Osorkon looked over his shoulder meeting the chief's gaze. He held it for a moment and then turned back to the horde. 'There is a growing darkness in my mind, a dread I cannot explain. Something is coming, but I know not what.'

'The war?'

'The night before I slew the last of the horde of Harelothis was one of the finest night's sleep I have ever had.'

Pediese laughed. 'And the night I heard of your victory I did the same.' The Great Chief trailed off, sobering quickly. 'You are not the only one I have heard speak so in recent days. The shamans have felt something. Something terrible.'

Osorkon looked over his shoulder. 'What do you mean?'

'It is better that you hear it from the mouths of the knowing. I will say no more.' Pediese turned and rode away, headings towards the centre of the column where the greatest cluster of wagons trundled over the sands.

Osorkon raced to catch the chief, shouting into the wind. 'Are you sure?'

Pediese pulled his headscarf down over his chin and his mouth was fixed in a grim line. 'One can never be sure, but their connection to the desert is strong. Come, Prince Osorkon. Let me show you the magic of the desert. Meet them and judge for yourself.'

KAROMAMA SWEPT THROUGH the halls of the nomarch's palace, moving as quickly as decorum allowed of a Great Royal Wife. A thin scroll held tight, pressed into her hand only minutes before, felt like a lead weight in her arm. The seal of Vizier Hory was already broken, her impatience getting the better of her, and she climbed the stairs to the top level with haste, ignoring the burn in her legs.

Takelot had taken to having meetings with his generals in their private apartments to prepare for the campaign against Shoshenq. Karomama had been unable to dissuade him, but the air of grief over the city was still strong and those who had been unswervingly loyal to the late Khonsefankh were a threat Karomama had not finished rooting out. A blade in the dark would end the war before it had truly begun.

The guards to the royal apartments, both loyal men of Thebes, half lowered their spears before they recognised their lady. They snapped back to attention, inclining their heads a fraction in apology. She favoured them with a smile before she burst into her own living quarters, rooms that now resembled the chambers of a war council.

'Apologies, my lords but I must interrupt.'

Takelot looked up in surprise. Kaphiri and Ukhesh launched themselves to their feet. The generals had come from Lahun after the fires had been put out, the question of the nomarch's dying words necessitating an emergency military council.

'Please do not stand on my account. I bring news from Thebes,' she said.

The generals glanced sideways at Takelot.

'You may stay,' said Karomama. 'These are joyous tidings from Isetweret. Thebes as we know it is secure,' said Karomama.

Takelot let out a long sigh. 'So, my brother lied? Thebes has not turned against us as the nomarch claimed?' Takelot had not yet said his brother's name.

Karomama continued. 'A border skirmish with Nubia, nothing more. Hory has sent the garrison south to deal with it before it has a chance to grow. Beyond that, I cannot say.'

Kaphiri shrugged. 'The nomarch may have sought to wound you and sow division where none exists. He was no longer himself, as you said.'

'Who can say how we all might act in our final moments?' said Ukhesh. 'May the Ibis-Headed One protect all our fates.'

Takelot rose to his feet and clapped Ukhesh on the shoulder. 'Thank you, both. I will see you this afternoon. If you would give me a moment with my wife.'

Ukhesh and Kaphiri bowed low, once to their king and once to the lady who ruled his heart and left the way Karomama had come.

'How goes the war?'

Takelot chuckled and led her out onto the balcony. It was her favourite spot in the city, a fact he well knew.

'The war within or without?' he asked.

'Both? Either?'

'The answer is the same,' he said.

She leaned against his side and wrapped his arm in her own. 'The Libyan fire in our blood pits brother against brother as often as it does against friend and enemy. The misfortunes of your brother's life are not laid at your feet. You are not him.'

Takelot looked down at her and kissed her forehead. 'Will you keep the city content while I am gone?'

'I will do as Pharaoh commands.'

'I do not command you.'

'But you do,' she said. 'And I may be the only one of your subjects who might speak truth to you without fear or reservation, so listen to what I say. Your brother's death will be seen as a sign of weakness to our family. One that we must cast aside with enough strength to silence the naysayers, for they will be many. Go north and break Tanis. We will be here when you return victorious.'

Takelot nodded. 'Our sons?'

'Will wish to go with you. Will feel a need to go with you. But you already have two capable generals by your side and if you can get past your aversion to our alliance with Osorkon's Meshwesh fighters then I am content for your safety. Leave our children here.'

Takelot turned and took Karomama gently by the arms. He looked tired, but there was a smouldering fire in his eyes that would burn away his grief in the battles to come. 'They are not children anymore, Karomama. Both have won great victories on their own.'

'I know. In truth, I would feel better knowing you were all together,' she replied. 'If Osorkon and Bakenptah go to war with you they will share in your glory. But if you stand against Shoshenq alone you will solidify our dynasty for a generation to come. Stand against Shoshenq alone and defeat him. Let no others share in that victory. It must be yours alone. The people will rejoice. The Pharaoh of Thebes is indefatigable and beats back the northern pretender single-handedly, the saviour of the land.'

Karomama went inside and poured two cups of wine, handing one to Takelot as he followed her in.

'You are smiling. What is it?' Takelot asked.

'There was one more part of the message,' she said, sweetly.

'Out with it then. My heart can take no more suspense.'

'Isetweret is with child. We are going to be grandparents.'

'All this gloom we have been discussing,' said Takelot, shaking his head. There were joyful tears in his eyes. 'My love, you might have started with that.'

TAKELOT LIT THE devotional incense, murmuring prayers of offering and worship and forgiveness for a brother taken beyond the edge of sanity. The king prayed, not for himself, but for his brother and nephew to find a measure of peace in the land of the dead. Gods knew that neither had ever found peace in the land of the living.

Takelot felt no guilt over his brother's death, though his grief remained strong. There could be no room for doubt on the path the gods had forced him to walk. Every action would lead to salvation or damnation, and Takelot had no energy to waste on regret.

The temple of Amun in Herakleopolis had become a sanctuary of sorts, as it had been in Thebes, a place of quiet contemplation and reverence so that he might be closer to, and identify with, the divine Father of the Theban Triad. He had left the daily services to the priests of the city, shunning the company of the city's religious hierarchs, wishing for time to commune with his god personally.

The precinct was otherwise quiet, though simple offerings had been left at the temple façade. Whether they were in appeasement to the god or to himself, he was not certain.

He rose to his feet, gazing upon the figure of Amun standing amid wafting incense smoke, low fires in braziers giving the statue's golden skin a gleaming sheen.

'Amun, father of all, grant me the strength to see your will done. Turn your face from Tanis and know your true servant.' Takelot suppressed a groan as he finished speaking, feeling a now-familiar pain inside his chest. He sucked in his next breath, his vision swimming for a moment as he steadied himself against the temple wall. The feeling passed, but it left him shaken with his eyes clenched shut. Already, the war weighed on him, burdening him with a fatigue he could not shake and a malaise he could not shrug off.

He would re-join the army soon, with Ukhesh and Kaphiri, and this weakness would pass. That is all this is, Takelot told himself, shaking his head to clear his thoughts. I have spent too long confined in this city. Too long sitting in a chair passing judgement. Too long indulging a treacherous brother. The weakness returned and Takelot went to his knees before the altar, breathing hard.

Pharaoh closed his eyes and prayed for understanding.

Was this a test or a trial of penitence? Had he erred in his quest to reclaim his throne? His cause was just, but were his actions pure? Was the god calling him from this earth already, with his work undone?

Clarity eluded him, and his thoughts turned to his fears for his family.

Karomama had always been his pillar of strength, stoic beyond mortal ken, but he worried for her facing this burden alone. Osorkon had fallen into a black mood, though Takelot hoped his son's lovely new bride would help draw him out of it. Bakenptah had simply retreated into himself, spending his time preparing for the war to come and resting only when exhaustion demanded it. His sons would hate him when he ordered them to remain behind, but there was a freedom in fighting without having to worry for his sons that he found agreeable.

Despite his doubts, a sense of fervour filled the king.

The kings of old had won their immortality by annihilating their enemies on the battlefield. Ramses had crushed the Hittites at Kadesh. Amenhotep had faced down the Assyrians and broken them in his glory. Horemheb had brought ruin to the heretic king Akhenaten and done so from this very city.

Now he, Takelot of Thebes, would win his throne from the usurper, he who had poisoned Takelot's own blood against him not once but twice. Let his grandfather and his brother watch from whatever realm held them and know that they had chosen wrong. Clenching his teeth, Takelot rose again and shuffled out of the temple.

It was time to re-join the army.

It was time to go to war.

# Chapter Nine

THE STENCH OF the battlefield was like nothing Sarasesh had ever experienced. The dead were beyond counting, and the priest stumbled through the field of bodies in an exhausted daze. Egyptian and Nubian alike covered the ground in every direction, putrefying where they had fallen. His legs were leaden, and his eyes were half-closed as he stepped around broken limbs and shattered weapons.

At Malkesh's command, Sarasesh had been forced to march beside the army he had once hoped to lead in the liberation of Thebes. Denied a place on the very ship that had brought him south, he fought, slept and marched beside men he had been raised to see as enemies. The tribes of the far south hardly seemed to notice the distance as they hauled their weapons and supplies on their backs. Sarasesh ran beside them until he was sick and then he ran some more. The fear of being left behind was enough to propel himself forward until he collapsed at camp each night, panting and thirsty and covered in dust.

When battle was joined against the Theban garrison, he had been kept away from the front lines, close enough to hear the screams and feel the fear of being enclosed in the dust clouds of the battlefield, but far enough to be well out of harm's reach. Sarasesh had almost expected to be sent into battle alongside the vanguard, but it seemed Malkesh was yet reluctant to get his bargaining chip killed. Now, with the battle won and the spoils picked clean, it was time for the horde to move on again.

Sarasesh wandered through the field of corpses. He thought to feel grief for his countrymen slain but felt nothing but fear for himself. He flinched at every sound, giving each of his allies a wide berth though he knew his connection to Malkesh made him untouchable, at least for now. Sarasesh looked down at the dead, noting the torn clothes fluttering in the low breeze, the discarded weapons, and the broken armour. So consumed was he by this vista of death that Sarasesh did not see the survivor until he had nearly stepped on him.

The Theban soldier's eyes were fixed on the sky above, his pupils trying and failing to focus on something beyond Sarasesh's sight. Recognition seemed beyond him for which Sarasesh was grateful, but the last spark of life clung stubbornly to flesh that would never heal.

Sarasesh started as a tribesman behind him hooted in surprise and trotted around to stand over the dying soldier. The warrior grinned at Sarasesh and said something in words the priest could not understand. Sarasesh shook his head, unsure what else to do, and the tribesman nodded, still smiling. Sarasesh saw the warrior's intent and shut his eyes as the tribesman raised his spear and brought it down deep into the soldier's chest. The Egyptian gasped and a long, rattling breath escaped his ruined chest before he was mercifully still. The tribesman wrenched his spear back out and dropped it beside the soldier's corpse, before he knelt and began picking over the body.

Around them, hundreds more warriors picked their way through the corpse field, looting their own as well as their enemies. They swept over the dead like a wave on their trek to the north, taking weapons and jewellery to use or sell, or cutting off ears and noses as trophies.

Scattered around the charnel ground, the disfigured dead were left to rot where they had fallen. Carrion birds circled high above, the vultures and ravens darting in to try their luck, which the tribesmen delighted in chasing and trying to catch. Elsewhere, thick clouds of flies clustered to drink greedily of the spilled blood and feast on the rotting flesh of the slain, buzzing over glassy eyes and bloodied lips.

Sarasesh closed his eyes a moment, no longer smelling the ripe stench or hearing the guttural chatter of the beasts that dared call themselves men. Malkesh was a monster, and not even the remaining might of the Egyptian south could stop him. With most of the Theban army marching under Takelot, the dead here must have been the city's garrison. Now it was no more, yet another instance of carnage wrought in the name of Senmut's great plan, one more massacre in a trail of destruction that led back to the First Cataract. The host of Malkesh was hurt now, though Sarasesh had seen no sign of the pirate warlord since the end of the battle.

The surviving Thebans had already fled northward, and it was all Sarasesh could do not to chase after them, to beg their forgiveness and go home. Senmut had entrusted him to leash Malkesh to their cause, but in that he had failed. Far from marching directly to attack Takelot in Herakleopolis, Malkesh had taken great delight in raiding every town they had come across, bloodying his horde again and again in a tide of destruction.

Malkesh had not risked the vengeance of larger towns, but fishing villages and hamlets had been easy targets. At least, until retribution had caught up with them.

For the first time, Sarasesh had seen hesitation in Malkesh's eye when the war horns had sounded and the northern horizon was aflutter with the silhouettes of regiments and their banners. The warlord had threatened his warriors into line as he waited for the ranks of soldiers to arrive, uncertain as to who had come for him.

Sarasesh had wondered likewise. Had Takelot already won the war and come south to punish their treason? No, Pharaoh was nowhere to be seen, and the Theban king was wrathful enough to come and take his vengeance personally. If he was not here, then it had to be another.

Then he had seen the battle standards, close enough now to make out the colours and patterns and he knew the truth. Far too many banners for a single unified force, this army was made up of several smaller cohorts from different towns and cities.

Professional soldiers then, fighting with desperation in place of savagery.

Sarasesh had watched from the heights of the ridge where Malkesh had made his camp. The warlord had stood beside him, drinking wine looted the week before and humming along to the terrified screams below.

Finally, the sounds of battle died away, followed by a triumphant roar as the city cohorts had broken and the real slaughter began. Fully armed and armoured, few had escaped the inhuman endurance of the desert tribesmen. Like lions among gazelles, the tribesmen pulled down the soldiers and set upon them with unrestrained savagery.

Sarasesh had turned to Malkesh, his expression pleading. 'Magnificent one, surely it would be wise to take hostages? We could sell them to Thebes for more supplies. Cut the war short.'

'Hostages?' Malkesh had rumbled. 'Only more mouths to feed. Now, go. Go down and see what battle really is and what you ask of me.'

Sarasesh had been compelled to obey the warlord, trudging down that long, winding slope to find a landscape seeped in death. The few wounded Thebans that were still alive were set upon for sport, murdered even as they screamed for their loved ones, their spirits plucked from them here on a nameless desert plain on Egypt's border.

Sarasesh had shivered as the murdering tribesmen stood and grinned at him as he passed each killing, a bronze bracelet clutched in a hand there, a nose taken as a trophy by another. As Sarasesh passed between the dead, he saw the first flies begin to buzz over a dead soldier's face, clustering around his glassy eyes and blood-stained lips. The priest muttered a prayer and trudged past him, imagining the oily scent of death already upon him.

The flutter of fabric caught Sarasesh's eye in the low breeze, and there he saw the fallen banner of the Scarab Cohort of Hierakonpolis. More movement stole his attention, the torn and bloodstained banner of the Lion Cohort of Asyut not more than two score paces away. It seemed that not even the lioness goddess Sekhmet could preserve Egypt against the ravaging horde of Malkesh.

Beyond the fallen battle standards, there were the men in the colours of Thebes. Men he may have met before, or at least seen in the marketplaces and temple services. Men who may have regarded his own position with respect and a touch of awe, trusting him to lead them in his own way as one among many in the temple brotherhood.

Sarasesh kept walking, following the trail of tribesmen toward the muster point, already noting that the horde vanguard was moving northward. He paused to catch his breath and fight the nausea when he felt eyes upon him. 'Move, priest,' said one of the pirates overseeing the muster. 'It is still a long way to your city.'

Sarasesh coloured at the pirate's laughter, but he nodded and kept moving, putting one foot in front of the other.

There was little else he could do.

THE FIRST SURVIVORS reached Thebes one week later. Exhausted, with dust and the dried blood of their comrades rubbed into the grooves of their armour, the fortunate few stumbled towards their city where they were picked up by the desert police outriders.

Hory ordered them brought to the palace immediately and the gate guards were forbidden to speak of the identity of the survivors lest the inevitable panic sweep through the city too soon. In secret and in small groups, the survivors were brought to the palace and given food and drink on the way to their audience with the vizier.

The war room was off-limits to the palace servants and only high-ranking generals and members of the vizier's inner circle were normally permitted to enter. Now it was the scene of sorrow and pain. Men who had never set foot in the palace now sat within metres of the vizier and the princess of Thebes.

Chancellor Pereftep stood behind them, though he remained a silent observer. Isetweret could not be sure whether it was the trauma of their escape or the nature of their audience that stunned the soldiers so, but they were slow to talk and spoke only with consensus, as though none of them were entirely sure what they had seen.

Hory summoned the palace doctors but most of the soldiers brushed off their ministrations. After their trek through the desert, any Theban with more than superficial wounds was already dead.

The highest-ranking survivor of Thebes, Captain Rekhtef, had delivered his report upon arrival, begging the vizier's leave to see his men fed and cared for before he met in this more informal audience. His features were yet wrinkled with dust and they creased in pain as a palace doctor cut through the rough stitches binding a vicious wound across his shoulder. Around him, the men of his company sat quietly, answering questions when asked directly, but otherwise trusting in their leader to tell their tale.

'They outnumbered us two to one. I don't know who supplied the intelligence, but they have the blood of thousands on their hands,' Rekhtef muttered. Exhaustion had stolen the anger from his voice, but a deep hurt lingered in his words. His retelling was marked with horror, though it granted the vizier precious little information he had not already learned.

A dozen of the most trusted palace servants flitted between the soldiers, topping up cups with wine or water and offering the famished soldiers platters of fruit, fish and bread from Hory's own larder. Each of the servants looked pale and shaken as they listened to the soldiers' accounts, knowing full well that with their defeat, the defences of Thebes had suffered a bitter blow. After a moment Isetweret ordered them gone, each of them oath sworn to never speak of what they heard. To gossip over a royal pregnancy was one thing but to let slip state secrets was treason and would be paid for with their lives.

'Five thousand to our two,' Rekhtef continued. 'We accounted for perhaps half of them on the field before we broke.' He broke off a piece of bread and chewed it slowly, deep in thought. 'The Hierakonpolitans broke and fled first. No stomach for a fight that lot. After the rout, we left them at their city gates. Gods alone know if Hierakonpolis still stands. After our left flank collapsed, the bastard Nubians spilled through and our lines buckled. It was all over soon after that.'

Rekhtef grunted and refilled his wine to the brim. The angry mouth of his wound was red and swollen and he grimaced as the doctor scraped out the corruption before packing it with a poultice and covering it with linen wrappings. Sweat beaded the captain's forehead and the red flush of fever marked the skin of his face and chest, Hory noted. The vizier called for more wine. Whether Rekhtef survived the next few weeks would be in the hands of the gods. The least the vizier could do was see that he was comfortable in the meantime.

'They will be here within the fortnight,' Rekhtef continued. 'Gods help us when they are.'

'How did you escape?' asked Hory.

Rekhtef narrowed his eyes for a moment until he realised the vizier's question was not an accusation, but a curiosity.

'When the lines were overrun, we ran. I cut through the straps of my armour and cast it into the river. Then I threw myself in too. The river swept me downstream for I don't know how many miles until I was washed ashore again. I found this lot a day after that trudging through the sand.'

'Two thousand men of Egypt. How could they run so easily? They were well-trained and well-supplied,' pressed Hory.

'Were they?' snapped Rekhtef, before he caught himself. He took a steadying breath. 'Fifty men from this district, a hundred from that village... This was an army cobbled together with desperation.'

'You are right,' conceded Hory. 'It was, but it was all we had in the circumstances.'

'And now it is gone,' said Rekhtef, clearing his throat. 'So, the question remains. What do we do now with just a few hundred soldiers left in this city?'

'Word will be sent to Pharaoh for aid,' said Hory. He glanced at Isetweret, who closed her eyes and nodded.

'Would that had been done sooner, many more old men and young boys would still be alive. Even your shiny bodyguards will be dirtied soon enough protecting these fine halls,' said Rekhtef.

'The palace guard will man the walls beside the city watch. You have my word on that,' replied Hory.

'As you say, Lord Vizier,' said Rekhtef. 'If there was nothing else?'

Hory nodded and dismissed them with a wave. Rekhtef's band of survivors followed him, but as they reached the door Hory spoke again.

'Give them quarters in the guest wing and see to their every need,' he told the tending servants. 'They have the gratitude of myself and the city.'

Rekhtef frowned. 'My wife-'

'Will be informed,' said Hory. 'Until then, please accept the hospitality of the palace until we can make an official statement.'

Rekhtef laughed, low and full of melancholy. 'Are we to be prisoners for our failure?' he asked.

'The city stands on a knife edge,' said Isetweret. 'Let the people believe in the illusion of safety a while longer, Captain Rekhtef. They will learn of it all soon enough.'

Rekhtef nodded wearily, glancing at the chancellor and vizier before he bowed his head. 'As my lady wishes,' he said, finally.

The survivors filed out slowly, leaving the vizier, princess and chancellor alone.

'This could not have come at a worse time,' said Hory.

'Amun makes a mockery of our plans, my lord,' said Pereftep. 'The city guards are few, and while the floods cover the farms in deluge, the farmers and fishermen will remain in a city that is already relying on its stores. Idleness could quickly turn to unrest.'

'What good will the farmers and fishermen be defending their homes when the army failed? The people will panic,' said Isetweret.

'It seems likely,' agreed Hory. The vizier rose from his chair to shut and lock the door. He poured a measure of wine for each of them and put one of the remaining platters between them. 'Pharaoh is a long way away fighting another war. I do not want to force him to quit his own field for our sake.' he said. 'So, what do we do?'

# Chapter Ten

IN THE PRIVATE office of the High Priest of Amun in Karnak, Harsiese read the scrap of papyrus with a trembling hand. Each time he read the words, scrawled in sloping hieratic, the writing remained unchanged. Herakleopolis burned. Pharaoh had slain his own brother, the city's nomarch. The people had risen up to challenge his rule, a short-lived coup put down by the Crown Prince. The missive went on to wish the priests of Karnak well and delivered the promise of victory against Shoshenq and the numerically superior forces of Tanis by the Theban army, who was even now camped outside the city of Lahun.

Harsiese set the scroll down, his gaze softly focused on the closed door to his office. The news was uncomfortable, to say the least. With the army well beyond the borders of Herakleopolis, the duty of first response would have fallen to Osorkon and his garrison at the Crag of Amun. The Crown Prince would be forced to keep the peace, while the bulk of the army marched against Shoshenq. Every force in the country then, was engaged or already destroyed, all except the horde marching inexorably north at Senmut's call.

The destruction of the Theban garrison had reached Harsiese's ears, despite the burden of secrecy placed over the palace. But for the palace guard standing watch over the Vizier and the princess, there were precious few trained soldiers left in Thebes. Osorkon needed to ride south, and quickly, if the situation was to be contained, but in the turmoil of Herakleopolis, many things could happen.

Harsiese rubbed his eyes and idly tapped the desk with his finger. The message had come directly to him, ostensibly so that he would share it among his most trusted brothers of the temple. A similar message had likely already reached the palace, but there was precious little Isetweret could do that Harsiese himself had not already done. In any case, ignorance was Isetweret's best defence as it was his own. While Senmut believed him ignorant of affairs, he was safe, but for how long. He did not dare to leave the city again for the towering walls of Thebes were his best chance for survival. But what then? Perhaps he would ask for lodgings in the palace, on the pretence of working with the Vizier to resolve this crisis. Yes, Harsiese thought, the palace was the only safe place left to him now.

He glanced down at the scroll one more time. 'There is not one man in this city that I would trust with this news,' Harsiese murmured to himself. He began to read it again, but stopped himself, and dangled the missive over the flame of his lamp. The fire caught quickly and within a moment, the news was nothing but a few strands of curling ash.

There was nothing left to do. By now, Harsiese's letter would have reached Osorkon's hand or else his friend Hekhenfer was dead somewhere in a ditch. Only death would stop his head slave from completing his mission and if that was so, Harsiese would likely see him again sooner than later.

Harsiese sighed. Perhaps there was another way. To slip into Senmut's chambers one night and slash a blade against his throat, filling his last seconds of life with the face of his killer. For a moment, Harsiese surprised himself at his own callousness, even as he dismissed the risk of it. Senmut had been a close friend once, long ago. But the thought of the self-serving toad lurking around the inner sanctums of the temples was almost too much for him to bear.

'I will purge them all when this is over,' he promised himself. 'By all the gods of this land as my witness, I will cleanse Karnak of this corruption once and for all.'

Tasenhor and Naroleth would follow Senmut screaming into the abyss, but it was Pedubast who gave Harsiese the most pause. The son of Bastet had wormed his way into the cult of Amun with a political fluidity that had caught Harsiese by surprise. He was a talented statesman, a gifted orator and seemed to have a grasp of the intricacies of the court that Harsiese struggled to match. Years of living in exile and shame had blunted his father's teachings, but Harsiese felt the power of the divine flow through him again.

Pedubast would fall with the rest, a short-lived political career that would end with a knife in the night. Harsiese's instincts told him the time for reckoning would come soon.

It was not yet noon, but few days of late had been easy and Harsiese unstoppered a jug of wine from his own estate. The familiar light-headedness had not numbed the pit in his gut, but it was a pleasant enough distraction and one that he could afford to indulge in.

Despite his family's destruction and his ancestral holdings seized, he had long ago managed to turn what little land had been left to him into dedicated and successful wineries. His vineyards outside of the southern border of the Theban nome had just the right amount of sand and lime to make the grapevines flourish. With his father's lands now restored to him as a gesture of good faith from Osorkon, he hoped to increase production by fivefold or more.

He savoured that first rich taste, leaning back in his desk chair and closing his eyes as hints of ripened dates and Anatolian spice tingled his tongue. The knock on the door made him frown, banishing his momentary contentment as his office door burst open.

Senmut eyed the wine and smirked. 'Am I interrupting something, Your Holiness?'

'Not at all,' replied Harsiese coolly. 'What can I do for you?'

'The tour of your estates was fruitful, I trust?'

'The grapes are nearly ripe and ready for picking, yes. It has been a bountiful harvest,' said Harsiese, setting his cup aside. 'But you did not come here to discuss viticulture with me, did you?'

Senmut shook his head and took a seat uninvited. 'There are rumours spreading through the temples that Pharaoh, beloved of the gods, has got himself into a spot of trouble.'

'Nothing he cannot handle I am sure,' said Harsiese, holding up a scroll from his desk at random. 'The last reports have informed me that all is well and even now he moves to crush Shoshenq outside Lahun. The Crown Prince is recently married and I have inquired whether he will tour Thebes in the near future.'

'Quite,' said Senmut. 'Be that as it may, the brothers of the priesthood feel that a holy representative from the temples should venture north to Middle Egypt to administer to the souls and spiritual needs of the fighting men of Thebes. The ravages of war affect us all, those that go and those that stay.'

'An excellent idea,' replied Harsiese, though his eyes narrowed at Senmut's tone. 'I will be happy to approve your request once you have found a suitable candidate.'

'Traditionally, once he enters office, the High Priest himself conducts a tour of inspection of all the temples under his domain.'

Harsiese set the scroll down. 'I see.'

'What greater inspiration would there be than to see the First Prophet of Amun lead the spiritual charge against the traitorous usurpers of Tanis? What glory!' said Senmut.

'I am flattered by your counsel, my friend, but I am needed here to tend to the god's needs and maintain the rule of Amun and Ma'at in the city of temples. It would be irresponsible of me to go,' replied Harsiese, gesturing to the sheafs of papyrus across his desk.

Senmut smiled thinly, his eyes never leaving Harsiese. 'Do not fear, Your Holiness. The prophets you have so nobly entrusted into your care will be able to handle matters until your return. The gods will not go unfed, nor the people unled.'

'Very good, but perhaps another time. The royal campaign is at a delicate stage and it would be foolish of me to impose on Pharaoh at this time. Now, if that was all?' said Harsiese.

Senmut frowned. 'Your Holiness, I must confess that I am surprised at your reluctance. I had thought you would be thrilled to venture into the wilds and guide our people towards salvation.' Senmut averted his eye. 'I beg your forgiveness.'

Coldness gripped Harsiese's heart and he stilled the first hint of trembles in his hand by drinking from his cup. His gaze met Senmut's over the rim of his cup and paled at the triumphant gleam so evident in Senmut's token regret.

'Why?'

Senmut rung his hands, a pathetic charade that demeaned them both. 'We had thought you would rejoice to go, so we have already made the announcement. The people already celebrate that you go to deliver their husbands and fathers from the demons of Tanis. Even now, they are preparing a festival in your honour.'

Unblinking, Harsiese watched as his prophet stood and bowed deeply.

'Forgive us, I will tell the people you have changed your mind,' said Senmut, a viperous glint in his eyes.

Slowly, very slowly, Harsiese set down his goblet and rose to his feet. Senmut would pay for this. By the gods he would burn screaming for his treachery. 'I would not wish to disappoint the people of this great city, for they are our masters and we are merely their servants,' said Harsiese. The High Priest of Amun fixed Senmut with a steely glare. 'There is much to do before I leave, for the safety and security of the realm. I must ensure that nothing befalls my beloved city in my absence. Close the door on the way out please, brother Senmut.'

Senmut bowed once more and slid silently out of the office, leaving Harsiese alone to his thoughts and his wine. Soon, the wine drowned the thoughts in fears as the High Priest of Amun quietly wept.

OSORKON FOLLOWED PEDIESE at a canter down the sloping dunes towards the entirety of the Meshwesh nation on the move. The tribal coalition, following their elected Great Chief Pediese, numbered in the many thousands, surely enough to populate a city of Egypt by themselves. Dust from their passage blocked out the sun, and both the vanguard and the rearguard were lost to Osorkon's sight.

Returning to the deeper desert, Osorkon found his mount becoming more agreeable, the camel more responsive to his commands and loping forward with measured, eager strides. The motion had been jarring to begin with, but he found himself moving to the creature's lolling gait, adjusting his balance with an ease that surprised him.

Pediese angled his own camel towards the centre of the Meshwesh column, gesturing with a nod as outriders peeled off from the main force to intercept them before they were even within arrow shot. Osorkon counted ten riders, then twenty, galloping towards them as fast as the camels could manage, weapons raised in salute as they raced to be the first to form the Great Chief's honour guard.

Pediese raised his spear and whooped with him, congratulating the first of them and commiserating with the last. 'We have come to see the holy men of the desert,' Pediese told them, and without a word, they wheeled their mounts around to target the column's dead centre, their expressions grim and sombre in an instant.

'There,' said Pediese, nodding towards a cluster of six warriors, conversing quietly together. Though they looked little different to the warriors around them, Osorkon noted the respectful distance afforded them, perhaps the only sizable gap in the whole column.

'Oh,' said Osorkon, sidling up beside the Great Chief.

'Did you expect something different?' asked Pediese.

'The holy men of my land rarely fight,' said Osorkon, by way of explanation. Each of the shamans was as rangy and lean as the other, inured to a hard life that would have been beyond most of the Egyptian priesthoods. They were as well armed as any warrior of the Meshwesh, light armour shining beneath low, flowing desert robes. Colourful headscarves wrapped their brow and they wore colourful beads entwined in their beards in the manner of chiefs.

Osorkon saw this all in an instant, but it was to the saddlebags on the shamans' camels that his eyes were drawn. No, not bags. Baskets, of the kind that healers and snake charmers kept to house their serpents. In that, Egypt and the Meshwesh shared a similarity.

'You ride with creatures of Set beside you?' asked Osorkon, recoiling. Every child of Egypt had been told stories of snakebites as soon as they were old enough to understand language. It seemed every family in the Two Lands knew of someone that fallen to the bite of an asp or adder, left swollen, bleeding and clawing for breath as the poison did its work.

Just one bite was a promise of death in mere minutes, feeling the life drain from your flesh, the breath seize in your lungs and the strength of your limbs betray you.

'Honoured mystics, I bring to you the one I spoke of,' called Pediese.

As though of one mind, the six shamans turned their collective gaze upon Osorkon.

'You are right to fear them,' said one of the shamans as the chief and prince approached. The Meshwesh mystic inclined his head a fraction to Pediese.

'I did not say I feared them,' replied Osorkon, pulling his camel into line with the shamans, keeping to their speed. Even for the Great Chief, they did not break stride.

'You did not have to. But you are right to do so,' said another, with a long drooping moustache and a vicious scar that drew the left side of his mouth up. On anyone else, it would have appeared as though he was constantly sneering, but it gave the Meshwesh a brooding, considering air.

'In the deepest desert, it is unwise to go quietly,' said a third, who was remarkably young, surely no older than Osorkon himself. 'To go loudly alerts the snake to your presence. It shows your strength. If you go quietly, you will surprise the serpent and it will strike out of fear. If it succeeds, it will learn that it too is strong, but mistakenly believe that it is the strongest creature in the land. This is folly, and will go ill for the serpent and the creatures with which it shares its home.'

Osorkon glanced at Pediese, but the Great Chief did not return the gesture. He was enraptured by their every word.

'Great Chief Pediese tells me you have news of import,' said Osorkon. 'There is much work to be done, and with respect, I do not have much time.'

'We are giving it to you,' said the first shaman again.

'There is much to do,' said the scarred shaman. 'We have looked upon your lands and your people and found them both pleasing. That is why we have advised the Great Chief to extend his hand of friendship to you, so that two branches of the Meshwesh might live together in harmony. We do not wish for war, but it is coming for you.'

Osorkon shook his head, feeling foolish he had come so far on Pediese's word. 'You inform me of the obvious. We are already at war,' he snapped. 'Why have you asked me to come here? Speak plainly.'

'You are born in the lineages of your temple priests and yet you do not have the patience to understand,' admonished the youngest shaman. 'We do not speak of your war where the river meets the sea, but another disturbance where you have walked firmly, but not firmly enough.'

'You speak of Herakleopolis? Or Thebes?' asked Osorkon. 'Both are under the firm control of my family.'

'Perhaps on the surface of the sand all appears serene, but it takes a mere breath of wind to disturb the sand and reveal the snake underneath.'

'How do you know this?' snapped Osorkon. He wanted to reach for a weapon.

'Do you trust us?' asked a fourth shaman, an old man with sagging jowls and leathery skin, tanned dark after a life spent under the desert sun.

'I have only just met you,' said Osorkon, casting another sidelong glance at Pediese. The Great Chief seemed amused, which only irritated Osorkon further.

The shamans laughed. 'When you fly as a bird you see far, but when you fly as a bee you see farther still. We can show you what we have seen, perhaps. The deep dream can be learned over years of patience, but it can also be induced if need be.'

'Unshackle your sight from your flesh and see further than you have ever seen,' pressed the first shaman. 'See the truth we have witnessed and return to us with tidings of what you will do.'

Osorkon did not reply, waiting for the mystics to say something, anything concrete.

'I will take him,' said Pediese, speaking for the first time since their arrival.

'Be his guide, Great Chief,' said the youngest shaman, turning to Osorkon with a thin smile. 'Go far, Prince of Egypt, and know that the Meshwesh stand with you in sharing one of our secrets with you, the uninitiated.'

The scarred shaman turned in the saddle and plucked a small leather bag from beside the wicker basket at his hip. He leaned over and held it out to Pediese, who took it reverently and tied it securely to the pommel of his own saddle. 'Consider our words when you fly as we do,' said the scarred one. 'Go deep into the desert and you will see we speak true.'

The taste of ash was a persistent irritation that neither water nor wine could entirely remove. Soot inked his skin and cuts and bruises marred his flesh where jagged stone had torn at him as he had led the Theban soldiers in clearing the debris of burned neighbourhoods.

Osorkon shifted in the saddle, trying and failing to find a comfortable position. The jolting motion of his camel sent jarring aches through him as his muscles pulled tight and tender welts were knocked and irritated against the beast's flanks.

Osorkon unstoppered his wineskin, ignoring Pediese's patient smile. He would have severely disciplined any man who dared drink on a scouting mission, but there had not been sight nor sound of another man or woman in two days. The only danger in this barren wilderness seemed to be dehydration and the myriad snakes and scorpions that the Meshwesh tribesmen insisted on hunting as soon as night fell.

The countryside was rough, and the hiding places of Set's creatures were numerous. Osorkon almost wished the vanguard of Tanis would appear over the horizon, if only to face an enemy that wouldn't kill him with a surprise bite to the ankle. The camels, at least, seemed to sense whenever silent death was near, though whether this came to them naturally or was a trick of the Meshwesh training, Osorkon did not know. Their splayed feet gave them an advantage over uneven ground that horses could not match, and upon sensing a snake hole, they tossed their heads and skirted around it, ignoring the guidance of their riders. Osorkon found a new appreciation for the beasts, but was mindful of their relatively slow gait. If they faced horsemen, they would have no choice but to turn and fight, but here in the dunes and ridges camels would outlast horses with ease.

Osorkon reached out to hand Pediese the wineskin, which the Great Chief took with gratitude, drinking a long draught himself. He wiped his mouth appreciatively and stood in the saddle, scanning the horizon. Apart from a smattering of rocky outcrops and the occasional sloping dune, the desert was utterly featureless. Seemingly satisfied, Pediese slipped from the saddle to the ground and began speaking to his warriors in the clipped tones of the desert dialects.

Following the lead of their chief, the Meshwesh warriors dismounted and began unpacking.

Osorkon watched them with amusement. 'I am not familiar with your ways, Great Chief,' said Osorkon, 'but even I know that this is a terrible place to make camp.'

'It is only for a short moment, Prince Osorkon. Come and join me.'

Osorkon did as he was bid, tying his camel's halter to Pediese's and stepping into the blessed shade of a hastily erected canopy. A rug of vibrant blue and red covered the pebbles and scree and a small wooden chest was brought to the centre.

'Great Chief,' said Osorkon, smirking. 'I am flattered, but I have a wife.'

'Who you have not lain with since you were safely behind city walls. Yes, young prince, your frustrations are a palpable force that we have all felt at one time or another, but do not fear. You are not my type.' Pediese flashed Osorkon a toothy smile and pulled out two vials from the chest, holding one out to the Egyptian prince. 'Do you know what this is?'

Osorkon cracked the lid of his vial, wincing at the bitter scent that assailed him. The liquid inside was clear, and there were little more than a few scant drops in the bottom of the vial. Even so, the repellent scent was unmistakable. Osorkon met the Great Chief's eye. 'It is poison.'

Pediese nodded, seemingly unperturbed. 'It is, but not in its purest form. It is drawn from the bite of a viper but changed far beyond its original potency. It will not harm you, but it will change you. Here, is the secret of the Meshwesh, our most potent magic.

With this, we become one with the desert and see all that we wish to see.'

'You speak in riddles, Chief Pediese.'

'By necessity, not desire. It is a tool developed by our shamans. Even I do not understand the process fully, but I have experienced the effects several times myself. Your *ka* will temporarily free itself from your body and you will walk as a god walks.'

Osorkon chuckled and went to hand the vial back, but Pediese refused. 'I have never been able to clear my mind,' said Osorkon. 'My tutors at Karnak despaired at me for it. I fear your potion will be wasted on me.'

'It is impossible to clear the mind fully. Maybe the gods can, maybe they can't either. Do not attempt the impossible and then give up when you fall short. Focus on the here and now.' Still smiling, always smiling, Pediese drained his vial in one and settled down into the cushions as though he were merely taking a nap.

Osorkon regarded his own vial dubiously. Closing his eyes, he swigged it back, gagging on the rancid taste. He gulped down the last drop and lay beside Pediese. Though the canopy was large enough for them all, the Meshwesh warriors retreated to crouch beneath the shadows of their camels.

Pediese spoke again, his tone muted as though he were speaking from far away. 'Try to stay awake. Fight it as long as you can. Use your frustration. Use your pain. If you succumb too soon you will sleep for a few minutes and then awaken.'

'Will I see you?'

'Perhaps you will, perhaps you won't. The desert winds beyond this world are fickle and difficult to navigate.'

Osorkon tried to ask what winds he should expect but his tongue refused to respond. His eyes drooped closed, weighing more than they ever had and he slumped into the cushions on his side.

A low hum rang in his ears and his body was suffused with rhythmic tremors that throbbed from his toes to the crown of his head.

As the darkness took him, he was vaguely aware that he exhaled and then...

137

...LIGHT.

Bright light.

The sun, burning high in a cloudless blue sky.

Osorkon looked into the seat of Ra himself and did not flinch. The sun warmed him, suffused him with comfort and strength, but curiously it did not cause him pain. He could look right into its burning depths, his eyes unaffected by the blinding light.

He breathed, falling into familiar rhythms.

He looked down, but the red of the carpet had changed, reflecting the brown hues of the canopy. The pillows too were gone and so was Pediese and...

Osorkon's stomach lurched and he threw out his hands to catch himself, but his hands would not obey. He looked down and where his body had been only moments before was nothing but thin air.

His breath caught where his throat should have been. Long seconds passed and yet the burning need for air never presented itself.

The tremors ran through him again until he looked away.

His sight obeyed and he turned back to the canopy, seeing through the fabric now where his motionless body was revealed beside that of Pediese. The Meshwesh tribesmen seemed entirely unconcerned, and if their chief was unattended then Osorkon rationalised he was in no great danger himself.

He had no legs to stand upon so he considered that he could only be floating, defying Earth's hold and flying like a spirit in the realm of shadows. He willed himself to rise and his sight responded, floating higher and higher until the Meshwesh were like ants and the canopy was but a brown pebble in the sand.

He ignored the curious sense of dislocation and sent his thoughts to the north.

An eagle passed him by, circling him effortlessly on the warm thermals above the river. It seemed to follow his progress for several minutes before its head snapped downward and it tucked in its wings, diving like an arrow into the golden dunes below.

Osorkon willed himself to follow it, but his intent made him roll over like a mewling babe, flopping over where his back had been and giving him an unparalleled view of the sky. He swore through lips he had left far behind and willed himself to see the land once more.

He followed the course of the river as a guide, free from the constraints of flesh but losing none of the thought or emotion of true life. Was this what it was to be a god? Was this his destiny after death?

He passed fishermen oblivious to his presence, their vessels drifting in the currents even as he drifted in the air. He willed himself faster and faster until suddenly the river seemed to stop, a barricade of brown and white cast across the water.

Osorkon ventured closer, his sense of wonder evaporating in an instant.

The fleet was massive, wide enough to fill the width of river with war vessels.

Shoshenq had come with the might of an armada at his back. There would be no quarter given to the Thebans, who had dared challenge him.

Victory or extermination. That was the choice facing his family.

He swooped in on the flagship, hovering above its highest mast. A figure in a blue crown stood in hushed counsel with men Osorkon had last seen attending his grandfather's funeral in Thebes, men with the power to crush nations and command thousands with a word.

He reached out to the central figure, this rival king.

Be gone from this place, he willed. Turn around and take your warriors with you.

The figures did not hear him and he could not hear them, such was the pounding roar in his ears. His vision blurred and he lost all track of where he was. Sight returned and for a moment he thought he had returned to his body. He looked down, far below, and knew instantly otherwise. Take me back, he willed, but his vision remained the same, sparkling with sudden recognition.

He knew this road. It was the road north from Thebes. The hill below him was the last turn where one could take a final view of the City of Temples. Such was the grandeur of Thebes that a traveller would see its walls kilometres before he reached its gates, just before the road wound around a deep bend and the city was lost to sight. The road was vacant, but for a train of donkeys loaded with baggage.

A dejected rider sat astride the first of the pack animals and half a dozen guards and twice as many retainers walked beside him.

Curiosity piqued, Osorkon willed himself closer, his non-existent eyes widening as he recognised the central figure.

The figure's closest retainer fell on his face.

The soldier next to him took one step and clutched at his neck where an arrow shaft had appeared. More shafts hissed through the air, felling soldiers as they turned frantically trying to find their hidden foe.

Osorkon watched in horror as the massacre unfolded.

The unarmed retainers fared no better as the archers closed the gap. Men in desert garb, flowing robes and head scarves fell upon the column with murderous glee. Those that fell to their knees pleading for mercy died there.

The central figure kicked in his heels and sent his donkey racing for the next corner and the cover of a grove of date palms. The ambushers shouted after him and an arrow took the donkey in the flank. The figure landed hard, getting to his knees before a gloved hand cannoned into his jaw. He did not rise again as the bandits roped his wrists and ankles and tugged a rough sack over his head.

The sun dipped below the horizon and...

...OSORKON'S EYES OPENED to the canopy once more.

His heart — his real heart — thudded in his chest. He was breathing hard, as though he had just run in full armour. There was a sense of dislocation in his arms and legs, and his head swam as his normal senses reasserted themselves.

'What was that?'

'That depends. What did you see?' said Pediese, climbing to his feet.

Osorkon rose after him, but stumbled and nearly fell.

Pediese steadied him. 'Move around. It is the easiest way to readjust. The desert shows many wonders, but it often shows us things we have little desire to see.'

'I saw a fleet of ships as wide as the river. Shoshenq is coming. And I saw a murder. A man I know was attacked on the roads outside Thebes.' Osorkon took a shuddering breath. 'Did you see what I saw?'

Pediese shook his head. 'It is rare for even the most gifted of seers to share a vision. I saw my people walk through a land fed by the blood of our warriors, but afterwards green life sprouted and fed a new generation of Meshwesh children. It is a vision I have seen more than once. I lead them now into war to save them from a lingering slow starvation in our homelands. Trust in what you saw.' Pediese called for his men. The Meshwesh warriors moved to join their master under the tent canopy and brought food and drink with them. Osorkon took a crust of bread and strip of dried meat gratefully, his thoughts lingering on a scene of violence hundreds of kilometres away.

He turned to the Great Chief. 'Is this man dead, do you think?'

'I cannot say. Sometimes we fly close to the real world, other times we are closer to the world of dreams where our sights can be interpreted in many ways.' Pediese chewed thoughtfully.

'If there is strife in Thebes, I must know,' said Osorkon.

Pediese nodded. 'Eat and regain your strength. Then we ride.'

# Chapter Eleven

THE FIRST THING Harsiese felt upon awakening was a cold rock at his back and burning pain in his wrists and ankles.

If this was the afterlife, it was very disappointing.

He opened up eyes gummed shut with dried blood, but the darkness remained consuming and all-encompassing. His head throbbed, and the rank taste of iron made him gag as memories leaked into his bruised consciousness.

He did not fear death, not really. His life had been devoted to serving the gods, and when the call of Anubis inevitably came for him, he hoped he would face the darkness with quiet dignity, secure in the knowledge that his station in this life would be preserved and his memory and devotions along with it. Such was the natural order of the world.

But now, in this place, he was afraid.

If he were to die now, so be it, but the implications for his immortal soul of dying here filled him with terror. Even his father, condemned for heresy, had been granted the gift of mummification to rescue his spirit from the in-between. The obliteration of his father's name would have weakened his power considerably, reducing the soul of a god to that of a restless spirit. Even that, though, was infinitely preferable to the oblivion faced by the truly forgotten.

Harsiese tried to bring his thoughts back to the moment. He was not dead yet, but the fear muddled his thoughts and he struggled to get a clear grasp. A hessian sack covered his head and rubbed against his scalp, irritating him like a thousand insects crawling across his skin. His wrists were bound, as were his ankles, and his back was pressed against stone too smooth to be natural, but rough enough to be in a state of disrepair.

He tested his bonds, but the coarse rope tore open a stinging rash on the soft skin of his wrists. Gasping with pain, he let himself go slack.

His movements had not gone unnoticed.

A distant star peeked out from the darkness and Harsiese's aching eyes struggled to follow it. Within moments it had become a burning sun, and his vision was dazzled by thousands of tiny pinpricks of light as the torch pierced the rough thread of hessian cloth.

'He is awake,' said a guttural voice at the edge of his senses. It was not a voice of a native Egyptian.

'Good. You really are too heavy-handed. Take off the sack,' said a voice, smooth and rich with amusement and all too familiar.

Harsiese looked up, but his eyes stung with tears and focus came slowly. When it did, his lips curled in distaste.

'So, you do recognise me, brother. I was afraid Kafkher here had been too rough with you.' Senmut smiled and gestured to the man beside him, the one Harsiese now recognised as the man who had chased him down and knocked him unconscious.

He glared back at Senmut. 'You son of a whore. I should have known you would stoop to the basest treachery, you debased spawn of Set.'

A face soft with easy living and a taste for luxury smiled broadly, inches from Harsiese's own. 'You can thank Pedubast for this latest deception. I was content to let you wander into the middle of a warzone and see if you really were Amun's chosen, but this.' Senmut took a shuddering breath. 'This is something I have dreamed of for a long time.'

Harsiese looked past Senmut's gloating face to a cluster of figures by the door. Each of them went hooded, but the profile of the closest was unmistakable.

'Pedubast,' growled Harsiese, his lips thick with swelling and his throat dry and hoarse. 'You are the most disappointing of my initiates.'

The men at the door chuckled together, though Pedubast himself remained impassive.

Senmut spread his arms wide in apparent surrender. 'You betrayed us, Harsiese.' Senmut's voice was calm, but the menace was palpable. 'You sought to alert our enemies to our plans. You did not join us, and though that displeased me, I was content to leave you be provided you remained neutral. But you attempted to tell Osorkon of our plans, and that I cannot allow.'

Harsiese smiled thinly through bloody teeth. 'It doesn't matter. The letter is already in Osorkon's hand. Even now he knows of your betrayal. Remember what he did to the Meshwesh, his own distant kin? Ponder, in your last days, what he will do to you.'

Senmut chuckled, glancing over at his conspirators in the shadows of the ruin. 'Dear sweet Harsiese. You did not honestly think we would not suspect your treachery? You think we haven't been watching you every moment since Takelot gave you everything?'

'Hekhenfer will not have failed me.'

Senmut's laughter trailed off, and his voice was a sharp whisper. 'Do you not understand, you fool? Hekhenfer was one of us.'

The blood drained from Harsiese's face and Senmut laughed again in genuine delight.

'Now you finally understand.'

Harsiese shook his head, the motion bringing to him fresh waves of vertigo. 'No, I do not believe it. Hekhenfer is my friend. He would never betray me.'

'He was your slave. Now he is free,' shrugged Senmut. 'Don't feel bad. All men have their price. His was a premature end to his servitude. We granted him that. I suppose he must have cared for you once, before he found a higher purpose in our service.'

Senmut pressed the papyrus in front of Harsiese's face, the fine cultured script and rich ink the same as he had remembered it. 'This is your penmanship, is it not? Osorkon remains clueless, and Takelot looks to the enemy to the north and only to the north.'

Harsiese sagged against his bonds. 'What will you do now?'

Senmut shrugged. 'Simple, wait until they annihilate each other and then remove the victor.'

'Your Nubians are animals. They cannot prevail.'

'No man can rule as King and High Priest in this city. Your father tried, and your father failed. I will not make the same mistake. You could have remained High Priest with us, Harsiese, beholden only to a council of the wisest in our priesthood. Thebes needs a council to lead it, not a vainglorious monarch. Look to Hermopolis and see how they thrive. Why do you insist on not seeing the truth in my words?'

'You are a baseborn cur, Senmut. I would trust you as far as I can throw you, and a life of easy living has made that not very far indeed.'

'You disappoint me, brother.'

Harsiese strained against his bonds, trying and failing to throttle Senmut's pudgy throat. 'I am no brother of yours.'

'You might believe that now, but we really are more similar than you think. You were trying the same strategy, I believe. Hekhenfer told us everything before he died. "Oh, Prince Osorkon. Behold my loyalty to you for I have stopped the treacherous Senmut and all his wicked followers." Then, when the dust had settled and the soldiers are bloodied or dead you would silence him with a knife in the dark. I am right, aren't I?'

Harsiese spat at Senmut's feet. 'Why go all this way for an elaborate façade?'

'To give you one final offer. Your name would lend great power to our cause. You would keep your position, of course, but you would respect our advice and follow it closely. And invest in the security of the priesthood.'

'You want my gold.'

'A donation for the good of the priesthood. We can just take your lands, but you know them better than we do and we do not have the luxury of time.'

'A puppet ruler,' sighed Harsiese.

Senmut shrugged. 'As you like. It is better than the alternative.'

Harsiese shook his head. 'A puppet ruler who would die of heart failure or plague at the slightest inconvenience to his loyal and noble advisors. You would make me another heretic to be damned like Akhenaten.'

Senmut sighed theatrically. He spread his hands in mock defeat. 'You would live far more peacefully if you just nodded and kept your mouth shut.'

'I will not live in fear.'

'Then you will not live much longer.'

Harsiese strained against his bonds, letting the pain lend him strength. 'Your threats do not scare me. Kill me now and I will see you before long in the shadow lands.'

Senmut grunted and his fist cannoned into the side of Harsiese's head. 'You are your father's son. And for that you will die, in time. First, I want you to see your plans fail, your ambitions turn to ash. I want you to watch as Osorkon falls in the shadows of the walls of Thebes.'

Harsiese's head lolled groggily. 'You underestimate them,' he slurred. 'Osorkon has Bakenptah with him. The younger will crack open your defences and the elder will cut your heart from your chest.'

'Good. They will die together. Only then will I leave you hanging from the walls so that you can watch your last hope putrefy in the sun.'

Harsiese spat blood. 'Why not do it now, coward?'

Harsiese's head rocked back as Senmut punched him again.

'Regrettably, the people still side with their false pharaoh. When he dies, when his whole family dies, they will have no choice but to the turn to the priesthood for succour. Plenty of time to lament that the arch-heretic Harsiese had us all so fooled until the end. Pure of heart and righteous he claimed to be, but rotten to the core none could see.' Senmut sniggered at his own wit and Harsiese had never felt such repulsion.

'You're insane.'

'So are all visionaries,' replied Senmut mildly. 'I shall not lose sleep over it.'

'Your time will come before long, Senmut. You have the stench of Apophis about you.'

'As you say, brother,' Senmut smiled and thrust the sack back over Harsiese's head. The light of Senmut's torch faded, but his voice rang out, echoing as if he spoke down a long tunnel. 'Enjoy your last days, my old friend.'

THE WIND WAS conspicuously absent from this part of the river, the fleet of Tanis pulled along by a sputtering breeze that left the sails sagging and the men restless. The Tanite flagship, *Wrath of Tanis*, led the way as the king of the river, followed by a fleet of ambling courtiers. The last time Shoshenq had sailed this far south the wind had been enough to fill his sails and make the ropes and rigging groan. The wind here, a league north of Lahun, barely rippled the fabric of his robes.

He looked out over the countryside, but the date palms and sedge reeds were likewise motionless. He laughed mirthlessly. What a fine image he must make, wearing the blue war crown and charging into battle with the speed of an infant learning to walk.

'The gods truly have a sense of humour when it comes to the lives of men,' said Shoshenq.

Paameny, the royal physician, sat perched on a step beside Shoshenq's throne. He followed his king's gaze up into the rigging and snorted. 'Perhaps Ankherednefer will get there first and set up our camp for us,' the physician suggested.

The *Wrath of Tanis* slid through the river waves with barely a ripple at its prow. It was hardly an inspiring sight, as impressive as the ship was, but what it lacked in propaganda potential it made up for in a complete absence of crew sickness.

'Even Ankherednefer is not as grim as you, Paameny, and I have seen him smile exactly twice since my coronation last year,' said Shoshenq.

'The Inspector of the Palace has his own battles, namely marching all of our men through potentially hostile nomes. Why else do you think I came with you? I hate sailing.' Paameny went back to his work on Pharaoh's correspondence, but Shoshenq could not resist needling at the physician again.

'I should have left you in the palace at Tanis among your books. At least then you wouldn't spend all of your time idly fretting.'

'I would fret there too, Great One,' promised Paameny, without looking up. 'And it is not idle. Even kings need to be reminded of the worst of eventualities.'

'I need no help with that, royal physician. Trust me.' Shoshenq looked skyward and spied a dark dot drifting in the endless blue. 'Behold, physician, the sky god remains with us.'

The eagle had been following them for hours, circling high above, diving once when it spotted a rat or small fox, but swiftly returning to its vigil empty-handed. It drifted lazily on warm currents high above, seemingly content to watch the procession float by.

Shoshenq spread his hands wide in the gesture of obeisance. 'Mighty Horus, Lord of Royal Protection, lend us strength so that we might return the land to the Rule of Ma'at. The will of the gods be done.' The eagle dipped its wings in its flight and Shoshenq was satisfied. With or without the intervention of the gods, he would crush the Theban usurpers. *With* would just make the whole exercise that much quicker.

The flotilla was huge, but only a scant fraction of the ships held any soldiers. Most were crewed by skilled naval seamen, handy in ship-to-ship combat, but untrained in marching and fighting in land formations. The vast majority of the Tanite army marched along the highways adjacent to the river under the command of Ankherednefer. Each night, the army built a city of tents surrounded on all sides by a palisade, while the fleet anchored offshore.

'Will you give Takelot one more chance?' asked Paameny suddenly.

Shoshenq considered the question, just as he had privately for weeks. 'What good would it do? He is as tied to this path as I am.'

'Thousands of men will die for the egos of two men?' The words were said without venom or rancour, just the cold simple fact of an old man who had witnessed generations of war.

'I do not need your criticism in this final hour, Paameny,' said Shoshenq.

'I hope you will not need me at all. Such is the irony of my calling.' Paameny groaned as he stood, old bones creaking as he shuffled across the high deck. 'I have much to prepare before the battle. I pray we brought enough linen and natron.'

Shoshenq let the rebuke slide and dismissed Paameny with a wave.

He had heard similar critiques of his predecessor from the aging healer. If even Osorkon II had not been able to iron out Paameny's pessimism then Shoshenq would not waste his time trying now.

The physician lived with the knowledge of life and death, but what could a healer know of commanding men or safeguarding the realm? What could he understand about the collective psyche of an army, a city, a nation even? A pharaoh's gift was to forge an insight into the kingdom itself, far greater than any one individual. It was his burden to maintain through the balance of light and dark, but he would struggle to do so here from the throne of his meandering warship.

Shoshenq sighed, cursed, and gave the order to run out the oars. The sails were stowed and the thudding beat of the drum rang out as the *Wrath of Tanis* picked up speed. Shoshenq half-expected the wind to reappear as soon as he gave the order, but nothing was forthcoming.

It seemed even the gods held their breath.

THE NOMARCH'S HALL of reception in Herakleopolis was a wonder, a gallery and monument to Egyptian engineering and artistry. Only the halls of Thebes, and perhaps Memphis, surpassed it in majesty and even the haughtiest of nobles was humbled within its walls. The common people who came to petition at the nomarch's feet, Karomama had found, were rendered almost catatonic with awe. How else, but with the blessings of the god themselves, had their betters raised such a mastery of stone craft?

If Karomama never saw it again in her life, she would consider herself lucky.

The Great Royal Wife waited on the nomarch's throne, alone in the chamber but for her bodyguards who were stationed around the entrances and at the foot of the throne's dais. Blessed silence reigned in the hall, for now at least. She rubbed at her temples and sighed as the throbbing ache behind her eyes finally began to ease.

The nobles came in seemingly ceaseless waves, braying like farm animals for her attention and her favour. They poked and prodded with their platitudes and petitions, seeking to learn more about her and her family and their designs upon the city. They had adapted to the loss of their nomarch surprisingly quickly, swapping one master for another with a fluidity borne of a nobility that had long desired change.

Just what that change meant for them they were still learning.

There was potential in this city. Potential to be moulded and cast upon the anvil to form a new southern kingdom. Potential that her husband would see forged into spearheads, but that Karomama intended to cast into nails, bracings and fasteners to bind her family's new realm together.

Karomama was torn from her thoughts as the court herald knelt by her knee and waited for her to grace him with her attention.

'The Royal Temple Builder to see you, your highness,' he said softly.

'Send him in.'

The herald bowed low and trotted back down toward the atrium. A few moments later he re-entered the hall, with the master of building in Herakleopolis close behind him. Hamma was thickset, with the arms of a blacksmith and the hands of a carpenter. He marched forward, his skin shining with oils and sweat, and fell to one knee at the foot of the throne dais.

'Karomama Merymut, Great Royal Wife of the southern kingdom of Thebes and Herakleopolis. How might I serve?'

'By dispensing with unrequired formality. Stand, Overseer Hamma. You are a true friend to my family.'

Hamma rose to his feet, coming to stand at the foot of the dais. 'Apologies, my lady. It is always difficult for a simple draughtsman such as myself to remember royal protocol.'

'If I thought there were anything simple about you would you not be building my late brother-in-law's familial temple,' said Karomama.

Hamma tilted his head, conceding the point.

'I was sorry to hear of Nomarch Khonsefankh. He was always a generous patron,' said Hamma, genuine regret in his words.

Karomama smiled to see the streaks of sandstone dust running in drips over the overseer's arms and legs where he had hastily tried to wash the filth after her summons. The temple builder, last employed by the late nomarch, had been at work for months on a commission from Khonsefankh himself.

Losing his sons and wife had driven the nomarch to cloak himself in his grief and build a glorious temple to his family so that they might always be remembered and so prosper in the Field of Reeds. Priests to the cult of Khonsefankh would have worshipped the family as gods, giving daily offerings and singing hymns to their glory.

Now, the nomarch himself would be honoured in the temple's decorated sanctum.

Karomama accepted the consolation with a graceful hand. 'Despair of his last son's death drove him to take his own life. You were not deaf to the whisperings about him, I trust. Nonetheless, it is a terrible loss and this city is all the poorer for his absence.'

'And Pharaoh?'

'Will endure, as always.'

'If there is anything I can do?' Hamma smiled and dipped his head for a few moments before raising it to see the Great Royal Wife standing in front of him.

Karomama smiled and gestured into the shadowed alcove at the edge of the hall. 'In fact, there is. I understand work on the temple of Khonsefankh is progressing well. It is Pharaoh's will that some alterations are made to encompass the families of both Takelot and Khonsefankh. A symbol of unity, you understand. Brothers standing together, in the eyes of gods and men.'

A palace servant ran to Karomama's side, falling to his knees and offering up a papyrus scroll a metre long. She took it and helped Hamma unravel it, revealing blueprints that would double the temple's existing design.

'You say alterations, but I see an entirely new hall added to the existing design.'

'You have a good eye, Overseer Hamma,' said Karomama, with a smile.

'It will take some time to draw up these plans. We will have to completely rebuild the western façade and expand the entrance. The work will be difficult and the costs… substantial.' Hamma's eyes remained fixed on the designs, his eyes already consolidating the new changes with what already was.

'Yes, they will be, but the work should keep your builders and artisans employed for years to come,' said Karomama, taking a moment to appreciate the handiwork of the designs. In another life, Bakenptah would have made a similarly talented builder or artisan. 'In wartime, unemployment leads to strife quicker than you might believe. I will provide you with all the resources and assistance at my command. You will want for nothing.'

'That is most gracious of you, my lady. I will begin work immediately.'

'My sons are at the service of this city too. Bakenptah is a talented draughtsman with an eye for architecture. Perhaps you could make use of him.'

'I would be glad of his assistance, my lady.' Hamma bowed and went to withdraw. 'Forgive my forwardness, but I am glad the Beloved of Mut is here to guide our city. You are a mother to us all in times such as these.'

Karomama smiled graciously. 'See that the gods are honoured and all will share in their prosperity. We all serve the divine in our own capacity, Master Hamma. Your service will last for a million years in the sight of gods and men.'

Hamma smiled and bowed again, before he marched from the chamber with purpose.

Karomama watched him go. Weariness stole over as the master builder left the hall, and she sat back in her throne and sighed. Immortality beckoned, and she was glad of the work in achieving it, but it was a heavy burden in this life. Perhaps she would go to the temples herself and seek the rejuvenation of the goddess Mut, for the battle to maintain what they had won was almost as exhausting as winning it back in the first place.

RUIN OF SEKHMET

# Chapter Twelve

THE PRIESTS OF Karnak were called to council at dawn. From the youngest novice to the most venerable archivist, all were summoned to the shore of the Sacred Lake. Not since Takelot's humbling by Nakhtefmut had so many priests been in one place. Muttered curses and sideways glances marked the occasion, and the murmur only heightened as Senmut, the Third Prophet of Amun, strode forward to address the crowd.

Beside him, Tasenhor and Naroleth stood as an honour guard, lending their authority to his words though even they were ignorant of his intent.

'I bring terrible news, my friends. It has come to my attention overnight that High Priest Harsiese, First Prophet of the Precinct of Amun and Lord of Karnak, is dead. Slain he was, by bandits on our very doorstep on the eve of his tour of investiture. His bloodline was cursed by his father's actions and now the chaos of the world has claimed him.'

Senmut bowed his head as a cry of anguish arose from the crowd.

'Alas, he is gone,' said Senmut, raising his head once more. He looked out over the assembled priests and his lip curled at the sight of their despair.

'Only Pharaoh may proclaim a new High Priest of Amun, but Pharaoh is not here. Until he returns, you may turn to myself, and brothers Naroleth and Tasenhor for guidance. Under this darkest hour do we oath ourselves to serve the priesthood with humility and grace,' Senmut continued.

'I understand your pain, my brothers, for I share it in equal measure. But now is no time for mourning. We have an obligation, and we will not falter.' Senmut raised his hands above his head.

'The people will cry out for succour during this difficult time. The people are greedy and will look to protect themselves and their families first. This is not wrong of them, but will Thebes survive, will the priesthoods survive, if the food is holed up in the ground beneath the houses of the common people? I say no,' cried Senmut. 'All must be shared and equal before the gods.'

The assembled crowd roared their affirmation. Senmut grinned and continued. 'Go forth, my brothers. Beseech the people for donations of all they can spare. Help them to bring bounty to the temples and so bring blessings upon themselves, under Amun's guidance.'

Senmut ended his speech with a flourish and stepped down from the platform. Tasenhor and Naroleth were hard pressed to follow him. The cries of adoration and belief followed them from the platform down into the alleyway.

'That went well,' said Naroleth, mildly. His eyes darted between Senmut and the priests assembled behind them. Hundreds of pairs of eyes followed their passage. They passed beyond the boundary of the square and Senmut began to laugh.

'What have you done?' snarled Tasenhor, when they were out of sight. He grabbed Senmut by the shoulder and pulled him around to face him.

Senmut smiled again. 'I have just turned the people to our side, brother. When the priests talk of the threat facing us, as they will, who will the people cry out for to save them? Not Harsiese. Not anymore.'

'You murdered a High Priest of Amun? Only killing Pharaoh is a greater crime. By the gods, Senmut, your heart is fit for the belly of the beast of Osiris,' hissed Tasenhor. The priest let Senmut go and stepped back.

'It was a necessary evil to maintain the priesthoods as Amun intended. Do not fear for me, Tasenhor,' said Senmut. He smoothed down his shendyt and rearranged his necklace and arm bands.

156

Tasenhor shook his head, his eyes fixed on Senmut's. 'And your plan now is to starve the people? You think Malkesh will move on when everyone is already dead?'

'There are priorities to consider, Tasenhor. The common people can grow grain and catch fish, but only we can serve the gods as they deserve to be served,' said Senmut. He looked back at the burgeoning horde of priests still crying out in the courtyard and he smiled. 'The common people are many. There is no harm in trimming them to keep the rest in line.'

PEDUBAST SHROUDED HIMSELF with his cowl, keeping his head down and his finery hidden. In the weeks since Senmut's pronouncement, the mood of the city had changed and then changed again.

In the beginning, the people had been joyous to feel the firm hand of the priesthood take charge. The vacuum of Harsiese's disappearance, swiftly filled by the Third Prophet Senmut, had brought relief. Relief that had quickly evaporated in sight of the temple's new decrees, given authority through the Vizier's support. The streets of Thebes now seethed with restlessness and discontentment as Senmut's push for donations stretched a thin people even thinner.

Pedubast paused at the top of the street, his head cocked as he listened to a lone voice cry out over a jeering crowd. One of Hory's town criers stood on a step at the edge of the market square, his hands raised and his reedy voice carrying over the irritable murmuring of the merchants and peasants. The Vizier's morning announcements were spreading resentment at the speed of thought, and Pedubast listened as the muttering grew louder and angrier.

'It is the Vizier's Decree that martial law is now instated across Thebes. All able-bodied men are to report to the barracks for arming and training. All grain, barley and malt is to be taken to the royal treasuries for rationing at once. Failure to do so will be regarded as theft for which the penalty is the loss of a nose or hand.'

The crier ducked as a root vegetable hurtled towards his head. 'Have that one,' cried a voice from the crowd. More voices joined the first and the crier's face twisted with fury.

'Enough,' he shrieked. 'It is the Vizier's Decree that-' A second vegetable struck him in the eye and cast him down onto the street. The crowd jeered as he staggered to his feet, his fury replaced with a very animalistic fear.

Pedubast watched as the crier took a final lingering look at the crowd before he fled, jeers and curses following him down the street. With their source of ire gone for the moment, the crowd began to disperse, and Pedubast slipped the bands from his wrists and secreted them in a pouch at his waist. He reached the palace without further incident, joining the ever-present line of petitioners waiting for audience with the city's masters. He waited to be admitted inside the first atrium by the palace guard before he parted from the main group and took a side passage away from the audience chamber.

He risked a glance behind him but the petitioners had barely moved, a line of bored-looking statues focused on their own miseries. Hory would be busy for hours yet. That was good.

He slipped the cloak from his head and retrieved his golden bands, charms and pendants, distinguishing himself from common humanity in mere moments. Palace servants and royal scribes passed him in the corridors, recognising his station and respectfully nodding in greeting. He returned the gesture, walking slowly but with purpose as though he had every right to be there. The path he took was circuitous, winding back on itself through corridors and vacant halls until he knew for sure that he was not being followed.

The palace gardens were a place of quiet contemplation, an oasis sanctuary in the heart of a metropolis of sandstone and dust. Pedubast stepped out into the light of day, taking a welcome breath of cool air, the music of birdsong surrounding him as swallows and bee-eaters darted among the trees and shrubs.

While the palace staff were not technically barred from the gardens, only the highest ranked among them had the free time and inclination to sit and meditate here.

It did not take long for Pedubast to seek out who he sought. Alone in the garden, a young woman watched the birds flitter and play among the branches of an ancient fig tree. Beneath the branches, fallen figs bobbed and floated in the pool beneath as they were pecked at.

Pedubast moved silently up behind her. 'My lady,' he said quietly.

Isetweret started where she sat, her eyes wide as she twisted to look behind her. 'Pedubast,' she gasped. 'What are you doing here?'

'Business brings me here. We must speak.'

Isetweret drew her own cowl up over her hair and glanced around the garden, but the two of them were alone. 'You cannot be seen here with me. It is not proper.'

'Perhaps, but it is necessary and so here I am,' he said.

Isetweret scowled up at him. 'You might as well sit then.'

Pedubast took the proffered seat, reaching down to toss a fig towards the edge of the pool. The birds flocked to it, chirping excitedly, tired of the challenge of food that bobbed and dipped in the water.

'How are the people?' asked Isetweret then, turning her dark eyes upon him. Worry lines creased at her temples and the cosmetic shadows around her lashes did not entirely hide the bags beneath her eyes. She looked tired. Pedubast imagined he looked little different.

'They are angry. Angry and scared,' said Pedubast, after a moment. 'They know what martial law means for them. They know something big is coming.'

'It is necessary.'

'Even so, fear has spread through commoner and noble alike. War leaves no man untouched. And no woman,' he added.

Isetweret smiled weakly, her eyes never leaving the chirping birds. 'If only we all had wings,' she murmured.

Pedubast turned to her, keeping his voice low. 'What will you do? War is coming to this city, sooner rather than later.'

'I have written to Osorkon already. Gods be good that the letter reaches his hand safely.'

'You cannot be sure that it will. You must leave the city. Head north to your family. Stay in Herakleopolis with your mother until the situation in Thebes is resolved.'

'And abandon the people?' Isetweret laughed, but it was harsh and forced. 'Hory will never let the city fall. He will stay to the end to protect his family's legacy.'

'I did not say Hory. I said you.'

Isetweret recoiled and glared at the priest. 'I will not leave my husband. Not while-' she trailed off, and looked away.

Pedubast's gaze wandered to the hand on her belly. 'I know you are reluctant to leave, but I cannot guarantee your safety in all of this if you stay.'

'The palace is the safest place to be.'

'Your father-in-law probably thought the same once, until your brothers unseated him,' said Pedubast. 'Hory will have to stay behind, but in your... condition, it would not be unusual to see you retiring to the country.'

'I am a princess of Egypt. What can they do?' said Isetweret, recovering some of her former hauteur.

'I don't know and that frightens me. Hunger makes people do unfortunate things,' said Pedubast. 'The power of the priesthoods hangs by a thread. Something foul has befallen Harsiese, but I cannot say what.' Pedubast looked away as he spoke, lest the princess see the lie in his eyes. 'None of us can know how bad this will get, only that those that can leave should.'

'How did you not foresee this?' Isetweret snapped then. 'Southern savages are marching on our city, something that has no occurred in centuries. Your own High Priest has gone missing, presumed dead. And Thebes itself is under threat, with the power of the temples in doubt, you now tell me. So, I ask you again, how did you, who is in with the prophets, not foresee this?' Her eyes narrowed in suspicion. 'Unless you are complicit in his absence. The temples have always been secretive, but now I think there is something more. Tell me what you know.'

Pedubast bit back a retort. 'I am not a prophet. I am a simple brother of the precinct of Amun. Do not think me wise to the machinations of better men.' Pedubast stood and went to leave. 'If you will excuse me, my lady.'

He made it to the edge of the glade before Isetweret called after him. 'Pedubast, why did you come?'

The priest turned and plucked a ripe fig from the tree. He went back and pressed it into Isetweret's clasped hands, meeting her dark gaze with his own.

'Think over what I have said, but do not think too long,' he said, and left the princess with her thoughts.

As MARTIAL LAW took effect in the days ahead, Thebes fell into a sullen silence punctuated only by the metallic ringing of battle drill and the constant droning of priests in prayer.

The streets were devoid of men, for every man capable of holding a spear was drilled in its use day after day. Fishermen and cloth merchants stood side-by-side in hastily formed units, a paltry but necessary support of the overwhelmed city guard.

The market stalls were instead operated by the old men and young children of the city, peddling increasingly fewer goods. The women either haggled for a bargain or waited for hours outside the state treasuries for their daily ration of wheat and barley, under the watchful eye of a cohort of palace guard.

Pedubast looked out over the cityscape from the roof of the First Pylon of Karnak. A hot desert wind blew across the rooftops, plucking at his robes and brushing his bare skin with grit. Come nightfall, the rooftops would be the domain of the Hour Priests, the stargazers and calendar-makers, but for now he was alone.

Far below him, the Avenue of Rams marked the path into the city proper, but it too was devoid of traffic. Senmut had ordered the temple gates closed under the guise of safety as the rituals beseeching the gods for aid grew ever more frequent and powerful. In reality, the precincts of the gods were a kingdom of prosperity in a starving and fearful land and the threat of eternal damnation would only last so long.

Instead, the priests ate and drank within the precinct walls with fare that was a feast to the pauper's fare now enjoyed by even the city's nobility. None dared speak out against it, for they enjoyed a bounty and those that stirred the waters were threatened with banishment, not only from Karnak, but Thebes itself.

In the quietude, Pedubast felt a rustle of footsteps behind him. He did not bother to turn and greet the man, nor did the newcomer bother with pleasantries. They were both beyond that.

'The rumours are true?'

'Yes,' said Pedubast. 'The princess is with child, Senmut.'

Senmut gasped as he climbed the last step, his face red with too much indulgence.

'You should walk more,' Pedubast admonished. 'It is good for the heart.'

'That is between me and Anubis,' snapped Senmut. The prophet spat over the edge and wiped his mouth with the back of his hand. 'Look at them,' he continued, gesturing toward the city. In the distance, the people of Thebes were as ants, going about their business. 'See how they toil for us. And in return, they shall know the gods' power!'

'How long?' asked Pedubast.

Senmut frowned. 'Days at the most.'

'I hope you know what you are doing.'

'You have trusted me this far.'

Pedubast grunted. 'Trust is not the word I would use.'

'It would not kill you to address me with respect,' snapped Senmut.

'Perhaps, but it is not a risk I am willing to take,' said Pedubast, with a smile that quickly faded. 'Isetweret suspects something ill. You will have to move quickly.'

'Don't you mean, we?'

'No, I don't. You chose me to act as your mediator and I will continue to act in that capacity, but no more than that,' said Pedubast, forestalling Senmut with an upturned hand. 'If I can offer some advice, treat them gently. Hory comes from tainted blood, but Isetweret's family will still have many supporters. Bring harm to her and you will find resistance.'

Senmut's eyes narrowed with suspicion. 'I do hope you have not grown to be fond of the princess.'

'Have you met her, Senmut? The lioness Sekhmet has less of a temper.'

Senmut chuckled. 'Yes, she has the fire of her father with none of the tempering of her mother. Hory will go along with whatever she says and with that they are predictable. Do not fear. She carries Takelot's grandson. She is twice as valuable to us now.'

'And what of Hory?'

Senmut shrugged lightly. 'We will see. What does she plan to do?'

'Nothing,' replied Pedubast. 'She is content to weather the storm and hope the conscripts will be enough to fight back the horde.'

Senmut laughed again and clapped the other priest on the shoulder. It took all Pedubast's self-control not to flinch. 'You have done well, Pedubast. She trusts you?'

'She does.'

'Then I sing your praises before the gods. With your help this has become a lot less bloody. You are on the frontier of change, my friend, and the rewards for the faithful are rich indeed.'

'You honour me,' said Pedubast. 'But I act in the best interests of the city, the gods and Egypt. I do no more or less than any priest should do.'

Senmut snorted and turned to leave. 'Humility does not suit you, brother, so dispense with the act and embrace your new station. I will have need of men like you in the coming years. We will do great things together.'

# Chapter Thirteen

THE FIRST SIGN of the approaching horde was a thin pillar of dust marring the southern horizon an hour after dawn. A sentry on the southern gatehouse raised the alarm, followed by another as the watch commander himself raced to the walls to verify the fearful reports. By midmorning, every man, woman and child in the city knew that the war had finally reached them, here in Thebes.

Under the midday sun, the first shapes of men became visible amid the dust. From the walls, it was impossible to see exactly the force arrayed against them. Even so, the veteran soldiers, those deemed too old, weak or injured to endure the march north to face Shoshenq, muttered to anyone that would listen that their doom had come. Only a force of thousands could raise dust that high, they claimed, but they tightened the straps on their armour and put their spearheads to the whetstone, nonetheless.

Within the hour, the column of dust had grown, and men of the city guard and the conscripted militia jostled together on the walls for the first glimpse of the enemy.

The horde marched only loosely in formation, without rank or file. The garrison on the walls watched on with grim comprehension, every man realising that it would be a slaughter if the walls were breached. The warriors of the horde outnumbered their own career soldiers three to one, if not more. Most of the conscripts had never held a spear before the Vizier's decree, let alone swung one at an enemy, and few among the commoners had the strength to shoot a bow for any length of time.

All of this was relayed to the Vizier in the palace's throne room, the watch commander delivering his report with commendable calm. Gone were the long lines of petitioners and gone were the courtiers and advisors shadowing his every movement, the latter sent to hide in the deepest parts of the palace.

Hory listened to the report without comment, his expression set as his servants fastened his armour and bore his weapons to him. Beside him, Chancellor Pereftep directed the palace's messenger runners, receiving missives from other captains of the city soldiery before sending the runners back with fresh orders.

Isetweret sat on her throne and listened in silence. On matters of war she knew little, but the furtive glances in her direction revealed enough.

'Sire, the enemy seem to have struck camp, but we cannot be sure it isn't a ruse,' said the watch commander. 'They may attack at once.'

Hory slipped on his rings and checked the knots on his vambraces. 'We have waited for them for weeks, commander. They can wait for us a moment longer. The men are ready?'

'Of course, lord.'

'I hope so,' replied Hory, hearing the hesitation in the other man's voice. 'These are warriors of Nubia, warriors who have raided and pillaged their way deep into Egyptian territory. Those that have made it this far are worth ten pottery-makers and cloth-weavers.'

'The walls of Thebes are the tallest in the world,' said the watch commander stiffly. 'We will make them pay for every step.'

'No walls are impregnable, commander. The evacuation?' asked Hory.

'Ready at your word, lord,' said Pereftep, dismissing a final messenger and leaving the four of them alone, but for the palace guards.

'Good. You are a faithful man, chancellor. Escort my wife to the docks and see her safely to her father. If the walls fall, you must be swift.'

Isetweret looked up at her mention. 'Has there been any word from my brothers?' she asked quietly.

The chancellor shook his head. 'Regretfully, the scouts report no sign of either Prince Osorkon or Prince Bakenptah, my lady.'

'We are alone then,' said the watch commander. He bowed low to the princess and nodded farewell to the chancellor. 'When you are ready, lord?'

'You will give me a moment, commander?'

The watch commander's eye strayed to Isetweret and nodded. 'Of course,' he said.

Hory thanked him and climbed the dais. He looked magnificent in his gilded armour, the first, and likely last, time he would wear it to war.

Tears streaked Isetweret's face as Hory lifted her chin with a gentle finger.

'Remember me always, Iset, for I shall never forget you.'

'Come with me,' she said, holding the rough hand that stroked her cheek.

'You know I cannot,' he replied, and gently pulled her up. He embraced her and the veneer holding back her sobs broke down like a dam built of papyrus. After a moment, he pulled away and kissed her forehead.

'Stay safe, my love,' he said, and turned to leave.

Isetweret clung to his arm, which he allowed for a few moments before he gently slipped out of her grasp.

The chancellor stepped next to her, offering her his hand.

'My lady, please come with me. Time is short,' said Pereftep.

The chancellor was interrupted as shouts came from the hall's entrance. The palace guards stepped forward as one with spears levelled at a lone soldier, unarmed and red in the face. He gestured wildly, but his words did not carry the length of the hall.

Hory's hand went to his sword and the palace guard at the dais formed up as a protective line between the Vizier and the new arrival. The soldier held up his empty hands toward them and threw himself to his knees. The palace guard angled their spears down at him, ready to strike at the Vizier's command.

'My lord, my lady,' said the messenger, bent over and out of breath.

'What is it? Speak!' Hory snapped.

'The prophets, my lord. The prophets of Amun. They are gathered at the main gate and demand to be let out to face down the horde.'

Isetweret laughed but it was a harsh and broken sound. 'I pray they have a miracle for us.'

'Well, my lady' said the soldier, looking up at her with fever bright eyes. 'I think they might.'

HORY LED THEM through deserted streets to the southern gate, flanked by the watch commander and his captains. Behind them, Pereftep and Isetweret brought up the rear, borne aloft in litters. The palace servants that carried them struggled to match the Vizier's pace, accustomed as they were to a slower, more sedate duty.

Isetweret peered out from behind a thin cloth veneer at the silent houses and abandoned marketplaces. Market stalls stood untouched and homes and workshops had been left open as the city's occupants fled to the docks by the Vizier's command. Isetweret's thoughts turned to the women and children of the city. Even now, far away in the city's west, they would be clustered together, silent and in darkness, as the Theban ships waited for word that the city had fallen.

She suppressed a shiver and dabbed at her puffy eyes. The motion of the litter disturbed her stomach, but she clenched her teeth and muttered prayers to Hathor, Taweret and Mut for deliverance.

Silence gradually gave way to a low hum of voices in the distance, and soon after, she heard Hory call their column to a halt. Isetweret slid out of her litter and rushed forward into the crowd, ignoring Chancellor Pereftep's protests behind her.

The avenue before the gatehouse was an all but impenetrable mass of the city's conscripts, the crowd little different from that of market day, but for the fact each man carried a spear and cowhide shield. The sudden appearance of the princess within their midst made her passage somewhat easier as the people shoved themselves aside to clear a path for her.

As the ranks parted, Isetweret saw just how dire their situation truly was. On the walls, the city's professional soldiers watched the horde's passage, but they were few; a paltry line of spears and daggers to drive back a horde of ladders and ropes.

The final ranks parted before her and Isetweret came before the very gates of Thebes. Her husband was thunderous as he shoved through his soldiers to reach the priests.

'Third Prophet Senmut, what is the meaning of this?' demanded Hory.

Behind Senmut, the prophets Naroleth and Tasenhor stood before what seemed to be the entirety of the Amun priesthood. Only the prophets stood beside the gate, for many hundreds of lay priests watched on from where they could beneath the shadow of the walls.

'It is the will of Amun, Lord Vizier. I, Senmut, will face down this barbarian warmonger and compel him to go.'

Naroleth's and Tasenhor's expressions led Hory to believe that Senmut would not be going entirely alone. 'That is suicide. You would cripple your own priesthood?' he hissed, but only the Third Prophet met his eye.

'Your faith is lacking, Vizier. Amun has spoken to me and he is displeased with those who do not show him proper reverence.'

'I am as devout as any man, but even Amun cannot help you if you go out there,' said Hory, striding forth and addressing the other prophets. 'Make him see reason.'

'You speak blasphemy to the gods' chosen representatives?' asked Naroleth quietly.

'You are twisting my words. What say you, Second Prophet Tasenhor? Will you share in Senmut's madness?'

'Senmut is chosen,' intoned Tasenhor. 'He will not lead us astray.'

Senmut smiled again. When he spoke, he pitched his voice so that all on the gatehouse would hear. 'With respect, Lord Vizier, I answer to a higher power than you. Now, stand aside and let us pass.'

The gate guards glanced nervously at Hory. The Vizier shook his head and sighed. 'Do as he says,' he ordered the guards. 'Give them their martyrdom. May the Holy Family have mercy on you all.'

Isetweret stepped forward, and Hory took her by the hand. Together, they followed the watch commander up on top of the gatehouse. The sight made her heart quail.

Clusters of ramshackle tents dotted the landscape beyond for kilometres, stretching from the city's southern edge to beyond its northern boundary. In front of the makeshift city, thousands of men stood in loose ranks, motionless and with swords and spears already drawn. Ladders crafted of timber and rope were set beside every section and a thick tree trunk was tied with ropes to be used as a gate ram.

She felt a tremor beneath her feet as the city's gates were closed and barred again and the crowds from below pushed their way up onto the walls for a view of the prophets' miracle. Isetweret glanced sideways as the priests too climbed the stairs and crowded around them on either side of the gatehouse. She pulled her shawl tight around her, unsettled by their presence.

She went to tug on her husband's armour, but Hory's attention was fixed on the progress of the three prophets. Senmut led them towards what could only be the warlord, a giant of a man, holding a great spear as long as he was tall. Isetweret had never seen such a man, except perhaps the Tanite pharaoh's shieldbearer, but while Lamintu embodied control, this man exuded raw, unrestrained violence.

'He's the biggest man I've ever seen,' Isetweret whispered, her hand still clutching Hory's.

The prophets were halfway now and yet the host before them stood motionless, either transfixed by an unseen power or bemused at this pitiful show of resistance.

TASENHOR GLANCED BETWEEN Senmut to the towering warlord ahead and then back again. He followed a step behind Senmut, flanking the Second Prophet on the left as Naroleth brought up the right. 'If this does not work, I will find you in the Field of Reeds and kill you again. If the beast does not devour your heart first,' he hissed.

Senmut chuckled. 'Come now, brother. We both know that you will be right beside me for whatever fate has in store for us.'

Tasenhor grunted but did not speak. It was little more than fifty metres from the gatehouse to the first ranks of the assembled horde, but his legs felt leaden and heavy as though he had already walked a league or more.

Malkesh watched them approach, the warlord's spear unsheathed and held loosely at his side. He made no move to address them, none of them did. Hundreds of eyes watched their passage across the plain

Senmut stopped a few paces before the warlord and held his hands high in front of him.

'Hail Malkesh the Conqueror,' he cried. 'I command thee in the name of Amun. Go forth from this place and fight in the great god's name. Turn aside your spears from the gods' sacred place and sunder his enemies instead.'

Malkesh twitched once and strode forward, his spear raised to strike Senmut down.

Senmut threw up his hands again and shouted 'I command thee, savage of the south. Cast down your arms and hear my command. Kneel before the rightful lords of this land, by the word of Amun.'

Malkesh stopped dead, his spear held fast in a downward arc that would have skewered Senmut through the heart. The warlord grimaced. Slowly, he knelt with his head bowed before the trio of priests. Like a wave rippling along the shore, the horde followed their master in his show of submission. Senmut turned his back to the warlord and raised his hands to the city and the priests and soldiers watching from the walls.

'Witness the majesty of Amun, He Who Rules in Heaven, He Who is Master of all Life, the Divine Will and the One Who Brings Forth Light. Witness him, and be humbled!'

Senmut ignored the low rumble coming from Malkesh. The warlord was laughing.

'Go forth from this place. March north and fight for Thebes against the northern oppressor. I charge you to strike down Shoshenq. Only then will you know peace by the gods' grace.'

Senmut stepped forward and placed his hand over Malkesh's brow. Even kneeling, the warlord's head was almost level to his own.

Malkesh bowed his head before the gesture, his spear held point down in the sands.

Senmut leaned in and pitched his voice low. 'Where is Sarasesh?'

Malkesh grunted. 'He is here.'

'He still lives?'

Malkesh smiled and nodded once. 'For now. Know this, little priest. When I have defeated your northern army, I shall return to this city and take it for myself. The blood of your priests will fill my wine cup. Every last one of them, except yours. You will live to serve it to me before I flay you alive and sew your skin into the sails of my ship. I would do it today, but your walls are high and my men hunger now. There are easier prizes within reach of my spear.'

Senmut's mouth opened and closed wordlessly as he stared into the dark eyes of the beast of a man before him. For a moment, he was pinned by the abyss, the sheer brutality behind that stare.

Malkesh slowly got to his feet, his spear resting over his shoulder. 'Consider this in your last weeks, spent trembling in your cowardice. I will return. All shall know that I, Malkesh, am lord of your Two Lands.'

SENMUT BATHED IN the city's adoration as he walked back to the gatehouse. Behind him, the horde of Malkesh was already at work dismantling their shelters and forming up to march north. The gates swung open and the priests stepped through to the cheering throng, the people of Thebes crying out with relief. Some, he saw as he climbed the steps of the walls, were opening weeping.

Radiant, the Saviour of Thebes smiled humbly and raised his hands for the cheering to subside. 'People of Thebes, through me the power of Amun has turned aside the Nubian threat and yoked it to our cause. Amun has shown them the true light where no other could.'

Senmut rounded on the gatehouse where Hory and Isetweret stood watching on.

'Take them, my brothers! They who banished High Priest Harsiese to his death. They who commanded your fathers and sons to die at the horde's hands. Arrest the Vizier and his bride for they are filled with darkness and will lead us all astray.'

The priests around the couple did not hesitate. As one, they swarmed them both, holding them immobile as the shock of the crowd turned to jeers.

Isetweret shrieked and flailed, kicking and slapping at the priests but they were many and pinned her arms to her sides. Hory offered no resistance, too numb to register the betrayal.

Senmut ascended the gatehouse where they had stood, watching as the priests loyal to his cause forged a way through the crowd to place the Vizier under house arrest. The Third Prophet raised his hands for quiet and the people obeyed, awestruck by this demonstration of divine power.

'Return to your homes, my brothers and sisters! Rejoice in your sanctuary and give thanks to Amun for your lives. Truly, the Father of Heaven is content.'

# RUIN OF SEKHMET

# Chapter Fourteen

BEHIND THE WALLS of Karnak, the holy places of the Two Lands fell sway to unbridled celebration and uncharacteristic decadence. Tasenhor had seen the celebrations conducted by the common people, a toast to their safety and a meagre feast with whatever they had left. But inside the temple boundaries, within the dining halls, storehouses and private spaces of the precincts, the priests of the Theban Triad lived in gluttony. Solemnity and reverence became tainted with revelry and excess, and all shared in the drunkenness of relief as the horde marched north and disappeared over the horizon once more.

Tasenhor shoved past the temple guards standing outside the precinct's dining hall, pausing at the threshold as his eyes adjusted to the darkness within. The air was hot and heavy, and alive with the sound of song and animated conversation. Temple singers sang odes and common ditties, and musicians played out of time as the wine flowed. Priests of every rank reclined together on woven mats and shared carafes of wine and platters of food. Donations to the temple had only increased in the wake of Senmut's miracle, the dwindling stores of the city repurposed by the people in an effort to buy more divine favour.

Tasenhor stepped over the languid groups, lethargic in their drunkenness. He looked around for a familiar face but they were few. Most of the devotees here were among the very young, those newly inducted into the priesthood's service. At the edge of the hall, Naroleth was in deep discussion with a circle of initiate priests, no doubt regaling them of his close friendship with Senmut, the Saviour of Thebes. Beside him, Pedubast looked bored. The priest nodded as Tasenhor crossed the room, and the prophet returned the gesture.

The Saviour himself sat at the centre of the gathering, on a pile of cushions and skins, the most devoted of his newfound followers lying around him in a ring of stupor. Senmut's smile was serene with wine and his movements were as unbalanced as his speech was slurred. He grinned up at Tasenhor as wine dribbled down his chin onto his chest.

Tasenhor's lip curled at the sight. 'You're drunk.'

Senmut stared in the bottom of his cup. 'I am,' he giggled, beckoning for his cup to be refilled. The server bowed low, whispering praises as he poured another measure, his face alight with fervour at the favour.

Tasenhor shook his head. Within a day, the Third Prophet had formed a cult of worship around himself that even great kings would have been envious of.

Senmut took another drink and swished the contents of his cup, splashing wine over his own lap. 'Do you think it would be too much to ask that Malkesh and Osorkon just killed each other? Would Amun do that for us, do you think?'

'I think you speak too liberally in your current company,' replied Tasenhor. 'I would ask that you keep yourself proper. At least, as much as possible.'

Senmut glanced around, but even his closest admirers were in the depths of their own wine and drug-induced stupors. 'So proper you are Tasenhor. Have you not come to kneel at the feet of the Saviour of Thebes? You were there to witness the miracle.'

At that last word, Senmut's devotees stirred and murmured platitudes to the Third Prophet. Senmut basked in their adoration for a few moments, before he grinned back at Tasenhor. 'What do you think?' he asked.

Tasenhor was unmoved. 'I think that you have asked for too much and now the price is demanded of all of us. What are we going to do?'

Senmut chuckled sadly. 'There is nothing to do, except to enjoy our lives such as they are.' He raised his voice for the entire hall. 'For we all stand before the gods before long.'

The clamour, and its misinterpretation, made Tasenhor wince. Like a wave along the river the noise receded as quickly as it had come. The priest glanced around them, but even those close to Senmut were locked in avid conversation or stupefied by wine beyond comprehension.

'We have hostages. Valuable hostages. We could strike a bargain with Takelot. There is still time to reach him,' said Tasenhor.

'I think not,' said Senmut, his voice level. The slur in his words was suddenly absent. 'How are our royal couple, by the way?'

'Still locked at opposite ends of the palace. Isetweret rages whenever anyone enters her room. Hory has not said a word,' snapped Tasenhor. 'We can get nothing from them but that.'

'Perhaps I should try,' said Senmut. 'Pay them a visit in the middle of the night. People are much more susceptible to questioning when they are roused from sleep. Did you know that, Tasenhor?'

Tasenhor ignored the question. 'She bears Takelot's grandchild. Why is that not a good idea to at least try?'

'Because it will never work. Takelot does not forgive a slight.' Senmut sighed into his cup. Suddenly, he looked tired and worn. 'Did you like it, though? The way I ordered them taken?'

'Will you focus?' hissed Tasenhor. 'I thought to wait until you were sober, but you have managed to drink yourself blind for a day. Do you not understand?' Tasenhor knelt by Senmut's feet. His voice when he spoke was a harsh whisper. 'If Malkesh returns, he will kill us all. If Pharaoh returns, he will kill us all. What are we going to do?'

'Perhaps we could just offer them wives? How many each do you think would stay their blades? Ten?' giggled Senmut. 'A hundred?'

Tasenhor shook his head. 'You disgrace yourself, Senmut. You disgrace yourself and you disgrace the god you claim to serve. I am sick at the sight of you,' said Tasenhor. He spat on the ground and walked away, and so did not see the murderous anger that flashed across Senmut's features.

PEDUBAST LEFT THE celebrations as soon as propriety allowed. He had forbidden Iuput from attending, but in truth, his brother would have been little interested in the social decadence and having him outside the temple walls was far safer than having him within. The priest breathed deep of the evening air, clearing his lungs of the heady smoke saturating the dining hall. He shook off his lightheadedness and passed the Sacred Lake, watching the breeze cast ripples across the water and disturbing the perfect reflection of the moon and stars. He lingered by the waters, his cowl hiding eyes that never stopped moving.

Twice, he was stopped by staggering groups of his brother priests, and each time he was careful to match their effusive praise of Senmut. When they were gone, he continued his winding path to the outer gate, but an itch at the back of his thoughts slowed his step. He blinked in the darkness, looking this way and that, but found no obvious reason for his discomfort. Nevertheless, he moved into the shadows before he could be seen, rubbing his right temple to clear his thoughts.

A wretched cough disturbed him, and he looked back the way he had come to see four priests staggering towards the gate. They whooped as they spied the guards, one of them loudly ordering the gates to be opened. Not one of the soldiers moved to comply. They watched the priests' progress and a knot of foreboding settled heavily in Pedubast's gut.

'Open the gates men, we wish to go into the city,' echoed a second priest, receiving the same lack of response as the first.

'Did you hear what he said, idiot?' cried a third priest, stepping within reaching distance of the guards. 'Open the gate at-' The priest hit the ground hard, floored by a single punch by the guard at the centre of the gate. He stepped forward to address the other priests.

'No one is to leave, by order of His Holiness, Senmut. Return to the precinct at once.' The other three priests turned and fled without another word, leaving their comrade to pick himself up and scamper away after them.

Pedubast waited long minutes in silence crouched in a shadowed alcove, but the guards might as well have been carved from stone for all the life they displayed.

Swearing softly, Pedubast backtracked towards the precinct's centre. Confusion muddled his thoughts. What harm was there in letting drunken priests return home? The gates would be open for no more than ten seconds. Was Senmut expecting an attack?

Pedubast headed towards the Hypostyle Hall finding it completely silent. He made his way through the titanic pillars and out the other side without seeing another living soul, but it was not to last. The portals at the hall's western and southern edges led to gates guarded with men loyal to Senmut. Like the main gate, they were motionless but they remained ever watchful for those that tried to leave.

Pedubast turned back and headed toward the northern half of the precinct, his senses reaching out into the darkness for the barest signs of life. But for distant cries and clamour towards the hall, the precinct was silent. He balled his fists into his eyes as he searched his thoughts for another way out, but there was nothing to be done for it. Not now. Perhaps he would return and wait for the guards to change shifts. It was a slim hope, but a slim hope was better than no hope at all.

He wandered for a time, glancing into darkened windows and testing locked doors, for the precinct was large and there were many places where a man could go to be alone, even in this city within a city. By chance, a cool breeze from across the river swept through the courtyard. At the end of the lane, movement caught Pedubast's eye as a curtain was momentarily disturbed. Deep within, the dull illumination of a single lamp silhouetted a lone figure. Pedubast checked that he was entirely alone before he pushed aside the door and entered. He started with surprise as he recognised the room's sole occupant, but in that surprise, he saw sudden opportunity. Perhaps Amun had barred his escape for a reason.

'I did not think to think to find another seeking solitude tonight,' said Pedubast.

Tasenhor looked up, his eyes red-rimmed and his cheeks sunken. 'And yet you did.'

Pedubast hesitated. The lamp glow did nothing to hide the other man's sickly pallor. 'Brother, we must speak,' he said finally.

'Now is not a good time.'

'Good times are in short supply in days such as these. I must insist. Why are the gates barred?'

Tasenhor grunted and gestured towards an empty seat. 'Close the door behind you.'

Pedubast nodded his thanks but did not sit. He ran his hands over the shelves around the room, until he found a heavy clay jug, still sealed with wax, and two empty cups.

'Wine?'

Tasenhor shook his head. 'I no longer have the taste for it.'

'You won't mind if I do?' Pedubast shrugged at Tasenhor's silence. 'Very well, if this is Senmut's vision for Karnak then I no longer wish to be a part of it. He must be removed from power.'

Tasenhor's laughter was a jackal's bark. 'You have come to tell me something I already know?'

'Yes, but without giving voice to it, it remains an idle thought.'

Tasenhor shook his head, his gaze somewhere beyond the confines of the room. 'It does not matter anymore, my friend. It is done and nothing can stay our course now. Ammit will eat our hearts and we will deserve it for our foolishness.'

'It is unlike you to despair, Tasenhor. What do you speak of? Why are the gates barred?'

'For us, Naroleth and me and any he suspects we might have told of what is coming for us all. The Nubians' rampage will return. When Malkesh ends Takelot he will return to claim Thebes as his own. He will climb the walls and slaughter every man, woman and child. We are all going to die.'

The breath caught in Pedubast's throat and the feeling went out of his hands. He left his cup where it sat before it spilled from nerveless fingers. Even in his stupor, Senmut was astute enough to realise that releasing drunken priests into the city was an idea doomed to bring the entire city down around him. It would take only one priest, just one, to realise he valued his family more than his service to try the outer gates and flee for safety. Word would spread before sunrise and a mass exodus, or more likely a mass riot, would destroy any chance Thebes had for survival before Malkesh ever returned.

'Who knows of this?' Pedubast whispered.

'Senmut, Naroleth, me, and now you.'

'No one else knows…' repeated Pedubast. 'Why would you not spread this news? There would be panic, but many would turn against Senmut.'

'It would be my word against his and his word is the stronger. Tell me, how convincing did his miracle look from the top of the walls?'

'Convincing enough, but I believe you now and others will too. How would our brothers react if they knew what Senmut had inadvertently planned for them? If they knew what was coming for them, would they break their own vows and spill his blood on temple grounds?'

'Be the messenger if you wish,' said Tasenhor. 'But I choose to live my final days as free as I am able, if only to watch them all burn too.'

Pedubast shook his head and slammed his cup onto the tabletop. 'By the gods, what have you done? What is this defeatism I hear from the great prophet Tasenhor?'

Tasenhor's eyes flashed with anger. 'What have I done? What have we done? Don't be so quick to lay blame, you who joined our fraternity. The deed is done. Malkesh will return and murder this city. Do you not understand? There is nothing we can do.'

'Will Pharaoh win the war before Malkesh reaches him?'

Tasenhor sighed. 'Will Pharaoh win the war at all?'

The wine soured on Pedubast's tongue but he drank it down to steady his hands. 'It is into Osorkon that we must put our faith then.'

'He's a boy,' spat Tasenhor.

'A boy that destroyed Harelothis and sent the Meshwesh scurrying back into the deserts,' countered Pedubast.

'He defeated a pack of dusty savages and sent them back to huddle around their dirty puddles. And he needed Ukhesh and Kaphiri to help him do it.'

'Then what would you have us do?'

Tasenhor shook his head and laughed. 'There is nothing to do. Do you not understand that, brother? That blasphemy that Senmut is hosting is one last pleasure before we are all sent for judgement. There is no reasoning with that barbarian warlord and if you think Takelot would be any kinder after what we have done, then you are a bigger fool than the rest of us.'

Pedubast leant back in his chair and swore softly. 'We release the Vizier and the princess then. There are those still loyal to them in the city. There has to be. Release them, reclaim the city and prepare a defence. Not lie idle in this vulgar display of indulgence.'

Tasenhor shook his head. 'If they still have allies, they are not enough. The palace is barely guarded and yet they are still under lock and key. Senmut has people everywhere. It is some small consolation that they will die with the rest of us.'

'Then we get them out of the city. Until Osorkon or Bakenptah father children, Isetweret is carrying the next generation of heirs,' said Pedubast.

Tasenhor shook his head. 'Here is the safest place for her, brother.' He lowered his voice to a whisper, despite the silence of the night air. 'If you try to break them out, you will only earn yourself a cell next to them. I am already under suspicion. Your closeness to the princess means you will share in that suspicion.'

Pedubast's frown brought a grim smile to Tasenhor's features and this time his humour was unfeigned.

'Senmut has eyes everywhere and this latest façade will only increase his number of followers. Whatever privacy you thought you had, forget it.'

'He knows some because I tell him so,' said Pedubast.

Tasenhor shook his head. 'Senmut is cleverer than you give him credit for. I would not be surprised if he has someone beside the princess at all times.' He sighed. 'It matters not. He has overreached himself this time and he knows it.'

Pedubast put his head in his hands. 'What has become of you, Tasenhor? You cannot sit here in despair.'

'You have his ear, but you are still a lowly brother of the priesthood, invisible to all but a select few. My advice, brother? Say yes to everything he says and wait for your inevitable end. Distance yourself now, if you are able, and your end might be swifter and kinder. Anyone close to Senmut now will suffer. Whether by Takelot's will, Malkesh's or the wretch's own self-destruction. It is only a matter of time.'

Pedubast's lip curled. 'You pitiful bastard,' he snapped. 'Damn it, Tasenhor. Come with us. Half of the priesthood is blind and deaf to the world and it will not be long before the other half follows them. We have more of a chance together.'

'You have more of a chance.' A single tear cut through the dust on his cheek. 'But not much of one. You will not make it outside the walls of Thebes, not while Senmut lives. He will catch you and you will die today. Forgive me for wishing to see a few more days before my own end.'

'There is always a way and that way is to get Isetweret and Hory to Takelot. Not even Pharaoh would be callous enough to execute the men who saved his daughter.'

'The whole damned city just saw me walk out at Senmut's side. I am already dead, brother. By Senmut's hand if I go with you, by one of the savages following that whoreson Malkesh if I don't, and by Takelot's hand if by some impossible miracle you succeed. It does not matter what I do. I am just waiting for the sword stroke to fall.'

Pedubast looked down upon a man utterly broken. Tasenhor's features were lined with the weight of woes beyond the mortal, for the prophet was looking at his own eternal damnation. Whoever was fated to kill him would be loath to treat his body respectfully and so assure his position in the afterlife. Pedubast drained the last of his cup and set it down in front of the broken priest. He retrieved the wine jug and set it beside the cup and turned to leave. 'You disappoint me. I will trouble you no more and leave you to your pity.'

'Go with all the gods' graces behind you, for all the good it will do' said Tasenhor. 'Nowhere in this land is safe now.'

# Chapter Fifteen

OSORKON SENT HIS scouts south the day he returned to the Crag of Amun. Within hours of his arrival, six riders travelling light and swift were dispatched with orders to search the country around Thebes for signs of unrest. His father had dismissed Khonsefankh's warning out of hand, confident that any insurrection was powerless to maintain itself under his daughter's custodianship, but now Osorkon was not so sure.

He had left Great Chief Pediese's camp with his thoughts awhirl, the revelations shown to him by the Meshwesh magic filling his gut with a dread that he could not shake. Osorkon did not deign to share the nature of his revelation with Akhetep or any other of his senior officers, merely stating that their Meshwesh allies had heard rumour of distant strife. Akhetep's distrust of their Meshwesh allies would hinder Osorkon's efforts to find the truth, and the prince could not abide another of his friend's lectures.

Osorkon petitioned his father daily for an audience, seeking some spiritual clarity to what he had seen, but his entreaties were met with silence. The pacification of the city after the death of Khonsefankh and the ever-growing demands of war consumed Takelot's time beyond all other obligation, even to the king's own family. Each new day brought the conflict in the north closer to their new home in Herakleopolis, but now Osorkon's fears turned toward their ancestral home in Thebes.

On the day Takelot was to depart north, Osorkon left the Crag early, letting the fortress sleep and entering Herakleopolis alone.

Dawn was still an hour away, but the city was already awake with the army's mobilisation. To march ten thousand men northwards and coordinate a navy and fleet of supply ships was no easy task, and every hour of daylight was immeasurably precious.

The palace halls were still dark, but even the throne room still burned with the fires of tireless, logistical work. Servants conducted their business under the ever-watchful eyes of the palace guard and somewhere beyond, deep within the palace chambers, scribes would even now be bent over their writing tables, copying missives and movement orders under the dull glow of torchlight. Osorkon swept through it all, barely breaking stride as the guards confirmed his identity at each checkpoint.

The war room was a nondescript chamber with a central table but no chairs, just large enough for ten men but certainly no more. A large map was spread out over the table and the southern lords of war looked up as Osorkon darkened the doorway with his passage.

Takelot was absent, as Osorkon had expected at this hour, and he nodded a greeting to the commanders of the coalition as he passed. Kaphiri of Thebes bowed at the waist and Ukhesh of Hermopolis greeted him with a wink. Osorkon gave the map one last envious glance before he left them to their planning and continued on to what had, until recently, been the late nomarch's private armoury.

Osorkon spied a lone figure silhouetted against the flickering torch flame and despite himself, he crossed the threshold with a sense of trepidation. At the sight of his father, his thoughts of Thebes faded, his desire to win glory at his father's side becoming all-encompassing.

No servants assisted their master in his dressing, nor would any soul alive dare to interrupt their king's preparation, for the rites of the blue crown of war were as spiritual as they were physical. At least, most would not dare.

'You march today.'

Takelot looked up, surprised to see his meditations interrupted. He went back to buckling his sword belt, shaking the metal scales of his armoured shirt loose around his waist. 'I did not expect you until the parade,' replied Takelot.

Osorkon came around to stand before his father, content at least that he had not aroused his king's anger. The prince was dressed plainly in a utilitarian shendyt and loose travel robes, but Takelot looked like a king in all his ancient glory, a Ramses or Amenhotep of ages past. Each one of his bronze scales was polished until it caught the light, giving him the appearance of a glittering river fish. It was adorned with golden threads and inlaid with smooth polished discs of iron for strength. Smaller discs of lapis lazuli trimmed the shirt along each edge and thick cords of crocodile leather tied the armour together.

The armour gave Takelot freedom to move and fight, but kept him protected against all but the most grievous of blows should any enemy be fortunate and foolish enough to get too close. Beside Takelot, the great war bow of Pharaoh stood unstrung and strapped secure in its rack, its graceful timber curve almost the height of a man.

'I could still come with you. Give the order and I will muster the royal charioteers. There is still time,' said Osorkon.

Takelot shook his head as he tightened the strap on his vambrace. 'And who would hold the Crag? Who would protect your mother and brother? You would leave this city defenceless?'

'That is not what I meant, my lord.'

'And your Meshwesh? The ones I am leaving behind?'

'Might feel better about sending their fathers and brothers to war if the prince that brokered this alliance was watching over them. They will not betray us, and they are not mine, nor are they yours. They ally with us for common benefit.' Takelot held out his hand and Osorkon dutifully retrieved the war bow. Takelot sighed as he grasped the weapon, holding it up to his eye as if aiming before he glanced at Osorkon.

'Do you trust the Meshwesh to stand against the might of Tanis?'

'Pediese will not falter. He has shown me things. Things that could be of use in the war if you would allow me to join you. Father, please.'

Takelot turned and his expression softened, but only for a moment. His eyes were rimmed with kohl and his skin rubbed with oils of protection and strength. He was every inch the king, embodying the strength of his grandfather Osorkon II, whose decision to pass over his blood relatives in the line of succession had unleashed this civil schism in the first place.

'One day, we will fight side-by-side but for now you must do as I say and stay here. It is you that must safeguard this country should the battle turn against us. What strength we have left must be consolidated here before I spend it against Tanis.'

Osorkon frowned. 'You don't expect to win.'

Takelot met his son's eye and his expression set like stone.

'No,' he admitted, after a moment. 'But neither do I expect to lose. We are both of us, Shoshenq and I, on a collision course that neither can now turn from. We must face one another; else this is all for naught.'

'You cannot. Send another champion in your stead, if not me. If you fall, our cause is lost,' There was no emotion behind Osorkon's words, simply a statement of fact, a resignation to what they all now faced. 'This is madness,' he said, finally.

'It is,' Takelot agreed, 'but this is what you must know and accept if you are to be my heir.' Takelot strapped his final vambrace into place and flexed his arms and shoulders experimentally.

Satisfied, Takelot gestured to the final piece. Osorkon did as he was bid, collecting the nemes headdress and placing it reverently on his father's head. The blue and gold striped headdress sat firm on Pharaoh's brow, the lappets trailing down over Takelot's shoulders. Despite his familiarity, Osorkon was overcome at the sight of his king. He fell to one knee, his fears silenced, even if only momentarily, at the sheer presence of his father and lord. The pain of being left behind, of losing the chance to fight beside his king and the generals of legend, was a knife to his heart, but he managed to speak once more in farewell.

'Until the sun shines on our next meeting, Pharaoh.'

'Go with Amun, my son.' Takelot placed a hand on his son's brow, the skin smooth and hot with the life of a priest and warrior. It lingered there a moment before the king collected his bow and left Osorkon alone in the chamber.

HARSIESE'S EYES FLICKERED open as the torchlight faded, just as it did every night after his captors grew tired of tormenting him. The sound of footsteps followed the light into oblivion, and then he was utterly alone once more. The mournful hoots of nocturnal birds broke the silence, disturbing the land of the dead with their vigilance. The hysterical barks of hyena echoed somewhere in the distance, but beyond that there was nothing but wind whistling through the dunes, the music of the desert in this parched land.

The cycle of rebirth taught that only through death can life be remade. Here, sitting in his own piss with his wrists and ankles rubbed raw by his rope bonds, Harsiese was willing to make that payment. He peered into the darkness, his eyes aching as he sought for a sign that the torchbearer was returning.

Content that he was alone for the moment, Harsiese twisted, grinding his teeth as the bonds opened the sores on his wrists. He dug his finger, one of the few that were not broken, under his stained shendyt and up inside himself, searching for the key to his salvation. His finger snared a tattered piece of cloth and with a pained groan he dug it free. At first, he had wanted to weep at the indignity forced upon him, for his captors searched a three-metre radius around him each night, clearing away any rocks or scattered debris that possessed even the hint of a sharp edge. Soon enough, he had turned to emotionless pragmatism, using his pain to fuel his hate and his desperation to be free.

Harsiese opened the cloth behind his back, retrieving a fragment of stone chipped from the ruined walls above him. It was tiny, no bigger than a segment of his finger, but one side had a keen, serrated edge, gained when one of his jailers had ruined his sword on the wall in a drunken rage. The blow had missed Harsiese's head by inches, but it had given him a prize of immeasurable value.

Alert for the sounds of his guards, Harsiese begin to work at his bonds once more. The night air was cool, but the priest was soon out of breath and sweating freely. The fever was on him as it had been for a full day. From which wound the infection had come, he did not know, but he recognised the symptoms of the wasting weakness all too well.

Harsiese stopped to rest, then cut again, sawing at the rope frayed from days of effort. He prayed constantly, the litanies spilling from his cracked lips in little more than a parched whisper. He had his eyes closed, so he did not see the torchlight again until the glow hurt his eyes with its brightness. He jerked in fright and the last threads snapped free. He stared past the jailer's legs, from shock more so than the forced obeisance so recently beaten into him.

'Awake, eh?' The guard kicked his legs and through narrow eyes Harsiese looked up at the face of his jailer. There were four of them, but this one, Khontef, was the only one that spoke to him, degraded him, tortured him.

'Water,' rasped Harsiese. 'Please.'

'What?' Khontef cocked his head as though he was hard of hearing. This game was nothing new.

'Water,' repeated Harsiese.

'Of course, Your Holiness.' Khontef bowed as he withdrew, and in his heart, Harsiese knew that he would have to kill to be free. He had seen death before, but to bring it about with one's own hands was an altogether different matter.

Khontef returned with uncharacteristic pace, grinning as he approached. It made him ugly, uglier than the rampant snarl that seemed to be his natural expression.

Harsiese's throat ached at the sound of sloshing water, but at the last step, Khontef lurched forward and tossed the cup's contents into Harsiese's face. The coolness hit him like a solid blow. It soaked into his hair, flushed out his aching eyes and dripped down the ragged beard they made him keep, the latter so that his fevered mind would know how long he had been kept here in the ruins of this nameless, forgotten temple. His lips stung as he drank what little ran down his face.

At least it was water this time.

'How clumsy of me. Forgive me, great one,' Khontef laughed. He bowed and withdrew like a humble retainer, chuckling as he went. The well was fifty yards beyond the portal and Khontef was not known for his haste. Gritting his teeth, Harsiese pulled on his bonds, gasping with relief as the rope slid from his wrists. The rope was stained with blood and pus and as it fell, it took with it a line of scabs that began to bleed anew.

With trembling fingers, Harsiese untied his ankles, ignoring the swollen ache in his broken joints. Standing was a little easier. His jailers walked him beyond the camp confines to defecate every morning, so his legs were not entirely atrophied.

He padded across to the stone portal, feeling in the darkness for something, anything to defend himself with. Whether through time or the artifice of man, the temple ruins had been torn down beyond repair. Debris littered the site, and Harsiese's hand enclosed on a rock the size of his fist.

Satisfied, he crouched in the darkness, straining his senses like a wild cat in the deep night. Khontef returned, humming an upbeat tune, no doubt enjoying this latest evening of torment before he turned to wine until early morning.

Khontef, the guard who liked to question Harsiese with a dagger held to his eye. Khontef, the guard who threatened to sodomise Harsiese with a stick if his answers contained even a shade of disrespect. Khontef. The name tasted sour even to whisper.

Such was the darkness, Khontef did not even notice Harsiese's absence from his bonds until his own lights were extinguished. The priest stepped forward and swung with every ounce of strength left to him, and Khontef fell with a muffled grunt.

Harsiese paused. The other three guards were out there somewhere, though the main camp was some way off, the more superstitious among them doubtless refusing to sleep in the shadow of a god's ruin. Silence greeted his attack and for the first time in weeks, Harsiese's lips cracked into a broad smile.

He knelt by the prone body, enjoying the reversal of fortune in ways he had not known he was capable. It was intoxicating, and in a rare moment, he empathised with what drove Takelot to seek vengeance on Tanis.

He shook his head with a smile and drew Khontef's own dagger across the prone guard's throat. Khontef's eyes bulged open, the trauma of his own death giving him precious last seconds of awareness as his body convulsed. Harsiese held his victim's chin up, stifling his wet gasps and making sure the blood could flow freely onto the sands, a morbid offering for the priest's own deliverance.

'May the beast devour your miserable heart,' spat Harsiese, as the death rattle took Khontef. The priest rose unsteadily to his feet and staggered past the corpse into the night. The blade dripped blood down his leg; warm, wet and satisfying. It took all of Harsiese's fevered discipline not to drink the lifeblood from the blade, such was his thirst.

The blackness was serene, but he could see vague shapes in the landscape around him. Long nights of complete darkness, far from the comfort of campfires, had given him night vision he had never known before. He kept his gaze ahead and his step light, trusting that his peripheral vision would detect the slightest movement around him. Men were not the only dangers in the night-time desert, and the jackals and hyenas would soon be drawn by the smell of blood.

Harsiese gasped as the muscles in his legs sang with pain and he stumbled, slipping on some loose scree. Immobile for days and all but crippled by his restraints, it was a source of no small irony to him that his escape literally hung on the knife edge in his hand. The air was cool though, pleasant against his clammy skin, and though his muscles screamed with exertion, the promise of freedom pushed him on. A dim glow at the southern end of the temple grounds revealed the camp of Khontef's comrades, the savage desert tribesmen in Senmut's employ. Blindfolded and gagged, he'd had only sound to rely on, but if his memory served him correctly, he was certain that a mere four, including the dead Khontef, had dragged him to this makeshift prison and remained to keep him secure.

Senmut's perverse sense of revenge had spared Harsiese from a quick death, and he intended to cling to such a gift until Anubis finally took him. The dagger was a heavy weight in his right hand as he staggered towards the campfire, keeping to the shadows and leaning on the ruined walls for support.

He paused at the southern edge of the ruined temple, kneeling in the dark. Ahead, the camp was built by a copse of acacia trees with thick reedy grasses filling out the undergrowth. The grasses grew in clumps the height of a man's shoulder, likely fed by some underwater spring that had once sustained the temple. The thought made Harsiese's throat ache again.

He went to rise when movement in the camp sent him falling back into the dust. He risked a glance out and was rewarded with a pair of dark eyes looking right at him.

Or at least, he corrected himself, in his direction.

The warrior wore a headscarf with his fine, gaunt features uncovered. Dark eyes roamed the ruins. Khontef's absence had already been noted then, but evidently the warrior was unconcerned for now. Like Harsiese, this warrior must be well enough aware that Khontef liked to take his time in his torments.

The man seemed to shrug and turned back to the campfire. Embers drifted skyward as he stirred the coals before Harsiese saw his silhouette pass the flames and leave the camp.

Wincing as his knees popped, Harsiese pushed himself forward, running the fifty metres between cover and coming to a tumbling heap at the edge of the camp. He strained to listen over his own pounding heartbeat, but there was little to note but the deep snores of sleeping men.

Harsiese crept behind the tents, straining to follow the first warrior's passage. The silhouette faded into the inky blackness, and Harsiese was faced with an impossible choice. The first was to leave the warrior and steal his camel. That might grant him minutes only before he was discovered and killed. The second option was for he, a crippled priest who had never committed violence until tonight, to stalk and kill a trained warrior in the midnight desert, which might grant him a few minutes more of life before he was discovered and killed.

'Gods grant me strength and give Senmut haemorrhoids,' he silently prayed as he stepped out of cover and jogged after the warrior.

It did not take long to find him. It seemed something from tonight's fare had disagreed with the man, and Harsiese found him grunting and cursing as he evacuated his bowels behind a spinifex bush.

Even for Harsiese, who had not washed in days, the smell was rancid.

The priest crept closer, breathing through his mouth, and came around the back side of the grass. The silhouette was blurred, or perhaps that was just his vision, but he could see enough to tell that the warrior was crouched with his robes hoisted high.

Harsiese waited for one last grunt and then, when the warrior had exhaled completely, the priest lunged forward.

The warrior had time enough to grunt again before he was thrown onto his face. He drew a breath to shout but the dagger flashed out, missing the fatal shot but sawing through the front of his throat. The shout devolved into a gurgle of bloody bubbles as the warrior tried to hold his throat closed.

Harsiese gave him no quarter, stabbing first at the warrior's throat and face, and then at his hands and arms when the tribesman tried to ward off the blows. Finally, the warrior's life ebbed away, his lifeblood covering Harsiese's arms and robes like a surgeon or a butcher.

Breathing deep of the coppery stink and the rotting stench of human waste, the priest admired his handiwork for a moment before his legs gave out. Harsiese had never actually seen a man killed by a leopard, but he imagined that it would look something similar to this.

'Killed while taking a shit,' muttered Harsiese. 'I pray that the gods never let you hear the end of it.'

The walk back to camp took significantly longer. Harsiese no longer had feeling in his legs, and the only way he could be sure he was moving was that the firelight bobbed and grew with each passing moment.

Fortunately, the snores remained undisturbed. Taking the dagger that had saved his life twice and taken two others, Harsiese sawed through the camels' ropes. Bulging sacks of water hung from the camels' flanks and he drank greedily, clenching his teeth at the sudden waves of nausea, but going back for more until he was sure he would be sick.

Finally, he hauled himself into the saddle and pondered the final mystery before him.

Where, in Set's arse, was he?

But for a brief bout of unconsciousness, Harsiese was fairly sure they had not crossed the river, which meant they could only be east. Temples were always aligned to face the rising sun, and without a roof, the passage of daylight had been clear.

With that knowledge in mind, next to the heart-warming image of Senmut's butchered corpse, Harsiese kicked his heels into the camel's flank. Leading the other four beasts in a caravan, he set off west.

SWALLOWS CHIRPED AND twittered, darting through the trees faster than the eye could follow. What game they played the gods only knew, but Karomama enjoyed watching them nonetheless. The gardens here, on a river bank beyond the palace boundaries, were soothing to the body and a salve to the mind, though even here she could never be truly free of the weight of responsibility.

The bustle of the city behind her was an ever-present reminder of the knife-edge her family walked along. Months before those same streets had been a running battlefield, but now the damage had been undone and life returned to a semblance of normality.

She sighed as the swallows' game reminded her of the gardens in her house in Thebes. Already her bed had grown cold and her sleep disturbed, as each passing day took her husband further away from her and ever closer to his reckoning with Shoshenq. Word would come, sooner or later, but in her heart of hearts she knew not whether it would be for good or ill.

She picked sparingly at the modest lunch of fruit, bread and wine. Behind her, her guards, as still as tomb shabti, kept the curious populace at bay as their lady watched the fisherman cast their nets and their children splash in the shallows. It was easy to forget, confined as she so often was in the great halls of the nomarch's palace, that there was a world out here that went on heedless of the worries of nobles. Had self-confinement led, at least partly, to Khonsefankh's madness? Karomama could well believe it so.

'Mother.'

The voice made Karomama turn and smile. She put down her piece of fruit and rose from her chair to greet her son.

Bakenptah waited at the edge of the street, stiffly formal though she had admonished him for it in the past. A close-knit family was a sign of stability, not weakness. His eyes, always moving, always searching, swept the sloping hill, his eyes never meeting hers until she stood right in front of him. She had rarely seen him at ease since the siege of the Nomarch's Palace, and the dark circles under his eyes revealed the depths of his exhaustion. His dedication to the building of their familial mortuary temple had done wonders for her family's public image, but she worried at the cost of it all on her youngest son.

'It is just us here. Those men are Theban,' she said, answering Bakenptah's unspoken question as he stared at the guards standing by the street edge. She walked up to him and took his hand in her own, putting her other palm onto his forehead. He felt warm, very warm, but he sagged at the motherly gesture. The tension flowed out of him and he was once more her boy, not a man whose destiny had been laid out for him since his birth twenty years before.

'The work is progressing then?' she smiled at him.

Weariness hung from Bakenptah like a cloak. His fingers and arms were scored with cuts and grazes and his shendyt caked with dust. Not for the first time, Karomama noted the differences in her sons' temperaments. Where Osorkon was prone to solitary brooding, poring over his problems from every angle until he found a solution, Bakenptah threw himself into work, any work, to keep his mind as active as his hands. That was one reason she had volunteered him for the task, but she was surprised at the depth of the physical labour he embarked on.

Bakenptah rubbed at his hands and straightened his shoulders, aware of his mother's scrutiny. 'The foundation has finished being re-laid and the western façade is now waist high and growing with each day. The work is hard, but the men are good and Hamma knows what he's doing.'

'High praise,' smiled Karomama.

Bakenptah coloured slightly. 'All in all, progress is satisfactory. If you have time, perhaps I could show you the new additions. Hamma's men are artisans all.'

'I would like that,' she said. 'But in truth, that is not why I called you here.'

'Oh.' Bakenptah frowned. 'Has something happened?'

'Many things have happened as they always do,' said Karomama. 'But I wished to inquire after my second son. How are you?'

Bakenptah chuckled. His eyes alighted on a carafe of wine and he gestured towards it. 'May I?'

Karomama nodded and Bakenptah filled his cup almost to the brim. They sat back down and Bakenptah snatched up a handful of dates.

'I have not seen you so much of late,' said Karomama.

Bakenptah laughed. 'I have seen no one of late. The war preoccupies us all.'

'It does. There has been word from your sister. There seems to be some strife in the south but nothing Hory cannot handle.'

'Hory, or Isetweret?'

It was Karomama's turn to laugh. 'Your sister most likely. The gods blessed Hory with a kind heart but not much else. I suppose we can be thankful he is not his father's son at least.'

Bakenptah nodded, his gaze fixed on the eastern shore. 'I still dream of that you know?' he said.

'Of what?'

'Of storming the palace in Thebes. Osorkon would have killed him. There and then, he would have done it, but Nakhtefmut was gone. I wonder where. Have you truly had no word of his whereabouts?'

'He has fled as far north as north goes or he is dead in the ditch of some nameless road. So long as he is far from here, I do not care either way,' said Karomama.

'Cold of you, mother, but it is probably better that way. Our family disputes seem to have a way of spilling over. Presenting Hory with the corpse of his father might have strained Isetweret's marriage.'

Karomama almost choked on her wine. 'Yes, it might have done,' she said, wiping away a stray drip down her chin, accepting the linen napkin from Bakenptah. 'But enough of old enemies. You have not told me of yourself.'

Bakenptah shrugged. 'I keep busy enough.'

'You wish you could have gone north with your father?'

'Of course, I do,' said Bakenptah, looking away over the river.

'I understand. Parting from him is difficult for me as well.' Karomama held out her hand and Bakenptah took it again. His hands were rough and calloused, and he smiled though it did not quite reach his eyes.

'Your father needs you here. I need you here, and so do all your people,' said Karomama.

Bakenptah raised his cup in his other hand. 'Protector of Herakleopolis. Commander of the Garrison. A noble title when there is no one left to fight.'

'There is always someone left to fight,' said Karomama. 'Even when this war is over, we will have to fight to keep what is ours. Only the dead that have made it to the Field of Reeds truly know peace. You will still have a role, a purpose.'

'And Osorkon?' he asked. 'What is his role?'

From her chair, Karomama could see almost a league down the river, the walls of the Crag visible far to the south. 'Osorkon will remain Lord of the Crag of Amun, Great of Roaring.' She sighed. 'I fear for your brother. The Libyan fire in his blood burns brightly, perhaps too much so. But you, you are as tempered as a well-made blade. I am thankful every day that you were born after him. His destiny as the eldest is in the temples, but you must be the sword that defends us all. You will look after him, won't you?'

Bakenptah drank deep, staring into his cup. 'The dutiful second son as always, mother.'

'Your duties will only expand in time, Bakenptah. There was more news from your sister.' Karomama paused, but only for a moment. 'You are going to be an uncle.'

'Truly? That is wonderful news,' said Bakenptah, his eyes bright.

'I am writing back to her today. Isetweret has much to hear of. Is there anything you would like to add?'

Bakenptah thought a moment, swilling the dregs in the bottom of his cup. His smile faded and his expression hardened. 'Wish her the blessings of the mother goddess. And tell her that if anything should happen, if anyone should bring her to harm, then her brothers will bring down the wrath of the gods upon them until they are nothing but a pile of ash.'

# Chapter Sixteen

ISETWERET SAT ON the edge of the bed, fighting off the latest wave of nausea that wracked her trembling frame. She lost the fight and fell gingerly to her knees, heaving into a bucket already stained with the meagre contents of her dinner. Grateful that the oil lamps in her room had long ago burned out, she pushed the bucket away into the darkness, the moonlight just bright enough to make out in case she needed it again. She wiped her lips, swore an oath to the mother goddess, and spat the rancid taste of bile from her mouth.

For weeks this had been her gilded prison, a suite of rooms worthy of royalty, but a cage all the same. Her captors treated her well enough, but other than the guards at her door, the servants delivering her meals were her only company. They never spoke, nor did they make eye contact, and when she had tried to touch one of them to shake them from their apparent stupor, they had shrunk away from her as though she were a malevolent desert spirit. She had given up after that.

Her pregnancy was finally making itself noticed. Her belly had begun to swell and though her loose shifts covered her well enough now, she knew it would not be long until it made movement difficult. The weeks would pass by and she would be trapped here, confined by her own physicality as much as by her captors' will.

At first, she simply sought to leave, walking past her guards as if they were there to serve her. They had dragged her back, kicking and screaming, and tied her to the bed frame for the night. She was forced to sleep in her own urine, her vomit too when the nausea became too much. The next time she had screeched her rage at them, calling down her family's vengeance on them if they refused to help her. Then she pleaded with them, but the guards at the door ignored her attempts, and when they grew tired of that, threatened to lock her in a cupboard overnight if she tried anything again.

After that, she had taken the liberty of damaging the cupboard's hinges, weakening the joins so that the doors would simply break if kicked hard enough. Let them try to confine a daughter of Takelot, she thought bitterly.

Isetweret closed her eyes and focused on her breathing until she was sure the sickness had passed. She groaned as she hauled herself to her feet, glancing at the closed door to her chambers. Firelight still shone beneath the door, but as always, no-one came to help her. Only weeks ago, she would have had a flock of handmaidens coming to her aid, but now she was alone. No, not entirely alone, she thought and her hand went to her belly.

'I have to get out of here,' she whispered to the little bump beneath her dress. 'For both of us.'

Thebes was dying, she knew. Karnak had risen up as it had done in her grandfather's time, and beyond the relative safety of the city walls, marauders now ruled the land. She could not stay here, but neither could she leave. The north was a whole world away, but she had to try. Not for the first time, her indecision made her want to lash out, and she wiped away hopeless, stinging tears.

She crawled back into bed as the fear of attempting escape became too much. She pushed her thoughts aside, as she had done for the last four nights, sick at her situation and disgusted with herself.

Tonight, she would make it. She had to.

She checked the position of the moon as she had done almost every hour since dusk. It was not yet midnight, and gods be good, she would have many hours of darkness to hide their flight into the desert. The whole city was hostile to her now, and her hopes of finding Hory and slipping away under the cover of darkness were disheartening, at best.

They had taken anything that might be construed as a weapon, even a small knife to cut her bread and fruit. Whether it was to prevent her escape or her suicide, she was not sure, but she suspected a measure of both. They had not taken her dignity though, and her cosmetics, wigs and gowns had been left in her possession, ostensibly to laden down any thoughts of flight. What her captors had not known, however, was that among her possessions was a gift from her mother; an ivory hair pin, carved from the tusk of a great bull elephant of the far south.

It was small, no longer than her middle finger, but it had a keen edge and so she had left it in one of her more formal wigs. She plucked the pin out from the bands of hair and held it in her fist like a dagger. Despite herself, she laughed. Even in the hands of a warrior, it would last seconds at best against any real weapon.

Steeling her nerves, she rose and slipped on her shoes before bundling together the bread and fruit she had hidden away for just this moment. She slipped the satchel over her head and held the pin loosely in her grasp.

Isetweret put her ear to the door. Usually, the sounds of muttered conversation carried to her easily, but now, at midnight, all was silent. She whispered a prayer to the mother goddess as she eased the door ajar, for it possessed a lock only from the inside and the thought of a pregnant woman fleeing the city had evidently not been taken seriously by her captors.

She sighed with relief at the two slumped forms of her guards. Each of them snored softly with his back to the wall, the low light from the nearly-expired torches creating flickering shadows over their still forms.

Part of her wanted to pluck a dagger from one of their belts and bury it to the hilt in their necks, but she turned away, clutching her hair pin with white knuckles. The palace atrium would be heavily guarded, but there were numerous secret passages that she could use to escape these halls unseen. If only she could get to an entrance unnoticed. She took a step down the corridor, and the nausea chose that moment to reassert itself. She retched and staggered forward, clenching the muscles in her belly to still the motion. She gasped, louder than she had intended to and froze at the sound of movement behind her.

She turned very slowly, fear surging through her as she saw both guards staring right at her. They blinked with sleep, but the sight of her outside her room brought them to instant alertness. She turned and sprinted down the hall, screaming with rage and frustration and hating these men for robbing her of her escape so easily.

Rough hands grabbed her from behind, and she shrieked as they tried to immobilise her. Her vision blurred and she thrashed, seeing only white teeth and savage eyes. One of the guards held her from behind, dragging her back down the corridor.

She twisted in his grasp, tearing her arm free, and slashed at his face. The guard howled and let her go as the pin opened up his cheek. The second guard held her firm and she twisted in his grip, hot tears coming to her eyes as she gritted her teeth almost to breaking point.

'You bitch,' snapped the first guard. She smelled the stench of stale wine on his breath as he hauled her upright and hammered a punch into the side of head.

Her vision exploded into stars and the tears streamed down her face. Her legs went out from under her and both hands went to the bump under her dress, shielding her unborn child from the assault. The second blow never came, and she looked up into his eyes, defiant now if this was her end, but he was suddenly looking past her. Sadistic triumph had been replaced by very real fear.

At the end of the corridor, Senmut watched the commotion with narrowed eyes. Four soldiers made up his honour guard. Like their lord, they were unshaven and stank of wine, sweat and stale oils.

'What is the meaning of this?' he demanded, stalking forward, his expression thunderous. Isetweret shrank back before them, scrambling across the floor towards the open door of her chambers.

'She tried to escape, Your Holiness,' said the guard that had hit her.

'The princess carries Takelot's only grandchild. And what did you do?' asked Senmut, patiently as though he were lecturing a child.

'I- I- I stopped her escaping,' stuttered the guard.

Senmut gestured to his honour guard. 'Kill him,' said Senmut. He turned to the princess, with a face completely devoid of expression. He held out a hand to help her up, but she flinched away, trying and failing to block out the guard's feeble protests as the soldiers closed in on him.

Isetweret clenched her eyes shut, her hands pressed tight against her ears, but her efforts did little to block out the wet punching sound of daggers piercing flesh. When it was over, she took a shuddering breath. The soldiers returned to Senmut's side, leaving the corpse where it lay. The other guard stood white-faced in an alcove. She met his eye and the terror there gave her strength.

'Please,' said Senmut. 'Let me help you.' He knelt beside her and offered his hand. She was too frightened to refuse. Senmut led her back into her chambers and helped her sit on the edge of the bed.

Not even ten minutes had passed since she had last been in that exact spot.

Senmut's soldiers stayed outside, for which Isetweret was grateful, and she took a deep breath to steady herself. The ache in her belly made her wince, and she prayed to Mut that her child was healthy and well. It was all she could do to keep the sounds of the man's gurgling demise out of her head. Her hand went to her belly and she grimaced at the bruising that would soon show.

Senmut poured her a cup of water, glancing up and frowning at her apparent discomfort. 'I will send for a physician to tend to you,' he said, going to the door and ordering one of the soldiers to fetch a healer.

'I would like you to leave,' she said when he returned, taking the cup he offered.

Senmut ignored her and pulled up a stool to sit a respectful distance away. 'I am sorry for your treatment. I had hoped you would be comfortable, but some of my followers can be overzealous at times. You have my word that it will not happen again.'

Isetweret wanted to laugh, wanted to throw this cup of water in her captor's face, but her pained frown turned into a smirk and she glared at him like the lowborn vermin that he was.

'Your word means nothing to me,' she spat.

'Perhaps not, but I still hold it to some value,' said Senmut. He poured himself a cup of his own and resumed his seat. 'Do you know why I am doing this? Doubtless you think it is for some self-aggrandisement. The same crime your father is guilty of, perhaps?'

Isetweret did not rise to the bait. Behind those glassy eyes, a malicious intelligence was still at work, always watching. Always calculating.

'The old pharaoh is dead, and two claimants tear the land apart for their own ambitions. Is it them that suffers? Is it they that die on the front lines or starve to death in the wars to come? Is it you who suffers these deprivations, Princess Isetweret of the House of Takelot? Who suffers and starves and dies when lords go to war?' Senmut's voice rose with each accusation. He panted with the effort and remembered himself.

'It is the rightful place of the common people to serve their lords. It is decreed by the gods,' said Isetweret. 'So has it always been.'

Senmut leaned forward, fixing Isetweret with a level glare. 'Under whose decree? Amun does not speak to us, princess. So, tell me, my lady. Why were you born in this opulent palace, and I in a mudbrick hovel on the riverside that reeked of fish and cat shit? Who decided you were more worthy than I?'

Isetweret stiffened. 'Even if they do not speak, the gods make their will known to us. We just have to interpret their signs.'

Senmut grunted with amusement. 'And yet here I sit, Lord of this City of the Gods. Is that their will too?'

'The will of Apophis made manifest,' said Isetweret. 'Without order all we have is chaos, which you have now brought upon us with your actions. How did you do it, I wonder? How did you turn them all?'

'I didn't,' Senmut admitted. 'Not all of them. No man could command that, and in truth, I suspect I am losing some of them. I believe they plot against me, even now. For all the good it will do them.'

'You deserve it, usurper,' snapped Isetweret, her composure returning quickly. 'Why should they not turn against you? You think Amun approves of your betrayal?'

Senmut shrugged. 'I do not know. Amun has not spoken to me in a very long time. I was born with nothing. My parents were nobodies before they died. Their tomb is a pit in the ground. Where will you be buried? In a hall more resplendent than a noble's house? With food to eat, games to play, and ushabti to tend your crops in the Field of Reeds?' Senmut paused for a moment. 'Do you know how many dynasties have come and gone in Egypt's history?'

Isetweret frowned. 'No.'

Senmut chuckled. 'Neither do I. Not with complete certainty, but surely a dozen or more. Maybe two. Who can say? Kings come and go, but the people always remain. I fight for them, if only the great lords of this land could see it.'

Isetweret did not reply, and Senmut tilted his head, watching her closely.

'Your father as Pharaoh, professes to be a god. So too then, does Shoshenq. Which of them is true and which is false? Which of them do the gods truly support? It cannot be both.'

Isetweret glared at him. 'They support the one true pharaoh. The one whose blood runs with the legacy of the dynasty.'

Senmut nodded to himself slowly as though her words confirmed something. He stood to leave, taking one unsteady step after another until he reached the door. Isetweret called out to him as he reached the door.

'Why are you confiding in me?' she asked.

Senmut shrugged and turned around, his gaze fixed at some point over her head. Outside, the moon's glow stained the land midnight blue and black. The city was silent, as per his decreed curfew, and in the distance the hills and valleys of the river stretched on, blending seamlessly into the infinite darkness of the night sky.

Senmut smiled at her, his eyes sad, though they still burned with something that unsettled her. 'It is a rare occasion for a common man to speak to a royal,' he admitted. 'Despite my station as Third Prophet of Amun, it has taken until now, when I have taken the city for my brothers and I, that I have the chance to meet you. I do not speak of an audience in the throne room. I mean a simple conversation. I have always wondered, since I was a boy, if you were gods too, so removed were you from the common man.' He paused and sniffed. He swayed and his fingers brushed the doorframe for support. 'I wanted to speak to you, to understand you. And now, I think I do.'

Senmut turned and left her to her thoughts, but Isetweret found neither solace nor sleep until the sun stained the sky with a new day.

THE LAND WAS dust, and the dust was the land. Nothing penetrated the haze, but the vague outlines of the men in front of him. When Sarasesh dared risk a glance behind him, the view was much the same. The horde moved without rank or file, lumbering forward in one great rolling mass, raising a column of dust a kilometre high to mark their passage north.

Somewhere out on the river, the warlord Malkesh watched his army march from the relatively luxury of the *Sobek is Content*, but within the horde itself, the world shrank into a pitiful grey-brown coffin of choking dust and burning fatigue.

Sarasesh ran with the rest of them, forcing himself to put one foot in front of the other, pushing his body beyond the agony screaming in his bones. Neptef's former command seemed like a world away, the comfort of that cabin a paradise compared to the deprivations he had been forced to endure. He gasped the dust down his raw throat as though it were oasis water, his lips and nostrils rimmed with crusted saliva and mucous as his body fought to protect him against this manmade dust storm.

Around him, the horde of Malkesh marched at pace, keeping to a trot that ate up the distance and conserved their energy for fighting, for those few trained warriors who were used to it. The Egyptian priest was not so lucky. The forced march had shed the weight from his bones, giving him a lean, almost gangly profile. His legs burned with the effort, and each night he collapsed where he fell, eating and drinking his meagre rations before he fell into a deep and undisturbed sleep, only to be kicked awake to start the march again before dawn.

Sarasesh stumbled over to a rock at the edge of the horde, and pushed his way through to the left flank, getting knocked down once, then again as he shoved through the edge of the horde and the lip of the ridge they ran upon. With his rhythm broken and slumped to his knees with his head in his hands. He gasped for air like a man drowning, feeling the grit coat his throat but not caring until great heaving coughs shook his lean frame. He turned to spit, but nothing but a breath of dust came out.

He looked around, his eyes bleary and bloodshot as a hundred men or more streamed past him. Below the ridge, the lush green of the Nile Valley called to him, stretching out far into the north and following the snaking water far beyond his sight. He wanted to roll down the hill, to let the wind take him and feel the green reeds against his skin, to throw himself into the river waters and damn the fate that had brought him here.

Sarasesh looked away, knowing that to do so was death, one way or another.

In the middle of the river, the cutter *Sobek is Content* drifted sedately just offshore. It was too far to make out individual figures, but he was there. Malkesh would be watching his army's progress from the river boat, his archers ready to cut down any man that tried to desert by casting themselves into the water. Sarasesh knew he was not the only man contemplating such a fate, for after weeks of marching, many of the weakest among their number nursed their regrets, pondering whether to chance the spears of Malkesh's captains, or the denizens of the river who snatched unwary travellers from the riverbanks.

Sarasesh's previous assumptions of the horde had proven incorrect in his first nights making camp with them. Many of them were warriors of their respective tribes, not professional soldiers, used to intertribal skirmishes but overwhelmed at the prospect of the scale of battle ahead. Many more had been conscripted or coerced by Malkesh's captains as the pirates plied their trade up and down the coast of the Red Sea, either by force or with the promise of riches in plundering the neighbouring Egypt.

As Sarasesh steeled himself to rise, he heard the call to halt and would have wept with relief had he the tears to do so. One of the Nubians of the horde knelt beside him and glanced his way. More joined the first and a makeshift group dropped down into the dust around Sarasesh, sharing out meagre clumps of dried bread and brackish water in old waterskins.

Sarasesh accepted a crust gratefully, wincing as it cut his cheek as he chewed. It took him three attempts to swallow and he nodded at the Nubian, attempting a smile.

'Death by crocodile, or even hippo, would be kinder than this,' gasped the priest.

The man nodded, too exhausted to speak.

Another warrior came trotting down the line, glaring from group to group. His expression was one of relief and irritation as he spied Sarasesh. The warrior grabbed him by the arm, hauled him upright and led him up the column. Sarasesh and the warrior had run together for the last three days, the horde forming loose packs of familiar faces from among the mishmash of tribes and villages Malkesh had plundered for war fodder. The strongest and most vicious among them became the pack leaders, and the man who led Sarasesh's group was a pirate of Malkesh's own crew.

Sarasesh did not know the man's name. He had never cared to ask.

'You're with us now, priest. Don't you even think about running,' he snarled as he pointed to a gap in the seated circle.

'That is all I have thought about for the last six days,' sneered Sarasesh. 'That is all we have done.'

The man grunted and tossed a waterskin at Sarasesh's feet. 'Drink,' the man ordered.

Sarasesh looked down at the deflated pouch. Apparently, he still had some value after all.

It was nearly empty, and the priest greedily squeezed what little moisture remained. He swallowed the wet dust, feeling the grit slide down his throat. He coughed up a wad of the mud and spat it into the ground. Within seconds, the moisture had dried and become dry sand once more.

Sarasesh regarded the man in front of him. The pirate captain of his section, for cohort was too organised a word, was little more than the strongest hyena in a pack. Violence and brute strength were power here. He had spoken to few men, but none of them seemed to be men of even rudimentary learning. Sarasesh was though, and that was why he knew the horde was in danger. The pirate was distracted with looking out, longingly perhaps, at his master's new vessel, and Sarasesh took a rare moment of peace to study him properly.

His skin was dark, the colour of a man who has spent his life under the Red Sea sun, but he had a grey pallor to his face, chest and shoulders. Sarasesh had seen that colour before in men whose hearts were not long for this world. As he looked around, he noticed the same grey sheen covered most of these warriors.

Those that fell would be left where their strength finally failed them. Perhaps, they were the lucky ones. Sarasesh's flesh called for sleep, any sleep, even the sleep of the grave, but his mind clung to life, screaming and half-mad with deprivation.

The call to order came minutes later. The pack leaders, for Sarasesh could regard them no higher than beasts, called their warriors to rise and resume the journey north. There was no escape, and so Sarasesh turned to the only choice left to him. Silent sobs wracked Sarasesh's frame as he forced one foot in front of the other. No tears spilled down his face, for they had dried up long, long ago.

THE GLOOM OF her enforced sanctum only sunk Isetweret's spirits deeper. For days she had drunk little and eaten less, her despondency a mute companion to her silent jailors. Her failed escape destroyed what little hope she had of reunion with her family, but it was Senmut's words that caused her the most grief.

The priest was a broken man, a traitor and a heretic to boot, but within his blasphemous words was a core truth, one that she could not avoid. Her people suffered in this conflict, her family suffered, and for what? Senmut laid the blame squarely at her family's feet, but how far behind should the blame be laid?

Her father, who had declared his own royalty? Her father-in-law Nakhtefmut, the former vizier, who had forced him to do so? Her great-grandfather Pharaoh Osorkon II who had unleashed all of this with one decision, to pass over Takelot in the line of succession?

Isetweret sat at her vanity table for hours at a time, writing poetry, reading and then re-reading the texts available to her, or busying herself with her cosmetics, for want of something to do. Busy hands quelled an overactive mind, and she was applying a fine layer of darkened kohl to the edge of her eyes when she saw a shadow move behind her curtain. From the corner of her eye the soft fabric rippled where it draped across the exit to her balcony. She did not move as she watched it return to stillness. The wind could have disturbed it, but the light of her candles was steady.

She stood up, steadying herself against the table as her vision swam, her head dizzy with fatigue and hunger. She kept the curtain in her peripheral vision as she made her way back to her bed, running her hand over the items of her bedside table before settling on a solid bronze candlestick. She took a steadying breath before she turned and launched herself at the intruder with a snarl on her lips.

The curtain exploded under her assault and a cry of pain went up as she beat the shrouded figure with the candlestick again and again. Hands grasped her wrists and the curtain was torn from its rings in their struggle. A familiar voice cried out from under her assault. 'My princess, it is your servant.'

Isetweret paused for a moment. Her vision returned to focus on a face that now filled her with loathing. 'You!' she shrieked, heedless of who would hear her. She attacked him with the full force of her anger, lashing out at his face and his chest, anywhere that he could not defend. She screamed in fury, desiring nothing more than to tear his eyes from their sockets.

'Princess, be quiet, please,' he hissed, holding her wrists firm, but she fought like a snake, twisting and forcing her captor to give ground. Pedubast was forced to retreat until his back was to the wall and he fixed her with a glare.

'Guards!' she screamed, glancing towards the door.

'You would seek help from your own captors?' said Pedubast. He did not seem shocked. Disappointed, perhaps, but not surprised. She thrashed in response, her hands reaching for his throat.

'Iuput, please,' he called, over her shoulder. Pedubast's brother stepped forward and held her tight against his chest, pinning her arms to her side. To her horror she saw that he had come from outside her now-open door. Where her guards were, she could not see.

'You betrayed me. You betrayed my family,' she cried. Iuput was stronger than he looked, and she struggled against him for a moment before she slumped in his arms.

'I will let you go if you promise to listen,' said Pedubast. Her silence was her assent, and Pedubast bid Iuput to release her.

Pedubast crossed the room to fix the curtain back over the balcony before he returned to her side. Caught between the two intruders, Isetweret backed towards her bed and sat down, glaring at the brothers. While Pedubast was the very picture of regret, Iuput remained impassive, though she sensed nothing threatening from him.

Instead, she glanced at the open door to her chambers. 'Why did they not come?'

'A little something in their evening wine,' said Pedubast. 'Not enough to be lethal, but enough that you could scream until your throat was raw and they would not stir. Do not worry for them. They will wake in a few hours, none the wiser. Or you could kill them now, if you wish.'

Isetweret glared at Pedubast with disgust. 'I am not a murderer.'

'Nor am I, so I leave the choice to you,' said Pedubast.

Isetweret laughed bitterly and Pedubast shifted, crossing his arms at her recalcitrance. His robes shifted aside, and she was suddenly conscious of the forearm-length dagger at his hip. She had never seen him armed before, and a glint of metal under Iuput's robes showed that he was equally prepared.

'You are with them. If you are here to kill me, get on with it,' she spat, hoping they would not see through her bluster.

'I am not a murderer,' Pedubast snapped, his anger finally showing. 'Show some damned respect for those that seek to help you. We are leaving Thebes, tonight. Come with us.'

Isetweret laughed again, this time in shock and confusion. 'What?'

'Thebes is no longer safe. Senmut has lost his mind. That bastard warlord from the Red Sea will be back and when he is, he will conquer Thebes and rape and pillage the whole city. No one can say whether it will be days, weeks, or months. Only that we do not have the strength to resist him anymore. We must go.'

It was only then that Isetweret was aware of the satchels sitting fat with supplies at the door to her chamber. They had not been there an hour ago when the guards had brought her supper. The brothers were serious in their flight.

She sneered. 'Even I have heard of the guard placed on the gate. You are going to fight your way out? You?'

'I am no warrior,' Pedubast admitted. 'But there are some in the city that are not loyal to Senmut. Come quickly, we can help you.'

'Traitors betraying other traitors.' Isetweret laughed again, pleased as she saw the barb of her ridicule strike home. 'I cannot believe I ever placed my trust in you. I hope I live to see you all eat each other.'

Pedubast's hand lashed out, catching the princess across the cheek with a sharp slap. The impudence of the gesture stunned her more than the momentary pain.

'Forgive me, but you are not focused. Put aside your arrogance for one moment and see sense,' said Pedubast quickly. 'We do not have time to tarry. Get your things.'

Isetweret glared between the brothers but made no move to get up and pack.

'Where is Hory? We must find him,' she asked instead.

Pedubast hid his irritation well. 'I cannot say, Highness. We can look for him on the way out, but time is short.'

Isetweret's eyes shot towards the door, when she heard a muffled groan from the corridor outside. Pedubast swore softly and looked back to see the princess suddenly fearful.

'Kill them,' she whispered. 'Kill them quickly. They will find us'

Iuput pulled his dagger half from its belt sheath and glanced at his brother with a questioning look. Pedubast shook his head, though he shared in the princess's fear.

'Death by the blade will raise too many questions. They will know you had help. Now, it is if you saw an opportunity to flee and took it. Fewer will look for us, but we must go now.' Pedubast hauled Isetweret to her feet and towards the door. Iuput snatched up two of the packs, handing a third to Pedubast, who had his other arm around Isetweret's waist. Iuput quietly closed the door behind them, and she hoped it would be some time before the guards thought to check in on her.

She stepped over one of the stirring guards, recoiling as he vomited where he lay, coating his own arm in a vile soup of wine and bread. She glanced back at the interior of her bed chamber but once she crossed its threshold there was no going back in. She had nothing left. Nothing in her possession, but the dress she wore.

But now, she had her freedom. At least, until Senmut send his dogged followers after them, but first steps first. For now, she would find Hory. Then she would be free of this wretched city, and only after that would she think of ways to purge Thebes of its taint.

THE THREE OF them, the princess and the two brothers, crept through the palace's silent corridors and empty halls. The torches and braziers remained unlit on this highest level, and the scent of dust hung thick in the air. Pedubast should not have been surprised. He was not sure what had become of the host of palace servants, only that the palace had been emptied on the day of Hory and Isetweret's incarceration, replaced with the most fanatical and trustworthy of Senmut's followers.

They walked in silence, following the main arteries towards the heart of the palace, but its passages and corridors were likewise devoid of life and light. Even here, on the level given wholly over to the vizier's private residence, there should have been dozens of servants and guards patrolling the halls, tending to the ruling family's safety and every need. Now, there was only stillness.

Pedubast's footsteps were light, but they seemed too loud to the priest, almost echoing in the confined space. High above them, a light breeze came through the thin slit windows, built in the height of the walls. The wind disturbed the gathering dust, bringing fresh air to the staleness, but giving the priest the uncomfortable feeling that the palace was breathing.

'Where are they keeping him?' asked Isetweret quietly, the first to break the silence. Spoken in a whisper, her words nevertheless echoed down the corridor.

'I do not know,' replied Pedubast, stopping to take stock of their position. They had walked for minutes now. The other side of the palace could not be far. 'He must be on this level, and it only makes sense that he would be kept far from you to discourage an escape attempt. I pray we find him soon enough.'

Isetweret's mouth set in a grim line as she stepped past him, leading them further into the winding corridors. Pedubast could see the need within her, to rush forward and spring her husband out of this prison, but already he feared for the futility of their mission. To find Isetweret had been simple enough, but to spring her from her gilded prison had been another matter entirely, and it was not a feat that would be easy to replicate.

Isetweret moved with a surety and knowledge that was beyond Pedubast and Iuput, and the priests held back as she checked down corridors, tested locked doors and glanced into midnight chambers. The princess soon went up ahead, almost trotting in her haste to find any evidence that Hory was somewhere here, trapped as she had been.

Iuput moved with surprising speed, springing forward and grabbing her arm, putting a finger to his lips as he pulled her back. Ahead, unseen by the other two, was the faintest hint of the fire glow. It was like the first smear of light in the pre-dawn, but it was enough to give them hope. Pedubast took off his sandals and bid the others to do the same, the noise of their footsteps muffled without the hardened soles hitting stone.

'How many?' whispered Pedubast, as they reached an alcove before the corridor's end. He pulled Isetweret into the shadow next to him, shielding her from sight. The corridor ended, with two more branching off left and right. Against the wall, Pedubast could see the silhouettes of men standing at attention. For a moment, he held the hope that they were life-size statues. Just as the thought occurred to him, one of them moved, rolling his shoulders before he returned to his motionless vigil.

Iuput glanced around the corner and came back to where they were crouched. 'Four of them.'

'Awake? Alert?'

Iuput nodded once.

Pedubast swore softly and changed places with his brother. He moved up to the corner, frustration rising to the fore as he saw the futility of even attempting a rescue. He had held a thin hope that the men guarding the Vizier might be as similarly prone to drink as those guarding Isetweret, but all four soldiers guarded the chamber entrance with uncharacteristic discipline. Each of them was armed with a spear. Even if he had known how to fight, he would be run through before he could get in range with his dagger.

Pedubast padded back to the alcove, trying to find something to exploit. The Vizier was at the centre of it all, despite Isetweret's royal birth. In him, was the law upheld and the decision-making done in Pharaoh's stead. They knew enough of his character to know that he would never leave Isetweret behind.

'I am sorry, princess. I have never fought a man in my life. Nor has Iuput.' Pedubast sighed, trying to form the right words, to convey the right sentiment of regret.

'Do you have anything to knock them out? Like before?' she asked, not meeting his eye.

Pedubast shook his head. 'They are not drinking. It was by chance it succeeded once already. I would not trust our luck to hold much further.'

'How did you do it before?' she whispered.

Pedubast heard the need in her voice and sighed. 'They were already drunk,' he said. He glanced at his brother. 'Iuput also makes a convincing and cringing servant when the situation requires.'

Isetweret closed her eyes, taking a steadying breath. 'We cannot get to him,' she said levelly. She looked up at Pedubast, and a new resolve hardened her features. 'We will have to trust that losing one hostage will only increase the value of the other. Get me out of this accursed place. We will come for him when the time is right.'

'When the time is right,' echoed Pedubast, with a respectful nod. 'For now, the best way to help him is to get his wife and unborn child out of the city. Come, our window of escape grows ever shorter.'

Isetweret nodded, her gaze lingering on the glow of the braziers for another moment before finally, at Iuput's urging, she turned and allowed herself to be led away.

TASENHOR TRACED THE rim of Pedubast's empty cup, smearing a line of the red liquid with his fingertip. The man's plan was suicide. His life was measured in hours, no matter his confidence, for Pedubast was as a lamb among a pack of hyenas.

Tasenhor had been there when Senmut had given the order to shut the gates and isolate the city. He had been there when Senmut had received reports from the watch, detailing the beatings of civilians and the summary executions of the priests for breaking curfew.

Few within the city yet knew the extent of their situation, but most felt the oppressive air of curfew and realised something was amiss with the city, even if hundreds had not been privy to the impossible sight of thousands of Nubians marching past their gates.

No, Pedubast was dead.

He would be caught and he would be brought before a wrathful Senmut, who would focus all of his paranoia and fear onto the unfortunate priest, his brother and the... no, he would never even make it to the palace. The princess was secure for the time being, as she would need to be if there was any hope in keeping the last lingering royalists on side.

He had not been entirely truthful with Pedubast and he cursed himself now for the momentary weakness that the other man's optimism had sparked in him. No, there was no escape, but perhaps there was a way to rid them all of Senmut's waywardness and restore the honour of the priesthood. That too, the seed of an idea, was courtesy of Pedubast, though he would not live to benefit from it.

His discovery and subsequent execution were assured, but Pedubast was far from an unpopular man, working diligently and untiringly for the benefit of the temple. His connection with Senmut had become equally well-known and his sudden fall would surely drive doubts into even the most drug-addled and fanatical minds.

Particularly, if that death was long, lingering, and exceedingly painful.

Senmut's pride would see him deliver the sentence himself and the right whisper would see him exposed as the cruel tyrant he had become. A brief smile cracked Tasenhor's face and he glanced at the carafe of wine that Pedubast had left on the table.

'What harm is there?' he muttered. 'To my health and longevity.' He poured a half measure and sipped the vintage, his previous aversion disappearing in the face of his relief. It had not been possible until Pedubast had come to him, and Tasenhor silently thanked Amun for sacrificing one servant for another. He laughed then, the mirth spilling out of him in waves of trembling release and he drank again, filling up his cup when it had run dry.

The more he drank the more emboldened he became. He was not walking to the executioner just yet. His previous fear had been foolish and beneath him. He was Tasenhor, Prophet of Amun in Thebes and his fate was his own. Had he not been faithful to his god? Had he not been faithful to the true order of things? Takelot was a false king, but at least the new pharaoh had more than a donkey's wits about him.

'My path is strewn with obstacles, but I will endure,' said Tasenhor, holding his cup up in the wan light. 'The light sees me as I see it. I will walk from this place in the name of order and goodness.' He poured a libation onto the dirt at his feet, watching the crimson liquid splash and sink into the layer of dirt covering the stone floor.

He laughed, loud and rich, the sound fading into a strangled choke as he heard noise coming from outside. He crept to the window, and where before there had been darkness and quiet, now there was fire and a riot of cries, screams, and prayers.

No longer content with their hall of debauchery, Senmut's fanatics had come out into the open, capering and cavorting into the sacred avenues and holy plazas. Tasenhor watched from the window as a priest dropped to his knees and vomited into the dirt. The priests around him cheered their fallen brother and danced a ring around him, drinking from wine jugs they had taken from the hall. Behind them a pair of priests twirled and swayed holding burning torches they had plucked from the wall mounts. The light splashed over the gathering, casting deep shadows over the open space. The scenes were repeated a dozen times, then a dozen more, then beyond that still, again and again in a riot of sound, light, and drunken revelry.

The noise washed over Tasenhor and he clutched at his head to drive it out. The serene silence was gone, and it seemed he would never experience such a thing ever again. He drank more, but the sounds became muddled, an unending babble of doomed priests.

'Home. I need to go home,' he gasped. Tasenhor staggered to his feet, knocking the table and sending the jug of wine to shatter against the floor. Clay shards shot out in every direction, leaving behind a growing, blood-red stain. 'Cast off the shackles,' he cried, looking down at the shards, not knowing from where the words had come.

Tasenhor groped his way to the door, pulling it open and breathing deep of the outside air. Where before it had been crisp and cool, now it seemed heady and filled with smoke, as the hall had been. His fear turned to incandescent rage in moments and he stalked towards the gathered priests, hands balled into fists at his sides.

'What are you doing?' he cried. 'Have you no sense?' No one heard him, his pleas drowned out in the music, screams, and songs that came from a hundred revellers. He turned to the nearest priest and hammered a fist into his face, dropping him into the dirt. Few noticed the violence in their midst, and those that did, merely eyed the prophet warily before they turned back to their revelry.

Tasenhor shook his head and ran towards the Hypostyle Hall, the grand pillars and brilliant bas reliefs invisible to him in his need to be free of this place. The guards at the Avenue gate saw him coming and stood to attention, spears held ready.

'Let me pass,' Tasenhor ordered them, his voice steady despite the tremors in his flesh.

The captain of the watch shook his head. 'By order of Lord Senmut, no one is to leave the precinct unless he has ordered it. We have received no such permissions. Not even for you, sir.'

'He is not a lord,' Tasenhor spat. 'I am the Second Prophet of Amun in Karnak, and you are a lowly soldier of Thebes. Let me pass or I shall have you hung from the walls by your feet and your families tied into a sack and thrown into the river.'

The captain wavered, and he glanced sideways at his men for support.

Tasenhor stepped forward, ignoring the spears that levelled just a fraction. 'Move,' he thundered, his face blotchy with rage.

The soldiers shared one more look before the captain nodded and stepped aside, letting the enraged prophet pass before they quickly closed and bolted the gate behind him. On the Avenue of Rams, a sense of vengeance came over him. The warm fog of intoxication stole away the fear in his heart, relegating it to a dull ache deep down where it would not stir until sobriety was forced upon him again.

Tasenhor desired nothing more than home, to feel a familiarity in his surroundings that had been stripped from him in Karnak. He sought to recapture the surety he felt at Pedubast's demise, but as he walked away into the silent streets of Thebes, the thoughts eluded him. They were like trying to catch a tendril of smoke, fading as soon as they appeared, leaving behind nothing but an impression.

'Home,' he grunted, his frustration rising as his thoughts turned to wine, solitude and a coming reckoning. He raised his eyes to the stars above and whispered, 'Amun guide my steps. Let them guide me to order and let the chaos burn in the fires of their own making.'

THE CITY STREETS were silent, as they were every night under Senmut's enforced curfew. Though Malkesh had long since departed the nome, a feeling of fear remained heavy in the air, seeming to grow with each night the curfew remained in effect.

During the day, the talk of the marketplaces turned to the city-wide decrees issued from the religious lords living beyond Karnak's closed gates. These hushed tones quickly turned to speak of the presence of soldiers, whole squads of them that patrolled the neighbourhoods of commoner and noble in the dead of night. Hushed toned to whispers of rumours of those hauled away under cover of darkness, those unfortunates that had broken the sacred commands of the prophets and been disappeared.

Why, the people wondered, when the dire threat of siege had passed, did martial law still hang over the city?

The stories soon took on a life of their own, fear warping fact into unbelievable fiction.

Some believed the banished horde to be evil spirits made manifest that would return in the night to prey on the unwary. Others claimed that the Vizier and Princess Isetweret had already been executed, their spirits torn from their living flesh to linger in search of revenge on their own people. Yet more whispered that the priests were privy to hidden knowledge of the whole affair with the great horde. Perhaps the danger had not passed as convincingly as they had been led to believe. Perhaps the war would come for them soon, and perhaps the enemy's spies were already among them.

That none could even contemplate the debauchery taking place within the holy halls of Karnak was a source of disappointment, as well as relief, to Pedubast. The people would need the spiritual guidance of Karnak after this war was over, his senses straining in the silence that had fallen over Thebes. Quietly, and keeping to the lanes and alleys of the nobles' quarter, he led Iuput and Isetweret to the southern gate. Though he was hesitant to bring Isetweret to the site of her own dethronement, he had learned of the double garrison placed on the northern gatehouse. The bulk of Thebes' remaining forces were concentrated in the north, though none but Senmut's inner circle knew that they waited for signs of Malkesh's inevitable return.

Previously, even at this hour of the early morning, it would not have been unusual to see the houses of the nobility opened late to friends and acquaintances. A panoply of musicians and dancers would now be livening up the neighbourhood with song and spectacle under the light of the moon and stars. Friendships would be strengthened and promises of future business assured, under the influence of wine and a sumptuous feast.

Now though, the windows remained shuttered, the doors locked and reinforced. The fluttering lamplight within burned so low that only the softest glow revealed that there was still life here in the city. It was as though Thebes held its breath in the darkness, praying for peace and deliverance, until the morning light revealed the apparent folly of their fears once more.

Pedubast paused at the corner of a merchant's mansion, a three-storey structure, large enough to cover an entire block of common dwellings. Incense perfumed the air, as did the sacred herbs that the master of the house must have ordered burned in prayer. No sound was forthcoming, but it was not entirely dark within, and Pedubast strained to listen for any sign that they were discovered.

The priest ushered Isetweret against the wall behind him as Iuput brought up the rear, still bearing the bulk of their supplies. They had come through an alleyway between two houses, and ahead was a main road that, come daybreak, would be bustling with traffic. The street was narrow, but Pedubast paused to listen for the tell-tale rhythm of military marching, for it was the only sound that graced the city streets these nights.

Pedubast knew he could have crossed it at a sprint in mere seconds, but the street was too open and too exposed to cross so carelessly under the light of the gibbous moon. As Khonsu lit their way, so too did he corral them into the darker places of the city, the alleyways and narrow passageways that most of the city's folk would have normally avoided. More than once, they had been forced to retrace their steps and detour when Pedubast had deemed a crossing too dangerous to risk.

The patrols were few, but discovery meant certain death, albeit after days of interrogation and torture. The risks were great, and a flash of movement in the night would raise the alarm within moments if it was spotted by the wrong eyes. For men such as Pedubast and Iuput, men known to the new temple hierarchy and trusted with its secrets, a long-drawn out death was all but assured. Pedubast did not care to contemplate his fate when he added freeing Isetweret to his list of crimes against Senmut.

Pedubast forced the morbid thoughts from his mind and focused on the street before them. He drew his cowl over his head and motioned for the others to remain hidden as he crept forward on his hands and knees. Keeping low, he pressed himself into the shadow of a set of drying racks that were set up outside the mansion's front entrance.

After a moment, he raised a hand to usher his two companions forward, when the sound of marching came echoing off the neighbourhood's walls. Around the street corner, the torchlight of a military patrol grew until it was like the rising sun in the inky darkness.

Pedubast clenched his eyes shut and held his breath as the soldiers marched past, oblivious to the deserters only metres away. Pedubast watched their passage through the scant cover afforded by the racks until they reached the end of the street and turned down another corner.

He sighed and laid a hand on the rack as he pulled himself to his feet. By morning, there would be fresh catch from the docks hanging here, salted by the house's servants and ready for storage. Now, it was little more than cover in a land where death came all too easily.

Isetweret crept out of the shadow, followed by Iuput, to join Pedubast in the temporary shelter of the drying racks.

'The southern gate will be guarded,' she said, her eyes fixed on the last position of the patrol.

'The docks are more so,' said Pedubast. 'Every vessel that Senmut does not control is anchored offshore until first light. The river is closed to us, princess. Are you ready?'

Isetweret nodded. Together, they sprinted across the street, throwing themselves back into the cover afforded by the narrow alleys that separated the houses of the rich. All of them stopped then, listening over the hammering of their hearts and their gasping breath for the sounds of pursuit, but there were none.

Iuput whistled softly through his teeth as he peered out towards the empty street. He cocked his head and closed his eyes. 'Do you hear that?'

Pedubast listened for a moment and shook his head. 'I hear only you, brother,' he said, with a hint of remonstration in his voice. He went to rise from where he was crouched, but Iuput caught his arm, his voice a grim whisper.

'There is nothing. Where are the snores from the rooftop? Where are the servants grinding grain for the morning? The city is silent with fear.'

'I do not blame them,' muttered Pedubast. He turned to Isetweret and offered her a waterskin, which she took gratefully. 'We are not far from the gate now, princess.'

'I know where we are,' said Isetweret, levelly. 'I grew up in this city. It breaks my heart to leave it in these circumstances.' She passed the waterskin back. 'What is your plan for getting us through the gates? Do you have transport? Horses, camels, donkeys? Anything?'

'There are farmhouses only a few kilometres south of the city. We will find what we need there,' replied Pedubast. Before Isetweret could press the point, he pushed past her deeper into the alley. 'Come, time is against us,' he said, over his shoulder.

Though the southern gate was not far by conventional means, they were forced to turn back twice more by the presence of patrols, and instead followed a winding path back through a shuttered marketplace and then along the eastern walls of Karnak. The circuitous route exhausted them in mind as well as body, their senses straining for the moment their escape would be discovered. Pedubast estimated it was nearing an hour or two before sunrise as they came upon the towering fortifications of Thebes, looming suddenly into view over the low cityscape.

Against the dim glow of distant torchlight, Pedubast could only just make out the figures of guards on top of the walls. The twin guardhouses on each side of the gate were immense rectangular structures, almost twice again as thick as the walls themselves. Hundreds of thousands of bricks and a generation of labour must have gone into their construction in another age, thought Pedubast. How could any army in the world hope to conquer this city, let alone a rabble of southern tribes more bent on pillaging and ravaging townships than fighting a real war.

For a moment, Pedubast was struck motionless. Yet more guards patrolled the walls themselves, almost invisible against the night sky beyond. On the street level, just a block away from where they were crouched, two pairs of guards stood on each side of the gate, silhouetted by the flickering glow of lit braziers in front of the guardhouse.

They were alert and watchful, even at this late hour, ceaseless and untiring in their vigilance. Pedubast watched them for long minutes, searching for a gap in their patrol patterns, but the overlap was too slim. From where he was squatted, he could make out the outline of the wicket gate, the pedestrian door built into the greater defensive gate. It had been their best hope of escape, or so Pedubast had thought.

'We'll never make it,' whispered Isetweret, echoing his thoughts.

'How do we get past them?' asked Iuput. There was hope in his question, and Pedubast quashed it quickly and mercifully.

'We don't,' said Pedubast, with a bitter laugh. 'There is no hope here, so we will find a way over the walls themselves. There must be one section in this city that is relatively unguarded. Princess, where would that be?'

'Everywhere is guarded,' said Isetweret, with a sigh. 'But the south-eastern tower stands over the barracks of the nobles, where the sons of the richest families complete their military training. The barracks keeps its own watch, so there are only one or two men in the tower often enough. Lookouts, you understand? There is no need for more. No fighting force is required to be kept on the walls if you can summon one hundred more men in a moment's notice.' She turned back to the gate and the guardians surrounding it. 'Not like here,' she said.

'The south-eastern tower,' murmured Pedubast, glancing to the right at a solid black shape, squat and square, looming above the buildings in the distance. 'I pray to the gods of this city that you are right.'

'The gods no longer listen,' said Isetweret, setting off in the tower's direction. 'Us being here now is proof of that.'

THE FORTIFIED TOWERS of Thebes interspersed the great walls of the city with indomitable regularity, dominating the skyline when viewing the city from afar. Towering rectangular blocks of reinforced mud brick, the structures were metres thick from the foundations to the crenellations, and taller again than the mighty walls by the height of three men. They were a testament to Egyptian stonecraft, rugged and functional, while still adhering to the seamless aesthetic of the precincts of Karnak. Each tower was a fortress in its own right, lined with arrow slits and packed with defensive capabilities and battlefield supplies, engineered to be defended even if the walls had fallen.

Such an impossibility had never occurred, at least not to Pedubast's knowledge. Then again, it was equally unlikely that anyone had ever used those same defences to escape the city. The south-eastern tower was much closer now, as Pedubast led Iuput and Isetweret along the inside of the city's southern wall, giving the noble barracks a wide berth. The military complex remained well-lit even in the pre-dawn darkness, exempt as it was from the rationing of pitch and oil, though they were yet to see any silhouettes of soldiers within its walls.

Likewise, the patrols had thinned out in this part of the city, their presence deemed wholly unnecessary by the army's commanders, given the suicidal futility of breaking curfew in one of the most secure parts of the city.

'There, the entrance,' whispered Isetweret, pointing ahead towards the base of the tower. The only entrance at street level was a thick timber door, reinforced with three horizontal bronze bands hammered into the wood. Strong enough to withstand a battering by an invading force and with no latch on the outside, there was no way in but by the will of the guards.

'Amun help us,' Pedubast whispered as he looked up at the perfectly flat heights of the tower. No flaws marred the stone, no divots or imperfections to be used as handholds.

Pedubast put one hand against the wooden door and gently pushed.

To his astonishment, the door swung open without resistance or sound, the latch coming off the lock with a dull click. Pedubast's hand strayed to the hilt of the dagger belted at his hip. He nodded at Iuput, and together the brothers set down their packs and ventured within, blades bared and angled towards the deepest shadows.

The brothers spread, tracing each wall with one hand as their eyes adjusted, and trying not to stumble over coiled rope and around timber crates and bulging sacks. With each sound, they froze where they were, listening for noise beyond the room, but the only sound Pedubast could hear was the thudding of his own heart and the sawing of breath in his chest.

'There is no one here,' said Pedubast. He paused next to the staircase that led up to the higher levels and out to the ramparts. 'I thought you said there was always a lookout here,' he said, turning to where Isetweret was crossing the room.

'Consider it a blessing of the moon god Khonsu,' said Isetweret, stopping next to him. 'For blessings are in short supply. Now, lead on.'

Pedubast bit back the retort forming on his lips and turned to climb to the next level. The stairs to the landing above were steep but manageable, though Isetweret had to rest upon reaching each floor. Her breath came short and sharp, and a sheen of sweat beaded her skin. She refused Iuput's offer of water, and her hand went to her belly as she winced and straightened up.

The fourth level opened out onto the walkways along the walls, while the tower rose another two levels. It was at the very height of the tower that the archers would make their nests in a siege, firing arrows through narrow slits to strike down invaders with impunity.

Iuput went for the door, cracking it open and glancing out onto the empty walls. He nodded back at Pedubast, who forced himself up the narrow stairs to the final landing. He sucked in breath as he reached the top, looking out over a vista unlike any other.

The landscape outside the city was a deep, dark blue under the cold light of the gibbous moon. A line of rocky ridges separated the eastern desert from the fertile river valley, and clumps of acacia trees grew tall and strong in the shadow of the cliffs. Behind Pedubast, the city was a sea of low light, like a fleet becalmed. Isolated pockets of illumination marked Senmut's patrols, as well as the odd noble who was rich or careless enough to keep his household lit.

Pedubast tore his gaze from his surrounds and concentrated on the means of escape he had at hand. Unstrung bows lined racks around the walls and quivers of arrows were slotted into racks like scrolls in the temple library. Clay pots that could be filled with boiling oil, or used as a chamber pot in the heat of battle, sat empty under each of the arrow slits. Daggers and cudgels were arrayed beside each of the arrow slits, ready for the archers to strike down their foes should they be confident enough to scale the tower, but it was not the tower's weapons that caught Pedubast's attention.

The arrow slits at this height had another purpose beyond the defensive. Wide enough for a man to fit through, a complex system of ropes and pulleys ended in a wicker basket that hung a metre over the edge.

Designed for supplies or to admit a messenger from outside the walls, the basket was wide and firm, but precariously high. Pedubast glanced over the edge, barely able to see the ground more than twenty metres below them. He gritted his teeth and busied himself with the pulleys and supports holding the bucket in its place. He wrenched on the release lever in an effort to bring it to a more serviceable height, but it was stuck fast.

Isetweret leaned over the side. The sand far below was a dark blue and black and the distance made her vision swim as she steadied herself against the battlements. 'You are joking?' hissed Isetweret, coming up behind him. 'What if we fall?'

'You die,' said Pedubast, simply. 'Try not to do so.' He wrenched on the release again, but to no avail.

Isetweret tried to laugh but the sound died in her throat. She looked out over the city instead, her city, and tried to ignore the pain in her heart as her eye caught the distant outline of the Royal Palace.

'It needs weight,' said Iuput, joining his brother at the edge. Together, he and Pedubast loaded the basket with the clay pots under Isetweret's scrutiny, until the wicker sagged with weight and the rope groaned from where it hung from the pulley above.

'There, that should-' Iuput stiffened.

Pedubast followed his gaze, along the wall going north. In the darkness, a single speck of orange light bobbed and dipped along the wall. It was getting closer.

'The sentry,' murmured Isetweret. 'Khonsu preserve us.'

'I am asking for more than that,' said Pedubast. 'Khonsu guide me.' He leaned against the lever with all his weight, his face contorted in desperation as he heaved. The pulley gave with a metallic grind and the basket dropped with the speed of gravity, halfway to the ground below before any of them could react. Pedubast snapped the lever closed and the rope pulled tight. The basket halted instantly, stopping at the end of its tether and swinging back against the stone wall with the sound of a whipcrack.

The three of them froze. Pedubast knelt beside the rope and closed his eyes, as Isetweret edged closer to the slit, peering down at the wreckage of the clay pots.

'It was a bold strategy,' she whispered, and her hand went to her belly. 'Thank you for trying.'

Pedubast smiled thinly at her, then crawled towards where Iuput sheltered beside the arrow slit on the northern side. The torch-bearing soldier was gone, and the walls were entirely deserted once more. No sound of discovery was forthcoming, but the priest held his dagger tight all the same. He had never before used it against another man, and the thought of doing so coiled a knot within his stomach.

'Perhaps he went down to street level,' whispered Iuput, holding his blade through the gap and angling it like a mirror.

'Maybe,' said Pedubast, glancing up at the sky. The first pale smudge of dawn lit the eastern sky. They would still have time, but only if they went now.

The trapdoor behind them opened with a grind of old hinges and the youthful face of the guard peered sleepily up at them.

'What the- Who-' he managed to say, before Pedubast dived at him.

The guard flinched and turned away, averting Pedubast's blade. The dagger scored a deep cut across the guard's face, opening his cheek to the bone. The guard grunted as he fell back and Pedubast leapt after him, staggering down the steep steps, Iuput a pace behind him.

The soldier recovered quickly, quicker than Pedubast had expected. He did not know who attacked him, just that two men with daggers wanted him dead, so he turned and fled, falling as he misjudged a step and came tumbling down onto the third level.

He looked up fearfully to where Pedubast and Iuput pursued him, and threw himself at the open door he had come through just minutes before. The burning torch he had carried lay abandoned where it had fallen on the floor.

Outside, the walls stretched some hundred metres to the next tower. On the outer edge of the walls, crenellations like teeth lined the walkway, but to the right, the passage gave way to sudden, empty space. No railing or barrier would stop a fall to the streets below.

The soldier drew a breath to scream, but Pedubast lunged at him from behind, knocking the air from the soldier's lungs and sending them both cascading onto the stone walkway of the walls. The soldier scrabbled for his own, dagger belted at his hip, but only half-drew it before his hand was knocked away.

Pedubast pushed himself to his knees, panic seizing him as he lashed out with his blade. The dagger flashed down, slashing the soldier's wrist before catching his ribs and opening up a vicious score across his chest. The soldier cried out, his empty hands held up to ward off the next blow, but then Iuput was there, putting the soldier into a headlock and muffling his shouts.

Pedubast lined up the next thrust, his right hand angling the dagger's point and his left hand flat against the pommel. He stabbed forward, using all his weight to push the blade through the soldier's chest. For a moment, it stuck fast, but then it cut through the soldier's ribcage, sliding through flesh and deep into the organs beneath like a knife through a ripe fig.

The soldier sagged in Iuput's grip, all strength fleeing him as the knife pierced his heart. He took a shuddering breath, then his life ebbed away in a death rattle that seemed to stretch on and on.

Mercifully, then he was finally still. Somewhere far below, an owl hooted mournfully, and the city slept on, ignorant to a priest's first murder.

It was only then that Pedubast realised how narrowly he had come to death himself. Another tumble and all three would have been pitched off the edge of the wall. The yawning chasm down to the street below seem to rear up at him and he scrambled back, putting the corpse between him and the ledge.

Pedubast's hand trembled as he tried to pull the dagger free, but the blade snagged on the soldier's ribcage halfway out. He was surprised and irritated in equal measure at his own physical reaction. It was as if he were viewing himself from above, such was the dispassion with which he tried to retrieve his murder weapon.

It had been so easy, when it came to it, to steal another's life. The choice to kill had been no choice at all when it was him or another.

It took three firm tugs to slide the blade back out in a welter of blood. The crimson tide flowed down the soldier's front and over the stone beneath them. Pedubast's hands were shendyt were stained beyond any hope of concealment. There was no hiding now.

He glanced up at Isetweret, who was standing in the doorway, looking down at the blood-stained brothers. The words died on Pedubast's lips as Isetweret simply nodded, gratitude in the gesture. Pedubast managed a nod in return, his gaze drawn back to the tower. Such was his attention diverted that when the soldier's corpse shifted as he rose to his feet, Pedubast did not see the dead soldier's half-drawn dagger slip from its sheath and tumble over the lip of the wall.

Pedubast started as the dagger struck the street below with an echoing metallic clang. The silence reasserted itself, but only for a moment.

'Nemhon,' cried a strong voice from the street. 'What are you doing, stupid boy!' Silence again. 'Nemhon?' A few breaths later, the blade slick with the dead soldier's blood must have been discovered, for the next noise they heard was a great outcry rising from the base of the walls. Like a spark coaxed into a flame, the noble barracks erupted into light and sound. Shouts of alarm carried easily in the early morning air, and cold fear gripped Pedubast's heart.

He glanced back at Isetweret as the colour drained from her face. Of them all, Iuput seemed the steadiest, waiting calmly for his brother to tell them what to do.

Pedubast glanced down at the dead Nemhon. There was no time now. No time to let the princess down gently or for the brothers to slide down the rope after her. There was no time for anything but to flee.

'Run.' Pedubast snatched up his satchel as the first sounds of pursuit came for them. With his bloodied blade still unsheathed, Pedubast sprinted north towards the next tower, a mere hundred metres away. He turned, but Isetweret and Iuput were only steps behind him. 'In the name of the gods of Thebes, run for your lives.'

THE SOUNDS OF alarm died quickly as they fled deeper and deeper into the city. Instinctively, the brothers ran for their home, the last place of refuge in a hostile city. For now, the sense of alarm seemed to be confined to the streets around the barracks, but by first light the reports of attempted escape would reach the rest of the city's authorities.

Then escape would truly be impossible, Pedubast reflected grimly. He turned and spied Isetweret ambling behind them and paused to wait for her at the next corner. 'Hurry,' he snapped.

'You try running with a sack of grain tied to your belly,' she hissed back, coming to a stop beside him. She was breathing heavily, her fine features contorted in pain and exhaustion. Pedubast imagined he looked little better.

'We are close. Do not despair,' he said.

'Who said I was?' said Isetweret, between breaths. 'Stop talking and lead on.'

Pedubast grunted in reply and dashed across the next street, crouching beside Iuput in the shadow of a house. The satchels of food had suddenly become very heavy, but they would be as valuable inside the city as they would be outside it.

Pedubast waited for a moment, checked the street was clear, and then waved for Isetweret to cross. As he watched her run, Iuput leaned in and whispered in his ear. Curiously, there was no fear in his brother's voice.

'If we stay, we die. That is what you said.'

'I know.' Pedubast rose and moved through the next block of buildings, where the houses were smaller and the streets narrower. Familiar surroundings appeared, and there up ahead, the non-descript house they called home that would be their salvation.

'So, what happens now?' said Iuput, relief writ over his features.

'I don't know.' Pedubast sighed. 'If we are to live through tomorrow, everything must seem to be as it has been.' He turned as Isetweret caught them up. 'Take the princess and hide her well. Our survival depends on her remaining unseen. The alarm will sound soon, and we must be above suspicion.'

Iuput frowned then. 'And what of you?'

'I will wash and change. Then I must return to the temples. If this is to work then I must be in plain sight this morning. Senmut will turn to me for advice. If I am not there to give it, we will not see the sun set.'

'I do not want you to go back there alone,' said Iuput. He stepped forward, clearly warring with the idea of physically preventing his brother from returning.

'For now, I must,' said Pedubast. He put a comforting hand on his brother's shoulder. 'We are trapped inside a most dangerous game, and if we are to survive, we must play our parts. Keep quiet and remain unseen.' Pedubast unshouldered his carry bags and handed one each to Isetweret and Iuput. 'You will need these. I will send word for you when I can, but until then, do not draw notice to yourself. My lady, you most of all must be silent and invisible. Iuput will show you where to hide.'

'If these are to be my last days, I will spend them free,' said Isetweret, with a thin smile.

'Your last days are far into the future, my lady,' replied Pedubast.

'Then return to us soon and tell us how we can be rid of this plague upon my city.'

'You have my word,' said Pedubast. He bowed at the waist and gave Iuput a nod of farewell.

'May Amun watch over you, priest,' said Isetweret.

Pedubast smiled. 'And Mut over you, princess.' Pedubast turned to go, but one problem still weighed on his brother's mind.

'What about the palace guards?' asked Iuput. 'Won't they report us?'

'And admit a pregnant princess escaped under their watch? They will be in hiding too, Iuput. They might as well cut their own throats. It would be less painful than the punishments Senmut would devise for them. Now, be swift, brother. Our absence may have already been noted.'

Pedubast looked to the eastern skies. The lowest and most distant stars had already faded and first light had finally arrived. The journey had not been entirely unfruitful, and between the fearful hiding and endless waiting for patrols to pass, the kernel of an idea had begun to form in Pedubast's mind.

As he watched the stars, he could feel the weight of history settling over his shoulders. The gods were watching, and he would have to move fast to win their favour.

# Chapter Seventeen

SLEEP CAME IN disturbed fragments, short periods of blessed oblivion before the starkness of reality was thrust upon him again, more often than not by vicious kicks from his so-called comrades. Sarasesh blinked the sleep from his eyes, feeling the dust and sand scratch the skin around his eyelashes.

In the township below, the first stirrings of life moved between buildings as families rose and broke their fast together before attending to the chores of the day.

Squat, square buildings were built in long rows, the single room dwellings the standard of living for those beyond the walls of the great cities. Small flocks of sheep and the odd working donkey brayed and bleated as they gorged greedily on the first feed of the day. Groves of date palm and acacia dotted the town, towering over dusty streets and market stalls offering dried fish and rough linens.

To the east, a rock formation was a natural defence against the harsh winds and desert sands. To the west, the land sloped deep into the flood basin where the rich silt made the sedge grow tall and plentiful. The town was in a natural basin, sheltered from the world around it, but that would not save them in the hours to come.

In another life, Sarasesh would have wept for the cruelty that was about to overtake them, but now he had no more pain to spare for others. A quick death would be the kindest fate and he envied them for it.

He looked down the line of warriors crouched low behind the rise, hidden from view but numbering in their thousands. The pack leader, who took perverse delight in the title Sarasesh had given him, waited with barely repressed impatience. His leg twitched like a dog's as he watched the townsfolk go about their routine, waiting for the order to attack.

Somewhere, closer to the riverbanks, Malkesh himself watched and waited. Sarasesh had seen the warlord's prize ship dock before first light, the honour placed on him by his devotees sickening to behold. Malkesh took great pleasure in coming onto land, only when the time for pillaging was ripe.

As the light grew brighter and the darkness of the western sky changed to a pale blue, the first battle cry broke the morning stillness. The cry spread through the warriors around Sarasesh, feeling adrenaline surge through his fatigue as the men around him jostled one another in anticipation.

It could only come from Malkesh's own throat, the cry that had heralded the doom of so many towns before this one.

Sarasesh could only imagine the confusion, and then mounting horror, of the town.

There were no drums or trumpets, as the more civilised armies of the world sounded as they went to war, but a deep animal chorus, rising in crescendo as thousands roared their bloodlust.

The first of the men around him launched themselves to their feet, throwing themselves over the dune lip, their spears and cudgels held tightly and feral triumph on their features as the first of the villagers dropped their tools and ran.

Following them, more out of instinctual preservation of the herd than conscious will, Sarasesh cast himself out of cover and sprinted toward the settlement. He carried a spear that tore blisters into his palms, but it felt good to hold to a weapon. If he were to die here, he wanted to die with the illusion of protection at the very least.

The town had no static defences, no walls or palisades, but that did not mean its people would surrender to their fate meekly. Above his head, Sarasesh heard the tell-tale hiss of arrows in flight. Such was the horde's density that even an untrained peasant could not miss.

Dust choked the air as hundreds of men ran without rank or order into the town. The first screams carried over the charge and

Sarasesh narrowed his eyes against the grit, keeping the man in front of him within his sight.

He ran and kept running, almost wishing for an arrow to send him to eternal peace, but a deeper and more instinctual fear made him wary of keeping enough bodies between him and the archers in front.

Suddenly, the sand and stones turned to hard, smooth ground, and Sarasesh realised he had made it within the town's borders. Around him, the din of battle, such as it was, rang out as desperate villagers sought to give their families a few extra moments of flight.

Sarasesh staggered to a stop at the edge of the town square, the energy of his charge deserting him and leaving his emaciated muscles trembling with fatigue. He watched the butchery with curious detachment, knowing he should be horrified but feeling nothing at the scenes before his eyes.

The men were torn from their families and butchered in front of their homes. Their blood mingled in the sands of roads they had trod thousands of times in life, the horrified wails of their families mingling with their death cries.

Their wives, mothers, and daughters were thrown to the ground, the beasts who called themselves warriors of Malkesh taking their pleasure with the satisfied grunts of rutting swine. The women's screams seemed to only spur the animals onward and Sarasesh's belly recoiled with disgust.

The children were herded like chattel, terrified and crying, huddling together for the illusion of protection. Penned like animals, they watched the horror with wide, tear-streaked eyes, their childhoods stripped from them in an instant by the machinations of a prophet of their own gods.

The priest turned from this sight, wondering at the gods' wills and knowing that such questioning was futile. The gods had abandoned them. Senmut's actions had seen to that, and Sarasesh, in his youthful naivety, had helped him do it.

He ventured back the way he had come, trying to ignore the lustful faces of the men that were only now reaching the fight.

Sarasesh saw a house off the way, under the shade of a grove of acacia trees. He stumbled towards it, wishing for nothing more than a place of solitude and rest as he fought through the mass of rancid humanity.

He reached the doorframe, taking a breath of the cool air within, when mortality reached for him. He ducked under the spear thrust out of pure instinct, throwing himself backward into the dust. He hit the ground hard, scrambling away, but his limbs seized as the villager advanced upon him. Pain contorted the man's face, and between his legs, Sarasesh could see his family huddled together in the far corner.

The villager surveyed the devastation, and Sarasesh knew that the man must just now be realising everyone he knew was dead. The man looked down and saw the closest and weakest of his attackers.

Sarasesh froze, too tired to defend himself, too full of despair to care.

In a moment, the man's rage changed swiftly to fear. Sarasesh glanced out of the corner of his eye and found why. The priest was flanked by a pair of tribesmen, then two more as the horde's warriors closed in on the final pockets of resistance. He took a faltering step forward, then cast his weapon down and turned to flee the other way.

The villager managed a single step, turning into the deadly embrace of a tribesman who had come up behind him. The spear took him in the gut, tearing open his belly. The man fell with a strangled cry at his own threshold, watching as his killer moved towards his wife and children.

Sarasesh went to his hands and knees, crawling towards the man. He pulled him over, facing the sky. The man's face was contorted in agony, his face ashen and his wound pulsing with blood. The villager's wild eyes met the priest's, and Sarasesh put a hand over the dying man's heart.

'I'm sorry,' he whispered. 'It was not supposed to be like this.'

The man gasped his last breath, and his wild-eyed stare went glassy and still. Sarasesh bowed his head, hearing footsteps behind him as he closed the man's eyes.

'You are welcome, priest,' the warrior growled. The soldier of Malkesh grinned down at him, watching with satisfaction as his comrades tore the man's family from their home. Their screams made Sarasesh's eye twitch.

'Leave them alone,' he said. 'There are many more for you to glut your foul appetites.'

The man grunted. 'You're smarter than that.'

Sarasesh looked up, seeing the frightened children marched past their dead father, hearing the woman's screams as she was dragged away.

'You are less than beasts,' he said, without venom or censure. It was simply the truth.

He half expected the man to beat him as they had so many times before, but the warrior simply smiled. He gestured with blood-spattered hands to the grain silo. It would not go far among the thousands-strong horde, but it would bolster their meagre rations for a few nights and in turn, their ever-suffering morale.

'You may be right, priest. But even the hyena celebrates its victory. Come, let us revel in our spoils.'

The warrior turned and marched towards the market square.

Sarasesh got to his feet and followed. The words were not a request.

IN THE PALE light of pre-dawn, Pedubast made it back within the temple precincts with greater ease than he had left it. The guards were lax and numb with exhaustion and at some point, in the early morning, they had given into nocturnal indulgence. Their challenge was half-hearted and swiftly calmed. Of course, they had seen him leave only hours before, bearing the word of Senmut. Of course, they had allowed it, after he had shown them Senmut's seal and told them the nature of his task. They were a credit to the new cause, and he would relay his compliments to Senmut himself for their diligence and devotion.

When first light broke, he had met Senmut with all suitable decorum, relaying sheepishly his lack of constitution and his embarrassment at passing out behind a storeroom sometime after midnight. Senmut had accepted the excuse without further question, but Pedubast was not fool enough to ignore the suspicion in the other man's eyes.

In Tasenhor's absence, Pedubast played the dutiful servant, dogging Senmut's steps as the self-proclaimed High Priest went about the daily motions of temple worship and divine maintenance. After the midday service and the shared lunch of temple offerings, Pedubast bid his master farewell and made his way towards the northern edge of the Central Court, taking a moment under the immense, painted walls to contemplate the gods' plans and their humble places within it.

He went to seek Tasenhor again, to speak with him of a new plan, but the older prophet had vanished. None of the priests could tell him where, only that they had last seen him in a fit of rage in the temple courtyard. It was only later that an exhausted soldier revealed they had let the prophet pass for he was in a drunken rage and muttering about home.

Tasenhor's disappearance surprised Pedubast for the unwelcome attention it would bring to the prophet. When Tasenhor did not resurface by noon, Senmut summoned Pedubast to a private audience, one without the prophet's usual retainers and supporters hanging on. The hall of revelry was deserted, the detritus of excess still evident everywhere he looked.

Senmut himself sat at the back corner, slumped on a simple chair and propping up his head with one elbow on the desk next to him. His skin was blotchy with shades of red and purple, his eyes were bloodshot, and his chest and shendyt were stained with wine. At first, Pedubast thought that some affliction had come over him, but as he came closer, he saw that Senmut was trembling with apoplectic rage.

'Your Holiness, you called for me?' he asked, kneeling at a safe distance.

Senmut's voice was a wet growl. 'Princess Isetweret is gone.'

Pedubast was aghast. 'Gone, my lord? You had her killed?'

'No, you damn fool. I mean she is gone. Escaped. No longer in my custody,' snapped Senmut.

Pedubast flinched, hoping his cringing servitude was convincing enough as he adopted a confused tone. 'How is that possible? She was secure in the palace. How does a pregnant woman evade armed guards?'

'I don't know!' thundered Senmut. He shifted in his seat, but he seemed unbalanced and his speech was a barely understandable slur.

'The accursed guards are gone too. She had help. This I know as surely as my own name.'

'Who would dare work against us now?' asked Pedubast.

'Someone who is tired of life.' Senmut rested his face into his hands and shook his head. When he looked up the anger was cooling, replaced by a bone-deep exhaustion and nervous energy. 'We must recover her as soon as possible. You met with her and she took you into confidence. Where are her favourite places? Where does she feel safe?'

'In her own chambers and in the palace gardens,' replied Pedubast truthfully, deciding that a lie or refusal would not be wise. 'She enjoyed walking the walls too, but I cannot think of anywhere that would be safe for her now.'

Senmut shook his head, very slowly, almost swaying. 'I have heard nothing from the gate guards. She is still here somewhere.'

'Perhaps Tasenhor and Naroleth have heard something?' said Pedubast,

'Naroleth was here all night. And Tasenhor... where is he? Have we any leads?'

'I asked around for him but no one has seen him all day. One of the soldiers said he had ventured out into the city. I would check his house.'

'I did not give permission for him to leave,' said Senmut.

Pedubast risked a small shrugged. 'It is unfortunate timing, my lord. I would not dare to speculate, but it is possible that he knows something, or perhaps saw something.'

'I will have my soldiers go to his house and drag him back here screaming.' Senmut shot to his feet, but his eyes glazed over and he staggered on the spot.

'My lord, no,' cried Pedubast, guiding the other man back into his chair. 'I have a better idea, if you will allow me to venture it?'

'Speak,' slurred Senmut, closing his eyes and leaning back against the wall.

Pedubast bowed again. 'If Tasenhor is indeed a traitor, then he will have had help, as you wisely said. That he lives now in his own house and does not flee is monstrously arrogant and shows that he does not fear us. Even now, he may still be meeting with his conspirators. Let us place a watch on his house. We will learn who is in league with him.' Pedubast smiled and shrugged. 'Why fish with a single line now, when we could cast a whole net soon enough?'

'You speak sense,' muttered Senmut, eyes still closed. 'And who should we trust to do this thing?'

'Place your trust in me for this, my lord, I beg you. I will have my brother, Iuput, watch over Tasenhor's house. He has a fine attention to detail, endless patience, and often goes entirely unnoticed, such is his gift. Allow me to send word to him and we will find the answers we seek soon enough.'

Senmut opened his eyes. 'It is a good plan. Know that if this is deception on your part your death will be just as agonising as that which will be visited upon Tasenhor and the other traitors. Do not fail me in this, for my vengeance knows no limits.'

Pedubast bowed his head and kept his eyes fixed on Senmut's feet, lest the other look into his soul and see the truth. 'I will be by your side, always. If there is even a hint of treachery, you will not have to look far to mete out further punishment. I offer you my service and my life.' The silence stretched on for several long moments, until Pedubast felt a soft hand on his shoulder.

'Very well, send word to your brother and then return here at once. We have much to discuss if we are to root out this infestation.' Senmut handed him a clay seal from a pouch at his waist. 'This will see you through the gates. I have left instructions.' Senmut's gaze glazed over and his head lolled back again as his eyes closed. Pedubast frowned as Senmut began to snore softly, his breathing laboured under the influence of wine and heady smoke. Pedubast's gaze settled on the soft flesh of Senmut's throat and a manic idea took root in his mind of strangling the breath from the prophet.

No one would know, he thought, watching Senmut's chest rise and fall and the pulsing of blood in his fleshy throat. How easy it is to choke on one's vomit after imbibing far too much.

He dismissed the idea as soon as it occurred to him, not least for the risk in physically murdering another man. His killing of the guard in the tower had been borne of desperate self-preservation. To murder in cold blood with his bare hands was a different matter.

A second thought occurred to him. If he were killed here and now, Senmut would die a martyr, not as the disgraced tyrant he would become if Pedubast would just wait and plan. Amun's blessing had come to him in the early hours after his inquiry after Tasenhor, the formation of a plan that would unseat Senmut's underlings and the mind of the despot himself. Senmut snorted and for a moment his eyes flickered open before he fell back into a restless sleep.

Pedubast refrained from sighing in relief and left as quickly as he was able. He went from the hall into the sunlight and felt the burning eye of the gods on him. He straightened himself, smoothing out his shendyt and set off for the gates. Pedubast showed the gate guards the clay seal, and though they let him pass he felt their eyes on him until the gates were closed and bolted once again.

The idea in his head was a pounding force, one that could only have been placed there by the divine. He could focus on nothing else as he walked through the city streets, though the sights should have stirred and excited him at their renewed novelty. He was dimly aware of being stared at as he made his way through marketplaces and busy avenues, and he considered that it had been likely some time since the people of Thebes had seen a priest of Karnak in their midst.

The sight of his own house brought feelings of joy mixed with trepidation, as the thought of seeing his brother again conflicted with what he would have to ask of Iuput. Pedubast called out as he entered, as cheerily as though he had just come from the marketplace. If he were in Senmut's place, he would have had himself followed and watched, even now. Though Pedubast had his doubts, there was no guarantee that the disturbed despot's signs of imbalance were entirely genuine and that a cunning malice did not yet lurk beneath the bluster.

Iuput looked up from where he sat reading at the table, and his expression of pleasure and relief brought a genuine grin to Pedubast's face. The brothers embraced warmly and held one another at arm's length, enjoying the moment of reunion.

'We hadn't heard. I began to worry,' said Iuput, pulling away.

Pedubast's smile faded. 'I am sorry, but it was too dangerous to send word and bring attention here. Know that I am safe, but that I must return to Karnak immediately. Is she well?'

Iuput's gaze flickered over Pedubast's shoulder. 'Ask her yourself.'

Pedubast looked up to see Isetweret standing halfway down the stairs. Dark circles shadowed her eyes and she held her belly protectively with both hands. 'What has happened?' she asked quietly, a tremor in her voice.

'Upstairs,' said Pedubast. 'It is possible I am followed.' The brothers followed the princess to the landing above and settled in where they would remain unseen and unheard.

'You are well, my princess?' Pedubast asked when. He refrained from bowing.

'Well enough, now tell me. Has something changed?' she said.

'Senmut knows you have escaped. He believes you are still in the city. His signs of instability grow, but there are still many that are fanatically loyal to him. None but the temple leadership know the full truth, though more and more complaints are being whispered. I believe a turning point is coming.'

Isetweret frowned and glanced between the brothers. 'What are we going to do?'

'You will remain hidden. We cannot risk even the hint of suspicion falling onto us. I have a plan to shift Senmut's attention, if you will allow me a moment alone with my brother?'

'You are really going hold secrets from me? Even now?' she asked.

'It will be better if you do not know,' replied Pedubast. 'I would spare your conscience.'

'It is heavy enough already, priest,' said Isetweret, and waved a dismissive hand and reclined on her cot. 'Do what you must. When I am returned to power, not only will you be pardoned for everything, but you will be honoured for what you do here now.'

Pedubast nodded in thanks and gestured for Iuput to follow him back downstairs.

'There is something that I need you to do, something that I would do myself if my own task was not even more dangerous,' he said, moving to the wooden chest of drawers at the rear of the house. Dried bundles of herbs hung from the ceiling and dozens of small clay pots filled the drawers with powders, extracts and dried leaves and roots. Pedubast opened the bottom drawer and retrieved a small clay vial from the back.

'I place a heavy burden on you, but this thing must be done. I would trust no other with this,' he said. 'If you are successful, we go a long way to unseating a tyrant.'

'Anything, brother.'

Pedubast smiled at the earnest trust in Iuput's voice. 'I have convinced Senmut that Tasenhor has something to do with the princess's disappearance. You are to set a watch on Tasenhor's house on the pretence of identifying his conspirators. You will do this, at least for a while, until you get the chance to sneak into his house. Take this vial and as soon as you are able, slip the contents into his wine.'

'What is it?' asked Iuput, picking up the vial and peering within.

'A concoction of mandrake and strychnine. It will be certain and silent,' said Pedubast.

'Poison? You wish him dead?' Iuput put the stopper back in the vial, but there was no doubt in his words.

'I wished him to live but his own choices have forced our hands. He has given up and to avoid Senmut's suspicions another must take our place.'

Iuput looked away and blew air through his teeth. 'You are certain about this?'

Pedubast nodded slowly. 'Tasenhor is already dead. We are merely easing his passing.' He repeated the steps, pausing only to ensure that his brother was clear on each step, but as always Iuput's memory was infallible. Only at the end did his brother express his doubt.

'I will do this for you, brother, but it does not have to be this way. Tasenhor could help us,' said Iuput.

Pedubast had considered likewise and he was pleased to see his brother's thoughts firmly rooted in the practical, not the emotional. 'No, Iuput. It is too risky. Senmut suspects treachery around every corner. We can only trust each other.' As always, his brother needed the whole picture to appreciate the subtleties. 'Naroleth is too much of a sycophant to turn, and even if Tasenhor agreed to join us he is stained with the suspicions of this new Karnak. Their uses are few, but of import all the same. When you are finished, return to our home and sleep. You are still beneath Senmut's suspicions. Come to the temples after the midday service and find me in the Hypostyle Hall.'

'As you say, brother,' said Iuput, taking the vial and slipping it into a pouch at his waist. 'Consider it already done.'

THE LIGHT OF day would bring many changes to Thebes, though few knew it when they opened their windows to the morning sun and hugged their families with relief at the end of the night-time curfew. Fishermen tentatively left their hovels, and pushed their boats out onto the river, glad for the respite from the oppressive air of the city streets. Bakers waited for the bravest of their number to disturb the quiet and begin grinding the daily flour, but before long the life and bustle of the city returned. Marketplaces filled up and friends came together to talk and laugh, always with a cautious eye on the imposing pylons of Karnak.

Tasenhor woke with bleary eyes, the daylight filtering through the curtain and onto a face stained red with wine. He groaned as the pain behind his eyes blurred his vision and he rose unsteadily to his feet, drawing the curtain aside and letting the fresh air filter in. Tasenhor called for his manservant, but only silence greeted his command. With an irritated snarl he padded across the floor of his bed chamber, his eyes alighting on a full carafe of wine on a table by the door. At least the useless cretin had remembered his lord's need.

That he had not returned to Karnak would enrage Senmut, if he was lucid enough to even notice, but Tasenhor felt lighter for the freedom he had taken. He had debated returning the morning after he had met Pedubast, but a breakfast of fish, bread and wine enjoyed in silence had postponed those plans until night had fallen again and the stores in his cellar called for him.

His last days in this world would be lived according to his own desires, not those of a madman who had condemned them all with his hubris. He was not sure what day it was, but Senmut would surely forgive a day or two's absence, particularly if he remembered their momentary falling out. Pedubast's capture would turn all attention from him, and he would slide back into Senmut's circle just as the self-appointed despot's trust was shaken to its foundations. His indulgence now might even increase Senmut's trust in him, for surely Senmut would understand the call of the grape to salve the stress they and Naroleth had been forced to shoulder.

Tasenhor drained his first cup in one gulp, feeling the warmth suffuse his limbs. He sighed with pleasure, feeling the pulse in his head start to abate almost immediately. He chuckled as poured himself a second cup. Perhaps today, he would go and hear of Pedubast's fate. Idly, he wondered what method of execution Senmut had chosen. He was vindictive enough to make a spectacle of it. Perhaps he would have him dipped in honey and left for the ants, or tied into a sack and beaten to death. Or maybe he was tired enough to simply order his throat cut.

He took his cup to sit beside the window on the second storey, watching the morning traffic pass him below. Merchants continued to dress in their finest clothes and kiss their wives goodbye for a day of commerce, while mothers brewed the beer and baked the bread to the cheerful sounds of children playing. As though any of it mattered any more.

He was halfway through the cup when he felt a sudden tightness in his chest.

At first, he thought it was fear, a nameless terror sprung on him by his own mind, but within moments, a vice had closed around his entire body. His eyes widened and his hands went to his throat, dropping the cup to the floor with a clang. He gasped for a breath that would not come, and his eyes bulged from his head as the feeling of being strangled locked his chest and throat in an invisible hold.

He hit the ground hard, though he barely felt the impact. He clawed at his throat like a madman, his legs thrashing and knocking aside the chairs and table. Through tear-streaked eyes he saw a figure in the corner of the room.

The figure, in the shape of a man, crept forward.

Tasenhor tried to gasp, to accuse, to shout the man's name, but nothing more than a thin croak escaped his throat.

The other man's face was impassive, studying him the way a farm inspects his beasts for slaughter. Iuput collected the cup from where it had fallen and poured more wine.

'For what it is worth, I argued in your favour,' said Iuput. 'But Pedubast was right. It is never rational to give up, but through your death you will help us to bring hope to others. I hope that comforts you.'

Tasenhor tried to speak, but the tightness in his chest sent agony coursing through him.

Despite his thrashing, Iuput held his jaw firm and forced more of the poison down his throat. Within moments his movements subsided, and a deep numbness suffused his limbs as the burning agony of suffocation stole the last vestiges of strength from him.

The last thing he heard, as his eyes went dark and his struggles faded into a rictus paralysis, was his killer's solemn prayer.

'May Amun guide you to the peace you seek.' said Iuput.

Then, Tasenhor heard nothing more.


PEDUBAST LOOKED UP at the towering pillars of the Hypostyle Hall, as he had for three days since he had instructed Iuput of his plans. As he had promised, he furnished Senmut with details of those who had visited Tasenhor's house, though those details were fabricated and vague enough to have applied to any number of priests in the temple's employ.

Each day, at midday, he came here to contemplate the holy mysteries. At least, that is what he told his brethren. In truth, he wandered the columns without aim, keeping one eye on the hall's outer entrance and waiting for his brother's presence. It was not until the zenith of the third day that a familiar figure approached him, walking solemnly among the dazzling bas reliefs and admiring the illuminated stories of divine vistas and holy scenes inscribed in eternal stone.

Iuput made no secret of his passage as he had been instructed. He paused to speak with passers-by, if only for a moment, before continuing towards his brother, greeting and embracing cordially as any observer might expect. Their conversation began on theological matters, loudly proclaiming the beauty and wisdom of Amun's ascendance, and of course, the favoured place of his chosen servants. Pedubast gestured up at the scenes of the bas relief beside them. He had memorised them all of course, and began espousing on the attributes of the Theban triad as a gaggle of priests passed them by.

'Is it done?' he murmured, when they were alone, still looking at the reliefs. For all intents, the brothers had been struck speechless by the scenes above, held mute by holy awe.

'It is,' said Iuput. 'I waited an hour to be sure.'

'Good. Very good. Regrettable but necessary, you understand?' said Pedubast, his voice level and steady. His expression broke into a relieved smile, and finally he turned to face Iuput. 'Brother, you are a treasure. I could kiss you!'

'I would rather you did not,' replied Iuput, lowering his voice to a conspiratorial whisper. 'You will be pleased to know our guest remains comfortable.'

Pedubast grunted and glanced sidelong at his brother. 'She has not been any trouble?'

'Plenty of that,' said Iuput. 'But she is discreet and makes few demands, except for news of the outside world. Unfortunately, I have had precious little to give her.'

'Good, she will be a staunch ally, when we return her to the throne. I do not regret aiding in her escape, but we must be very careful. Any misstep now and we may yet be undone.'

'I would follow you into the Field of Reeds if you asked it of me, Ped,' said Iuput.

'I know you would,' said Pedubast, laying a hand on Iuput's shoulder with a smile. 'But we need not grace those golden fields just yet.'

Iuput's eyes flickered with alarm, and Pedubast had the presence of mind to smooth his expression to a more pleasing servitude before he turned and greeted the new arrival.

The High Priest's face was a furious shade of crimson, his expression pinched and his hands balled into fists at his side in the manner of pharaonic statues. Behind him, Naroleth looked pale, the fear apparent in the set of his mouth, no matter how much he tried to hide it with sneering hauteur. Several of Senmut's sycophants attended him likewise, each of them looking drawn and haggard.

'Where have you been? I have been searching for you,' snapped Senmut, halting Naroleth and the others with an irritable wave and crossing the last few paces alone.

Pedubast bowed low at the waist. 'We have been here all along, revered prophet. I do hope our service has not gone so far beneath your notice?'

Confusion crossed Senmut's feature, but only for a moment. He glanced at Iuput over Pedubast's shoulder. 'You, be gone,' he ordered. 'I must speak with Brother Pedubast alone.'

Iuput started, but Pedubast held out his hand to halt him. 'You remember my brother of blood, Iuput, noble First Prophet?' prompted Pedubast.

Senmut's eyes narrowed. After a moment, the dawn of recognition spread across his face. 'Ah yes, of course. The simple brother. Good, stay then. Tell me of your task.'

Pedubast suppressed the irritable curl that came to his lips and continued, his voice unwavering. 'Perhaps somewhere more private?'

Senmut's frown deepened. 'Do not presume that was a question. Out with it.'

'Tasenhor is dead, my lord. It seems he took his own life,' said Pedubast, deeply bowing before he risked looking up. Emotions of every stripe coloured the High Priest's face, confusion, grief, satisfaction and, most of all, anger. 'My lord?' Pedubast prompted.

Senmut glanced once more at Iuput and then turned on his heel. 'Follow me,' he snapped. Such was the sudden change in him that the priests attending him parted like the bow wave of a ship, spilling over each other to get out of his path. Naroleth flinched as Senmut passed him, the priest giving the brothers a warning look before he trotted after his master. The High Priest led his followers back through the pillars of the Great Hypostyle Hall into the open courtyard beyond. Pedubast noted that many of the priests here contemplating the hall watched their passage guardedly, many of them sidling behind the enormous pillars as the new temple leadership passed them by.

Pedubast kept his expression neutral, ignoring the stares as he kept pace with the rest of the group. They followed Senmut as the High Priest trudged towards the great hall where so much of the fear-laden celebration and riotous excess had taken place. Senmut made for the entrance before he stopped, seeming to awaken from whatever momentary stupor had come over him. He shook his head and turned left, bypassing the hall towards the storeroom-turned-meeting place in which Pedubast had last seen Tasenhor.

Pedubast tried to ignore the sick grip of fear over his heart, but he lurched.

Senmut pushed open the door and sat inside, calling out the names of the most influential among his followers to attend him, including Pedubast. When the rest of the hangers-on had been dismissed, Senmut said, 'Naroleth, summon the others.'

Naroleth paused, clearly unsure to whom his master referred, but he demurred with a bow and fled, ignoring Pedubast's attempt to catch his eye. He closed the door behind him and the silence of those left behind was total and complete.

'The rest of you will stay here,' said Senmut. 'We have much to discuss.'

THE CANDLES BURNED bright, the light the intensity of a jailer's torch, a dancing inferno that cast a hundred different shadows against the sparse, stone walls. For all the blindness they invoked, the figures clustered around the chamber's central table stared into its flame, none of them willing to meet the gaze of the man who sat at the table's head.

In the hours it had taken to gather everyone, no refreshments had been offered and none had been asked for. The tiny chamber, barely worthy of being called a storeroom, was in the shadow of the eastern walls of the Precinct of Amun, a non-descript place that had been the site of clandestine whispers until those whispers had found their voice and unseated the social order of Thebes.

All but one man wanted to leave this place as soon as they were able.

Senmut glared down from the head of the table, as befitted his right as the High Priest of Amun. To either side of him, the high priests of the neighbouring brotherhoods, Merenmut of the priesthood of Mut, and Nebneteru in the service of Khonsu, watched the new hierarch with wary expressions. Though they were lords of their own domain, the High Priest of Amun was the de facto ruler of Karnak. By their will or not, his words heralded their salvation or damnation.

Senmut's lip curled as he surveyed the gathering. More than a dozen men were in attendance, the high priests and their ranking prophets from the priesthoods of the Theban triad, all seated and awaiting the reason for this unconventional meeting. Collectively, they were the most powerful men in the country, discounting their distant and uncaring pharaoh.

'I am disappointed, my friends,' Senmut began. 'I work to the will of the gods, and yet there are those that still speak against me, against Amun himself. More than that, they act against my decrees, spit upon them. I do what is best for us all,' said Senmut, shouting the final word.

Half of the gathering flinched in their seats.

'Though I care little for the opinions of one troublemaker, the temples must be of one accord if we are to successfully lead Thebes into a new age of prosperity. How can I lead us through these turbulent times otherwise? And you are telling me now that none of you have any idea of who has brought this about?' The High Priest's words were slow and his speech slurred, without the intonation of the learned. His eyes were unfocused, and he swayed like a cobra as he spoke, entranced but ready to strike.

The silence stretched on, none willing to be the first to break it.

'Cowards, the lot of you,' hissed Senmut. 'Brother Pedubast, tell them the news.'

Pedubast bowed sycophantly low, coming to kneel beside Senmut's chair. He sniffed as the overpowering stench of old wine flooded his senses, but managed to hold his High Priest's gaze.

'It seems apparent that there is indeed opposition to your leadership, Your Holiness,' he said. 'Tasenhor's suicide would suggest a conspiracy of some strength against you.'

The news of the prophet's death had shaken the priesthood, but none could deny Tasenhor's melancholy and his abandonment of the precinct. Poison was the obvious choice. It was a coward's choice, one that left the body intact for ritual mummification, though Pedubast did not dare to speculate what would become of the prophet's mortal remains under Senmut's control.

'Tasenhor. My viperous friend. Dead by his own hand. Cowardly, as I said,' slurred Senmut. 'And if he has proven false, then who else might falter? You, Naroleth? You, Nesperennub? Or do these crimes go higher still? My brothers, in the precincts of Mut and Khons, do you wish for your own ascendency at the expense of mine?'

Those named stiffened with fear, their eyes as motionless as their flesh as they sought to be beneath Senmut's notice.

'I am sure, Your Holiness, that all in attendance are loyal to you. Would they not have taken the coward's way out as their leader did? Have faith, as we have faith in you.'

Senmut placed a hand on Pedubast's shoulder and smiled, a crocodile's smile devoid of warmth. 'Look at you. Craven and cowardly,' Senmut spat, glaring at the gathering. 'Any one of you may have turned against me and I would not know it. Let me be clear, here and now. My rule is given to me under the mandate of Amun. It is mine!' he roared, spittle and acrid fumes billowing into the open, flickering flame.

The priests flinched at his outburst and the candles danced before his wrath, casting the light unevenly and marking Senmut's expression as demonic. The High Priest's anger vanished as quickly as it came, and he leaned over the right arm of his chair, his eyes fixed on the priests gathered at the end of the chamber as he spoke to his trusted confidante.

'Brother Pedubast, what would you do?'

Pedubast paused for a moment, conscious of every eye in the chamber fixed upon him.

'We cannot put aside the possibility that others from without colluded with Tasenhor,' said Pedubast. 'Perhaps it would be beneficial to put more guards on the outer walls? A show of force? Why not call for recruitment, a newfound regiment in service to the priesthood itself? Let the people know that we are building our strength and that there is reward for those that stand with us.'

'Do you see how high these god-devoted portals rise? No army in the world could hope to breach them. We have all the food. We have all the wine. There is no threat to us. The savages will get bored soon enough pawing at our city gates,' said Senmut with a snigger.

Pedubast flinched at Senmut's words and the murmur that spread throughout the room. He glanced around quickly, seeing scowls on some faces and hushed whispers coming from others, though whether the priests thought Senmut referred to their own people or the horde of Nubians he did not know. He pressed on quickly.

'Then a show of force to let the people know that we are in control. That is what is required, my lord. In my own humble opinion,' he added, averting his eyes once more.

Senmut nodded and grinned. 'What say you, my loyal followers? A show of force to let our enemies know that we are not to be challenged?'

The chorus of assent was tragic, in Pedubast's mind, an empty cheer for want of anything else to do. Even the High Priests of Mut and Khons joined in half-heartedly, a shared glance between them revealing far more than the praises spilling from their mouths. The bright torches rendered the shadowed features around the table almost skeletal, a gathering of the damned with none present wishing to be the most vocal nor least enthusiastic in his praises. Pedubast noted there was little risk in the former. Naroleth fulfilled that role easily enough.

'What is your command, Your Holiness?' asked Pedubast, once the chamber had quietened sufficiently. 'Shall I send the order to increase patrols in the noble's quarter? Then perhaps a parade through the waterfront so that all may gaze upon our ascendency? It has been some time since the priests have moved among the people. Surely the people will be more content knowing the holy servants of this city hear their pleas and know their hearts.'

Senmut laughed again. He was the only one to do so. 'The common people will serve as they always have. It is their gods-given place to toil in the fields and the river. Let them see the fate of a highborn once, and they will be brought into line. The death of a noble will hasten their cringing pledges of allegiance. Let them all see that none are beyond divine punishment.' Senmut leaned back in his chair, his eyes roaming over the faces of those present, always watching for the slightest hint of treachery. 'Perhaps the princess Isetweret,' he ventured. 'She is with child, you know. Two offerings of divine blood where before there was only one. Yes, Amun would be pleased.'

No one spoke. No one dared even to breathe.

Only Pedubast and Naroleth knew of Isetweret's escape and yet none of them spoke up. Not one man protested the murder of mother and child and Pedubast hated them for it. Knowing the impossibly of Senmut's threat, Pedubast played his part, bowing even lower, his forehead pressed to the arm of Senmut's chair. 'Sire, I must caution you against such action. The princess is still the daughter of the false king Takelot. Apophis and Set may yet lend him strength to overcome his enemies, and keeping her under our control would lend great strength where arms do not. I would beg you, as your humble servant, to reconsider.'

Senmut turned his gaze on Pedubast. For a moment, Pedubast feared Senmut had forgotten their plan, but the High Priest laid a hand on his shoulder and addressed the gathering.

'Very well, not the princess. But another must be made to pay for Tasenhor's crimes. Now get out while I consider who. All of you, get out!'

The priests closest to the door all but fell over themselves to escape the chamber's confines. The two other high priests stood and left without a word. Merenmut nodded almost imperceptibly to Pedubast, while Nebneteru grunted with the effort of rising and followed his counterpart from the hall without looking back.

Pedubast had almost reached the door when Senmut called after him.

'Brother, a moment.'

Pedubast turned slowly, his expression once more one of sincere loyalty bordering on sycophancy, his tones soft, soothing and dripping with platitudes. He knelt beside Senmut's chair arm again, listening as the footsteps of the priests outside faded into silence.

Once more the idea of murder rose in Pedubast's thoughts. He could kill Senmut now, surely. The High Priest's movements were slow, and his speech slurred as if he had been drugged. Likely he still was, by his own hand. It would be simple enough to wrap his hands around Senmut's neck and squeeze the life from him, but what then of his followers? The hundreds of priests that owed their newfound power and privilege to Senmut's ambition would surely begin a schism that would burn Thebes to ashes.

'You are a trusted friend,' said Senmut. 'I appreciate your loyalty when so much else is unbalanced.'

'I have always been a true friend to the righteous,' replied Pedubast.

'Good, good.' Senmut nodded, his eyes fixed on the doorway.

Gone was the raging tyrant. Now there was just a frightened man whose actions had brought downfall to all that he had known, a man whose plans had been ruined by the scale of his own ambition.

'Which of them do you judge false?' asked Senmut.

'In truth, Your Holiness, I do not believe any of them are behind this insult to your majesty. See how they fear you? Who among them would dare?'

Senmut's gaze seemed to see through the stone wall and beyond, to the thousands who made up his new kingdom, to both those that worshipped the ground beneath his feet and those who wanted him dead. That dreadful gaze turned on Pedubast.

'But it would do harm to investigate it further,' he said quickly. 'Your mind is better spent pondering the mysteries and the will of Amun. Leave such mundane matters of security to your humble servant. I will take control of the forces we have left and safeguard your office.'

Senmut sighed and his hand drifted absently towards a cup of wine that was not there. He frowned at the emptiness of the table and sighed. 'I know you mean well, brother, but I must stay in control. I must guard myself from all threats, you understand? What if someone were to bewitch you?'

'Then I would die before I let the curse turn me from my purpose.'

Senmut smiled and cupped the other man's face in his hand. 'You are faithful, Pedubast. I remember when you came to us in the wake of Takelot's call, a provincial priest of a backwater temple.'

Pedubast's lip curled, but Senmut's eye had already wandered. To call Bubastis a backwater was to call the nemes headdress a mere scarf and the great Imhotep a modest dabbler in architecture.

'I was humbled when I first came to Karnak, Your Holiness,' Pedubast replied truthfully. 'I have seen many things since then that have changed me.'

Senmut seemed not to hear him, and long seconds of silence stretched on until Pedubast would have been sure the High Priest had died but for the twitch in his eyelid.

'Can I confess something to you, brother Pedubast?'

Pedubast nodded. 'I am here in your service, my lord. To ease your conscience if I am able.'

Senmut sighed again. He looked deep into the fire of the oil lamps, watching it transfixed. 'Harsiese has escaped.'

Pedubast blinked in a surprise, an emotion he had thought lost to him. His mind reeled at the possibilities. 'Harsiese is still alive?' he asked. 'How?'

'Someone must have been helping him. I do not know who, but if one of our brothers have broken faith I must know. Swear to me now. You will find out who it was.'

'I swear with all due honour,' said Pedubast. 'I will find out who has broken faith with you and will not rest until I know.'

'Good, good,' said Senmut. 'Now we must talk of practicalities. I will retain command, but you must withdraw all our forces to the walls of Karnak. Leave a token force on the city's outer walls, enough to fool the people, but bring the rest back.'

Pedubast nodded, his thoughts afire at this latest confession. 'As you say, sire, but what of the common people? They are but sheep, and a shepherd never abandons his flock.'

Senmut chuckled, but the humour did not reach his eyes. 'When Malkesh comes for us, where do you think the people will run? We do not have the strength to man the outer walls. Takelot took it all with him, thinking Thebes too safe in its position, too far from danger to be worth guarding properly.'

'As you say, Your Holiness,' said Pedubast. 'I would beg your leave to return home in the city. My brother Iuput will have need of me.'

'Yes, go home for all the good it may do you. Leave me now as so many others have done.'

Pedubast bowed and withdrew, leaving Senmut alone with his thoughts. He passed by brothers who looked to him for guidance and answers, but he ignored them entirely. He passed through the outer portals without incident, flashing Senmut's seal as he had done previously.

Pedubast found his brother sleeping peacefully, and extinguished the flame left burning in Iuput's bedchamber. He smiled down at the sight, the sense of peace bringing on weariness that struck him like a physical blow. He climbed to the next level, checking behind a partition to find Isetweret too sound asleep. Satisfied, he took his sleeping mat to the roof and slipped out of his shendyt, enjoying the cool breeze over his naked flesh. Sleep came uneasily to him and his dreams were filled with dread and bitter accusations, a persistent doubt that he would survive each new day.

In the morning, Pedubast woke to a city in turmoil.

Patrols of soldiers, not in pairs or small groups but in whole cohorts, swept the streets, detaining and interrogating seemingly at random, and arresting noble and commoner alike on the merest suspicion. If the people were terrified before, they were paralysed with fear now. Within Karnak's walls, the priests who had enjoyed the privilege of lordlings under their new master finally began to wonder if perhaps they had overstepped their bounds.

# Chapter Eighteen

A SEA OF rippling white stretched far across the desert plain, hundreds of tents laid down and ordered with military precision. The sounds of blacksmiths at the anvil and the smoky aromas of cooking fires completed the scene, the industrious sounds and smells as familiar to Takelot as the music of the temples and the scent of divine frankincense.

He breathed deep of it all.

Few moments in a generation changed the course of history, and for good or ill, it was a fine thing to savour the anticipation. He had endured trial after trial, and yet he remained. He was here, at the head of his host, facing the man who had persuaded Takelot's grandfather to pass over his own blood in the line of succession. The gods were with him, but they were fickle beings and their favour was far from guaranteed, regardless of the daily offerings and sacrifices he had ordered. He would be remembered for eternity or he would fall into oblivion.

When the choice was as stark as that it became no choice at all.

Takelot had taken to walking through his camp, eschewing the unreachable sense of divinity that many pharaohs, including his own grandfather, had fostered about themselves. Such familiarity could only be taken so far though, and he was mindful of preserving the vanities of his stations. He maintained the blue crown of war, and bright pigments burnished his skin to a flawless bronze lustre, balancing his appearance between that of a man and that of a god. He passed the chariot cohorts and the clusters of tents hosting the archer regiments and the legions of spearmen, thousands of men from the southern cities standing side by side for him and him alone.

The camp was built on a low rise, looking down onto featureless plains that stretched far into the distance. Clusters of rock lined the horizon where there was a natural bend in the river, promising the Thebans more than ample warning once the Tanites came within sight. The camp, itself the size of a small town, was surrounded by a wooden palisade the height of two men. An archers' walkway three paces wide spanned the inside edge, providing enough room to shoot freely but with little room to move. Against a determined foe it would not last long, but Takelot hoped it would at least slow Shoshenq's warriors if the worst should happen and they were beaten in the field.

'I commend you, my generals. You have chosen well,' said Takelot, leading his entourage onto the ramparts where they could survey the battlefield proper. Barely a rock marred the surface of the plain now, but it would be littered with thousands of corpses in the days ahead, if Shoshenq refused to back down.

Such was the cost of securing the dynasty.

Kaphiri and Ukhesh bowed their heads, the former grim and reserved, while the latter, the commander of the Hermopolis forces, smiled contentedly.

'There is no better position. At least, not with the time we have,' said Ukhesh. He lowered his voice, directing his next words for Pharaoh and the two others standing with him. 'With respect, my king, it's going to be a bloodbath when Shoshenq lands.'

Takelot's eyes narrowed, but Ukhesh stood his ground, meeting Pharaoh's flinty gaze with his own. The king turned away first and greeted the fourth member of the war council. 'Great Chief Pediese, you honour us with your presence.'

'The honour is mine, Pharaoh Takelot,' said Pediese, bowing low at the waist. His robes flowed around him, the beads in his beard jingling with his every word. He smiled at the grimness around him, ignoring Kaphiri's pessimism. He was always smiling, Takelot noted. 'Long have my people held the great cities of Egypt in awe and admiration,' continued the Great Chief. 'My bow arm aches to wage war beside you.'

'I am glad to hear it. We have the high ground, so it may not come to that. Perhaps the fool usurper can be reasoned with when it comes time to fight.'

Kaphiri snorted. 'You truly have hope that any of this can be avoided?'

Takelot fixed Kaphiri with a level glare. 'I always have hope. The gods work in mysterious ways that even their most devout servants cannot fully comprehend, and we cannot know Shoshenq's thoughts entirely. Mind your tone, general.'

Kaphiri grunted and crossed his arms, looking out over the battlefield once more.

Takelot turned to the others. 'We will fight defensively and attack only if attacked first. I want to make that abundantly clear to you all. Understood, Ukhesh?'

Ukhesh nodded but Takelot could see the hunger in the other man's eyes. 'Understood, lord. A few hundred more chariots would be no bad thing though. That would send them scurrying back home. To have your sons standing beside us would make my heart sing.'

'Bakenptah remains in Herakleopolis, Osorkon in the Crag of Amun. Should we fail here, the legacy of our kingdom falls to my sons. I will not order them into a suicidal attack.'

'Just us, my lord?' said Ukhesh.

'If you want to leave the main force and try for a flank attack against men who have faced the Assyrian cataphracts, then I will take that under advisement, General Ukhesh. In any case, Great Chief Pediese will act as our flanking reserve. His riders are faster than our chariots and his archers no less accurate.' Takelot acknowledged the Meshwesh leader with a nod. 'Send out your scouts, Great Chief. Harry their supply lines and break their formations as they land upriver. Burn their food and make them terrified to sleep. I would see them stung like a hyena at a beehive before their banners show on the horizon.'

'As Pharaoh wills,' grinned Pediese. The Great Chief nodded to the Egyptian commanders in turn and then, with a flourish, swept away to rally his men.

'A curious man,' said Kaphiri, watching the chief disappear inside the fort.

'Osorkon places great faith in him, and so shall I,' said Takelot. 'Now we have much work to do. Our best hope, if it comes to it, is to break their front lines with arrows and fire. A crushing first blow will damage their resolve more resoundingly then a protracted campaign.'

'The potters and magicians report they are on schedule,' said Kaphiri, answering the unspoken question.

'Good, inform them they have two more days to finish their preparations. Then we must put their work to use,' said Takelot, turning from the vista before him to leave his generals on the ramparts. 'We cannot afford to be unprepared when Shoshenq finally reveals himself. Gods know that we need every advantage we can find.'

THE ATMOSPHERE OF the Crag of Amun, Great of Roaring, was quiet and subdued, the fortress falling into familiar rhythms as they waited for word from the war. Few among the garrison did not know men who had marched north under the king's banner, and the brutal arithmetic of battle meant that many would never see their friends, brothers, or cousins again.

The idleness of life in a defensive garrison suited them not at all, for the charioteers were men of action, addicts of speed and the glory of charging into battle on an open plain. Standing behind walls was little different to being imprisoned to many of the garrison and when frequent petitions to the Prince of the Crag had fallen on seemingly deaf ears, Akhetep had been forced to make concessions, allowing the charioteers to conduct scouting missions of no more than a single day's travel.

Osorkon knew of this, and yet he could not bring himself to leave his quarters. The visions he had experienced under the influence of the Meshwesh poison scarred his waking vision. The sight of the armada filled him with dread. He had not known there were so many ships in all of Egypt, let alone those under the command of the Tanite king. Even against every ship from Aswan to Herakleopolis the naval battle to come would be a bitter and gruelling fight, and for the life of him, Osorkon did not know who would emerge the victor.

The vision of the bloodshed outside the gates of Thebes likewise filled him with foreboding. Who would dare attack travellers on the road so close to his city? Had bandits taken control of the countryside? Osorkon had never heard of such daring, no less seen it, and the truth of what it might mean filled him with foreboding. Had Isetweret's rule failed, somehow? Was she even now in danger, waiting for her brothers to come to her aid?

The last words of his uncle, the Nomarch Khonsefankh, came back to him, dredged from his memory by a new and fearful conjecture. *You are betrayed. Thebes has turned against you*, the nomarch had said, even as he fell to his own brother's blade. The thought of the nomarch's betrayal had been unthinkable enough, but had Thebes followed Herakleopolis into treachery? Did those words, dismissed as the ramblings of a spiteful and dying mind, hold some truth?

Fear and doubt warred within his mind, each gaining ascendance and then fading away, only to regain its strength as inevitable as the cycle of night and day.

Perhaps neither of them was right. Perhaps it had been a poison-induced dream and his greatest fears had simply taken form in his tortured, dreaming state.

Then again, perhaps both were real.

He had heard of such power before. The High Priests, after years of divine communion, were said to gain an insight granted by their god that went beyond mortal comprehension, possessing knowledge and sight that they had no other possibility of knowing or seeing.

Was the Meshwesh method a shortcut to that power?

He had prayed for guidance, spending long hours in quiet contemplation, surrounded by incense smoke and piles of devotional texts, seeking some insight into what he had seen. The room was dim and the windows drawn, keeping his thoughts in the perpetual twilight between wakefulness and sleep. He told himself the darkness was required, the candles unlit to encourage his mind to turn within, but the truth was rather more pained.

The candles had been extinguished on his wedding night, an extravagance that he had bought for the occasion when oil lamps would have easily sufficed. He could not bring himself to light them again, some part of him wishing to leave everything as it had been, as though it were a bas relief of a night he would remember with a bittersweet fondness until his dying day. Grimly, he recognised that if his visions were true, that day could be sooner rather than later.

He opened his eyes as the sound of commotion outside his door stirred his thoughts to wakefulness. He frowned at the intrusion. Unless Shoshenq had already won and now marched upon them, he had given express orders to be left in seclusion. So far, every man under his command had respected his wishes. The door burst open and suddenly he understood why.

'Karoadjet,' he murmured, looking up at her through sleep-crusted eyes.

Rage contorted her features, her beauty terrifying and alluring at once. Behind her, Irbekh, one of his chamber guard, followed her in, his expression pained and fearful.

'My lord, I am sorry. She would not listen,' he said, falling to his knees.

'If the walls of this fortress could not stop her, then you did not stand a chance, Irbekh. You are dismissed.'

Irbekh nodded and closed the door with a soft click, leaving Karoadjet alone in the doorway trembling with anger. She had been crying, Osorkon saw.

'Since you will not see me, I thought I would come myself and see what was so important. Who is she?'

Osorkon's thoughts were still sluggish, but this was not the direction he imagined this confrontation would take. 'What?'

'Who is she? The woman that keeps you occupied while I languish back in the house of my parents. One of your charioteers' widows, or is it an army whore? Answer me!'

Osorkon laughed then, overcome with the humour of utter hopelessness. Karoadjet crossed her arms, momentarily wrong-footed. Her confusion only made Osorkon laugh more. It was likely that no man had ever dared laugh at a beauty like Karoadjet before.

He wiped away tears and reached out to her. 'My love, there is no other woman. There never will be. I love you and only you.'

Mollified for the moment, she accepted his touch though her movements were stiff. 'Then why do you avoid me? Answer me that at least, coward.'

Osorkon smiled at her. 'You are right. I am afraid. I am afraid that when I march south, I will never see you again. I fear that you will be widowed before your time.'

Her anger gave way to confusion. 'South? The war lies north.'

'The war lies all around us. Thebes has betrayed my father, betrayed me, I think. I am a prince without a kingdom. I must go south to find the truth of the matter and set it right if the Rule of Ma'at has been upset in my absence.'

Karoadjet sat beside him on the bed and took his hands in her own. 'How do you know these things? Has there been word from your sister?'

'No, and it is that too that concerns me. The ways of the Meshwesh are strange, but they reveal things beyond mortal means. I flew as an eagle flies, and I saw strife in Thebes. At least, I think I did. I cannot explain it any other way,' said Osorkon.

To his surprise, Karoadjet accepted his words without argument. She laid a cool hand on his cheek and he sighed at her touch. 'What does your heart tell you?'

'That my father was both right and wrong. Thebes has been upset, and there is only one power left in that city that would dare turn against Hory and Isetweret. If Thebes is lost, it is the priesthood of Amun that has betrayed us. I do not know under whose design, but my home has been taken from me by men I once called friends.'

Karoadjet frowned. 'How could the priests have taken the city? They have no soldiers to call upon. They would not dare.'

'I do not know, but that too unsettles me. Something has changed. I can feel it. Tell me, the mood in Herakleopolis. Is it stable?' he asked.

'Stable enough,' replied Karoadjet. 'Bakenptah's works on the temples have employed many and your mother has managed to mollify most of the nobility.'

'Then I will empty the Crag of the Royal Charioteers. I do not know what I will face on the road south, but I will need every man in this fortress in the coming days.' Osorkon rose unsteadily to his feet, feeling unused muscles ache and pull tight.

Karoadjet reached out to steady him. 'Then why do you hesitate? Return south and crush them before they have the chance to amass before our walls.'

'That is not all I saw. Shoshenq has amassed an armada the likes of which the world has never seen. My father is outnumbered. The army will not survive battle with Tanis.' Osorkon slipped his hands from Karoadjet's and rubbed eyes that felt filled with grit. 'It is an impossible choice.'

'You saw beyond your own eyes. I would have thought that impossible,' said Karoadjet. 'Now you are seized by indecision. That is unlike the prince I first met. You have spent too long in the dark.' She stepped away and pulled the curtains aside. Bright light flooded the room, making Osorkon clamp his eyes shut and wince. The smoke swirled as fresh air blew into the room, disturbing the sanctum he had built for himself. 'You cannot wait here until the choice is made for you,' she said.

'Forsake my father or forsake my city?'

'I never said it was an easy choice,' snapped Karoadjet. She softened her tone. 'Your father knows what he is doing. He has the armies of three cities with him and a few more charioteers will not change the outcome if it turns against him.' She stood before him again, lifting his chin up with gentle fingers to look her in the eyes. 'If what you say is true, then a dire threat to our security is in the south. Whatever the designs of the priests, they do not bode well for our family. You will have to fight them one way or another. At least now you can choose the battlefield.'

Osorkon's heart ached. For the love he bore for this fierce woman and for the need to send his men back into the fray. 'I do not know what awaits me in Thebes, nor do I know what madness has seized the land, or if Karnak has found its own military strength. There is much gold in the vaults beneath Karnak and no shortage of mercenaries in the land. Whatever has happened, I will cut the head of the snake and leave it hissing in the sands.'

Osorkon nodded slowly as he spoke, his mind turning over the logistics of a campaign he had never thought he would need to fight.

'Irbekh.'

The door opened once more and Irbekh stepped in. His eyes darted to Karoadjet, standing beside his lord, her previous anger gone.

'Send word to Herakleopolis. I need to speak with my brother. Today,' said Osorkon.

Irbekh nodded and closed the door, but not before Osorkon caught the crease of a smile tease the corners of the guard's mouth. His men would have what they desired, a chance to chase the glory they craved. Though in what form that would come was yet to be seen.

Most of the charioteers had family in Thebes, and it would be a delicate thing to set them on the warpath against their own city.

Karoadjet looked sideways at him and a new look came over her. 'I believe we were interrupted before,' she said. 'Once more before the war?' She reached under his shendyt with her right hand as her left worked at the ties at his waist. The breath caught in Osorkon's throat as the desire stirred within him. He groaned at her touch and allowed himself to be pushed back onto the bed as Karoadjet leaned over him.

She took him in her mouth, and he closed his eyes and thought of nothing else.

# Chapter Nineteen

THE STEW WAS brackish and bubbling, filled with grit and coated with a fine layer of floating dust. The few slivers of fish were almost rotten and mostly bones, and the scant chunks of root vegetables were hard and unripe. A few sprigs of wild herbs, found by a hunter in Sarasesh's section, gave it a bitter and stringent flavour that burned on the way down.

Sarasesh gulped it all without hesitation, holding out his broken clay mug for more before the last man had had his first. The pirate leader of his section laughed and filled it up from the boiling cauldron in the middle of the circle of men. Though the cup billowed with steam, he finished it in one, feeling the warmth suffuse his belly and a comfortable numbness fill his limbs.

'Damned fool,' grunted the man next to him, a bearded fellow with thin hair and hanging jowls. Like the section leader, Sarasesh had never bothered to learn the man's name. 'You'll have to shit soon. We've been living off nothing but water and bread crusts for days.'

Sarasesh smiled and did not care, licking the last of the stew from the bowl. Around him, the warriors of Malkesh joked, placing bets on when Sarasesh's bowels would loosen.

The priest ignored them all, used to their cruel jibes and taunts. Though the horde around him was a mix of peoples from Nubians, Meshwesh, and even dispossessed Egyptians from beyond the cataracts, they treated him, and him alone, as an outsider. He was a priest of the enemy. He was representative of the people they preyed upon.

And since his discovery that he was still useful to Malkesh, and so beyond their punishment, he had never stopped reminding them of it.

'Perhaps I will use your eating bowl,' he said to the jowled man. 'You could do with more food, and being from beyond the First Cataract you should be used to the taste.' The others laughed at the jibe at the jowled man threw down his empty bowl and stormed off.

'You have hurt Tesh's feelings,' said the pirate, with a wry grin.

Sarasesh shrugged and helped himself to the scraps crusted on the edge of the cauldron. 'I care not,' said Sarasesh.

The grin slipped of the pirate's face. 'We know, priest. And don't think we have forgotten it.'

Sarasesh ignored the man's threats, constant as they were. Over the weeks since his indenture, he had slowly inured himself to the threat of death and the unceasing pain. Most of all, he had inured himself to the poison in his spirit. He sat shoulder to shoulder with men he hated. He knew it in his soul, or what was left of it, that he hated them, but as he lapped thankfully at an offering that would have offended him mere months ago, he felt curiously light.

The beatings had lessened, in intensity if not frequency, and the exhaustion and privation of the campaign had given his body a curious, emaciated lightness. He wondered if the others felt it too, but as he looked around the campfires, he saw hollow faces and grey pallors.

Men stronger than he had ever been now lay dead on the road behind. Men of all colour and creed, none were immune to the deprivations they had suffered. Those that could pass for Egyptian from the coastal lands of the Red Sea, like Malkesh himself, were starved just as much as the dispossessed warriors of Nubia or the tribesmen of the Western Desert.

Few had the strength for more than muttered conversation, and even fewer bothered looking up, their eyes fixed on their own thin brackish soup as they fished out the few lumps of mushy grain as though they were sublime delicacies.

A disturbance far along the ridge drew Sarasesh's attention, the sound of scuffles and raised voices reaching them like a wave. A tall and terrible shadow moved between the campfires, low light casting long shadows along the rocky ground. Ripples of unease swept through the gatherings as recognition spread at the speed of thought, and warriors who only days ago had slaughtered villagers so cruelly and mercilessly now whined like frightened dogs.

Sarasesh knew the shadow would be coming for him and fixed the warlord and his retinue with level stare. Malkesh came to stand at the edge of their firelight, his bodyguard spreading out around neighbouring fires and watching, always watching.

Malkesh's eyes bored into Sarasesh and the priest was pinned, his mind going blank but for the image of the terrible yellow eyes of a lion in the moment before it springs to attack. The men of Sarasesh's section went silent, their eyes fixed on their feet or the dregs of their meal.

Even the pirate leader, a self-proclaimed member of Malkesh's original crew, averted his gaze and all but crawled out of the warlord's eyeline.

'Come with me,' the warlord rumbled. He turned and walked away without bothering to wait for Sarasesh to follow him. Malkesh's retinue fell in behind their leader, but for a pair of warriors that formed up behind Sarasesh as a rear guard and prisoner escort.

Sarasesh wanted to laugh. What hope was there for escape in a horde such as this?

For all their poverty, Malkesh's warriors still numbered in their many thousands, but their attacks had taken on a more frantic undertone in the last fortnight. Word of their coming had begun to spread, and the horde came across more and more villages that had been entirely abandoned and stripped of everything of value.

There was no hope of following their prey. At each abandoned town, clusters of single-mast fishing boats were spied tied together on the far bank, where the townspeople had made their escape across the river.

Frustrated and hungry, the horde tore apart the humble huts and houses, searching in vain for something, anything that had been left behind. Every building and store had been picked clean of tools and cloth, and the last three villages they had encountered had poured water over what little grain they could not carry with them, spoiling the crop into a rancid mess, fit only for rats and other vermin.

The scraps they did find were viciously fought over. In the last village they had found, a hundred men lay dead where they had fallen in storerooms and town squares, abandoned and left to feed the creatures of the desert.

Malkesh sent hunting parties into the desert, but after the failures of the first few nights, subsequent hunting parties had vanished into the desert, never to return.

Dead or deserters, no one looked for them.

Sarasesh followed the warlord through the camp for a few minutes more, weaving his way through campfires and passing by hundreds of silent and wary faces. Haunted eyes followed his passage and as he looked closer, he realised his section's fare was a feast compared to that endured by some.

Then there was silence and darkness and blessed open space. Away from the confines of the horde, Sarasesh breathed deep of the cool desert air, feeling it brace him with phantom strength. The night-time temperatures swiftly brought a shiver to his wasted flesh and he pulled his rags a little tighter around him as they walked.

Malkesh led them down into the valley basin and the sweet sound of the river lapping at the shore stirred a surge of emotion in the battered priest. In the darkness, the great black shadow of the *Sobek is Content* gently rolled with the river's tides, straining at the mooring ropes hammered into the riverbank. A single lantern fluttered into life at Malkesh's return, a soft beacon in the darkness, guiding its new master to his prize.

Sarasesh waded into the shallows, feeling the water tug at him and waiting for the moment a crocodile would tear him apart as divine punishment from Sobek himself. The freezing chill bit deeper as the current reached waist-high and then to his armpits.

His arms were weak and frail and he clung to the rope ladder, needing two men to help haul him onto the deck. He hit the timbers hard, laying there breathless for a few moments until a nameless sailor hauled him to his feet.

Malkesh stood beside the helmsman, the priest's presence momentarily forgotten as the *Sobek is Content* slipped its moorings and floated downriver. Sarasesh did his best to keep out of the way, the warlord's finest sailors from their days of pillaging the Red Sea given the honour of crewing his new vessel. Their expertise made getting the small sailing ship underway a choreographed dance of effortless efficiency.

Sarasesh settled in as the ship drifted north under an endless tapestry of stars above. He did not dare ask their destination, and the crew largely ignoring him but for snarled commands to move when ropes needed adjusting. They sailed for hours, and Sarasesh slept fitfully, pressed up against the railing, nestled against a coil of rope for comfort.

He was awoken to the sound of feet thudding against the deck. He sat bolt upright to see the lookout steady himself against the mast before he clambered up towards the helm.

'This is the place, lord,' assured the lookout. 'The scouts said they saw it from the heights of that cliff. The finger of stone.'

Malkesh followed the lookout's finger to a rocky outcrop at the top of the valley basin. True to the lookout's description it was a pillar of rock jutting like a pointed finger, bent and craggy. 'Bring us in,' he ordered.

The *Sobek* docked a few minutes later, and Malkesh led them ashore, climbing the steep slopes to the ridge above.

The march up to the clifftop filled Sarasesh with dread. Twice, he stumbled in a snake hole and was rewarded with a rough shove from the man behind. His breath came in ragged gasps, the stew churning in his belly as he climbed higher and higher. His vision swam as he finally reached level ground and he fell to his hands and knees to retch, but nothing came out. He clambered to his feet and stumbled towards the warlord and his followers at the edge of the cliff, where the lookout was now pointing animatedly.

The sight stole away what little breath Sarasesh had left.

A thin horizontal band of flickering lights broke the night, high above the ground and spaced at even intervals, dimly illuminating high walls of towering stone. Within those walls, the soft glow revealed a city of thousands upon thousands. Sarasesh knew this place, had walked its streets and drunk deep of its wisdom. It was a place of unparalleled knowledge, and steeped in the mystic arts. The city was not as immense as Thebes, nor did it rival the architectural splendour of Memphis, but it was a jewel of the Two Lands all the same. Few cities were as grand as the one before him, and there was only one place of its scale within hours' travel from where they had last made camp.

Malkesh turned from the sight. 'My scouts found this city. What is its name?'

You don't even know where you are, thought Sarasesh with disgust. Instead, the priest bowed low and replied, 'That is Hermopolis, seat of the great god Thoth, He of wisdom and writing, Lord of Heka-'

Malkesh silenced him with an impatient wave of his hand. 'Who rules this city?'

Sarasesh shrugged. 'The priests of the ibis-headed one. I do not know who leads them, but they rule the city as a council.'

'Priests like you?'

Sarasesh shook his head. 'No, I serve Amun, not the Master of Magic.'

'But priests all the same,' said Malkesh, a smile twitching at the corner of his mouth. 'And tell me, priest. How would a man take such a city, so mighty are its walls and rich are its treasures?'

'A man wouldn't. This is no village rabble. The walls of Hermopolis are high and its people well-armed. Unless you plan to burn down their walls and slaughter your own forces in the process, it is useless to even consider. This is not some village rabble. Not to mention its leaders are steeped in the mystic arts. Their knowledge of magic is unparalleled. If you attack that city, you will fail and you will die.'

The warlord's warriors bristled at his tone, but Malkesh barked a command and they ceased their menace. 'You misunderstand. It was not a request. When your kings fight each other as they do now, how do they break open cities like this one?'

Sarasesh frowned. 'Our deal was to head north and confront Takelot, not to attack Hermopolis. It was-'

Malkesh moved faster than a man of his size should have been able, his meaty fist clocking into the side of the priest's head with the force of a blacksmith's hammer. Sarasesh crumpled, his ears ringing and his vision wavering. The warlord knelt beside him, his eyes glittering dangerously in the dark.

'I know the bargain we made. I am altering it. Do not forget, it was your former master who bid me raze your country and I have done just that. To take this city as the seat of my new kingdom would lend your cause tremendous strength.'

'Your new kingdom?!' hissed Sarasesh, spitting a mouthful of blood onto the sand. 'You have no kingdom, nor are you fit to rule one. Those are my people. You have already preyed upon enough Egyptians. No more.'

Malkesh grunted. 'I grow tired of your protests. Cease to be useful and you become one more useless mouth to feed. Remember that.'

'We have already tarried here too long. We must press on to the war. Takelot is still out there,' shouted Sarasesh, but Malkesh had already turned his back.

'We will take those boats from the last village and ferry our people across to the western bank,' said the warlord to his men.

'That will take days,' protested Sarasesh, groaning as he climbed to his knees.

'Yes,' agreed Malkesh, over his shoulder. 'And when we do, we will crack open this city and drink deep of the spoils within. Aren't you hungry, little priest?'

'We all are. Your army is starving to death,' snapped Sarasesh.

'Then we will feast like kings, tended to by an army of slaves.' Malkesh turned and began the trek back down into the valley. 'Come. Tomorrow, we begin. Pray that you are still of use to us.'

Sarasesh felt his bowels spasm. It was not from the food.

IN SIMPLER TIMES, the nobility of Thebes served as the divide between Pharaoh and the masses of common humanity. A vital structure in the fabric of Egyptian society, it was the nobility that kept the poor toiling the fertile flood plains and harvesting the bounty of the river. It was the nobility that served in the priesthoods, maintained the officer corps of the army, and conducted the commerce and mercantile pursuits that maintained Thebes as one of the most important commercial hubs in the known world. Had any bothered to consider their position, with their military leaders absent, their merchants growing ever poorer, and their priests seduced by corruption, the events of the day might not have come as a surprise, but rather as an unfortunate inevitability.

Under Senmut, the nobles of Thebes were little better than the commoners they professed to lord over. None were beyond fear, and none, Senmut had crowed, were beyond his retribution.

In the early hours of the morning, when the protection of sun and moon were at their weakest, the district of the nobles was emptied. Soldiers of the temples, loyal only to Senmut, went from house to house, driving the noble families out onto the streets in various stages of undress and disarray. Priests of the new First Prophet walked among them, shouting devotional prayers and platitudes to the great god Amun on behalf of Blessed Senmut.

Few were fool enough to argue. Those that did were beaten and dragged away, leaving behind screaming and terrified families who were nonetheless herded onwards. As the streets converged and the threads of disparate nobility became one, the lords and ladies of Thebes slowly began to realise the magnitude of their complacency.

Pedubast walked among the crowds, Iuput trailing at his side. The soldiers largely ignored them, their priestly vestments an assurance of their loyalty. Despite the fear around him, Pedubast smiled at that. It had not taken much to goad Senmut into rash action and turn the whole city, or at least those that mattered, against his insanity.

As Pedubast had known it would, the thought of conspiracy against him would send Senmut's thoughts into a self-destructive spiral, but as the brothers marched onward, the hint of misgiving grew in Pedubast's heart.

Though Pedubast expected some kind of spectacle, surely even Senmut could not execute the entire city. Likely, the High Priest had captured some unfortunate that had crossed the High Priest's impossible standards one too many times and decided to make an example of him.

Pedubast found himself ushered into a vast square. He pulled Iuput close to him as the flood of humanity filled out the space, stretching from the edge of the buildings to the stairs ascending to the Vizier's palace. Despite its size, the square was almost filled to capacity with the city's nobility. Even in their dishevelment, there could be no mistake as to their identity. Their finery was too well-crafted, their cloth too well-woven and the hairlessness of their bodies too perfect to be anything but servant-shaven.

At the top of the palace stairs, beneath the great portal of the entranceway, two priests came to stand before the mass of humanity. High Priest Senmut strode forth, raising his hands for quiet as the murmur of the crowd reached a new height. The ever-faithful Naroleth stood behind him, his arms stiff by his side in the manner of pharaonic statues, but with none of the grace nor majesty. To Pedubast's surprise, the nobles complied, hundreds of faces staring fearfully at the portly figure on the palace steps.

'My friends, my people,' began Senmut, his voice carrying over the hush. 'I have dark tidings, but also those of light. The gods have spoken. The war in the north will soon be over and the punishment Takelot deserves shall come unto him. Your countrymen, your own husbands, fathers and sons die for his vanity, but that will come to pass now that Thebes is in the rightful hands of the gods' servants.'

Pedubast heard the hum of the crowd and felt the ripple of discontent thread through every woman and man. With that, he could have owned them all, but Senmut was not to be denied his spectacle.

'But I have darker news. Within this very city, within these walls, there are plots afoot to upset the new order. Karnak is your rightful lord. Only those who hear the words of the gods can guide you through these uncertain times to a future of glory. The desires of men have led us all astray. None are more anguished than I at Takelot's folly, but the gods of this land will guide us true and I am their chosen voice.'

A murmur erupted at his proclamation. None knew whether to acclaim him or stay silent and out of sight. Pedubast could not blame them. He gave Iuput a warning glance that even his brother would understand.

'Some of you doubt me. I see the truth in your eyes. There are false men and women among you. Liars and corrupters, they who work against our people. I will show you what happens to such lost souls. Behold!'

Senmut threw his arms above his head, pointing towards the top of the palace façade. Every face, young and old, looked skyward to the height of the palace wall.

Pedubast squinted in the glare of the rising sun. Three figures inched towards the edge of the roof, a soaring height of some ten metres or more. The men and women of Thebes craned their necks to look up and a hush descended upon the crowd once more.

Senmut grinned as he looked down at them all.

'Behold the death of impious nobility!'

His arms fell and the central figure was cast down over the edge.

The only sound to split the air was the man's terrified scream as he plummeted toward the steps far below. His scream was abruptly cut off as the ropes fastened around his ankles snapped taut and he slammed bodily into the façade with bone-breaking force.

Pedubast hoped the man was dead. He watched in horrified fascination as the rope around the figure's legs jangled. In death spasms or in agony, he could not tell, but a thin trickle of blood spilled from the man's head down to the stone steps at Senmut's feet.

'You have seen the death of cursed blood,' proclaimed Senmut. 'For here, Hory, son of Nakhtefmut, shall hang until his bones fall to the earth. Look upon his ruin and despair.'

Hory was dead. If not now, then soon, as the blood rushed to his head and he died in prolonged, throbbing agony. Fear lanced through Pedubast's heart, even as the rational part of him rejoiced in the horrifying display. The boy's death was regrettable, but Pedubast knew he had made the right choice in provoking Senmut to this dreadful excess.

The silence of the crowd was absolute, the horror and disgust in the air an almost tangible force. Pedubast's thoughts turned quickly to Isetweret, still hidden away in the upper storey of his home.

'The flame that burns brightest burns out the fastest,' he murmured as he watched the spasms of the Vizier fade into trembling, then stillness.

The High Priest was not done.

'Behold the price of blasphemy. None may stand in falsehood before Amun's light. The ruin of Sekhmet shall come for the false ones, and I will send them to it! Go back to your homes. The marketplaces shall cease for today in penitence, but tomorrow you may resume commerce under the eyes of the gods. Go now. Go and pray for deliverance.'

No one spoke. No father offered hollow words to comfort to his family, and no mother tried to hush her frightened and confused children, for even the littlest among them was already tight-lipped with fear. None dared say a word as the square emptied and the Theban nobility returned to the false comfort of their homes.

In contrast to his father, Hory had been a gentle soul. Ineffective, and nothing more than a footnote in the histories of greater men, but possessed of qualities all too often lacking in the powerful. None present could have honestly spoken against the boy's character.

As Pedubast walked back to the street of his own house, he felt the stirrings of dissent, the sideways looks between friends that transcended religious and political loyalties. Like a clan of hyena waiting for the first of their number to move against a lion, the nobility checked their strength.

Pedubast walked through the front door and sat down at the table, his head falling into his hands as he heard the sound of footsteps padding across the floor above his head.

There was no going back now.

THE FIRST SAILS of the fleet of Tanis came over the horizon just two days later. Against a backdrop of blue sky and golden sand, the first white speck was joined by another, then a dozen more, and finally a fleet of more than a hundred sails floating upriver with alarming alacrity.

On the walls of Takelot's fort, the first cries went up, the alarm spreading to all corners of the army within minutes. Flags stained black with ash were waved from the fort's ramparts and the combined fleets of Thebes, Hermopolis and Herakleopolis set their mainsails in response, weighing anchor and clearing the decks one last time of anything not needed in the fury of battle.

Takelot was knelt in morning prayer when his camp came alive. A small altar to Amun had been erected in his private tent. It was a poor substitute, but one that Takelot hoped the god would notice in all his beneficent wisdom.

He left the tapers burning and rose on protesting legs. He winced at the tension, a pained smile tugging at the corner of his mouth. The kingship was a heavy burden, at times a physical weight that seemed to accelerate time's curse upon his mind and body.

He limped to a desk and took up his burnished bronze mirror. A stern, patrician face gazed back at him with the high cheekbones and dark eyes of his Libyan heritage. Dark shadow marred his cheeks where he had shaved himself and already his scalp prickled with new growth. His eyes were tired, deep circles staining his skin like bruises, seeming to grow with every sleepless night. Wrinkles at the edge of his eyes deepened as the cares and worries of campaign settled upon him, and his cheekbones were more prominent than he remembered them being.

He rinsed his face, the cool water going some way to bringing his thoughts into focus. He sat at his desk, his mirror held in his left hand, and began to reapply his cosmetics. He allowed himself this vanity, for he was Pharaoh, and he would face his enemies as such.

A cough at the tent's entrance made him turn.

Berekhef of the Theban Royal Guard stood a discreet distance away and coughed again. 'My king, the Tanites are here.'

'Thank you, Berekhef. Help me here, please.'

Berekhef laid his spear against the wall and tied the clasp to his king's gold-link necklace. He glanced at the blue war crown, and Takelot nodded, allowing the soldier to touch the divine artefact and place it on Takelot's brow.

Takelot held up the mirror again. 'Suitable, I hope?'

'Like Amun himself, sire.'

Takelot smiled at the flattery and slipped his dress of bronze scale armour over his head, letting Berekhef secure the knots at his sides and hips before he belted his sword and dagger to his waist. The armour was heavy, but he felt a new power flow through his limbs as he studied his reflection again, noting the divine perfection in every scale.

He nodded once and readied himself for what was to come.

'Lead the way, Berekhef,' Takelot commanded, and followed the soldier outside.

Takelot stepped into the sunshine and was greeted by the sight of an army on the move. The Royal Guards fell in behind their king as he made his way through the sea of tents to the front walls. Camp fires were hastily extinguished, sending plumes of smoke up into the air. Spare equipment was stowed away, and tents were left in order as the men made their way to their units' muster points. Soldiers bowed as he passed, keeping well clear of the Royal Guard, though they craned their necks for a glimpse of their lord and master. Here and there, soldiers checked and rechecked their equipment, while others spoke quiet sentiments to their friends and brothers.

Takelot climbed the ramparts, taking his premier place among his chosen warriors. Generals Ukhesh and Kaphiri were already there, bowing to their king as he nodded in greeting. The archers and spearmen on the walls watched their leaders in awe, these titans among men that could command the obeisance of thousands with a single word.

The plains were vast and empty, utterly featureless but for the odd rock or patch of recently disturbed earth. His craftsmen and magicians had worked long into the night, and now slept soundly at the rear of the fort, their service complete.

Takelot hoped their magic would be enough.

The northern horizon was broken up by rock formations that his scouts had assured him were nigh impassable to standard formations and chariots. As Takelot watched, the ridges and shadowed areas of the rock line seemed to bend and buckle, shimmering like heat haze. The rock line rippled and seemed to grow and thicken and Takelot's eyes narrowed as he witnessed the folly of his scouts. The army of Tanis marched over rock and sand in long thin lines, coalescing into ranks on the far side of the plain, streaming over the geological formations like floodwater after a long drought.

Takelot turned his back to the approaching enemy and raised his hands for the attention of his army behind the walls.

'Men of Thebes,' he began. The silence stretched out and the king could hear the flutter of regimental pennants on the walls behind him. Rank upon rank of soldiers, drawn from every city between the garrison to the First Cataract in the far south, now hung on his every word.

'Men of Hermopolis, Herakleopolis and the Western Desert. The hordes of Tanis descend upon us. Shoshenq's warriors failed to defeat the Assyrians and they will fail in their aggression against their own kinsmen!'

Takelot raised his spear as the rallying cry went up.

'My heart breaks that it has come to this. I loved Shoshenq as a brother when he was still called Senneker, but vile ambition wormed its way into his heart, and he took my throne from me. Even then, I held him in high regard, but I will not be party to the Tanite belief that the southern cities, all of us here and now, are theirs to bleed dry!'

Takelot slammed the butt of the spear down onto the rampart. The sound was lost but the gesture drew fresh roars from his men.

'My own nephews died in Shoshenq's foreign war and the grief drove my brother mad. Shoshenq asks everything of us. No, not asks. He demands it, at the point of a spear! He takes our men to bleed for him, he takes our food to feed his own people, he takes our supplies from our temples and our gods. And now, he wants to take our land. To force us into slavery to fuel his own glory!'

Anger now rolled through the ranks at the king's words, jeering cries that shouted vile abuse at the very men now coming over the horizon.

'I ask everything of you, my friends. More than I ever wanted to ask.' Takelot pitched his voice low, his expression mournful and filled with regret. 'If we lose, our way of life is forfeit. Our sons will grow into slave warriors fit only to die on foreign sands. Our daughters will work bent-backed in the fields to feed the nobility of the Delta cities. Thebes, Hermopolis and Herakleopolis will fade, their glories forgotten.'

Takelot let their anger burn, their jeers and insults and cries of disbelief a sweet music to him. They would need all of that anger if they were to repel Shoshenq's forces. The king raised his hands for quiet, waiting for every murmur to fade away before he spoke again.

'If we win, if we throw Shoshenq's hyenas back to Tanis yelping and crying, we will have secured a future for our people. We will have won a generation of peace. Follow me this one last time and your sons and daughters will grow up in a land without the need to bear a sword. We will live in peace and security, without fear and without enemies. We will win glory for the ages. None shall be forgotten.'

The soldiers roared with approval, crashing spear and shield together in a deafening chorus of assent. Takelot smiled down upon his followers and flung his right arm out.

Ten thousand heads turned with his gesture and his voice rang out once more.

'Look to the east, and know our battle is joined by our noble sailors. Now, archers to the battlements, spears follow me. It is time to send these curs howling back to the Delta.'

RUIN OF SEKHMET

# Chapter Twenty

THE FLAGSHIP OF the Tanite fleet cut through the river waters with all the grace of a raging bull. Its prow, carved into the form of the falcon of Horus, cut through the river, bearing down on the Theban coalition fleet with gleeful retribution.

The wind had picked up, and it was blowing with the fleet of Tanis. The breath of the gods howled from the north, filling the sails and straining the tack with a supernatural enthusiasm for the battle to come. Behind Shoshenq's throne, the ship's captain hauled red-faced on the tiller, the coxswain struggling next to him. Both men wrestled with the vessel to keep it in formation and face the coalition fleet straight on.

The *Wrath of Tanis* was not alone in its struggle.

What the wind provided the Tanite fleet in speed, it took back in stability. Ships of every class, from the battleships like Shoshenq's own vessel to the cutters and sloops that flanked them as escorts, yawed and pitched in the unnatural swell. The river was a sea of spray, and each of the Tanite vessels bore down on their enemy with bow waves foaming at the prow like the maw of some rabid beast. Teams of oarsmen on each side of the deck hauled the vessels forward to the tempo of each ship's drummer, adding to the fleet's charging speed.

The Tanite king himself faced the southern fleet from his throne. He watched the fleet formations without expression, following the interplay of vessels with an understanding borne of a lifetime studying warfare.

Beside him, Lamintu, the Nubian royal shield-bearer, watched the coalition fleet approach with his teeth bared. The royal bodyguard carried a brace of short stabbing spears at his waist and an enormous full-length shield on his left arm. Larger than a standard chariot shield, the Nubian warrior used it as much as a weapon as a means of defence. Shoshenq had seen him fight many times before, using that formidable shield to clear space around Pharaoh Osorkon II in the midst of battle and protecting his master from stray arrows when the royal chariots charged the archers of Assyria. That was long ago now, but the fire in the Nubian's breast remained undimmed.

To the south-west, Shoshenq made out the jagged battlements of the Theban camp. A long, sloping hill led to a sudden rise, protected on either flank by rocky terrain, anathema to the regimented formations so favoured by the Tanites. Somewhere, in that gods-forsaken pile of lumber and stone, the grandson of his predecessor challenged him. He hoped Takelot was watching now to see his fleet sunk beneath the waves of his ambition.

Shoshenq brought his attention back to the river. The coalition fleet had folded in on itself, clustering in small wedge-shaped groups and adopting defensive formations as Shoshenq had expected they would against a numerically superior foe. Outmanoeuvred, they would have to stick together and concentrate their efforts if they were to make a dent in the Tanite assault. Shoshenq's own ships hunted like leopards, each searching for their own measure of blood and glory alone, confident in the strength of their rearguard.

'Take us through them, captain. Stop for nothing,' called Shoshenq over his shoulder. The momentum from the wind carried them well, but even with the superior force he had no desire to get bogged down in ship-to-ship combat.

'As you say, sire,' replied the captain, aiming for a gap to the left of the main Theban spear-tip. To a man, the sailors onboard watched the incoming fleet with relish, willing their vessel faster into the fray.

The coalition ships had their own sails furled, the great mainsails tied away and teams of oarsmen desperately trying to reach attack speed. Their fatigue would be all the greater for the wind's fickle favour and they would be forced to keep their distance and so avoid a boarding action by the Tanites.

From his throne, Shoshenq could almost see the faces of the Theban sailors, praying to their god and beseeching the wind to turn. He imagined the sight they must face, a river's width of shining white sails bearing down on them with no quarter given or expected.

'Drummer, sound the advance,' Shoshenq commanded. 'Charging speed.'

The hollow tempo increased and the Tanite flagship started to pull away from its escort. Shoshenq smiled as he saw the ships on his flank increase their own speed to match, wishing to earn a measure of glory within sight of their king.

'Stow oars.'

The oarsmen shouted their obeisance, hauling on their great oars and stowing them behind the gunwales. Without them, a ship was at the mercy of the wind, and as the Thebans were about to discover, mercy was in short supply.

The archers nocked arrows to their bows, each man standing at position with a quiver of arrows at his hip, and stationed by spare quivers at the railings, mast and tiller. There would be no excuse for anything other than a withering concentration of fire, favouring Shoshenq's own battle philosophy: obliterate the enemy with overwhelming force and move on. Survivors would surrender or flee. It mattered not.

The flagship tacked in close, close enough to hear the insults and challenges from enemy vessels as a wave of rising noise. The Tanite sailors were silent, as Shoshenq expected of them. Save your breath for the battle to come, he had told them, and let them shout themselves hoarse so that their cries for help choke in their throats and go unheard.

The king himself shouted only one word, his voice carrying to every man on deck with ease.

'Loose!'

Dozens of arrows hissed up from the deck, rising in a high arch. The wind caught many of them, sending them to spin and fall harmlessly into the river but many more hit their mark. The Theban ship did not have the chance to reply, but Lamintu held his shield high over his king nonetheless, as agonised cries went up from the other ship.

The *Wrath of Tanis* passed the Theban spear-tip by, and Shoshenq saw his handiwork firsthand. Only a handful of the Theban sailors were down, but the deck was littered with buried and broken shafts and the king could see the Theban captain gesticulating wildly, trying desperately to restore some form of order.

The Tanite king did not give them a second glance.

'Draw.'

The second wave of Theban ships loomed ahead as the sounds of battle rang out behind the flagship's stern. Shoshenq saw the closest Theban ship was nothing more than an escort vessel, separated from its charge and floundering like a hippopotamus calf lost among a bask of crocodiles. Perhaps twenty men crewed this vessel, either hauling on oars or drawing their own bows.

In a gesture of suicidal defiance, the ship's captain brought his ship in close, the archers firing their volley up at the deck. Most of them thudded into the flagship's starboard side, wasted and desperate.

Shoshenq grunted at their defiance as an arrow thudded into the deck at his feet, snapping its shaft with the force of impact. A metre left and it would have hit him in this chest or perhaps even the side of the head. What a short end to the war that could have been, he thought with amusement.

Lamintu's lips curled, taking the arrow's presence as a personal insult.

'Fear not, noble Lamintu. Give the order,' said Shoshenq.

The Nubian grinned and roared the word like a battle cry. 'Loose!'

A second flight of arrows buzzed from the flagship's deck, arching high towards the escort vessel. Screams of pain and fear reached the king's ears, but his attention had already diverted to the battleships ahead.

Three vessels that rivalled his own flagship in scale and splendour made up the core of the coalition fleet. Two of the ships flew the colours of Herakleopolis and Hermopolis respectively, but as the distance between them closed, Shoshenq's eyes were drawn to the vessel in the centre, a monstrous battleship flying the colours of Thebes.

The *Pillar of Eternity*. Takelot's flagship.

Whether the bastard king of Thebes was on board or not, Shoshenq would have to let it pass. The two escort ships would not be so fortunate.

'Bring us in close,' he ordered. 'Come about on Herakleopolis. Let them witness their folly first.'

The sailors rushed to obey, stowing away anything not tied down. Ropes were fastened, sails loosened, and bows were secured into their racks as spears and shields were handed out. Shoshenq watched them work, keeping an eye on the enormous vessels bearing down on them.

'All hands,' he shouted. His sailors held tight to the rigging and gunwales; weapons ready but out of sight of the opposing deck. Shoshenq sat where he was, eyes peeled for a matching blue war crown on the deck of the Theban ship.

'Brace,' shouted the ship's captain, hauling on the tiller at the last second to send the armoured prow crashing into the Herakleopolitan ship with splintering force.

The air cracked with the sound of rent timber, and the entire ship lurched in the swell as the ship's bow ground against the enemy ship's flank. Shoshenq was thrown forward in his throne, and even the implacable Lamintu fell to one knee.

The Tanite flagship floundered for a moment as it regained its balance. The sail, flattened with the impact, caught a full breath of wind once more, and lurched the ship forwards again past the trio of battleships.

The ship of Herakleopolis had been damaged but not destroyed, but Shoshenq smiled with contentment that the formation had been broken. Let the treacherous southerners see that even the vessels of their lords were not immune to the wrath of Tanis.

Shoshenq led his ships through the heart of the coalition fleet and beyond, shooting down deck crews and barging aside smaller craft to open up room from the following Tanite ships. Like the blade thrust through a shield wall, Shoshenq's ship broke apart the coalition defences, forced to react to a superior battle plan.

The wind remained strong, and suddenly the river was empty. Shoshenq peered astern, at the rear of the coalition fleet, gauging how many of his vessels had made it through.

Two had already managed to break through the defences, and more were in the process of disengaging, but he counted far fewer than he had hoped. Likely his captains were taking their time and cutting apart the coalition fleet with a butcher's thoroughness.

'Run us ashore, captain. It is time.'

The ship's captain leaned hard against the tiller, pulling the flagship into the shallows high above where it should have been able to go. The *Wrath of Tanis* was of a make not often favoured by the Egyptian Empire. Shoshenq had first learned of the design from Phoenician traders when the Tanites had landed at Tyre at the outset of the Assyrian campaign.

The flagship had been designed with a proper keel, a shallow foundation letting it ride high in the water even with a full complement of chariots or cargo. The ships of the south were deeper but narrower, and so were incapable of rapid landings away from port.

Shoshenq rose from his throne, stepping down the gangway as the *Wrath of Tanis* skimmed the shallows like a bird. From the hold below, the first chariots were led slowly up the ramp onto the main deck and the blinkers and ear padding removed from the horses now that the worst of the naval engagement was over. Rock anchors were dropped into the shallows, sinking into the soft sand and bringing the vessel to a sudden halt. The water was no deeper than a man's shoulders, but the flagship drifted over it without hindrance. The portside gate was opened and planks the width of two chariots were run out, secured with clamps to the deck at one end, and sinking into the sand at the other.

Shoshenq mounted his chariot and gave the driver the signal to advance. On the driver's other side, Lamintu hung his shield on the front brace and set out the rack of spears for ease of access. Unlike most of the regular chariots, his own war machine had an extended footwell, large enough for three to mount comfortably.

The chariots of his bodyguard were likewise modified. Wide wheels kept the chariot from sinking into the wet sand, and a stripped back chassis maintained a lightweight and flexible frame that handled a wider variety of conditions than the heavy chariots of the main force.

The last charioteer pulled ashore and the gangplanks were run back onto the deck. The portside oars were run out, pushing against the riverbank as the *Wrath of Tanis* sought to return to the battle.

'Good hunting, captain,' called Shoshenq, as the flagship drifted back into deeper waters.

'The gods be with you, sire,' said the captain, saluting with a clenched fist over his heart. His cargo delivered, he bellowed orders to his crew and within minutes the oars were out once more, powering the flagship downriver to attack the coalition fleet's rear.

'My king, what are your orders?' Lamintu's voice was a leopard's growl.

'Take us to where he can see us,' said Shoshenq, looking up at the fortress walls. The gates of the camp had opened and a steady stream of Theban warriors spilled from it, the front ranks reforming at the bottom of the hill.

'Takelot has seen what our fleet is capable of,' said Shoshenq. 'I will give him one final chance to surrender.'

OSORKON LOOKED TO the north and prayed that he was making the right decision. His bow felt leaden in his hand and his voice was unsteady in command as he led the men of the Crag to an unknown war. He had wished for a ship to take them south but every vessel worthy of transporting troops or supplies had already been taken north, and Osorkon was reluctant to requisition fishing vessels from a city that had already lost so much.

Smoke drifted lazily from Herakleopolis. Fires burned in every neighbourhood, for cooking or smithing this time, not the mindless chaos that had consumed the city mere months before. Some of those scars yet marked the cityscape. Whole neighbourhoods had been wiped out, leaving behind little more than piles of scorched, cracked mud bricks. Healing such marks completely would take years of rebuilding.

'Let us hope it doesn't fall down in our absence,' said Akhetep, drawing his chariot up level beside his prince.

'It has almost done so already,' said Osorkon. 'It is out of our hands now.'

Akhetep grunted by way of reply. 'Still, I think we should have kept a bigger garrison. I would hate to have to retake it. Even the civilians fight like bastards.'

'Every city has its secrets for those that know where to look,' said Bakenptah, with a wry wink. He rode up on Osorkon's right flank. 'Even your Crag has weaknesses.'

Osorkon's meeting with his little brother had been terse and short, culminating in Bakenptah's insistence that any expedition south also included him. Though Osorkon had hoped to bypass their mother on the matter, Bakenptah's absence from Herakleopolis would require a replacement for his duties, and so they had been forced to petition her like any other supplicant of the city.

Karomama had not taken the news well, berating her sons for their abandonment of the nome until Osorkon revealed the truth of his vision. Finally, she had accepted, if not supported it, Osorkon's reasoning, but not before forcing the brothers to swear oaths before Amun that they would return together alive.

'The Crag is mighty, sure enough, but a skilled siegemaster would quickly find its faults,' continued Bakenptah.

Osorkon raised an eyebrow. 'Oh? Enlighten us then, little brother.'

Bakenptah smirked as he told them. 'Your gates are strong and your walls are high, and it would be nigh impossible to breach or climb them, but the feed sheds and animal shelters have roofs of thatch. Animal feed and hay are sheltered beneath, and you have only two wells and shallow water troughs for the horses. A firestorm would tear through half of the fortress before you could fill a bucket. Imagine the horses breaking their confines, mad with fear. Would your warriors stay within or flee outward, I wonder?'

Osorkon rounded on his brother, his expression furious. 'By the arse of Set, why have you said nothing of this until now?'

Bakenptah shrugged, unfazed. 'It did not occur to me until recently. I have spent long hours helping the surveyors replan the ruined districts. The ruined houses were often clustered closely together and filled with timber furniture and woven cloth. I imagine animal feed will create a similar furnace effect.'

'Make a note, Akhetep. If we return, the Crag is undergoing revision.'

Akhetep frowned. 'If? Your confidence fills me.'

'I cannot say what we will face, only that we face an insidious enemy that thinks it has the element of surprise,' said Osorkon. 'We will show them their foolishness in that belief and come prepared for every eventuality.' Osorkon gestured behind him at a supply train that ran the length of the chariot formation twice over. He had all but emptied the Crag of supplies. Wagons filled with food, and jugs of beer and water, were pulled beside those almost spilling with replacement axles and wheels, spare bows, spears and arrows, as well as the fortress's supplies of gold and incense for bribery and gifts. The priests of the Crag, and the skeleton garrison that had stayed behind, would have to draw what they could from the people of Herakleopolis.

Karoadjet sat perched upon the lead wagon with her chosen handmaidens, picked from among a dozen charioteers' wives. They chatted gaily, as though the procession was a trip into the countryside and not a march to war.

Osorkon had steadfastly refused to let Karoadjet come, but his resolve had slowly crumbled through her repeated petitions, within and without the bedroom.

'I will not be left behind like some old crone while the fate of my country is decided. You will need healers after the battle. Think of the morale when it is the men's wives tending them,' she had said late one night.

Osorkon had countered, asking her pointedly if she would be the one comforting any newly-made widows. He had seen the grief of war, and such scars cut deep and often permanently.

Karoadjet was not to be denied, and over a period of days she needled at his arguments until he had thrown up his hands in exasperation. Finally, he had granted her permission as she had known he would, but his words of warning left her cold when he spoke of the torment they would face if the men were killed in battle and the women captured by an enemy.

After that, Karoadjet had ensured each of her women had a blade concealed between their breasts or strapped beneath their skirts, but not even the threat of rape and death had dulled her curiosity of his home city.

'I have always wanted to see Thebes. Is Karnak as big as they say?' she had asked.

'Bigger,' he had replied.

Osorkon's thoughts returned to the temples. It was a homecoming of sorts, but gone was the nurturing comfort that the walls of Thebes and the portals of Karnak had once provided. Home was nowhere now but the land upon which he walked and the men and women he called his kin.

Akhetep broke the silence, his thoughts similarly running towards their inevitable destination. 'Do you think Thebes has changed in our absence?'

Osorkon's mouth was set in a grim line. 'Yes, but not in any way that we will like.'

# Chapter Twenty-One

HUNDREDS OF KILOMETRES to Osorkon's south, the siege of Hermopolis ended as it began, in fire. Discontent to find the towering walls of Hermopolis standing against him, and the priest Sarasesh useless in his defiance, Malkesh spent liberally the only currency he had: blood. Timber that could have been used for cooking fires was tied into bales with ropes looted from the increasingly derelict ship *Sobek is Content*. The ship's meagre stores of linen were also tied into bundles and soaked with the few buckets of pitch left in the hold.

Under the cover of a moonless night, the horde of Malkesh fought their final gambit, hurled themselves at the city gate unarmed but for their incendiary cargo. Howling their animalistic rage to the stars, they cast bundles of burning material against the reinforced timbers, smouldering at first, then building to a roaring fire, and finally a blazing inferno licking hungrily up into the floor of the gatehouse.

Without knowing that the Hermopolitan forces were engaged in the war against Shoshenq, the warriors of Malkesh fought and died against a skeleton defence of the city.

The city's bells tolled in alarm at this surprise attack, and the citizen militias were called to arms. They flocked to the walls, bows held high and broken masonry stacked to cast down on the invaders. Ash mingled with blood as arrows hissed through the air, striking down screaming warriors who seemed heedless of their own survival. Bodies fell into the fire, skewered by shafts, becoming the very fuel they sought to carry.

Sarasesh watched it all from the heights of a hill far beyond arrow range. Beside him, Malkesh stood with his officers, cursing his men to hasten their progress. For all his desperation, the warlord was still beyond taking personal risks, letting the weakest of his horde bring fire to the gatehouse. Malkesh watched with satisfaction as the flames took and crackled up the gate, nodding with approval as the next wave of his men prepared themselves. Each man was heaped with bundles of cloth or wood, lining up to receive a measure of the sticky, viscous pitch that was poured over their burdens like honey over bread. As soon as they were ready, the men were sent running in their twos and threes at the inferno under the watchful, unforgiving eye of their lord and master.

The roaring crackle of the bonfire did little to drown out the screams of Malkesh's dying warriors. Darting silhouettes dashed towards the flames, and Sarasesh saw one man struck down on the cusp of the fire, a shard of brick falling to crack open his skull. One of his comrades bent to retrieve the bundle, but he too was struck down, the arrow taking him through the shoulder and burying itself down into his lungs.

Another tribesman ran past the carnage, howling in either blinded terror or rage, Sarasesh could not tell which. The tribesman went to cast his bundle onto the fire but stumbled on the edge and fell, load and all, onto the roaring flames, his pitch-soaked flesh catching instantly alight. By some miracle, he regained his feet and ran back towards his comrades, making it further than Sarasesh would have thought possible before he collapsed and his screams faded.

Once, he would have felt something at such a horrific sight, but now it was as though he were watching the unfolding siege in a waking dream. Yes, it was horrible, but it was not real, could not be real. And yet, he knew as the fire burned with yellow intensity that it was indeed real, and that it was he who had condemned this city to death.

Sarasesh had thought his advice moot. To starve out a city as grand as Hermopolis would take months, if not years, and no army in this world would stand against the slaughter they now endured and keep fighting. There was not the timber for ladders and a ram would be useless against the reinforced doors. Fearful for his life, Sarasesh had gambled on something he had thought impossible, to burn the walls down for all the good a frontal assault would do them. That Malkesh had taken his idea and corrupted it should not have surprised him.

'See your handiwork, little priest,' rumbled Malkesh. 'You will feast by my side for this victory.'

Surprisingly, proximity to the warlord no longer filled Sarasesh with fear, only revulsion. He ignored the offer, instead fixing his gaze on the gate and willing it to hold as dozens, perhaps hundreds of tribesmen died at the foot of Egyptian greatness.

Sarasesh had barely completed the thought when the sound of crumbling stone reached them on the hill.

'Amun, no,' he whispered. Heated from the fire below like a stone cauldron, the gatehouse disintegrated, falling inward to smash the fire-weakened doors to kindling. Smoke and embers plumed upward as an entire section of the wall fell apart, crushing beneath it another two score of warriors of the horde.

Malkesh favoured him with a demonic smile. 'Time to go, priest. Do not leave my sight.' Malkesh raised his monstrous spear in the air and the legion of warriors behind him roared their fervour as their lord led them into the grand city before them.

Sarasesh jogged after the warlord armed with nothing more than a short stabbing spear, its wooden tip dull and fire-hardened rather than forged from metal. He wore no armour, running into battle almost naked but for the scraps of cloth he had left from his old shendyt.

The gate may have fallen but the slaughter continued unabated, and many were crushed into the fallen stone or pushed into the fire by the sheer weight of the horde behind them. Others fell to the blades of their comrades, lunatic screams piercing the air as warriors lost themselves in the slaughter and lashed out in the press of bodies.

The soldiers and militias of Hermopolis rallied quickly. The rain of arrow fire continued, cutting down the outer edges of the horde, but it was a bee sting on the hide of a hyena. Within minutes, the horde had scrambled up the debris, charged along the walls and hacked the hapless archers to pieces. The horde cast their remains over the side onto the city streets below, smashing through the fortified doors of the guard towers and dashing down the stairs to break into the city proper.

Sarasesh followed Malkesh through the main breach, an aura of fear giving the master of the horde clear room to move. A tribesman of the western desert ran ahead of them and stumbled on loose scree, pitching backwards, unaware of who was behind him. Malkesh's spear launched through his back, punching out of his chest, and the warlord roared as hot blood splashed over his arms.

The fighting at the gatehouse was brief but intense, a brave stand by a handful of defenders against a far more numerous foe. Somewhere far beyond, the din of the warning bell increased in tempo and elsewhere, the first screams of civilians rent the air.

Malkesh fought like a man possessed, his spear stabbing out like a viper, extinguishing lives with every thrust. He was drenched in blood already, some of it his own as a lucky soldier of Hermopolis desperately lashed out, slashing open the warlord's thigh. Malkesh roared at the affront, hammering his left hand into the soldier's helmeted head. The Hermopolitan crumpled, hitting the ground hard. He stirred, but was impaled into the ground before he had a chance to rise. Malkesh wrenched the spear back out and ran on, ignoring the wound as though it were a scratch and leaving the soldier to shudder in his death throes.

Deafening noise and the stench of blood and spilled viscera filled Sarasesh's senses, overwhelming him in a riotous blur of unrestrained violence. Tears streaked his face, a profound wrongness setting heavily in his heart at the sight of so fine a city as Hermopolis falling prey to such uncultured savagery. He staggered, unable to catch his breath and looked around at the piles of dead filling the streets.

He dropped his spear at his feet, reaching up to tear at his face as he shrieked to the stars.

Malkesh and his retinue turned at the sound, weapons raised ready, but the warlord laughed as his eyes settled on the pitiful figure of the broken priest.

'No more, you bastard,' cried Sarasesh. 'No gods-forsaken more, you cursed savage.'

Malkesh turned and lunged at him, stopping after a single step but it was enough to frighten the priest. Sarasesh recoiled from that leering face and tripped over the corpse behind him. Black blood spattered from the wound in the corpse's chest and splashed over Sarasesh's skin and rags. He felt the clammy wetness stick to his leg and fought down the urge to retch.

The warlord had already turned to leave, but Sarasesh called after him.

'Enough, Malkesh. This has gone on far enough,' he said, pushing himself to his feet. 'Your men are dying in droves.'

Malkesh watched the blood congeal on his spear tip. A thick droplet dripped low before it hit the road. 'I grow tired of your protests, priest.'

'These people are innocent.'

'These people are prey,' growled Malkesh.

Around the warlord, warriors with looted weapons and armour came running to rally around their master, waiting expectantly for orders to join the slaughter where it was thickest. Sarasesh spat on the ground at the sight of the ragtag bunch of invaders.

'The enemy is to the north, you barbarian,' Sarasesh shouted. 'I am a representative of Karnak and you are honour bound to serve the priesthood.' He turned away and pointed to the north, his gaze fixed on the northern sky and the promise of victory against Takelot, the true enemy of Thebes. He spoke without looking at Malkesh for he did not know whether his venom would survive gazing upon the monster behind him.

'Withdraw your men at once. Show me you have any control of this pack of lice-ridden dogs. These are not men. They are beasts, lapping at the richness of their betters. By Amun, you will obey me in this, or I will call upon the gods themselves to strike you down.'

Sarasesh heard one word before his world exploded in pain.

'Fire,' said the warlord.

The arrow took him high in the chest as he turned, causing him to stumble. A tribesman next to the warlord lowered his bow and confusion muddled Sarasesh's mind as it made the connection a moment before the pain took hold.

Blinding agony lanced through Sarasesh's chest and he gasped as the breath was punched from his lungs. His vision swam and he looked down at the shaft of wood protruding a palm-width from his chest. Hot wetness spilled down his belly and he had a moment to be offended that Malkesh had not bothered to kill him himself before his legs gave out beneath him.

All sensation fled his limbs as he hit the ground, and the warriors of the horde ran around him and over him in their eagerness to push further into the city.

'Talk to your gods yourself,' he heard Malkesh growl as his vision swam and his world began to dim.

Hot tears wet the ground beside an expanding pool of his blood as he called out once more. 'Amun, forgive me,' he cried, and his vision went dark.

THE TWO KINGS of the Two Lands met face to face for the first time since Nimlot had been entombed in the hillsides of the Theban necropolis. Upon landing at the river's edge, the northern king erected a canopy of brilliant white in full sight of the southern fortress, a site that would drown in blood within the day unless an agreement was reached.

The bulk of the northern king's army waited a kilometre beyond that, a sea of tents that sprawled from the river's edge to so far inland that a man might walk through the camp for twenty minutes without seeing the other side.

'Behold,' said the self-proclaimed king of the south from his chariot. 'See how many men our enemy fields? Why then does he requisition our sons to die in his wars if not to preserve his own people first? We fight for our survival, my friends. One way or another.'

The charioteers escorting the southern king shouted their assent to the sky as they made their way down the hill in an arrowhead formation aimed directly at the Tanite king. While Takelot himself went unarmed, his men held no such discretion. Lances and war bows were stowed in braces, and swords and daggers hung at the waists of driver and archer alike.

Like Shoshenq, Takelot wore the blue crown of war, a legacy of the blood he had been forced to spill in the time since his father's death.

Pharaoh Shoshenq waited patiently and enthroned, while his retainers hovered behind him. Takelot dismounted far beyond the tent and walked alone past the mighty Tanite guards.

Neither king deigned to glance at the river. The naval battle raged on and the screams of men and the splintered groan of sinking ships carried easily to the parlay.

'Hello, Senn.'

The Tanite king gestured towards the empty seat. 'It is Shoshenq now, Takelot. Rightful Pharaoh of the Two Lands as named by Osorkon II.'

'You are not his blood. You are not my king.'

'Your stubbornness only confirms his decision.'

Takelot looked over Shoshenq's shoulder to the vast host arrayed against him. 'What would you know of my stubbornness, Senneker? You know nothing of the workings of the south. What did Pharaoh say? He cannot rule that which he does not know?'

'You speak his name in vain.'

'He was my grandfather. His name is my name. And he is responsible for the downfall of his own blood. If it were not for him, we would not be here. Perhaps he should have been wiser in his appointments,' Takelot smiled, content to twist the knife a moment longer. 'Where is he, by the way? Our errant Vizier? I have long searched for him, but he has disappeared. He's not with you, is he?' Takelot made a show of looking behind Shoshenq's throne.

'Nakhtefmut is in Tanis under lock and key, where he belongs. His heresy is regrettable and his actions against your family a stain on the honour of this kingdom, but your reaction is unacceptable to the continued security of the Two Lands.'

Takelot ignored him, smiling at the figure seated behind Shoshenq's chair. 'Paameny, I trust you at least waited until my grandfather was cold before you crowned your new master?'

Paameny met his gaze with sad eyes. 'That is unworthy of you, my lord.'

'There has been a lot that is unworthy of late, physician. Some wounds even you cannot heal.'

To the east, sounded the crack of splintering timber and a chorus of screams rose in crescendo before being abruptly cut off.

'Dynasties end all the time. I have more of a claim to these lands than you do with your Libyan blood,' said Shoshenq. The Tanite king watched his rival over steepled fingers.

'You must know that you cannot win this cleanly,' said Takelot. 'What does this accomplish except weakening us both? I would be more frightened of Shalmaneser's vengeance against Tanis than I would Nubian savagery against Thebes.'

'And yet, here I am.'

'Ruling in my grandfather's name.'

'Because Pharaoh decreed so,' snapped Shoshenq, hammering his fist onto the arm of his throne. 'I am Pharaoh now, Takelot, by the will of the god Osorkon II.'

'So you never tire of saying.' Takelot smiled up at the great Nubian giant, standing beside Shoshenq's throne. The royal shieldbearer had changed not at all since Takelot had seen him at Nimlot's funeral, nor in all the years before when the Two Lands had been nominally, if not practically, united. 'Lamintu. In another time you might have stood at my side. I would have welcomed such a legendary warrior into my retinue.'

Lamintu might have been carved from black granite for all the emotion he showed. Whatever thoughts were raging in Lamintu's head at the sight of Takelot were his alone to know, if indeed he possessed individual thought at all. He had a function, an unavoidable destiny that seemingly defied the natural need to age. He would never hang up his spear, not until the world around him was ash or he himself was finally ended. Takelot had seen the man fight and figured the former more likely than the latter.

'It seems we are at an impasse. You will not turn your men from your course,' said Takelot, rising and stepping out from under the canopy. 'And I will not kneel to you.'

'Takelot, you cannot win. Even with your savages on their camels, you cannot win,' said Shoshenq.

'Pediese is closer to my family than you will ever be, Senn. And he is a distant relation indeed.'

'By the laws of this land, I am your uncle and yet you stand before me, acting with insolence that I would expect from your sons, not you.'

'You turned my own brother against me,' roared Takelot.

Lamintu stepped forward, spear levelled and dark eyes glittering in that impassive face. The charioteers reached for their weapons, but none of them wanted to be the first one to draw.

Only Shoshenq remained unmoved by Takelot's outburst. 'He saw what you cannot. Egypt can only survive if the Two Lands are united.'

'He saw many things. Not all of them true,' countered Takelot.

Shoshenq snarled and launched himself from his throne, coming to stand in front of Takelot at the edge of canopy's shadow. Shoshenq's next words were little more than a whisper, for Takelot's ears alone. 'If your pride forbids it, do not kneel. Just say the words. Disband your coalition and acknowledge the throne of Tanis. Fight with me against the Assyrians and help me usher in a new age, one untorn by internal strife.'

'I think you know I cannot do that.'

Shoshenq hissed through his teeth and looked away. 'I know.'

'Then why meet with me at all?'

Shoshenq walked back to his throne and sat back down. 'In sight of your own walls? So that when I rout your army, they will know that you could have saved them. Every man that dies, dies because you refused to kneel.'

Takelot laughed quietly. He nodded once at Shoshenq and stepped into the sunlight and up into his chariot. He turned and looked past the Tanites. 'See that rock there?' he asked, pointing to a jagged stone perhaps twenty paces beyond the tent.

Shoshenq frowned, slowly turning his head. 'What of it?'

'That is the range of our arrows. I will give the order to fire when I return. I suggest you not be here when I do.' The chariot driver cracked the reins and led the charioteers back to the fortified camp.

Halfway up the hill, the driver could no longer contain himself. 'That was well done, sire,' he grinned.

'Thank you,' said Takelot, smiling indulgently. 'One of my finer moments, I think.'

'Your orders, sire?'

Takelot looked back down the slope, where the Tanites were already taking down the canopy and remounting their own chariots. Shoshenq was clearly taking no chances. 'Now we dangle the bait and hope they bite.'

THE ROAD WAS long and threatened to lull the charioteers into the plodding contentedness that has doomed many an unwary traveller. Osorkon rotated the formation every two hours, dividing the two hundred and fifty chariots into five groups of fifty that took turns riding out to scout ahead before falling back into the comfortable numbing fog of monotonous travel.

The rotation also had one additional benefit that Osorkon had kept to himself. Dark thoughts could now only spiral so deep before they had to be put aside for the action of the present. All of them, from the prince himself to the lowest soldier, could feel the fickle winds of fate blowing around them, threatening to tear down all they had built, and it did no good to dwell upon it too deeply.

'Ho!' called Akhetep, pulling his mounts to a stop as a lone figure staggered out from the copse of trees. Akhetep's hand went to his bow but Osorkon stopped him with an outstretched hand.

The figure was unarmed and barely standing. The woman, for her bare breasts and ragged dress revealed this fact, simply stared blankly at the charioteers, pinned by their presence like a deer in the moment before a hunter's arrow finds its mark.

Her eyes were listless but filled with fear.

Osorkon called the column to a halt and stepped down from his chariot, going to her slowly with his palms out. She whimpered and Osorkon saw the full extent of her torment. Her dress had been ripped and torn, deep purple bruises covering her chest and arms, and dried blood coated the insides of her thighs. He held back his revulsion at the sight of her injuries, letting the anger simmer hotly in his belly.

'I am Prince Osorkon of Thebes,' he said softly. 'You are safe now. We won't hurt you.'

He reached out for her, but her legs gave out and she fell soundlessly into the dust. He knelt beside her, letting her be for the moment. He offered her his waterskin, and called for a horse blanket to cover her with, but she seemed to be only dimly aware their presence at all.

'We are of Thebes and we have come to help you. What is your name?' asked Osorkon.

The woman whispered something, but it did not carry above the wind. Osorkon leaned in to listen again.

'Kill me,' she whispered, and a single tear spilled from her bloodshot eyes before the dam burst from within. Tears spilled down her dusty cheeks as great sobs wracked her wasted frame and her fingers curled into claws as she cradled herself.

Osorkon knew in that moment that she would never recover. Terror stole away her thoughts so that she knew of nothing else. Joy, contentment, even sadness, all had been washed away in the presence of unspeakable terror. Whoever had done this to her had already killed her, her heart had just yet to stop beating.

Osorkon called for Karoadjet to join them and glanced around the convoy. He was grateful to see Bakenptah already directing the charioteers to search the surrounding countryside for others and setting up a defensive picket in case her pursuers were close.

Osorkon tried to look the woman in the eye but she refused to look at any of them. 'No-one here will harm you. You have my word as a Priest of Amun,' he said softly.

The woman flinched at his words and made to crawl away, but her exhaustion and terror seemed to sap the strength from her limbs. She made it only a few paces before she fell back into deep, uncontrollable sobs.

'Who did this?' Osorkon pressed, kneeling beside her. He reached out to her, to let her know she was not alone, to stir her from his waking nightmare, but the woman began to tremble, her eyes haunted by horrors she could still see.

'My children,' she whispered, staring misty-eyed in the direction in which she had come.

Osorkon glanced up at the shadow behind him.

'Bandits?' murmured Akhetep, and passed his prince a blanket to cover the lost woman. She flinched as the fabric hovered over her shoulders, as though the blanket itself would harm her. Osorkon frowned as he drew the blanket back, unwilling to force the issue as necessary as it was. She was delirious and exposure in the desert was a constant risk.

'Or worse,' the prince replied.

He turned at the sound of footsteps and went to speak, but stopped himself as he saw Karoadjet's features twisted in concern and fury. 'What are you doing?' she snapped.

Osorkon glanced at Akhetep, but the chariot commander only shrugged.

'Give that to me,' she said, snatching the blanket from Osorkon. 'Go. Form your perimeter, and look to your scouts. Leave this to me, husband.'

'I only meant to help,' Osorkon replied, wounded.

Karoadjet rounded on him. 'In some things, you cannot. What were you thinking? That she will talk to more men, armed men at that, after what has been done with her?' Karoadjet softened her tone. 'When we find who is responsible, you will do your duty and you will have my gratitude for it. But you cannot help here. Now go.'

Karoadjet shooed him away, standing between the charioteers and the lost woman like a protective parent. Karoadjet knelt in front of her, wrapping the blanket over the woman's shoulders. This time, she did not flinch, and Karoadjet laid a gentle hand on her arm. 'You are safe now, but we need your help to find who did this. What is your name?' she asked.

The woman looked up at Karoadjet, seeing properly for the first time. 'Amaket,' she stuttered.

Karoadjet smiled with effort. 'My name is Karoadjet,' she said. 'I will look after you, Amaket.' A few of the charioteers' wives had followed her over, but Karoadjet waved them back, not wishing to crowd a poor woman already at the limits of her endurance.

The memory of her torment stirred deep in Amaket's psyche and her fragile grip on reality faded, as her eyes took on the furtive, frantic looks of the hunted and the haunted. Karoadjet headed off the next panic attack before it could begin. 'You are safe now, Amaket. You are safe,' she whispered.

Amaket shifted in her position, drawing her knees up her chest. Just for a second, as her torn dress shifted around her legs, Karoadjet saw the ruin that had been done to her.

Anger burned bright in Karoadjet's breast, tinged with revulsion and fear at the beasts, for they could not rightly be called men, that had tortured the poor woman.

'I escaped, but they are hunting me. They will never stop,' Amaket whispered. Her eyes, wild and unblinking, fixed on Karoadjet's.

'You poor thing,' Karoadjet murmured, reaching out to touch Amaket's matted hair. 'You are beautiful, Amaket. We will save you.' Karoadjet edged closer, sitting in the sand beside Amaket, her touch going from the woman's hair to her back. 'We can help your people too. Where are you from? How many attacked your village?' Karoadjet asked.

Amaket's eyes roamed over Karoadjet's face, never fixing on any one detail, but seeing her now.

'Hundreds,' she whispered. 'Hundreds of them.'

Karoadjet glanced to where Osorkon and Akhetep were speaking with Bakenptah. The perimeter was already complete and the charioteers watched the darkness, arrows to bow strings. Osorkon's soldiers were efficient and skilled, but they too numbered in the mere hundreds. 'And where are they now? These hundreds?' she asked, but Amaket's grip on reality had already faded.

'Not of this world. Walk in shadows,' Amaket whispered, clenching her eyes shut as she wept. 'Monsters, spirits, demons.' On and on she babbled, as her lucidity retreated deeper and deeper into her tortured mind.

Karoadjet tucked the blanket tight around Amaket and stood without a word. She was suddenly unable to be close to the woman, for Amaket was a living reminder of the potential of evil, not just violence, but violation and defilement and the destruction of all that is peaceful and good.

With a gesture, she bid the charioteers' wives take over Amaket's care, and within moments food, water, and clean clothes were set out before her, though she took no notice of any of it. Karoadjet's skin crawled as she walked back to where Osorkon waited for her by the chariots, hating herself for the revulsion she felt at Amaket's condition.

That could be any one of us, she thought darkly, drawing her shawl a little tighter across her shoulders.

Osorkon's mouth was a grim line and he held out a hand to her, which she gratefully took. 'What are we dealing with, do you think?' Osorkon asked, her previous censure of him already forgotten.

'Amaket says there were hundreds that attacked her village. She speaks of spirits and demons.' Karoadjet's words were delivered flat, surprising even herself with her lack of emotion.

'Perhaps she exaggerates,' ventured Akhetep. 'Fear can warp perceptions beyond measure. In the dark, a few bandits can look like an army.'

'Even a broken mind knows the difference between a dozen and hundreds,' snapped Karoadjet. 'She speaks the truth. I heard it in her voice. This is no roving band of marauders. Whatever is out there is much larger and more dangerous.'

'I believe you. And her,' said Osorkon. 'We will know this threat when we see it. Or when it sees us, but by all that is holy, I swear that whoever did this, man or spirit, dies for what they have done.' Osorkon spat on the ground and set off for his chariot.

'What are your orders?' called Akhetep after him.

'Unhitch the horses and empty the wagons. We will make camp here tonight, until we know what we're facing. Send out more riders when the first scouts return, but have them back before moonrise. We will need to be well-rested.'

Akhetep nodded and began to shout orders to the men, leaving Karoadjet alone.

She glanced back at Amaket once more and shivered in the cool evening air, her hand drifting to the dagger secreted at her hip. Spirits, demons or men, it mattered little.

She swore to herself that Karoadjet of Herakleopolis would not go so easy.

AMAKET DIED THAT night. The trauma done to her was too severe, the wounds to her body too deep and her despair too great to cling to life. Perhaps it was a blessing that Anubis had come for her, to guide her to her family in the Field of Reeds.

The Thebans wrapped her in a linen shroud and buried her deep in the desert sands. They had neither the time nor the means to provide for her the mummification process, but the desert sands would dry out her body and the meagre belongings and supplies they had buried her with would sustain her until she was reunited with her family.

Osorkon spoke the words of warding, beseeching Amun himself to intervene and deliver this messenger into his embrace.

'May you find the peace denied you in life,' Osorkon finished. No manmade marker existed over Amaket's burial site; the lessons of the royal burial valleys applied here on a smaller, immeasurably more humble scale. Instead, a lone date palm stood over her grave, a living memorial to a life cut short.

Osorkon rose from where he knelt, letting a handful of sand fall through his fingers. 'Akhetep, it is time.'

The commander of the charioteers nodded and raised his voice to disturb the silence, ordering those chosen to make ready for the night's travel.

Amaket had revealed little before she slipped into the underworld, but what she had said had made Osorkon's blood run cold. She had hailed from Khnefen, a small village in the Hare nome, home to some one hundred and fifty farmers and reed cutters. Two nights before, Khnefen had fallen to a force of Kushites, howling shadows that had raped and pillaged the town in the dead of night, burning huts and putting the men and boys to the sword. They had come on foot, but Amaket had seen them during the day hunting for her on horseback, riding their plunder from her burned out village. Osorkon bade her to skip over the other details, and yet that was not the worst of it by far.

Hermopolis itself had fallen that night. With the majority of its fighting men engaged in Takelot's campaign, the City of Scrolls had not seen the threat from the south until it was upon them. Scant kilometres from Khnefen, the fall of Hermopolis saw the end of an entire nome and the fall of one of the most influential and learned cities in Egypt.

Even without its army, the force required to take a city that size must have been considerable. Osorkon tried not to imagine what horrors would have been inflicted on the scholars of the city and any others too weak to offer resistance.

Whoever had allowed this to happen would answer for their crime in time, but for now Osorkon needed to see the truth with his own eyes.

'Mount up and move out,' Akhetep ordered, once the men had made ready, each selecting his favourite mount from the chariot teams. A mere six charioteers, including Osorkon and Akhetep, rode on horseback, leaving the rest of the convoy encamped under Bakenptah's command.

'If we are not back by morning, then we are dead. The survival of our people is of greater importance than vengeance,' Osorkon had told his younger brother.

Bakenptah had nodded, following Osorkon's gaze to where Karoadjet worked with the other women to take an inventory of their supplies after the evening meal. 'Good hunting, brother,' Bakenptah had replied. 'Amun watch over you.'

Behind four of the riders, a lone wagon trundled along the uneven path, covered with a thick linen shroud. Behind the wagon, a final pair of riders brought up the rear guard. Together, they presented a sight that would not be out of place anywhere in the Two Lands.

The riders moved out, taking a slow path south, a single rider going ahead to scout before returning, before another would take his place. Each time, they brought back nothing but empty roads ahead.

'You should not have brought Karoadjet,' said Akhetep, as the sun began to dip in the sky.

Osorkon grunted in his saddle. 'Try telling her that.'

'That girl, Amaket? She was little older than we are,' pressed Akhetep. 'Now she lies beneath the sands. She was not stabbed. She was not bludgeoned, and still she is dead.'

'I know.'

'Is that all?'

'There is much horror in war, Akhetep. We have unleashed violence ourselves, many times,' said Osorkon.

Akhetep shook his head and spat. 'Not that. Never that. We fight soldiers.'

'Not all conquerors are as merciful as those that follow Ma'at.'

'Tell me truthfully, my friend,' said Akhetep, urging his horse forward and blocking Osorkon's path. 'Who do you believe we are facing? Who has corrupted our home and unleashed darkness against us?'

Osorkon fixed his friend with a level stare. 'That is what we are here to find out.'

'You have your suspicions. I see that much,' said Akhetep.

'I will not spread hearsay until I am sure. Keep your mind on the task at hand, commander. If they are demons, we will banish them. If they are men, they will bleed slowly.' Akhetep went to argue but Osorkon rode around him, pitching his voice to the men behind him. 'We must be close. Get into formation and play your parts well. Our entire venture may depend on it.'

The riders nodded and slouched in the saddle. The wagon driver struck a spark in the darkness and lit a pitch-soaked torch, letting it burn in a brace beside the driver's seat. He pulled a sack from the wagon's depths and set it where he had been sitting, tying a smaller bundle to the top. Satisfied with his work, the driver ducked between the bullocks and led them by a rope through the nose. The animals snorted, but a bribe from the feed bag was enough to send them plodding along in the darkness.

Osorkon too slumped in the saddle, leaning over the pommel with shoulders hunched and head lowered. Around him, Akhetep and the other rides mirrored his posture, a plodding escort for a dimly illuminated wagon, the very image of an exhausted escort pushing through the night for the safety of Hermopolis.

Or so the prince hoped.

The darkness stretched on, silent and limitless but for the soft glow at their backs. Osorkon considered the possibility of more survivors. Would the glow represent an island of safety to any refugees watching? In seeking safety, they would likely spell their own doom, and Osorkon made a silent prayer that the only eyes upon them would be those hungry for treasure. His thoughts were interrupted by Akhetep.

'Riders on the ridge,' the commander whispered.

Osorkon glanced up at the valley heights to silhouettes of men and horses on the rise. The night was dark, but the moon gave just enough light to see. 'I see them.'

As soon as the silhouettes appeared, they were gone, vanishing back over the top.

Keeping an eye on the ridge, Osorkon unlimbered his bow, holding it loosely in his right hand. It was a lighter bow than he was used to, but it would still discourage a leopard or hyena from venturing too close. Or knock a man from his saddle.

'Maintain your positions. Fire only when I say,' said Osorkon, pitching his voice low. 'Keep your eyes on the darkness.'

The Theban riders did not have long to wait. The first sign of attack was a low rumble, like a rock rolling down the hill, almost imperceptible but for those expecting to hear it.

The noise grew as the Nubian scouts crested the rise and charged into the basin. They howled like jackals, all pretence at secrecy cast off in favour of this one charge.

Osorkon was prepared for it, but the sound still grated on his nerves, and after hours in the saddle the lull he had sought to portray was not entirely an act.

An arrow hissed overhead, thudding into the wagon behind him, but no cry of pain was forthcoming.

'Fire,' snapped Osorkon, drawing his bow in one fluid motion and firing his shot into the dark mass of riders.

The Theban riders were instantly alert, casting off their mantles and kicking their mounts into the charge. Wrong-footed in the dark, the Nubian riders faltered for a fraction of a second in indecision before they charged in kind.

Osorkon rode low in the saddle, hearing but not seeing arrows hiss past him before striking flesh with a meaty thud. Kharafa fell with a burbling cry, a feathered shaft appearing in the centre of his chest. Moments later, Refta went down silently, his horse shot out from under him, pitching him headfirst onto the rocks.

Osorkon gritted his teeth, stowing his bow and drawing the merchant's sword belted at his knees. The blade glinted dully, the edge not much keener, but he needed at least one of their attackers alive, if not unwounded.

An arrow kissed his cheek, the feather sting bringing tears to his eyes. The devils could shoot for sure, the darkness beholden to them in a way those raised in the light of cities found it difficult to match.

White teeth and fervent eyes broke the darkness, a floating visage of hate that lunged at Osorkon. The Nubian screamed, not a war cry but a howl of ecstatic bloodlust.

Osorkon's sword lanced through his throat, ending the scream in a wet gurgle.

The Thebans and Nubians came together in a clash of blades, bows discarded in favour of short swords and stabbing spears. The whirlwind of blades was no more than a minor skirmish but for each of the riders, Egyptian and Nubian, the whole world shrank down to warding off the next blade in the shadows.

Osorkon cut, sending other Nubian screaming into the dust, but a third took his fallen comrade's place, stabbing with a short spear like a coiled adder striking out. Sensing an opening, Osorkon leaned forward in the saddle, slashing at the grinning face, but his reach fell short and he nearly toppled into the sands.

The Nubian shouted in triumph, stabbing forward and catching Osorkon on shoulder, gouging a deep cut over his collarbone. Osorkon let himself fall, rather than facing the return stroke that was sure to end him.

He grunted as he hit the ground, rolling underneath clashing hooves and losing his sword in the turmoil. His hand went to his belt on instinct, drawing the *Tooth of Sobek*, his fine iron dagger and the one affectation he had allowed himself.

He rolled to his feet, moving, always moving. He sensed, rather than saw, the Nubian bearing down on him and he threw himself aside, feeling the breath of the rider's horse pass behind him. His shoulder stung, grit and stone flakes working its way deep into the cut. Elsewhere, he was vaguely aware of the sounds of battle dying down, the last Nubian riders dead or disengaging, but his eyes narrowed on his impending death.

The Nubian was silent as he charged. He bore down on Osorkon, his spear held tightly and Osorkon knew that a last-minute dive would not work a second time.

He held his dagger out before him, judging in that moment that the blade was too uneven for an accurate throw and too short to deflect the coming blow.

The Nubian's charge faltered halfway, and the rider was thrown aside with the force of an arrow lodging in his side. His mount skittered and bucked in fright, darting through the Egyptian warriors and leaving its master in the dust.

Osorkon raced to the prone figure, kicking the man's spear out of reach. The arrow had bitten deep into the man's shoulder, piercing through the meat and coming out under the shoulder blade. A lung shot and one that was likely a death sentence even under the care of the most gifted physicians.

The Nubian hissed as Osorkon rolled him over. The surviving Thebans rushed to their prince's side, their foes dead or fleeing the field.

'Are you well, my prince?'

Osorkon looked up at the concern in the eyes of his men. 'Thanks to you, Nemetu, yes.' Osorkon looked around, seeing every face but the two that had fallen. 'Check the fallen. See if they yet live. Do it now.' Osorkon returned his attention to the wounded Nubian, trying not to let the first tendrils of fear infect his voice.

'Tell me what I want to know, and I will grant you mercy.'

The Nubian simply glared up at him, which Osorkon took for assent.

'How many men do you have in Hermopolis?'

The Nubian grinned, a manic showing of teeth. Osorkon mirrored the gesture as he gripped the arrow shaft and twisted it. The Nubian's lips rent the night, bloody foam flecking his lips.

'Do you know who I am?' Osorkon asked the Nubian. The warrior was bathed in sweat, his eyes clenched tight and teeth gritted together so hard that Osorkon thought they might shatter in his mouth. 'I am Amun and Ra, Horus and Set. I have come for you. Now tell me, how many have taken Hermopolis?'

The Nubian stared up defiant and Osorkon's held the man down with one hand and gripped the arrow's shaft, gently pulling it out. The arrowhead slid back through the man's lung tissue, eliciting an agonised gurgle.

'Two thousand,' gasped the Nubian, twitching under Osorkon's grip. 'Two thousand.'

'How long will they stay there?' Osorkon demanded.

'As long as the Great Chief demands. He rewards his warriors for their efforts.'

'Who is your chief? Tell me,' Osorkon snapped when no answer was forthcoming.

'Malkesh.' The Nubian was gasping for breath now, his lungs labouring as they filled with blood.

'Who sent you? Who has betrayed us?'

The Nubian gurgled, bubbles of blood flecking his lips. It took Osorkon a moment before he realised the warrior was trying to laugh.

'Everyone,' the Nubian hissed. There was a rattle in his chest and the wildness in his eyes slowly faded. Osorkon dropped the dead Nubian, suddenly aware that he had held him by the shoulders.

The prince steadied himself, the adrenaline of the moment fading and leaving him faint. He looked up at the men around him who had come to hear the dying Nubian's last words.

'We will return to the camp and continue towards Hermopolis in the morning. When we do, neither the gods of this land nor the spirits of the sands will be able to save the men that have done this.'

The remaining charioteers nodded grimly and silently, for there was nothing more that needed to be said. A great crime had fallen upon their people and a quick and ignoble death was far more than these invaders deserved.

Seeing the ruin done to Amaket, it was also far less than they would suffer themselves if given if they failed.

# RUIN OF SEKHMET

# Chapter Twenty-Two

BALLADS, HISTORIES AND even the bas reliefs that adorned the tomb walls of kings made battle out to be a glorious endeavour, worthy of celebration and remembrance. Like a spearhead fresh forged or an iron blade worked over at the blacksmith's anvil, the crucible of war tempered boys into men, warriors into heroes and won monarchs their immortality.

All of this was true, but the reality was rather more ignoble.

The poets always left out the blinding dust and deafening noise, choking the senses of sight and sound so that battle passed in a series of flashing images rather than one complete memory. An arrow shot here and a sword stroke avoided there was often all Takelot recalled of his hours amid the fray.

He was aware of the thought, even as he knew his memory would later numb the experience. The unfortunate Tanites that fell before him would not have that luxury.

Takelot's world existed solely within ten paces of each side of him. He could see no further than that, and the trumpets at his command post had taken on a muted quality that he could only hear if he strained to do so over the cries of fighting men and the clashing of weapons upon shields.

The baked leather guards on his paired stallions turned aside spear and sword both as he bore down on Shoshenq's left flank. Men scattered, men ran, but there were another fifty of the war machines close behind him that cut them down. The wheel scythes reaped a heavy toll cutting through men's bellies like threshing wheat, dismembering as often as disembowelling, and leaving shrieking soldiers writhing in the dust.

Takelot's driver, Olekh, crouched in the footwell, keeping the horse team steady as his master launched shot after shot into the mass of men. The king's right shoulder began to burn with effort, the war bow's tension strong enough to throw a man from his feet.

He paused in his efforts, trusting the charioteers behind him to continue their murderous volley unabated. The Tanites fell in droves, their lives plucked from them by arrows too fast to see, or simply trampled beneath the stampeding war horses and heavy war machines.

Grief settled upon Takelot's heart with every death, for these men should have been his loyal subjects, fighting under his command instead of against it. Run, he willed them, flee and rout and this will all be over.

Far beyond the impenetrable dust, Great Chief Pediese's riders would be reaping a similar toll. Their marksmanship rivalled that of the Egyptians, surpassed it even, if Takelot was being generous. They were the bees stinging the exposed rear of Shoshenq's forces, while Ukhesh and Kaphiri drove forwards with ranks of spearmen and archers.

Takelot had no idea if they were winning. For all Shoshenq's complaints about the wars in Assyria, his army now seemed endless. Frightened and angry faces flashed past him, the unfortunate immediately cut down while others lived to disappear back into the gloom. Takelot risked a glance behind him, and though the dust obscured everything in sight, his instincts tugged at him to fall back.

Takelot leaned in to shout into his driver's ear. 'Take us about.'

The driver gave no response but a slight pressure on the reins, guiding the horse team in a lengthy arc back towards the flank's edge. The formation followed in a sweeping crescent as they cut and hacked their way from the press. The Tanites died in droves, but it was not enough. They clung doggedly to their formations, unwavering even as their brothers and comrades fell, torn and screaming around them.

Takelot admired and hated them for it.

Takelot held on as his driver cracked the reins with renewed vigour, freeing his war machine from the press of bodies. Like a swimmer coming up for air, the chariots burst through the formation's edge and onto open ground once more. The ragged tear they left behind took time to heal, but soon enough the soldiers of Tanis shuffled back into line, spears pointed out and shields held high.

A stone, painted white on its southern edge, flashed by his sight, then another. As the heavy chariots churned up the battlefield next to the stones, black sand mixed with the pale topsoil.

'Back. Out,' shouted Takelot.

This time Olekh nodded in affirmation. There could be no mistake now.

The chariots continued in their arc, kicking up dust and obscuring themselves in a cloak of blinding haze. The Theban lines flashed past, and Takelot was back at the command tent even as the dust was still settling from his break-out.

'Thank you, Olekh. A little rough, though,' he said.

Olekh grinned and nodded at the familiar joke, moving to brush and water the horses, caring for them as he would his own children.

'Pharaoh,' said General Ukhesh, coming forward and kneeling. The other commanders joined him, and Takelot was touched by the genuine concern he saw in their expressions.

'Sound the retreat,' Takelot commanded, relishing the piercing shrieks of trumpets moments later. The sound carried across the vast open space of the battlefield and slowly the warriors of the south disengaged and fell back toward their own lines. The withdrawal was gradual, ordered. Not the hasty flight of men in terror, but the seasoned retreat of battle-hardened men against a superior force.

And Tanis was indeed the superior force, though Takelot would never give voice to the thought.

Ukhesh watched the retreat with an old desert scout trick, shielding his sight from the sand's glare with hands held horizontal under his eyes. 'Sire, we can wait no longer.'

Takelot narrowed his eyes, willing more Thebans to escape from the press, but the first warriors in the uniform of Tanis pierced the dust clouds and he knew he could wait no longer.

'Give the order.'

In the same breath, Ukhesh roared to the archers perched on the camp walls. Officers on the ramparts echoed him down the line. Hundreds of bows were raised to the sky and at the general's command they let loose a devastating volley of smouldering fire. In the daylight, the fire-wreathed arrowheads were all but invisible, the heat held in the core of the pitch-soaked linen that shrouded a smooth head.

The Tanites raised their shields by reflex, catching the deadly rain against hardened cowhide. An unfortunate few fell to the volley, pierced through the legs. They screamed as the fire scorched their wounds, and wherever they fell, their comrades rushed to their aid. Some among the Tanites laughed at the attack, as many more of their number lowered their shields, emerging entirely unscathed.

The turn of battle had stripped away the top layers of desert, exposing black, clumpy sand underneath. Clay pots the size of a man's head had been buried a finger-length deep, their contents black and congealed and turning the top layer of sand into thickened mud.

More than a hundred pots were buried across the battlefield, in a stretch of earth some fifty paces wide marked by white painted stones and churned up by thousands of trampling feet, as the Tanites charged forward in their lust for honour and vengeance.

And for their heroism, they burned.

As Takelot watched, the fire-laced arrows stuck home, lancing into the black sand and lighting the pitch-soaked earth. The sand rippled with heat haze an instant before it exploded. The flames raced across the ground, hungrily seeking out the hidden pots and igniting them with concussive explosions, throwing up great clumps of earth and tearing men apart with the force of their detonation. Those closest to the epicentre were torn limb from limb, while those further away were thrown from their feet, knocked senseless and deafened by the blast.

The Tanite vanguard suddenly found themselves caught between their enemy and a wall of flames from which the agonised screams of their comrades sounded, burned alive by Theban sorcery.

At a gesture from their king, the Thebans returned to the fray, charging down the hill and screaming savage war cries as they fell upon the very men they had just been retreating from. The Tanite vanguard broke almost instantly but had nowhere to go, their retreat cut off by the wall of flame engulfing the middle of their force. They died where they stood, cut down in vengeful frenzy, a merciful death compared to the fire behind them.

The inferno was short-lived. Starved of fuel, the flames guttered and died, leaving charred corpses in their hundreds. The Thebans cut and chopped at the survivors, careful not to stray into the smouldering strip, for there was no guarantee that all of the pots had exploded.

Smoke choked the battlefield, and the sand shimmered as burning fragments of flesh and pottery littered the land. As a final infliction, a lone pot detonated deep within the Tanite ranks, casting aside fleeing men like a petulant child throws their dolls.

The smoke rose high as the Thebans retired from the field. Through the haze, Takelot could see the bulk of Shoshenq's force well beyond the trap he had set. The thought did not trouble him for he had no desire to kill more Egyptians than necessary.

He tore his gaze away from the horror and took off his blue crown.

'That will be all for today,' he said. 'I want reports at the war council in two hours.'

Of his officers, most stood to attention, watching the scene with grim fascination. Two vomited noisily, but he did not begrudge them that. War was filled with horror, but fear won wars as often as numbers did.

He handed the war crown to his attendant and set off for the camp gates. 'Now, let us see if the Tanites still have the stomach for a fight.'

OSORKON WENT TO war with hatred in his heart. His moods were black enough that Karoadjet could not reach him, and even

Bakenptah was at a loss of how to draw him out again. The convoy passed Amaket's village a day later, the once-thriving town now little more than smouldering ruins and corpse-littered streets. More than a hundred Egyptians lay dead and bloating in the sun, butchered senselessly in the name of what, Osorkon did not know.

The scout reports only darkened his moods.

Hermopolis was overrun. The villages of the Hare nome were destroyed, and their people killed or enslaved to serve the growing Kushite force. As far as the scouts could tell, the horde was made up of disparate peoples under the overall command of a pirate lord turned conqueror. Nubians from the south, Egyptian peoples from the coasts of the Red Sea, and nomadic Libyan tribes from the western oases had all answered the call, united in their hatred for Egypt and doubtless their love of gold.

Such an alliance should have been fraught, each tribe falling upon another for the slightest insult. That it had held together long enough to not only reach Hermopolis, but take the city, spoke of the implacable will of the barbarian chieftain that ruled this host.

Malkesh.

The name was repeated with every report. Every scout relayed the same dark tales of public executions, smouldering ruins and mass graves. The screams of women, the laments of men and the cries of children wove their way into each telling, a gruesome tapestry of tales that brought fresh horrors and darkened Osorkon's thoughts still further.

These were his people, these lands under his protection, and they were suffering. The people of Hermopolis still lived, spared a quick death, but if even half of the reports were true then many would gladly walk into the embrace of Anubis sooner than later.

Malkesh.

Osorkon let the name roll off his tongue every night as he drifted towards restless sleep.

Malkesh was responsible for the murder and rape of thousands. Malkesh was responsible for the death of the City of Scribes and the loss of the holy relics and great libraries of knowledge that lay within the city's walls. Malkesh was responsible for keeping Osorkon from reaching Thebes and ascertaining the truth of what had happened there.

The thought sustained his hatred as his army of charioteers trod the well-worn roads south. On the morning before they approached Hermopolis, Osorkon ordered the women and children to remain in camp while the charioteers pressed on. For once, Karoadjet did not argue, and though she tried to be strong for the families she led, Osorkon could see the fear in her eyes as the men took their leave of their wives.

The first sign of the city was the smoke. Great plumes drifted lazily in the breeze, too thick and too black to be the gentle haze of cooking fires. To the south and to the east, more pillars of smoke marked villages like grave markers, all but obliterated by the malice of souls touched by darkness.

'Orders, my lord?' Akhetep halted his chariot a respectful distance from his prince's and saluted with a closed fist over his breast. Bakenptah did likewise, his face grim and dust-streaked.

Osorkon smiled, for the first time in days, at their formality. He stepped down from his chariot and looked over the city as he leaned on the edge of his friend's chariot. 'Forgive my ill temper these last days. These are my people and I have failed them. They are dead because of the choices my family has made. It is a burden that does not sit easily.'

Osorkon considered the problem before him. Where the city gates should have been was a ragged tear in the stone, as though a massive fist had gouged out a section of the city's defences. Broken masonry lay where it fell, but a hastily erected timber palisade plugged the gap. Though it was a poor replacement, almost laughably so, it would stand against chariots with ease. 'We brought no siege equipment with us. We have no hope of breaching the walls and even if we did, we leave our most precious resource behind.'

'We wait them out then?' asked Akhetep.

'We cannot afford to. Every day the people inside those walls suffer and die. If Thebes has betrayed us as my uncle believed, then every day they will dig their claws deeper into our home. Every day my father's army bleeds.'

'Then we politely ask them to come out and fight,' said Bakenptah.

Osorkon's mouth split into a grim smile. 'In a manner of speaking. How do the warriors of Nubia fight?'

Akhetep shrugged. 'Screaming?'

'Beyond that.'

'In a horde without formation,' said Bakenptah. 'Seeking their own personal glories.'

'Exactly,' replied Osorkon. 'They fight frenzied, their strength lying in the knowledge that they have numbers on their side.'

'Which they do,' countered Bakenptah. 'We number no more than five hundred. They have two thousand, at least.'

'A fact that I am well aware of, brother. They will fight like beasts when they think they have the upper hand and while they have the numbers. We lull them out and tempt them with their own savage nature.'

'And their garrison?' asked Akhetep.

'What garrison? Which of them will volunteer to stay behind when the right bait is laid?' said Osorkon. 'Start collecting timber. We will need a lot of it. Move the wagons beyond the rise and let us get some sleep. We have a long night ahead.'

GENERAL KAPHIRI SWEPT the figures off the planning table, the wooden blocks representing the Theban and Tanite forces cast across the room to crash against a timber chest.

'This will scar a generation,' the general shouted, as he paced back and forth like a caged lion. The officers and commanders in the royal tent shrank before his wrath.

Only Takelot and Ukhesh met his eye unblinking.

'Let me remind you, general, that you were at the council that decided on this course. I will forgive your outburst for you are weary, as are we all. It is late and we have lost many friends today, but do not presume to speak like that to me again,' said Takelot levelly.

Kaphiri glared at his king. 'And how many more enemies have we just made today? How many of our countrymen have we condemned in the world beyond with fire and vengeance? Half of them have nothing left to bury.'

'How many more will soon refuse to fight and die and instead broker for peace?' countered Takelot.

The fire in Kaphiri's eyes faded, an exhausted disquiet coming over his features. He pinched the bridge of his nose and rubbed his stinging eyes. When he spoke again his voice was quiet, the voice of an embalmer conducting the rites. 'Mark my words. In that fire you ended any chance for peace. Men will not bow to the man who burned their brothers alive. If you bring peace, you bring the peace of the grave. No, not even that. You bring the peace of eternal oblivion.'

Kaphiri shook his head and made for the tent opening. 'And what now?' he said to everyone and no-one. 'We have shown our first and only trick.' Kaphiri did not wait for the answer and pushed through the tent doors into the night.

'They do not know that,' called Ukhesh after him, but Kaphiri was already gone.

Takelot stooped to pick up one of the war figures scattered by his general, and within moments his staff had scurried to collect the rest. The king spent long moments rearranging the armies on the map precisely how they had been. 'Is there anyone else that wishes to air grievances. You may speak freely.'

No-one moved.

No-one but Ukhesh.

'My king,' he began, falling to one knee at Takelot's side. 'You have led us this far and suffered as we have suffered. You lost your own kin as we have lost friends and brothers. I do not pretend the road ahead is free of blood. I fear we may spill far more before this day is done, but I believe in the future you promise us. I believe in you.'

Ukhesh bowed his head. 'I cannot speak for other men, but I will follow you into the depths of the underworld itself if you ask it of me.'

Takelot's stony façade cracked and like a priest administering rites, he laid a hand on Ukhesh's shoulder and gently led him to his feet.

Pharaoh and general clasped arms.

'Hermopolis stands with you, sire. For the glory of Thoth and Pharaoh.'

'You are a credit to your people, general. I am grateful to have you, all of you, at my side,' said Takelot. 'Sleep well, men of the south. The war begins anew tomorrow.'

THE CAMP WAS set out according to Egyptian military protocol, a grid of shelters with the command tent at its heart and fires burning at set intervals. Five hundred men could sleep here comfortably, but the camp could hold a thousand or more warriors and camp followers if necessary, and the stores left out in the open were designed to give just that illusion.

The camp boundaries had been hastily erected and with little thought to a full-scale attack. At main thoroughfares, clusters of pickets pointed into the night and caches of arrows were never far from hand, but no palisades had been erected nor ditches dug to discourage a sizable assault.

Lone figures stood motionless at the camp's edge, leaning heavily on their spears and silhouetted against the torches and braziers.

To the west, Osorkon crouched at the edge of a ridge, watching the firelight flicker and burn in his camp. From such a distance, the glow coalesced into one light, the brightness of the torches tricking his eyes.

The night was cool, but the temperature did not bother him. His blood was running hot, as it always did before a battle. Behind him, his five hundred charioteers waited patiently beside their war machines, the drivers checking and rechecking their mounts while the archers tested their bows and spears in silence. Their ranks stretched back in three columns perfect and still, putting in Osorkon's mind the image of tomb ushabti awaiting their master's summons. When the time came for Anubis to pluck him from this life, he knew that he could ask for no finer guardians than the men standing with him here and now.

Osorkon checked his bow string for the fifth time that hour, testing the tension and searching for frayed edges in the darkness. He was about to check his quiver again when he heard a hiss.

Akhetep heard it at the same moment, and prince and commander each silently nocked an arrow as they watched the ridgeline.

A lone figure, crouching low, tumbled over the heights, springing back to his feet and making a beeline for the head of the columns. The runner came to a breathless stop before his commanders and saluted. 'My lords, Hermopolis has opened.'

'Thank you, Kotef. You have my gratitude.'

Kotef bowed again and scurried toward the back of the column and his own war machine.

Osorkon turned to the charioteer behind him. 'Pass the word. We move soon.'

'Finally,' growled Akhetep, and stepped up into his chariot, rolling his shoulders.

Osorkon did likewise as a low hum reached his ear and he gestured for silence. The thunder of hundreds and hundreds of feet grew louder and louder, reaching its crescendo as the destroyers of Hermopolis crested the distant rise, heading straight for the empty campsite.

Osorkon watched them sweep over the ridge like water, flowing over the landscape in a single, rippling mass. No battle formations nor sense of cohesion bound them together, but for a singular desire to shed blood and loot whatever was left.

The closest of their flanks, if such a thing could be referred to with any precision, was still half a kilometre off when, with a silent gesture, Osorkon led his chariots to the charge.

Despite his instructions to grease the axles and the wheel mounts, the chariots creaked and groaned as the charioteers rode across uneven ground. The horses whickered and whinnied as their hooves pressed into the sand, and Osorkon willed the battle madness of their enemy to hide them for just a few moments more.

The horde's vanguard had reached the camp borders by the time the last of them had come over the ridge. No Theban remained in this camp, the families and followers kept hidden in another camp kilometres away with instructions to flee back north at dawn should they receive no word from the charioteers.

The thunderous charge of the chariots did not go completely unnoticed before battle was joined. As Osorkon had sighted his first shot, one of the closest warriors turned, ears pricked at the sound of chariots like a jackal in the night. The moment stretched on as Osorkon saw the surprise in the man's face. His eyes widened and his mouth opened to scream a warning when Osorkon fired his shot, his lips pulled back from his teeth in a feral snarl as he loosed the arrow into the writhing mass of men.

The warrior threw himself forward, stumbling in his stride, but such was the press of bodies that the prince could not miss. Over the first man's shoulder, another of the warriors pitched forward, pierced by the arrow that took him high in the ribs. The men that followed ran past him, assuming he had simply tripped until more of their number began to fall.

Within moments, scores of shafts hissed through the night, striking down men indiscriminately. The darkness made true accuracy all but impossible, but the charioteers did not need to see their enemy to kill them, such was the horde's size.

Osorkon raised his bow above his head and shouted in his driver's ear. In reply, his driver pulled hard on the reins, sending the chariot skirting along the flanks of the horde. A thousand men or more, driven to the edge of insanity with bloodlust, were suddenly aware of the danger in their midst. Those closest turned to fight this new and hidden threat, while those furthest away continued on toward the camp, oblivious to the slaughter being wreaked upon their comrades only a few hundred metres away.

From the corner of his eye, Osorkon saw Akhetep lead half of the chariots further to the south, running across the horde's rear ranks and cutting off their escape. Akhetep knelt in the footwell, firing with practised precision, his arrow arm never stopping as he burned through the quivers secured to his machine. For every warrior shot dead, ten more men seemed to emerge from the darkness and Osorkon ordered his contingent to break from the massed flanks lest they be caught and overwhelmed.

The Thebans reaped a fearsome tally, but they did not emerge entirely unscathed. Throwing spears pierced man and horse both, and a lucky strike here and there slashed the tendons in a horse's leg or bit through a charioteer's armour.

The chariots under Osorkon's command rode in a long arc, riding hard past the camp to come in a circle back along the horde's edge. Osorkon's expression hardened as he saw the camp burning. Deprived of sating their bloodlust, the sackers of Hermopolis had unleashed their wanton destruction on the unoccupied tents instead. Osorkon grimaced at that. They would be sleeping under the stars for many nights, one way or the other.

The firelight shone like a beacon, casting long shadows over the battlefield and throwing the expressions of fighting men into stark and terrible relief. Theban and Kushite both fought with desperation and hatred in their hearts.

Within the press of bodies, Osorkon discarded his bow and took up his long sword, its iron edge glowing red in the light. It rose and fell as his chariots cut through the edges of the formation, butchering men with every stroke. The fortunate died in silence, dead before they hit the ground. The unlucky ones fell wounded, only to be crushed beneath the wheels of chariots further behind.

Osorkon turned as he heard a horse scream in pain. Holding onto the chariot railing, he watched helpless as one of Terekh's horses fell thrashing into the sand, its throat opened up by an unlucky spear thrust. Its partner, suddenly hauling the weight of a chariot and its dying companion, stumbled and lost its footing. Osorkon heard the twin cracks of its front legs breaking, bringing the chariot to a sudden, grinding stop.

Terekh was thrown from his mount, landing in a crumpled heap among his wounded horses. His driver managed to keep his footing, but he screamed as he was thrown bodily against the chariot's chassis. The horde was upon them both in seconds, hacking and cutting them to pieces with feral abandon.

Osorkon cried out in frustration and rage, pointing with his sword where he wished to go. His driver hauled on the reins again, forging a path deeper into the horde's flank.

Osorkon was wrath incarnate, the burning exhaustion in his arm only fuelling his rage as he hacked and cut at any of the horde within his reach. He roared as he killed, his chest and face spattered with blood as tribesmen were torn apart by his wheel scythes.

He killed for what seemed like hours, though later he would learn only minutes had passed before he caught sight of Akhetep carving his own way through the smoke and sand.

For the first time, Osorkon detected hesitancy in his enemy. Fractious and divided, they possessed none of the kinship and sense of duty and brotherhood that the Egyptians possessed. The Nubians turned to their own, while the Libyans sought out their kin and those of the Red Sea coast sought out familiar faces. In the darkness, the vicious visages of fighting men were replaced by wide-eyed fear, pushing back against their own allies to escape the hewing ferocity of the Theban charioteers.

Just as the first frightened buffalo heralds a stampede, so too did the first tribesmen break and fall back, bringing the entire horde into flight. In a disordered mob, the warriors of the infamous Malkesh turned and ran.

Osorkon gave them no respite. Shouting to Akhetep over the terrified screams of the horde, he charged after them with all the ferocity he could muster, even as the battle fury brought trembling fatigue to his flesh. He led the charge after the horde, but their number was still beyond counting and the gates to the palisade were rapidly closing.

As Osorkon watched, the light grew thinner and the prince begin to realise that Malkesh was ready to sacrifice hundreds of his men for the safety of his new realm.

'Faster or this battle is lost,' shouted Osorkon over the hissing wind. With practised precision, the chariots of his cohort fell in behind their prince, scything through the slowest of their enemy in a spear-tip formation as they aimed for the only way into Hermopolis.

# Chapter Twenty-Three

THUNDER RUMBLED ACROSS the desert as the chariots of Thebes rode down the fleeing invaders without mercy. The gates of Hermopolis, rebuilt from ruined timber loomed up ahead, a sliver of pale light between the open doors. The horde were silent as they ran, a far cry from the screeching savages they had been only minutes before.

They died just as silently.

Osorkon shot them down with impunity, launching shaft after shaft into the backs of men fleeing in terror. He had returned to his bow when the horde broke, striking down at range and relying on his war machine to clear a path through the press of men.

Dozens more were torn apart beneath the whirling blades of the chariot's wheel scythes, some as they fled, others as they turned to fight in a last futile gesture of defiance. The wet splash of iron through flesh was repeated again and again, leaving a bloody feast for the vultures when dawn came.

The tribesmen were not without their luck, however. The war machines of the royal charioteers were swift and gilded, forged for speed not strength, and more than a few were undone on the rocky terrain. Timber axles splintered, and reinforced wheels fractured from days of constant use with only rudimentary maintenance afforded to them.

Without a stable foundation, archers and drivers alike were tossed from their platforms and scattered across the rocky ground. Those that fell within sight of the Nubians or Libyans were set upon before they could defend themselves. The tribesmen's triumphs were short-lived though, and the next wave of chariots scattered them to bloodstained sand.

'Die as you lived,' snapped Osorkon as he let off another shot. 'Choking on dust.'

A Libyan warrior heard Osorkon bearing down on him and he turned in alarm, terror etched across his features. The man was lean and hard from a lifetime in the desert, his colourful robes a mirror of the Meshwesh style but torn and ragged in his flight.

Exhausted and pale with fatigue, the warrior held a single throwing spear in trembling hands. Facing the chariot formation with no change to escape, the Libyan's eyes fixed on the horses and he threw with what little strength remained in him.

Osorkon's eyes widened and he hauled on the reins with his free hand. His driver tried to correct, turning to his master in confusion before the spear took him in the chest. A low gasp escaped the driver's lips before he was gone, thrown from his footing by the force of the throw.

Osorkon resisted the urge to look back. If the spear had not killed him outright, then the fall almost certainly would have. He swore as he snatched up the flailing reins, the horse team swaying off course without a firm hand to guide them. Osorkon was almost thrown off as he brought them back under control, but their rhythm was broken and he drew them back into a canter as the other chariots surged ahead.

The Libyan had watched his throw strike home and grinned as Osorkon brought his chariot to a halt not twenty paces away from him. The horses were skittish as Osorkon snatched up his spear and shield and went after the Libyan with murder in his heart.

The tribesman saw the spear in the prince's hand and realised his only weapon was gone.

Without word or challenge he turned and fled. Osorkon snarled at being denied and calmly walked back to his chariot. He snatched up his bow and nocked an arrow to the string, taking a moment to rub his horse between the ears before he sighted the Libyan down.

Around him, the hiss and rumble of chariots speeding past left a twinge of unease in his gut, but he was assured that they had all so far given him a wide enough berth. He closed his eyes for a moment, feeling the complete absence of wind, and fired.

The arrow disappeared into the chaos of the melee and Osorkon watched the retreating tribesman for a moment more. He almost reached for a second shaft when the Libyan lurched and fell forwards.

Whether it was his arrow or another's did not matter to him, only that his driver was avenged. Osorkon remounted, securing his bow back in its brace and brought the horses back up to a steady gallop.

The tribesmen were being funnelled into the gate, the fortunate few pushing past their comrades for the safety of Egyptian-made walls. Osorkon cried out in hatred as the gates narrowed to a fraction of what they had been, his chance for vengeance slipping away with every push against the makeshift gates, but moments later the tribesmen hauling on the defences scattered as the Theban vanguard fell upon them.

The first chariot to reach the gates was a fraction too wide for the gap, its chassis catching on the doors and breaking apart in the impact. The horses screamed as their momentum was broken, and their halters snapped with the force. They reared up in fright, lashing out and shattering bones with flailing hooves.

The second and third chariots slid to a grinding stop, bottlenecked as more of the vanguard suddenly found themselves with nowhere to go.

'Open it,' cried Osorkon. 'Open it now.'

He was on them in moments, leaping from his chariot and snatching up his spear. Holding up his spear in guard position, he lent his strength to pushing the door back, throwing his shoulder into the timber and roaring with effort.

The Nubians on the other side ran as the Thebans spilled through the gates on foot, hacking and slashing until the defenders were overwhelmed. One of the charioteers was struck down by an unseen archer and Osorkon called for covering fire as the Thebans secured the improvised gatehouse.

Osorkon left his men to hold the doors and took his first steps inside the city. Charred husks smouldered where homes and warehouses used to be, but he recognised the main thoroughfares well enough. Already, reinforcements were massing in the centre square, drawn to the sounds of battle and rallying where there were the most numbers.

'Remount. Go through. Remount,' shouted Osorkon, leaping back onto his chariot.

The ruined chariot was dragged away, and the horse team released out beyond the walls. The bodies of the unfortunate charioteers were quickly shrouded and hauled away as the rest of the charioteers remounted.

As in many Egyptian cities, a great highway split Hermopolis down the centre, linking the primary gate to the market districts and palace. Wide enough for traders pulling oxen teams and wagons, it was easily expansive enough for the chariots to ride down at a charge.

The first chariots made it through with only token resistance, most of the tribesmen too focused on preserving themselves to offer much of a challenge. Stuck to the rear of the formation, Osorkon could only listen as the vanguard cut down the stragglers from the earlier battle. So close to safety, the routed screamed for help that would never come. Osorkon felt no sympathy. Such aggression could only be met with unyielding vengeance.

The charioteers in the front ranks pulled hard, slowing their charge down to a canter. Osorkon peered through the gaps, cursing at the sight. What, at first, he had taken to be the drifting smoke of burned-out houses had only intensified since their breach of the walls.

The Hermopolitan highway was choked with fire, a burning barricade the height of a man lashing the road and surrounding buildings with flame. Nothing could pass the inferno, and Osorkon knew that it would soon spread.

Osorkon wheeled his chariot around, gesturing back towards the gate.

'Back,' he shouted. 'The savages use fire to stop what their spears cannot.'

Trapped in a dead end, the milling Thebans found themselves under fire from the tribesmen beyond the barricade. Nomads and huntsmen all, their aim was remarkable, and horses and men fell shrieking as the deadly shafts pierced armour and horseflesh alike.

Osorkon returned fire, but the chaos of the moment was too great and shot and shot went wide. Here and there, charioteers followed their lord's lead, firing to cover their comrades, but the shots were hurried and desperate and too few found their mark.

Osorkon steered his way back through the throng, finding Akhetep in the heart of the broken formation. The commander's eyes were wild in the firelight and he cursed as he ordered his warriors to fall back.

'Akhetep, take your detachment along the river. Secure the libraries and warehouses and meet me at the palace when you are done,' shouted Osorkon, gesturing towards the plaza they had passed three blocks earlier.

Akhetep saluted a clenched fist over his heart. 'Cohort of Anubis, to me!' he called, leading the way from the front.

Osorkon searched for Bakenptah in the chaos, but his brother was lost among the blockade of chariots. He prayed to Amun for deliverance and tried to put his brother's fate to the back of his mind.

'Cohort of Osiris, on me! To the royal standard. Fall back.'

The charioteers fell back in short order, a trickle and then a flood of horses and war machines thundering down the way back towards the city gates.

Akhetep's cohort peeled off right, heading east along the riverside roads and into the port district where the widest roads would lead back to the central plaza. Osorkon led his own cohort to the left, deeper into the residential and administrative districts.

At this hour, the sight of torches and burning lamps in the windows of houses and offices should have been commonplace, but the streets of Hermopolis were shrouded in complete darkness, the city's inhabitants nowhere to be seen.

'Onward,' ordered Osorkon, leading his men deeper into the shrouded streets. Not one of them spoke, nor were there any rallying cries now, just a fierce and bitter determination to avenge the destruction around them. Osorkon could hear the roaring flames of the barricade burning streets away, and the rhythmic creak of tortured axles sounded with each hard turn they made as they navigated their way further into the city.

Up ahead, the looming silhouette of an obelisk stood tall, where humble houses gave way to large, grand temples and administrative buildings. No firelight disturbed the scenes here and Osorkon paused at the junction, judging which way to go.

An arrow buried itself deep in the timber of his chariot frame, and within moments a second had joined the first. Osorkon dropped to his knees in the footwell, searching for the source of the shot. From high above, the whining hiss of arrows continued unabated, and Osorkon snarled as he heard men and horses struck down screaming around him.

'To the palace,' he called. 'Forward.'

At the end of the junction, over a hundred spearmen spilled out of their hiding places and into the streets to form their own living barricade against the oncoming chariots.

Osorkon charged them down without pause. He crouched in the footwell, holding the reins in one hand and couching a spear in the other. The charioteers around him fired into the ranks directly ahead, waiting for the crucial moment before the charge when the death of a comrade causes the most pause. Taken aback by the sudden deaths in their midst, the spearmen either side of the slain wavered for just a moment.

It was enough.

Osorkon's horses bludgeoned the spearmen aside and the wheel scythes cut them down a second later. Their lines were shattered, the survivors on the flanks throwing themselves back into cover.

'Fall before us,' Osorkon roared. 'Your death has come!'

No sooner had the words escaped his lips then the sound of the earth rending caught his attention. A grinding crack split the sound of battle and Osorkon hauled on the reins as the noise eclipsed his sense of direction. A moment of silence was followed by a titanic thunderclap that shook the ground beneath his feet and sent the horses into a frightened whinny. The enormous obelisk, taller than any object in the city, had been brought down, blocking the road and obliterating the houses beneath it. Its ruined base was a patchwork of pick strikes and axe marks as the mercenaries had hastily unmade the work of years of Egyptian masons and artificers.

The surviving spearmen fled down the road towards the central plaza, casting their weapons aside in blind flight. With the way to the temple district blocked, Osorkon hauled on the reins and went after them instead. He turned to his cohort and pointed beyond the orange glow of the burning barricade. 'Follow them in,' he ordered.

Until now, none of the charioteers had dared to give voice to their fears. One of his charioteers looked back at him wild-eyed and fearful. 'Sire, it's a trap. They'll pull the city down around us.'

'Then kill them faster,' Osorkon snarled, sending his horses into a gallop. He brought his spear up again, ignoring the now familiar burn in his killing arm. Another routing spearman fell but there was another and another to take his place.

Osorkon's eyes narrowed as he honed in on another fleeing form. 'Thoth, Lord of Hermopolis, deliver us in this final hour,' he said. He laughed with savage joy as he felt the spear recoil, jarring back into its shoulder as he reaped yet another life.

THE THEBANS EMERGED from the smoking battlefield like the dead reawakened. Caked in dust from headscarf to sandals, they were a far cry from the gleaming soldiery that had set camp here less than a week before. The only bare flesh not covered in dust was that washed clean by rivulets of blood and sweat. Takelot could only hope the Tanites were in a similar state.

One day had felt as long as a week, the Thebans testing and probing the Tanite lines, skirmishing across the battlefield but refusing to commit to a full-scale battle. They had been pushed back at every turn until the fading daylight prohibited further attacks, lest the Thebans become lost, surrounded and destroyed.

The Pharaoh of Thebes looked out over his battle-wearied companies and hardened his heart. He was a king, and kings did not have the luxury of mortal emotion, least of all fear, but an all too ordinary tension hung over him as the camp gates were opened and survivors of the latest skirmish filtered through.

Takelot greeted them at the walls, wishing them well and offering words of encouragement and benediction. Many of his soldiers simply looked up or nodded at their king, throwing down their shields and weapons as soon as they reached the safety of the camp walls, too tired to make the trek to their own tents. Takelot could not begrudge them that, and called for water, beer and food to be brought to the gates.

Five days of battle had seen his army exhausted against the well-disciplined Tanite force. Five days of losing as much ground as they gained, of losing brothers and friends new and old, of losing entire units in the maelstrom of civil war.

Five days of spilling Egyptian blood.

Ukhesh was gravely wounded on the third day, dragged down under Tanite spears. By some miracle, he had been found still alive when his charioteers had pushed back the northern lines and recovered their leader. By the grace of Amun, he yet breathed, but he had fallen into a deep twilight sleep from which neither the entreaties of priests nor the ministrations of healers could awaken him.

A shout came from beyond the gatehouse and the men trudging through quickly shuffled aside as a contingent of chariots pushed through. The gate was wide enough for two chariots across, but General Kaphiri nonetheless led alone as the first through.

Kaphiri saluted and stepped down, barking instructions to his driver who quickly led the chariots to the camp's stables and workshops.

'Good hunting, general?' greeted Takelot.

'As good as any other day, sire,' replied Kaphiri.

Takelot called for water and a clay cup was pressed into Kaphiri's right hand. The water was warm and brackish but Kaphiri drank it in a single swallow, tossing the vessel back to the attendant and wiping his grime-covered lips with the back of his hand. When he spoke again, his voice was pitched low, beyond the hearing of the exhausted men reclined only metres away. 'We cannot endure much more of this.'

There was no accusation in his tone, simply cold fact. Takelot nodded, the words of comfort and hope that came to him so easily abandoning him now in the face of reality.

'How went the battle?'

'Our centre gave way, but their left flank broke almost immediately after. We were lucky. Had our right flank not broken through, far fewer of these men would be sitting here.'

'Amun, guide us,' intoned Takelot.

'Would that he came down and fought beside us,' Kaphiri grunted.

Takelot's jaw clenched but he let the blasphemy pass.

'Sire, we must begin preparing for all possibilities,' said Kaphiri. 'Today, we were lucky. Tomorrow, I am not so sure.'

Takelot nodded again, words failing him. He wanted to retort, but defeatism was rapidly becoming a matter of practicality, not pessimism. 'Feed yourself well, then summon the commanders that still stand. We meet in an hour. We may yet find a way out of this mess.'

Kaphiri saluted and ventured to do his lord's bidding, leaving Takelot alone by the gate.

Takelot glanced west, as the last hour of day stained the landscape in reddish-purple hues. There were a hundred matters and more that demanded the king's attention, but for now he wanted to be here, among the men that had fought, bled and grieved for the dead with him. He climbed the ramparts, leaving the soldiers to their recovery, and looked out over the battlefield. The Tanite camp was a smear of white on the northern horizon, almost invisible unless one looked for it. The dust of the battlefield was slowly settling. By nightfall, it would be gone, leaving behind a charnel house sight that would soon be thankfully smothered in shadow.

Soldiers from both sides collected their dead and wounded under the flag of truce, but already the stench had drawn carrion beasts that lingered at the peripheries. The wounded numbered in their hundreds, the dead in their thousands, and for every walking wounded that was brought back, the bodies of three of his comrades were dragged to the embalmers.

The king made himself watch it all.

This was his responsibility, try as he might to justify the sight before him. He had been manoeuvred into it and the circumstances surrounding his incarceration had left him little choice, but surely the gods had not intended the story of the Two Lands to be steeped in so much blood. The wounds of this war would take generations to heal, and Takelot knew that enemies, both within and without, would look to this civil strife and see the advantage. Shalmaneser, the King of the Assyrians, had been beaten but not vanquished, and the stirrings of unrest in the lands of Nubia were a constant threat to Egypt's southern borders. Tribal conflicts were a nuisance, but might the grand armies of distant Nubia risk a full-scale invasion of Egypt?

Would Thebes have the strength to push back against external enemies? Would Tanis?

The civil war had drained the fighting spirit and strength of both cities, the battles and skirmishes lasting more than a week with no clear victor, but the inevitable mathematics of war had firmly swung in the favour of Tanis. A complete victory, one of routing the enemy entirely, would come at a cost that even Shoshenq would be loath to pay. Veterans as they were against the Assyrian kingdom, they beat the southern coalition back time and again, winning through patient and dour resoluteness.

He was losing, Takelot knew. Not in a glorious last stand, nor with a battle to carve into the stone of eternity, but through the brutal arithmetic of attrition. It had taken days to reach this point and it would take days more to quit the field. Perhaps half of his men were still in fighting condition, while best estimates from his spy networks put the Tanites at under three-quarters fighting fitness.

To the east, the lights of the Tanite fleet illuminated the black water of the river like floating candles. The coalition fleets had fought valiantly but could not match the experience of the Tanite navy, veterans as they were against both the Phoenician navy and Cypriot pirates. Forced to retreat days ago, the coalition fleet gave way and this stretch of river now belonged to Tanis, and therein lay yet another problem. Without ships, Theban supplies were diminishing by the hour.

Leaning on the ramparts, Takelot watched the embalmers pull a wagon loaded with the wounded. Most of the draught animals had been slaughtered for food already, the coalition army voracious in its appetite, and the priests as non-combatants had been forced to fill in the role. Unused to physical hardship, the king saw one of the priests slip in the sand as they hauled the cart up the hill. One of the wounded let out a scream as the cart rolled over a rock. The extra joint in the man's leg rolled with sickening fluidity.

So, this is what we are reduced to, thought Takelot. Men working as beasts and the only salted meat in sight is our own dead. His hands clenched into fists as he looked back over his camp and the difficulties it now faced. His ships were gone, but resupply by land had become an even more difficult proposition. Tanite raiders and opportunistic tribesmen attacked his caravans whenever they saw them, and recent battlefield losses made it impossible to draw too many men from the front lines to guard their passage.

At least, that is what he convinced the officers who had petitioned him. The threat of desertion was all too real and would seal the coalition's doom sooner than anything else.

The mortuary cart made it through the gates and Takelot went down to meet them. He had dismissed his guard, wishing for silence and a moment of contemplation, and it felt oddly freeing to simply be a man again. The priests dipped their heads in greeting, though he waved away their deference. Takelot went to speak, but the screaming man's eyes rolled back into of his head and his screams faded into a stuttering groan. The agony had at last pushed him into merciful unconsciousness.

'Take care of them,' said Takelot, regretting the obvious words as soon as he spoke them. He left the priests to their work and made his way back to his command tent.

As Takelot passed the hospital tents, he lingered and listened. The healers did what they could, easing men's suffering with strong beer as often as medicines, but the lack of supplies meant infection was rife and only the superficially wounded had any real chance at a full recovery. The screams of the wounded and the occasional moans of the dying were by far the loudest sounds in the coalition camp. Gone were the crude jokes and rousing songs, the stories told and retold, and the casual laments of leaving families and friends behind. The army was wounded, but the spirits of his men were already dead.

Takelot hovered at the entrance to his command tent. The guards at the door went to push the curtains aside, but Takelot stilled them with a gesture as he listened to the seditious talk taking place within his own sanctum. His expression set hard and immovable and he stepped through with a flourish, enjoying the startled faces of his commanders.

'Finish your thought, Nekhera. I am keen to hear the opinions of my staff,' said Takelot, taking his rightful place at the head of the table.

Nekhera looked everywhere except his lord as he searched for the words.

'Speak man, we do not have all night,' snapped Takelot.

At the raising of the royal voice, the guards at the door entered, spears ready to safeguard their king. Nekhera's eyes flickered from the king to the guards and back again. 'I- I believe we should begin exploring alternative options.'

Takelot smiled thinly. 'That is why we are here, Nekhera. Why do you fear to say it?'

Nekhera looked as though he might be sick.

'He means we should sue for peace.' Kaphiri stepped forward, his arms crossed. His voice was level, neither in support nor denial of Nekhera's position.

Takelot turned back to Nekhera. 'Shoshenq is winning. What makes you think he will come to the negotiating table?' Takelot grunted at Nekhera's continued silence and turned to his officers. 'Well?'

Kaphiri spoke up first. 'He is losing men too. He won't want to rule over a pile of ashes and bones.'

'He won't want to rule over those he hasn't entirely subjugated either.' Takelot shook his head. 'Understand well, my loyal followers, that any surrender to Shoshenq will be unconditional. And in his mind, we have committed treason.'

Takelot caught the look that passed between his officers, so subtle it was that he would have missed it had he not been looking for it. 'Speak plainly, Khefra. No sanction will be placed upon you for speaking your mind.'

Khefra squirmed under his king's gimlet gaze. 'His issue is with your position, my lord.'

Takelot's grim smile broke into a laugh. His officers, with the exception of Kaphiri, flinched at the sound. 'And now we come to the crux of the matter. You would commit treason against one who is already accused of treason? Is that half as bad or twice so?'

'No-one is breaking faith today,' said Kaphiri, standing in front of his king and holding up a placating hand to the commanders.

Herefkne stepped forward and pushed Kaphiri's arm aside. The Hermopolitan's face was flushed with wine and his expression purple with frustration. He thrust an accusing finger at Takelot. 'No, you promised us our freedom. This is your fault, son of Amun,' he snapped.

Kaphiri pinned Herefkne's arms to his side, his eyes blazing in anger. 'Shut up, you damned fool. How dare you?'

Takelot laid a reassuring hand on Kaphiri's shoulder. 'Release him, general. I wish to hear what Herefkne has to say.'

Herefkne threw off Kaphiri's grip and took an unsteady step forward. 'You have led us into an unwinnable war and now we will lose everything. We are defeated. What is left but to be sold into servitude, or worse?'

Takelot shook his head. 'Is your memory so short? Shoshenq was already bleeding us dry.'

'You promised us our freedom,' Herefkne cried.

'I still hold to that promise,' said Takelot.

Herefkne's laugh was the bark of the desert dog. 'It is only a matter of time until Tanis crushes us beneath its heel. Will your empty platitudes shield us from Tanite spears? You are a fine talker, my lord, but your words are meaningless and laced with fear. Nay, cowardice!'

Takelot's fist flashed out, smashing into Herefkne's jaw and sending him careening over the table. The battle map and military tokens were cast over the ground, and the Hermopolitan fell into a groaning heap.

When the king spoke again, his voice was low and level. 'You think me afraid? You are correct. I fear for my family, not myself. I fear for my people, not myself. As I always have. But I tell you now, if you think you would ever rise again under the rule of Shoshenq, then you do not know his heart. His is a vengeful soul, not prone to cruelty or malice, but possessed of a long memory grudges that burn deep. If the thought of toiling on a barren farm for the rest of your days appeals to you, then go and surrender yourself now. I will not stop you, but instead go to my own death laughing at your wasted, pointless life.'

'Surrender is not an option,' cut in Kaphiri. Takelot looked sideways in surprise, but the general was not finished. 'Not anymore. We lost that option when we burned his men alive on the first day. As you say, sire, his memory is long.'

Nekhera stepped past Herefkne's supine form, wagering that his king's rage had already been expended on another. 'That leaves the question of what's to be done now. We cannot weather another frontal assault.'

'No, we cannot,' agreed Takelot, watching as his guards dragged the groaning Herefkne out. He spread the battle map on the table once more and replaced the tokens, letting his hand linger on the ships of Tanis.

The king settled his gaze on his commanders and other officers. 'We cannot fight them head on. They have the numbers and they have the experience. They are better provisioned. We can only do something about one of those things.'

'That's one more thing than I can see, my lord,' said Khefra. 'How do we fight when we are bested in every way?'

'By fighting fire with more fire,' said Takelot, with a thin smile.

Kaphiri's eyes narrowed. 'Sire?'

'How many of those fire pots do we have left?'

Kaphiri shook his head. 'Not again. I will not be responsible for burning more men, my king. These are our countrymen.'

'Calm yourself, general. I have no intention of burning more men. Answer the question, please,' replied Takelot.

Kaphiri's expression was cold as he dug through his memory for the figure. 'I would have to check the exact tally, but certainly no more than fifty.'

Takelot nodded, still smiling. 'And how much pitch?'

'About the only thing we have enough of, my lord,' added Khefra.

'Good. They have the greater numbers, but we can turn that against them. Burn their supplies and they will have to retreat.'

Kaphiri snorted. 'They bring their supplies in by ship. How are you planning on getting out there? Swimming?'

'Why not?' said Takelot.

Kaphiri crossed his arms and searched the faces of his colleagues for similar incredulity. 'If the current does not drag you down, the crocodiles and hippopotamus will.'

'Sobek can be reasoned with. The buffalo, as is its nature, splashes and alerts the Lord of Crocodiles to the feast, but go slowly and calmly and leave no trace behind you and he will look the other way,' replied Takelot.

'As you say, but how do we get fire across water?' asked Kaphiri.

Takelot raised a burning candle from the table and tipped the scalding liquid onto the desk. It solidified instantly and the king scraped it away with his fingernail.

'We can seal the pots with wax. They will float on the river if they're watertight. Seal the wicks in a wax lined bag and use the firebrands that are undoubtedly burning on their ships.'

Nekhera shook his head at the thought. 'And who is going to go?' he said. 'It's a suicide mission.'

'I will,' said Kaphiri, raising a hand to forestall the protest he could see forming on Takelot's lips. 'If this is your will, sire, then I trust no-one else to see it through. I will only take volunteers.'

Takelot nodded, placing one hand over his heart. 'As you wish, general.'

'And what will we be doing, sire?' asked Khefra. 'We cannot sit idle.'

'We won't,' said Takelot. 'Kaphiri will need a diversion to get through unseen and we will provide it. I will lead the chariots into the heart of Shoshenq's camp and see if we can end this another way.'

Kaphiri laughed, but it was short and harsh. He held out his arm and Takelot gripped it, meeting his ranking commander's gaze as at last they reached an understanding.

'Tomorrow night, then?' asked the general.

'Tomorrow night,' replied the king.

RUIN OF SEKHMET

# Chapter Twenty-Four

HERMOPOLIS SCREAMED AT the torture inflicted upon it. Fires gutted whole neighbourhoods, and homes that had stood for generations collapsed under their own ruined weight as timber supports turned to ash. Stone walls that had taken months to build were torn down with reckless abandon and the spoils within plundered.

More than once, Osorkon's cohort had to turn back as avenues were closed over, blocked by debris and fire. Flickering tongues of flame lashed out from broken buildings and overhead, embers and ash rained down in thick, choking clouds.

The sight had become all too familiar to Osorkon in recent months, and he breathed thinly through his mouth as he led his charioteers deeper and deeper into the maze-like inferno. Streets choked with soot and smoke stole all sense of direction, and the only choice left to the charioteers was to keep moving. To stop here was to be trapped, to be felled by an arrow or spear, or choke to death on the billowing fumes that blanketed their passage. The destruction spread quickly, sweeping through the city's quarters as the tribesmen of Nubia looted what they could and set to the torch everything else.

Osorkon's charges cut through tribesmen taken completely unawares, their weapons discarded and their arms laden with looted treasures, fine clothes and ceremonial trinkets. Such was the noise of the inferno that the screams of dying men carried little further beyond those that killed them, and so the Egyptian advance continued in relative secrecy.

The central plaza of Hermopolis was an open forum as much as it was a marketplace. Statues of long dead thinkers and artisans graced the gardens and boulevards, standing watch for eternity over the merchants, philosophers and priests and who plied the public space with their wares and their discourse.

All of it was gone.

No, not gone, for that was too simple for the scene that greeted the charioteers as they burst through into the open square. The plaza had been obliterated, destroyed by the wanton malice of avaricious minds. Statues had been torn down, their features disfigured, and the beautific scenes painted on the masonry daubed with blood and faeces.

Rage threatened to overwhelm Osorkon again, and he blinked his eyes, focusing his anger into every thrust of his spear. He charged into the milling masses, even now crudely profaning this place and entirely unprepared for the vengeance of Thebes. The plaza was replete with the recoiling forms of the invaders, the tribesmen falling back into familiar patterns, gathering together in their mistaken belief that there was safety of numbers.

Osorkon looked beyond the square, seeing that even the temple complex had not escaped the flames and predations of the city's occupiers. Though no flames yet consumed its walls, the Temple of Thoth, the patron god of Hermopolis, was already smouldering. Among the pillars, barbarians ransacked the god's sacred spoils, his divine statues shattered and his sanctum corrupted by the mere presence of unworthy souls.

Osorkon snapped out his orders, his voice grown hoarse from the thick smoke, and watched with a measure of pride as his chariots manoeuvred around burnt-out market stalls and crumbled masonry to organise in wide ranks. Osorkon raised his spear and lanced it forward, lashing his horses from a standstill to gallop within seconds, his men only a fraction behind him. Osorkon was silent as he rode, the agony in his heart beyond words, and his anger was laced with a sick bitterness as he lined up a tribesman at the end of his spear.

Without an organised formation with which to offer defence, the chariot charge sliced through the tribesmen like water flowing through reeds. The Thebans rode them down a dozen at a time, trampling the panicked tribesmen where they stood. Those of Malkesh's horde that were gathered in the central plaza numbered in their hundreds, but they fled before the Theban assault, throwing each other aside to escape the spinning wheel scythes.

Osorkon's spear thrust out, catching a Libyan tribesman between the shoulder blades. He fell soundlessly, or if he screamed Osorkon did not hear it. The prince's chipped and battered spear ran red, his chariot wheels awash with the lifeblood of those that had defiled the city.

Osorkon cut down another with impunity, the tribesman almost throwing himself onto the spearpoint. Another dashed forwards towards a gap between two chariots, misjudging the distance and losing his right leg at the knee for his trouble. He fell screaming as still more sprinted heedlessly at the line of chariots bearing down upon them.

For a moment, Osorkon's face creased with confusion. Tribesmen were fleeing towards him, running onto his blades and throwing themselves beneath his chariot. What madness had possessed them to cast away their lives so readily?

From the other side of the square, Akhetep's Cohort of Anubis came thundering into the fray. Men fell like wheat beneath the thresher's scythe, dozens felled by bow and blade.

As the cohorts converged, Osorkon saw that Akhetep's men had not been without loss. Half of his men still rode, and those still fighting were on the edge of fatigue, man and beast coated in blood and ash. One charioteer, unrecognisable beneath the soot, fought with an arrow lodged in his shoulder. Another rode with a deep gash across his chest. The shadows playing over their faces showed the truth of the turmoil within their souls.

'Commander, report.'

'Nothing you haven't already seen, I'll wager,' replied Akhetep. 'Hundreds of them were heading north, but we cut them off before the gate. The bastards are everywhere, but there's no sign of the command.' Akhetep spat black phlegm onto the road. 'Many are fleeing. I saw hundreds more heading for the port.'

'You let them go?'

'I thought Malkesh would still be at the palace.'

Osorkon shook his head and cursed. 'We can't be sure of that. Whatever dark will has bound them together has fragmented. Where does a beast run when it's facing death?'

'Wherever it can.'

Akhetep looked over the two cohorts. Savaged and mauled, but unbeaten. 'My men are reaching their last and yours look the same. We almost didn't make it back, and I will feel better for fighting at your side again. We must consolidate, but it's your call, sire.'

'The fires are getting out of control. There's no guarantee we'll make it to the palace.'

'To the port, then?'

Osorkon nodded. 'You can bet that Malkesh will be among the first on board. Lead the way, commander.' He raised his killing spear and realised he had been holding it white-knuckled for some time. Fresh blood dripped from his fingers as he adjusted his grip, the iron reek of it filling his senses. The sight should have stirred him, for exultation or revulsion, but instead he felt a molten fury and a burning need to rid this city of the detritus that had sullied its beauty. 'Standard spear-tip formation. Kill anything that gets between us and that port.'

The spear-tip formation swept through the road to the docks like a ship's prow cutting through water. The Thebans rode to battle in silence, hunched in their war machines, spears lashing out to reap life with every thrust. Those that could not flee were cut down without remorse or celebration, but with a cold and methodical precision. Others threw themselves into the alcoves of burning buildings, running blindly into the very inferno they had created to escape this sweeping death.

Like the river delta far to the north, the Hermopolitan harbour road branched out into tributaries that each led to a different nexus of the port. The temple docks branched out to the north, while the centre held the main merchant hub, and the south, in better times, was busy with the traffic of fishermen and local traders.

'There,' shouted Osorkon, over the howling wind. 'Head for that galley.' Eclipsing the cutters and feluccas, the galley was twice the size of the rest of its flotilla, taking pride of place in the centre hub.

Its sails were unfurled even at rest, fluttering in the night breeze, and its braziers were lit, washing the deck with a soft orange glow. The ship sat deep in the water, likely filled with the warlord's personal spoils. As the two cohorts came up to the dock, prince and commander could see a commotion about the gangplank.

'Someone is preparing to leave,' said Osorkon.

'My lord, look! Prince Bakenptah,' shouted Akhetep, gesturing with his spear to the dockyards. Akhetep's earlier estimate of the tribal exodus had only grown. Hundreds upon hundreds of Malkesh's followers swarmed the dock for passage out of Hermopolis. Panic-stricken men pushed each other aside with little thought for anything other than escape.

In the heart of the horde, an ever-diminishing circle of Egyptians held their ground. One hundred Thebans stood against of hundreds of terror-crazed tribesmen, the charioteers fighting in a makeshift fort of their own making. Their chariots had been aligned in a defensive wall, a ring of timber and iron from which the Egyptians stabbed and shot into the mire of men. Bakenptah's personal standard was held high in the centre, and the young prince cried bloody oaths to Amun and Ra with each swing of his blade. The Egyptians were forced back inch by inch against the edge of the dock and the black waters below.

Osorkon raised his spear and charged with a wordless battle cry, the desperate need to reach his brother pushing him beyond the limits imposed by exhaustion. Without a driver he was unable to shoot, but the men beside him had no such difficulties. Dozens of tribesmen fell in the opening moments, cut down by arrows they never saw coming as the line of chariots made straight for Bakenptah's defences.

Several of the horses reared up in panic, their battle indoctrination crumbling in the face of the bitter fray. Others were driven mad by the fire and the noise, kicking and lashing out as their animal instincts overrode years of patient training.

Osorkon held tight to the reins, holding his spear loose and ready as his chariot covered the last of the ground. The chaff amassing in front of him were irrelevant, unyielding in their numbers but meaningless to the final victory. All that mattered was reaching

Bakenptah and hunting the warlord that had brought this ruin to Hermopolis.

'We have to go for the throat,' shouted Akhetep, spear lashing out and opening the neck of an unfortunate Nubian.

The arrow took Akhetep high in the shoulder and threw the chariot commander from his footing. His driver was knocked aside, losing the reins and sending the horses kicking into the horde. The chariots behind swerved around Akhetep's slumped form, but then he was gone, lost in the mindless fray. Osorkon cried out in frustration and fear, torn between the brother of his blood and the brother of his choosing.

He turned in the footwell, pointing his spear back the way they had come and shouted at the closest charioteer behind him.

'Ikhet, recover Commander Akhetep. The rest of you with me.'

Ikhet raised his spear in salute and peeled off from the main attack, dropping his speed and waiting for his comrades to pass him before he made straight for the prone commander. In a moment, he too was lost to sight.

Osorkon fought back stinging tears as all of the hatred and anger uncoiled in his stomach. He screamed for all the friends he had lost, for the blood that stained his family's hands, for the choices that had been thrust upon him that weren't choices at all.

He screamed for the death he knew was certain.

Osorkon braced his legs for the impact every muscle tensing for the bone-jarring deceleration he knew was coming. The spear-tip punched through the masses, forcing those closest to push back against their comrades or to die where they stood.

Silent death came for them, followed by the grinding collision of chariots against flesh. Dozens more fell when the chariots crashed into the swarming mass, catching the horde between Osorkon's charge and Bakenptah's defences. Spines were splintered and bellies were opened as the writhing blades mulched through the masses.

Osorkon's chariot cohort followed him in and formed up, creating a second defensive cordon of war machines, the horses kept within the inner ring to keep them from the spears of the enemy. Those that were caught between the two rings were cut down, but the tribesmen fought with animalistic desperation and dragged down several of the charioteers even as they dismounted.

Bakenptah's standard dipped, the bearer dogged by three tribesmen climbing up and over the chariot ring. The Egyptian charioteers, on foot now, fell upon them a moment later, butchering the tribesmen with methodical precision before they returned to the position.

Osorkon caught sight of his brother in the melee, the dull bronze scales glinting in the torchlight of the galley, a mirror of his own armour. He tore the shield of his chariot housing and fought his way towards the inner circle, where Bakenptah's chosen warriors faced the bodyguards of the warlord, Malkesh.

Bakenptah's face was awash with blood, his headscarf gone and a vicious gash over his brow. His scale armour was torn, his shield dented, and his spear dulled with use. He fought for his life, always on the defensive and forced to turn aside three blows for every one he dealt.

The man he fought was a bronze-skinned giant. His armour was tanned leather, ornate and gilded, his arms bare and a headpiece studded with shining brass gracing his heavy brow.

Bakenptah's eyes darted in his brother's direction, the movement betraying him. Malkesh caught his look and turned to regard the newcomer. The warlord's gaze lingered on Osorkon's armour, his eye roaming back and forth to Bakenptah's own battered scales. His bearded face split into a broad grin.

'Two of you?' he laughed. 'Two little lordlings come to die?'

'Do not talk, fiend,' snarled Osorkon. 'Your voice insults me.'

Malkesh's smile never faded. 'I am the Lord of the Red Sea, the Reaver of Sinai and the Butcher of Hermopolis. Come then, boy. Die well.' He brought his spear up to his brow in a mocking salute, though in truth the weapon was like no spear Osorkon had ever seen. It was a harpoon, its killing edge the length of an infantry sword and its reach half again that of Osorkon's own spear. Like his own weapon, Malkesh's spear tip ran red, clumps of hair and flesh congealing on its edge. For the first time, a cold sense of calm pierced the raging heat inside Osorkon's heart, and he sized up the warlord, circling to force Malkesh between himself and Bakenptah.

Out of the corner of his eye, Osorkon saw Bakenptah shift his balance, an almost imperceptible movement but one that Malkesh was looking for.

Osorkon's spear lanced forward, scraping a cut across Malkesh's breastplate as Bakenptah aimed low, his sword slicing across the back of the warlord's calf. Malkesh snarled, battering aside Osorkon's thrust and throwing him off balance before lashing out and driving Bakenptah back.

Malkesh fought with raw aggression and unfettered power, a primal force encased in flesh. Around them, Osorkon's royal charioteers fell into the fray, throwing themselves at Malkesh's bodyguards. Few of Malkesh's chosen wore more than a few scraps of armour, their chests and backs criss-crossed with scar tissue and a latticework of fresh wounds.

Malkesh laughed as he fought, his harpoon-spear whistling through the air with each strike. Osorkon's arm ached where he turned aside a thunderous blow on his shield. He held his spear loosely, waiting for an opening that never came.

Bakenptah circled around behind the warlord, but Malkesh was faster than the princes had expected. Every blow was battered away with brute strength, forcing the brothers off-balance and open to a murderous return stroke.

Bakenptah shouted, in pain and defiance, as Malkesh's spear caught him with a heavy blow across the back. His torn scale armour prevented the sharp edge from cutting him in half, but the force knocked him to his knees and he rolled with momentum as the harpoon speared after him, scoring a line in the earth where Bakenptah had just been.

Malkesh dashed after Bakenptah, covering the distance in three bounding steps, to stand over the supine prince, grinning from ear to ear as his spear raised high. The warlord tensed to deliver the killing blow before his face contorted in agony.

Behind him, Osorkon twisted and pulled the spear from the meat of Malkesh's thigh, watching thick blood jet down the back of the warlord's leg.

A wet leopard's growl escaped from Malkesh's lips as he stalked towards Osorkon, who was forced to give ground, backtracking through the melee. The harpoon-spear shot out again, punching through his timber shield. Pain flared in his wrist and he felt something give inside his shoulder as his shield was torn from his forearm.

Osorkon darted back, retreating over the line of chariots and opening up some distance between himself and Malkesh. From the corner of his eye, he saw Bakenptah still on his knees, surrounded by his charioteers in a defensive ring.

The warlord's smile was gone and Malkesh regarded his prey with pitiless cruelty. The warlord went to step over the chariot housing, favouring his good leg. His weight shifted forward for the next step and that was when Osorkon lunged forward.

Taken aback by the sudden attack, Malkesh went to step back and put all his weight on his wounded leg. The torn flesh gave out, and with a cry the warlord toppled over the chariot bracing and landed on his back in the dust.

Malkesh made it back to his knees before Osorkon was on him, the prince's spear thrusting down with all his weight behind it. The warlord's breastplate held for a moment before the spearhead punctured through deep into the meat of his chest. Malkesh's whole body convulsed, and Osorkon almost lost his grip on the spear. The warlord rolled and thrashed like a crocodile, trying to escape the deathblow after it had already been delivered.

'Unfortunate to die so far from home,' hissed Osorkon, leaning forward and savouring the pain on Malkesh's face.

Malkesh's fist shot out, grasping for Osorkon's throat. The prince recoiled, his hand going to his dagger and slashing out in panic. The blade slashed against Malkesh's wrist, opening up arteries and severing tendons. The warlord recoiled and howled in pain, holding his ruined stump to his chest even as he sought to pull the spear out with his remaining hand.

Malkesh gasped in a wet, gurgling breath and his face became a jackal's snarl as he tried to rise. Osorkon twisted the spear in both hands, eliciting a moan of agony. 'You are nothing. Your deeds will be forgotten, your name vanquished. Such is the fate for all who stand against the Dynasty of Takelot.'

Osorkon put one foot on Malkesh's chest and pulled up and out. The spear came free with a wet, sucking sound and Osorkon lanced it back through the warlord's throat, pinning him into the dust. The warlord's face contorted in shock, crimson vitae spurting from the mortal wound, and he gave one last pained gurgle as the baleful light faded from his eyes.

Osorkon climbed up onto the closest chariot and raised his bloodied spear in the air.

'Malkesh is dead,' he thundered. 'Stand down in the name of Pharaoh Takelot and your lives will be spared. Surrender and there will be no more bloodshed.'

The closest of the warlord's bodyguards stared down at the lifeless body in disbelief, their own duels seemingly forgotten. Without their master, the tribesmen found themselves overpowered for the first time, their strength called into question at the seemingly invincible warlord's death. Freed from the will of Malkesh and surrounded by vengeful Egyptians, exhausted warriors so very far from home wavered and broke.

The first spear dropped as a warrior of the Red Sea coast fell to his knees beside his master, his face white with shock and fatigue. A second followed him into capitulation, then two more, then ten, but many others turned and fled back into the firestorm of the city streets.

'Men of Thebes, form up.' The three cohorts fell in before Osorkon and he raised his spear in salute to them all. 'My brothers, we have won, but there is still work to do. Disarm those that stood against us and bind their hands. Kill any that resist.' The fallen tribesmen closest to him threw their hands up in abject surrender and the Thebans worked fast before any could change their minds.

A charioteer jogged in from the plaza's edge as more chariots came out of the smoking city in their ones or twos, regrouping where they had lost contact with their cohorts. The runner saluted before Osorkon's makeshift platform, taking in the butcher's tally around his lord. 'My prince, the barbarians are fleeing through the gates.'

Osorkon stared out over the orange cityscape. He did not have the men to cover all three gates and guard the prisoners. The fires still raged through the city and they too would take a small army to stop.

'Run down as many as you can. Tell them that Malkesh is dead. They are to throw down their weapons and come to the central plaza where they will be escorted safely south. If they resist, they will be killed and thrown into the river as crocodile feed. So speaks Prince Osorkon of Thebes.'

'Your will, my prince,' said the charioteer, saluting with a closed fist.

Pained laughter startled Osorkon from his fervour. Bakenptah's face was contorted with pain and he clutched his left arm to his chest. 'Escorted to safety?' he asked.

'The life of a slave is safer than that of a warrior,' Osorkon replied, stepping down to meet his brother. He looked at Bakenptah, as if seeing him properly for the first time.

'Where were you?' said Osorkon. 'How did you know?'

'To come to the docks?' asked Bakenptah. Through the soot and grime, Bakenptah was deathly pale, his fingers trembling with post-battle fatigue. 'Truthfully, I didn't. I lost you in the opening charge and I followed their flight until they led me here.' Bakenptah sucked in a great lungful of air as whatever pain inflicting him heightened for just a moment. 'But we needed ships and now we have them.' Bakenptah clutched Osorkon's arm, almost disbelieving. 'Brother, we can go home.'

SARASESH WOKE IN agony. Pain was not new to him, but his body was paralysed by the hot fire spreading from his chest out to his hands and feet. He cried out as he tried to move, and his vision swam just with the effort of breathing. In the distance, he heard voices calling out, but their Egyptian was cultured, their words unmarked by animalistic hate.

In his tortured unconsciousness he had rolled, pushing the arrow through the meat of his chest, so that it protruded beside his shoulder blade. 'You are a priest of the city?' asked the soldier, taking in the rags of his pleated shendyt. 'Thoth smiles upon you then.'

The soldier took hold of the arrow and snapped it at the fletching end. 'Hold still for a moment. I figure the arrow has missed your heart by a feather on Thoth's head.' Sarasesh spasmed as the soldier took a hold of the arrow shaft, the delicate touch sending waves of nausea radiating through him.

'I said hold still. Hold him down, will you?' grunted the soldier to his comrade. Before Sarasesh could protest, the soldier grabbed the arrow by the head and yanked the other end through his ruined shoulder. Sarasesh bucked in agony, the blood flowing freely, and he vomited on himself as the pain set his nerves on fire. The soldier stuffed a linen wad into the wound in his back and rolled him over so that he could look up into the faces of his saviours.

'Breathe,' the soldier ordered. The soldier grunted with satisfaction, watching the wound ooze steadily, without any of the tell-tale bubbles of a mortal wound. 'Missed your lungs as well. Damned lucky.'

Sarasesh twisted as the soldier stuffed another linen bundle into his chest wound and hauled him to his feet. 'Here, easy now. Prince Osorkon has established an infirmary towards the docks,' said the soldier, gesturing for his comrade to take Sarasesh under his other arm.

Sarasesh gasped for breath, his voice little more than a ragged wheeze as he took faltering steps. 'Prince Osorkon is here?'

'He speaks,' said the second soldier with a laugh. 'Yes, Prince Osorkon is here. We, his royal charioteers, are at your service.' The pair all but dragged him through streets paved with blood and bodies. In the distance something burned, the dark orange glow casting the horror of the battlefield in an unnerving light.

The streets were a butcher's shop, some of the bodies barely recognisable as human. Severed limbs and spilled organs glistened in the firelight, and the priest finally made the connection between the identity of his saviours as charioteers and the fact that he was still alive.

Soldiers in the colours of Thebes swept through the streets, checking the fallen for signs of life, but there were few to be found. Sarasesh staggered over the corpse of a tribesman, and the soldiers led him gently to his knees as he vomited a thin trail of yellow bile down his chest.

The soldiers nodded approvingly. 'No, blood. You might survive this yet.'

Sarasesh retched and spat once more.

'Aye, the barbarians are dead, or as good as,' said the soldier. 'I don't know how many of them will make good slaves, but at least they'll fertilise the fields when they drop.'

'Mal-,' he whispered. 'Mal... the warlord?'

'Ah, their leader?' said the second soldier. 'Biggest bastard I've ever seen.'

'The sons of Takelot put him down though,' said the other. 'Cut him apart together, by the grace of Amun. Finest work I have ever seen.'

The soldier dragging him along mistook his dazing for confusion.

'Yes, Prince Bakenptah is here too. You may have been too buried in your books to know, priest, but Thebes has turned against Pharaoh. We're here to take it back.'

RUIN OF SEKHMET

# Chapter Twenty-Five

THE FIRES OF Hermopolis burned throughout the night and well into the next day before the inferno was finally exhausted of fuel. Scores of captured tribesmen were put to work, tearing down buildings in the path of the blaze and creating fire corridors to contain the flames. By sunset the following day, Osorkon estimated a full third of the city had succumbed to the ravages of Malkesh's horde, leaving behind a charred and blackened wasteland.

The priest lords of the City of Thoth had emerged from their holes, blackened and bloody. Crying to the heavens, they regarded the ruin of their city with horror. They grasped at Osorkon, beseeching him to kill the rest of his captives, they who had dared desecrate their home. The prince had been forced to detain the city masters, their hysteria doing more harm than good to a frightened people. The theft of several icons of Thoth had been a bitter blow, spreading a miasma of despair through the ranks of the few priests left alive, but miraculously the cult statue itself had survived the fires.

The populace, those that had not fled the war or been killed in the days of Malkesh's reign, were found chained together like beasts in the dockside warehouses. Thousands of men, women and children had lain shivering together, listening to their city burn and their captors die. With few homes to return to, Osorkon had seen to it that the palace was converted into a temporary camp. The sight of soot-blackened, dirty, starving refugees eating bread crusts in gilded halls struck something of an incongruous chord, and Osorkon left a few veterans to oversee the distribution of food and other supplies.

Unable to bear witness to this most wretched condition of humanity any longer, the prince joined the work crews clearing the city of debris. He kept his hands and his mind busy enough to forget for a while the need to return to Thebes and the thought of what might await him there.

Osorkon sifted through the ruins of a merchant's house, yet another in a lone avenue that had succumbed to the flames. Nothing but ashes and mud brick fragments rewarded his efforts, though he looked for the tell-tale gleam of something more. A modest amount of gold and silver had so far been recovered from the ashes, along with the occasional heirloom weapon warped from the heat, but the inferno had obliterated anything not forged of the hardest metals.

The ashes blew aside to reveal a shining speck of white among the charcoal and Osorkon reached in to brush away the cinders before he recoiled with a grimace. A crack ran from the brow ridge to the top of the skull, and the jawbone hung open impossibly wide as though the corpse's last action in life had been to scream.

It was impossible to tell to which side of the conflict the body had belonged. Flesh and fat were long burned away, and as Osorkon disturbed the rubble, a foul-smelling smoke escaped from below. Glowing embers burned luminous beneath the body and Osorkon called for a bucket of water from the chained men that worked beside him.

The work gangs, comprised of the enslaved tribesmen, were organised in human chains from the river to the merchant's quarter, and within minutes a bucket had been brought up from the riverside and the embers were snuffed out.

Osorkon grunted his acknowledgement, ignoring the look of hatred on the Nubian's face as he sullenly returned to work. The Nubian should have considered himself lucky, for those that had identified themselves by rank in Malkesh's horde had been whisked away under secrecy to face Theban interrogation. Within the deepest and darkest chambers of the palace, their secrets were wrung from their flesh, their tongues loosened under knife and firebrand, and every scrap of information flensed away from them under the vengeful eye of Osorkon's charioteers. Between their screams and cries for mercy, Osorkon learned much.

The invasion had not been the work of Malkesh, cursed forever be his name. The warlord had been invited into Egyptian territory by a priest of Thebes, who, by all accounts, had been recently slain in the battle to take Hermopolis. The true target of the horde, the survivors claimed, had been a false king of Thebes, who the priests wanted dead. The priests had not given a reason, but the wealth of their temples was Malkesh's to spend if he did as they asked, though both parties had overestimated the value of gold. Without a supply chain to feed the ravenous host, the horde had fallen in on itself soon after leaving Thebes, eating its way through townships and villages until hunger had forced them to risk a bigger prize. The rest of the story was known to Osorkon well enough.

None among the horde could give him names of the priests responsible, despite the tender ministrations of Theban care, but Osorkon swore he would sweep through Karnak and learn the truth of it himself. With their gambit destroyed, the traitorous priests of Karnak were now defenceless, helpless in the face of the inevitable royal wrath that would come for them. Let them hear of their failure and face the nights ahead with terror in their hearts, thought Osorkon, declaring to his men that he would see Hermopolis restored before he set his sights on Thebes.

The Thebans were too few to halt another rebellion, so he had seen the work crews made up of different tribes and ethnicities to reduce the risk of collusion. Still, they warranted a jailer's attention, and Osorkon dared not trust the oversight to any other.

There was another reason, beyond the image of a prince helping the dispossessed, that kept Osorkon sifting through the rubble. Ikhet had found Akhetep unconscious but alive, but by all accounts, the commander's mind had been scattered by the impact.

Osorkon had sought long for a healer, but many of the priests of the city had been murdered while hiding in their temples of riches. Instead, he had found help from an unlikely and surprising quarter. A man called Amenmose, introducing himself as a snake charmer and healer of the tomb builders' village of Deir el-Medina, assured Osorkon that Akhetep's affliction was temporary, but that deeper injuries he sustained in the fall would take much longer to heal. Despite the healer's misfortune to be travelling through Hermopolis at the time of Malkesh's attack, he had a cheerful, phlegmatic aspect to him that Osorkon had immediately warmed to.

Osorkon had brought the camp followers into the city by noon, and Amenmose had quickly set himself to work, establishing a field hospital in an emptied warehouse. Amenmose taught many of the charioteers' wives, including Karoadjet, how to dress and stitch wounds along with the foundations of medical cleanliness, though he kept bone-setting and the treatment of internal injuries for himself. Osorkon saw little of his wife during that time, stealing glances when he visited the hospital and sending her messages of love and support via messenger, but their respective duties kept them apart until they collapsed into a cot together late at night, too exhausted to even speak. Osorkon's heart sung with pride at her devotion to a people unfamiliar to her. One day, when he took the throne of Egypt and Karoadjet became Great Royal Wife, she would watch over every man, woman and child in the Two Lands.

The children of the Theban chariot cohorts were likewise set to work, carrying supplies and messages from the warehouse headquarters to Bakenptah, who had been tasked with shoring up the city's defences and maintaining a garrison on the gates.

Osorkon would inspect Bakenptah's handiwork later, when his body was exhausted by the manual labour of clearing rubble. Without the fatigue brought on by physical exertion, his sleep was disturbed and haunted. He stepped over the buried skeleton and called over the work crew, giving them orders to collect the body and shroud it for burial. He hoped it was one of the tribesmen. No true Egyptian deserved such a fate as to be without form for eternity.

Satisfied that the captive crews were working as hard as the lash could make them, Osorkon made his way to the hospital. A few of the critically injured had been afforded cots, but by far most of them lay groaning on sleeping mats or slumped against stone walls.

Akhetep lay level on his left side, his back to the door and a brace of hide and leather keeping his shoulders and hips immobile. Long leather strips ran down the length of his spine and others wound up to his neck and chin. It was unlike anything Osorkon had ever seen before, like the halter of a horse but shaped for the body of a man. As he came closer, Osorkon noted the deep purple bruise that spread from the centre of Akhetep's back like a bloodstain in water.

Amenmose's face was creased with concern as he pondered his patient from the foot of the cot.

'What is it?' Osorkon asked quietly, coming to stand beside him.

The healer did not look up immediately, his gaze fixated on the deep bruising. 'It is a break of the bones. A serious one. The arrow wound will heal cleanly enough, but Lord Akhetep will need to stay immobile for some time to ensure the bones in his back heal correctly.'

'How long?'

'Two months, at the least. Three would be ideal' said Amenmose, with a sigh. 'Then he must regain his strength slowly.'

'Two months?' hissed Osorkon. 'He cannot move for two months?'

Amenmose nodded slowly, pointing towards the centre of the bruise. 'I have heard of such injuries before. A break in the back interrupts the flow of *ka* energy. Such injuries can sometimes prevent the use of the legs.'

'I'm coming with you.' Akhetep's voice was a parched whisper.

Osorkon and Amenmose moved around to his front. The chariot commander's eyes fluttered open, but remained unfocused, fixing on somewhere beyond Osorkon's shoulder.

'No-one is going anywhere, not any time soon at least. We stay until the rededication of the Temple of Thoth,' said Osorkon.

'I can ride,' protested Akhetep, looking up at the healer. 'Tell him. Tell him I can.'

'If you ride now, you will not walk for a lifetime. Put aside your foolishness for one moment and let me fix you. Do you know how many young men like yourself thought themselves beyond the laws of flesh?' hissed Amenmose.

Akhetep's eyes fluttered shut again.

'He is fading. The lucidity does not last long,' said Amenmose, retrieving a long, thin knife from his surgical kit. 'My lord Akhetep, can you feel this?' asked the healer, pressing the knife's point into

Akhetep's big toe on one foot and then another. A slight tremor ran through the flesh before Akhetep once more faded into unconsciousness.

'What in Set's name are you doing?' baulked Osorkon.

'A test. If he can feel it then his *ka* still flows freely. If not...' replied Amenmose, moving back around the cot to a steaming pot of clear liquid. The healer poured the hot water over the probe and rubbed it clean with white linen. 'I will try again later.'

Osorkon turned to the healer. 'If he tries to rise, you have my express permission to chain him to his bed.'

'I had the same thought, but the harness keeps him secure enough. If you wish to make yourself useful, then speak to the men while I tend to them.' Amenmose collected the remainder of his instruments and moved on to the next of his patients. The man looked unwounded, but for the linen bandaging his chest. He was deathly pale and his face was covered in a sheen of sweat. Amenmose knelt beside him, watching the gentle motion of his chest slowly rising and falling, a pained grimace etched seemingly permanently on his features.

'Heshpe,' said Osorkon, recognising the man's face. 'What is wrong with him?'

'His ribs were crushed in an impact.' Amenmose held out a small cup to Heshpe and gestured to Osorkon with his free hand. The prince knelt beside the charioteer and helped ease him into a sitting position.

'What is it?' asked Heshpe, eyeing the cup suspiciously.

'Wine,' replied Amenmose.

Heshpe managed a weak smile and drank deep, swallowing the cup almost in one gulp. His lips twitched in a momentary smile of pleasure before the pain returned. He sighed as he lay back and closed his eyes.

'Can I have some more?'

'Soon. We don't want you getting up and dancing when you need to be resting.' Amenmose favoured him with a fatherly smile and moved to the next patient. He paused as he regarded the cot-stricken charioteer and glanced back at Osorkon.

'Did you mean what you told Akhetep? That you would stay here for some time?'

Osorkon nodded. 'Our victory here was divinely inspired. I will not leave until the temples are restored, the gods are honoured once more, and the people are safe.'

'What of the survivors who fled during the night? You could not catch them all.'

'The Libyans among them will run west, the villagers of the Red Sea will run to east. The Nubians will run south past the city. Let the conspirators in Thebes know they are beaten. Let them know I am coming for them,' said Osorkon.

Amenmose grimaced. 'They will run far. I will pray that you do not reach them and that they will never return.'

'The burden of a ruler is to know the minds of men as well as he knows his own,' replied Osorkon.

'Quoting our father now?' said a voice from behind them both.

Osorkon turned to see Bakenptah smiling at him from the warehouse entrance.

'Little brother, good of you to come,' said Osorkon, embracing Bakenptah in a clatter of armour. Neither had deigned to remove it yet for the prisoners of Malkesh's horde still outnumbered the Thebans by two to one.

Bakenptah was the first to step back. 'Of course, you summoned me.'

'I am not your master, Bakenptah. But I do need your help,' said Osorkon.

'As you wish, provided it is not yet another suicidal assault.'

Osorkon turned and led the way back to where Amenmose was tending to the wounded.

'Malkesh is dead,' he began, 'but Thebes still stands against us. I have no desire for the flames of war to spread further than where we stand. We must take Thebes quickly and without fuss.'

'What of the warriors that fled before us?' said Bakenptah, echoing Amenmose's earlier sentiment. 'We cannot ignore them forever.'

'They will run and keep running until they are home and the next bastard chief comes along to unite a raiding band. Then we will put them down too,' replied Osorkon.

Bakenptah met his brother's eye unflinching. 'I would rather it did not come to that.'

Osorkon clapped his brother on the shoulder. 'The prisoners have told me Malkesh was a great pirate lord of the Red Sea. A legend approaching mythos. If he had been Egyptian someone would have built him a temple. With him dead they will squabble among themselves until they find a new leader. Until then, they are no threat.'

'There are always threats, brother,' pressed Bakenptah.

'Then I will send Malkesh's body to be strung up at Abu Simbel. Let them witness what it is to stand against Thebes.'

'My lord, no,' said Amenmose, aghast. 'They are beaten and that is enough. Best not to rub salt into the open wound.'

Osorkon's eyes narrowed at the healer's objection. 'You agree, little brother?'

Bakenptah rubbed a hand over his chin as he thought and Osorkon was once again reminded of the changes wrought upon him. He was a child no longer, and yet some days the image of Bakenptah playing with wooden soldiers was stronger in his mind than the man standing before him now.

Bakenptah frowned. 'Brother, fear does not win wars. It creates a temporary armistice. How long until the resentment builds up enough that war seems a favourable enough prospect again?'

'Then we will destroy them a second time. I have been fighting too long, Bakenptah. I am tired. You are tired. I want to go home, and if it takes making a public example of those that stand against us then by the arse of Set, I will do it.'

'I worry for you, my brother,' said Bakenptah. 'We do not have the strength to put down another uprising.'

Osorkon laughed. 'When we return to Thebes, we will be doing just that.'

# Chapter Twenty-Six

AFTER MORE THAN a week on the road, sleeping under starlight and trudging across seemingly endless desert on camelback, the walls of Thebes felt as comfortably enclosing as the shawl wrapped over his shoulders. Towering and indomitable, the great stone fortifications that surrounded Harsiese arose in him a sense of comfort and nostalgia, mollifying at least some of the terror of his recent captivity.

His escape from Senmut's men could not have gone unnoticed for more than a few hours, and the suspicion that he was still being tailed and toyed with plagued him even now. He had slept little and ate less, certain that each night spent huddled beside his stolen camels would be his last. No-one ever came for him though. The mercenaries had either lost his trail or simply given up, though his dreams were beset with fear that they would suddenly appear over the horizon and come for him.

Harsiese looked back toward the crowded gatehouse, to a thin line of soldiery standing before a long, winding snake of traders and travellers. Entering the city had been difficult. Each traveller to Thebes was now routinely interrogated on where they had come from, how long they intended to stay, before having their wares inspected and reinspected. Harsiese counted that four out of every five travellers were turned away, all but those bringing the freshest and richest commerce to the city. He had almost given up his ruse, until the guards stepped forward and waved him through after only a brief line of questioning.

He walked with a limp now, exaggerated but not entirely feigned, and the dirt and bruising masked his features well. For all that, he held himself erect, and possessing liberated weapons, clothes, and a camel from his captors, he had passed well enough for a veteran of the wars, and not the fugitive vagabond he had become.

He breathed deep of the city air, the scent of spices tinged with the stench of human waste, and the musky odour of common humanity stirred in him a sense of homecoming, even as the strangeness of his position threatened to unbalance him further.

He was a stranger now, a foreigner in a city he knew so well. He was no longer a hierarch but just another face in a crowd of traders and refugees. What choice did he have though, but to exist on the fringes until fate interceded? His estates would be watched, his home in the city confiscated, and to go anywhere near Karnak was as good as a death sentence.

What had he hoped to do? Ride into the temples and strike Senmut down himself?

The familiar weight of despair threatened to smother him again, and he closed his eyes and fell back to whispering comforting prayers he had memorised by rote decades ago. The panic faded, and he took a shuddering breath as he surveyed his surroundings.

Noon was a high point of mercantile traffic, and Harsiese's stomach growled as the smell of hot food wafted over him. He reached into a saddlebag to retrieve the meagre coin purse he had also liberated in his escape, and frowned at how light it had become.

Harsiese bought a couple of fried fish and half a loaf of bread from a vendor and sat down at a public table nearby to eat, savouring the simple flavours and enjoying the novelty of anonymity as life in Thebes continued unabated. He listened to the talk of the street merchants and their customers, rumour and hearsay spreading from merchant to merchant with each transaction.

He smiled as he heard stories of the war in the north, most of them outlandish and many of them contradictory. Some claimed Takelot and his sons had been slain, and that even now Shoshenq sailed south to reclaim what was his. Others asserted that Amun himself had come down to earth to smite the wicked Tanites and that Takelot was returning as a god in mortal form. Yet more argued that Takelot had destroyed Shoshenq and now ruled from the throne of Tanis, abandoning his seat in the south entirely.

The only thing the rumours shared was that they whispered the name of Pharaoh with hushed breath, as though to speak his name aloud was to invite some evil fate. With Senmut in charge of the city, it likely was, Harsiese considered grimly. A pair of soldiers passed by, and Harsiese drew his cowl tighter around his face as they bought fish and beer. His gaze was fixed on the ground when two shadows loomed over him.

'Welcome home, my lord Harsiese. Do you mind if we join you?'

Harsiese paused with the fish halfway to his mouth. The two soldiers smiled at him and before he could speak, they dropped their platters on the table and sat down.

'It's good fish, this. Teb does fine work,' said the first soldier. He was young, very young. Not much older than a boy, but with a glint in his eye that Harsiese did not like.

The second soldier raised his mug in toast. 'Come, my lord, this is an occasion to celebrate.' This one was older, more haggard, and with a lethargy in his eyes from one who has imbibed too much for too long.

Harsiese raised his own mug uncertainly. 'Who are you?'

'Ones with a great interest in finding you,' said the boy with a wide smile.

Harsiese looked away, his heart threatening to beat right out of his chest. 'Senmut's men?'

The soldiers laughed with genuine amusement.

'My lord, you're not a fool,' said the older one. 'If we were Senmut's men, you would be dead already. You killed Khontef sure, but we could kill you now with little enough trouble. Even out here in the open. People aren't exactly questioning soldiers these days. At least, the smart ones don't.'

'Thank you for your service, by the way,' said the younger one grinning. 'Khontef was known to us before our... change of allegiance. He was, if we're being honest, a cunt.'

'Not as much as Senmut, mind,' replied the grizzled one, shaking his head.

The soldiers ate hungrily as the conversation lulled into silence, but Harsiese's food remained untouched as he waited for something, anything to happen. The soldiers finished their food, the older one belching with pleasure as they both went to rise.

'Anyway, we should all be going,' said the first one again. 'Someone is expecting us.'

'I'm not going anywhere,' said Harsiese with much more bravado than he felt. He paused. 'Who is waiting for us?' Harsiese reached for his mug, watching the smiles fall from the soldiers' faces.

'I said you were not a fool. Do not make me change my mind on,' said the older soldier.

The younger man shook his head. 'He's being difficult as the master said he would.'

'Well can't leave him here for others to find. Kill him.'

'Wait.' Harsiese threw up his hands as the older soldier drew his dagger. 'Wait. I will come with you for all the good it will do. I have nothing left,' he said, gesturing to the saddlebags and the camels tied up not far away. 'This is everything.'

The soldiers' demeanour changed in an instant and they smiled again. 'The master said you would be changeable. You had best come with us.'

'Where?'

'Bring your food,' smiled the older one. 'Trust us, you will be glad we found you first.'

'What will happen to me?'

'If you say the right things,' said the older man. 'This will be the best decision you've ever made.'

Harsiese hesitated and the soldiers' friendliness faded again. Their attitudes became serious and the laxity they displayed before vanished in an instant. Harsiese realised then their attitude had been a front. The younger was no inexperienced child and the older one was deadly in his attention.

'Follow me but a few paces behind,' said the younger soldier. 'My friend here will bring up the rear. Keep a sharp eye.' The boy turned and led the way through the streets, taking turns seemingly at random and doubling back on a whim. The presence of the older man behind Harsiese was constant but not at all reassuring. Whether his purpose was to guard against outside attack or discourage Harsiese attempting to escape, he did not begin to guess.

The younger soldier led them through an alleyway onto a wide-open street, belonging to neither the very rich or the very poor, and loitered outside one particular dwelling, his gaze wandering over the crowd a moment before he turned and slipped inside.

From the outside, the house was dark and nondescript, little different to the hundreds of similar residences built on the edge of the noble quarter. It was a merchant's house, or perhaps that of a gifted craftsman, teetering on the edge of noble and commoner.

With the older soldier's presence behind him, Harsiese followed the younger man in. The curtains were drawn and Harsiese blinked away afterimages, momentarily blinded as his eyes adjusted to the gloom.

As he stepped through the atrium into the living area, Harsiese saw that his assessment of the house had been entirely correct. A single table ringed by four chairs was the house's main feature, and there was a chest of drawers in one corner beneath a drying rack of herbs hanging from the ceiling. A cooking fire in a low, mud-brick oven made the interior hot and heavy, the ruddy glow all that illuminated the interior.

A lone figure sat at a windowsill behind the table, watching the traffic go by through the gap in the curtain's edge. The figure turned at Harsiese's approach. He nodded at the soldiers, who returned the gesture and left to take up station inside the house's single door.

'We have much to speak of, my friend, and I am afraid little of it is good,' said the figure.

Harsiese peered into the gloom, his lips peeling back in a snarl as he recognised the figure's face.

'Pedubast.'

'I know you are angry,' began Pedubast.

'Angry does not even begin to cover it, you traitorous bastard,' snapped Harsiese. His hands bunched into fists at his sides, but even in his anger he was mindful of the soldiers standing behind him.

'But I need you to listen,' finished Pedubast. He stepped around to the other side of the table and fixed Harsiese with a level stare. 'Much has changed since your departure. How have you returned?'

'You should be fawning at Senmut's side. How are you here?' countered Harsiese.

'I had heard you escaped and someday I would like to hear the tale of it, but time is short, and we have more pressing matters to attend to,' replied Pedubast.

Harsiese watched the other priest silently. Though he tried hard to hide it, Pedubast looked nervous. The worry lines around his eyes had deepened, his skin becoming more mottled, and he frequently glanced at the stairs, his only line of escape should Harsiese deem his explanations insufficient.

'Speak then, or let me leave. I have made it this far on my own,' he said.

'As you wish, I will not dally,' said Pedubast, leaning forward over the table. 'Senmut must die, as must those that follow him too blindingly. It is an end we are working towards but one that will hasten with your presence.'

'That was obvious months ago,' hissed Harsiese, crossing his arms.

'We are slowly turning the tide of opinion against him. Some of Senmut's excesses have been… well, excessive,' said Pedubast slowly.

Harsiese let out a derisive snort. Keeping the soldier's in his peripheral vision, he moved towards the stairs and leaned against the wall. 'So, you whisper in the shadows, binding loyalty to you in secrecy? That is how this all started, you cursed fool.'

Pedubast's lip curled at the insult. 'And this is how it will end. Just listen.'

'I will never trust you.'

'I don't need you to trust me. I just need you to agree with me,' pressed Pedubast. 'You were the chosen of the gods and you are of the high nobility. Despite Senmut's assertions to the contrary, that still means something. The nobles will follow you. The priests will follow. Stability will reign once more if you fill the vacuum left by Senmut's untimely death.'

'Stability that you destroyed. You were involved from the very beginning,'

'And I broke faith soon after,' said Pedubast, coming to stand before Harsiese. 'I do not need your help, but this will go a lot more smoothly with you by our side. I swear to you we will bring about Senmut's downfall. There is no other way to save Thebes.'

Harsiese looked away. 'How do I know this is not some perverse trick? This reeks of Senmut's cunning.' He glanced sharply back at Pedubast. 'What do you mean "our"?'

Pedubast sighed and stepped back. 'Perhaps someone else can convince you of my good intentions.' He glanced up the stairs over Harsiese's shoulder, directing his next words to someone unseen. 'It is safe, my lady. You may come down.'

Harsiese spun on his heel as he heard footsteps from the landing above. He glanced at the door, but the two soldiers still guarded the entrance and Pedubast was too close to dash past him if this was indeed some trick. Pinned as he was, he looked up to the top of the stairs, feeling suddenly foolish at his previous fear. He dipped his head, partly in deference and partly to hide his surprise. 'My lady Isetweret.'

'You can trust Pedubast, Lord Harsiese. I have come to. He saved my life,' said Isetweret, stepping past him and moving to sit at the table. She groaned as she lowered herself, her skin flushed and ruddy in the low light. Her condition, Harsiese thought, seemed a scant improvement to his own. Darkness ringed her eyes and not from kohl or cosmetics, and she walked with a slight stoop of someone decades older. Vivid purple streaks, visible through the thin fabric of her shift, covered a belly that could surely stretch no more. It was her face though, that Harsiese was drawn to. Her expression was set, a terrible blend of anger, despair and exhaustion that Harsiese identified with all too keenly.

He had asked the question before he was even aware of forming it.

'What of Hory?'

'Hory is dead. I will say no more,' said Pedubast quickly.

Isetweret's eyes fluttered at Pedubast's words, but she remained firm. Something terrible had happened then, thought Harsiese, and he sent a silent prayer to Amun for whatever foul fate had befallen the vizier.

'So how is it that you come to speak to me now, risking your life harbouring a fugitive. Senmut is not a forgiving soul,' Harsiese asked instead.

'Tell him, my lady. Please. Better he hears it from lips he trusts,' said Pedubast.

Isetweret nodded and fixed Harsiese with a penetrating look that was the very image of her mother's. 'Pedubast has been my eyes and ears inside the temple for some time. When the temples recruited after Nakhtefmut's demise, the new palace looked to those same recruits and sought out the more promising candidates. Pedubast has been making sure that Senmut hears what he wants to hear, and I have heard much of interest,' she said.

'If Pedubast is so clever, how did you end up here, I wonder?' asked Harsiese, waving his arms to encompass the meagre dwelling.

'The same way you ended up kidnapped and stolen away, Lord High Priest,' said Isetweret without venom. 'We were outmanoeuvred at every turn. It is a mistake I will never make again. First though, those that have wronged us must be destroyed.'

'How do you intend to go up against Senmut? If he can move against the High Priest of Amun and the Vizier of Thebes, you do not scare him now.

'We are gathering allies to our side even now,' said Pedubast.

'How many?'

'Not enough,' Pedubast admitted. 'But the tide is turning.'

'Not enough,' repeated Harsiese, feeling the taste of the words on his tongue. He glanced at the door. 'You have soldiers?'

'Enough to secure ourselves.'

'But not enough to make a difference,' finished Harsiese.

'My brothers will come. I am certain of it,' said Isetweret, the light of fervour in her eyes.

Harsiese frowned. That changed things. 'Have you received word?'

'No word enters or leaves the city but by Senmut's will,' said Pedubast.

Isetweret shook her head, her hand going to the golden icon of the mother goddess at her throat. 'They will know something is amiss and they will come for me.'

'When?' pressed Harsiese.

'When the time is right.'

'I have placed a watch on the northern walls just in case,' said Pedubast, though Harsiese heard the doubt in his voice. 'So, will you join us?'

Harsiese grunted but in their words, he felt the first stirrings of new opportunity and dreams forgotten reawakened. 'It seems I have little choice. We will have reckoning, Pedubast, but for now I am listening. Tell me it all and leave out nothing. Amun's vengeance is ready to fall.'

IT HAD BEEN little more than a week since the battle between the Egyptian navies, but already the bitter marks of battle were fading. Shattered hulls lay sunken at the bottom of the river, and broken masts, torn sails, and other debris and detritus were swept northward to the sea, along with hundreds of bodies from both sides.

On the first night, the sound of crocodiles feasting on the dead had carried far, sending a shiver through every restless sleeper.

General Kaphiri put the thought from his mind. One did not need to be a priest of Sobek to know that the beasts were creatures of habit, and where they had found food once they would likely return.

Kaphiri whispered a prayer to the crocodile god as he swam, a promise of sacrifices before the next dawn if only holy Sobek granted him safe passage across the river. Around him, twenty of his volunteers prayed for the same. Whatever the outcome, success or failure, the children of Sobek would feast tonight.

Kaphiri shifted in his stroke, treading water for a moment as he readjusted his load. The pots were bottom heavy and the size of a man's head, bobbing together in a secure rope brace in the current. The saboteurs swam naked, their skin daubed with ash mixed with oil to mottle and darken their outlines. Sheathed daggers hung on straps around their necks, and flints dangled in waterproof pouches beside the daggers.

The darkness was almost complete, for the ships were at rest on the far side of the river and lamp oil was becoming a scarce commodity. Each of the Tanite ships seemed limited to three points of illumination. Dim lamps burned at the forecastle, the main mast and the wheelhouse, interrupted every so often by the midnight watch trudging slowly between the pools of light.

Kaphiri smiled. The river water was cool and prickled his skin, banishing the mental lethargy of recent days. The delicious thrill of fear gave him vitality and the surety of his mission gave him strength, even as his arms began to ache and his legs burned with effort.

The Tanite flagship, the *Wrath of Tanis*, sat high at anchor, not far from the eastern shore. Kaphiri's numb fingers reached out and grazed the ship's hull, and he rolled onto his back to track the progress of his men.

Though they had entered the water far upstream, the current had spread them wide, and while all of them were capable swimmers, the endurance required to reach the other side had dispersed them even further. Only from the waterline were the shaved heads of his men visible, bobbing in the waveless water.

Only two were missing, Kaphiri noted. An acceptable sacrifice, Amun rest their spirits. The lost cargo was undesirable, but most of his men had made it to their target undetected. Whether the two lost ones had drowned or been taken by crocodiles before they could scream, he did not know, only that the dead had fulfilled their final duty and not betrayed their comrades' position.

The saboteurs clung to their floating cargo as the river current pushed them deeper into the anchored Tanite fleet. Kaphiri reached out and clung to the flagship's hull, checking his pair of pots for cracks. Satisfied that there were none, he waited in the water for the others to reach their allotted positions and for the final signal. Takelot had been insistent on the timing. A mistimed attack was an invite for discovery, and discovery was death.

Far to the west, the Tanite camp in the foothills was one mass of torchlight, an orange stain on the blanket dark. South of that, the Theban camp was more subdued. Pale light lit the walls, but it was the sparse and dotted light of stars, not the sun that Tanis was.

Kaphiri kept his eye on the Theban camp, murmuring a greeting as Uhman and Heshka hauled themselves up onto the ribs of the flagship beside him. As they settled, they looked back at their camp, keeping the same vigil as their general.

'Soon,' Kaphiri whispered, as the chill began to set in and his teeth started chattering. 'Have faith, my friends.' Elsewhere, under the other ships of the Tanite fleet, those vast grain behemoths and military command vessels, other teams of saboteurs in their twos and threes waited for their king's command.

Even now, Takelot would be riding out, heading for the heart of the Tanite camp with host at his back in one final gambit to stave off their inevitable defeat.

After an age of waiting, the signal came. A single dot of light rose high above the Theban fort, arching in the air and falling just as silently. Another of its kind rose a moment later. The second fire arrow faded like the first and then all was still.

Kaphiri gave a single nod and pulled himself up the side of the ship. The pots were little heavier than his usual armour and weapons, but after the swim and the wait in the water his fingers were numb and his muscles burned with fatigue. Uhman and Heshka followed him up, pausing with their commander at the base of the ship's railings.

Kaphiri paused, listening for the slow and heavy footsteps of the patrol. His hand paused, reaching for a handhold, as a shadow loomed over him. The guard stepped within a metre of Kaphiri's head, oblivious to the Thebans below. He continued in his patrol, spear and shield held low and his steps shuffling and groggy. Sloppy, thought Kaphiri, a floggable offence had the guard been his to command. He waited for the footsteps to fade before he pushed his pots through the gap in the railing and slipped himself over the side, crouching beside the main mast.

He checked the guard's progress and beckoned his men to follow. Few Tanites remained on the flagship, and the skeleton crew would be billeted belowdecks with most personnel already transferred to the on-shore camp for comfort and ease of supply. With the Theban navy put to flight, even the Tanites had fallen victim to complacency.

Kaphiri collected his fire pots from the deck and headed for the aft hatch, shadowing the guard's progress around the deck even as

Uhman and Heshka shadowed his. The Tanite paused at the railings on the opposite side and Kaphiri froze as the guard set down his spear and shield. He relaxed when the guard grunted with relief and a soft trickle over the side reached the saboteurs. Satisfied that the guard was preoccupied for the moment, Kaphiri slipped through the hatch and into the gloom below.

The soft snores of seamen and naval personnel broke the quiet, but they were even and undisturbed. Even so, Kaphiri paused at each step, listening for the slightest change in sound. He gestured ahead at another dark portal, a second hatch to the lowest deck and cargo hold. It was already open and unbelievably unguarded.

Kaphiri slipped down first. He held his breath, straining his senses for the slightest sound. But for the creak of rigging and the soft lap of the river against the hull, all was quiet. His eyes adjusted slowly, taking in the vagaries of crates and sacks full of foodstuffs and weapons as his men clambered down after him.

The greater bulk of supplies would be on the trade ships, he knew, but others would bring those to ruin. The burning of the *Wrath of Tanis* would be a symbol. Shoshenq's might vanquished when he thought it safe, his pride turned to ashes before his eyes.

Kaphiri was not a vengeful soul, but the loss of so many Thebans against fellow Egyptians hardened his heart. He steeled himself for the escape to come and set one of his pots between two sacks of linen, feeling his way for the rope snaking out of the pot's wax seal. The fuse would burn for two full minutes before it reached the pitch within. Kaphiri intended to be well off the ship when that happened.

Uhman passed him, heading to the fore.

'Put it by the grain,' whispered Kaphiri as he reached for his flint. His fingers wrapped around the dry stone and he passed thanks to whichever god was listening. Uhman slipped past him, any acknowledge lost in the dark, and moved to the front of the ship's hold. A second shadow revealed Heshka's passage towards port where the water on the other side of the hull would be deeper.

Kaphiri flexed his fingers to drive the numbness away and struck the flint, the sparks painfully bright to his eye. On the third strike, the fuse began to glow and smoulder, the layer of pitch coating the wick burning with rapacious hunger.

Kaphiri went to rise when a heavy crack shattered the silence. In the darkness, he could not tell who had dropped what, but it did not matter. Raised voices thick with sleep filtered down from the deck above, and Kaphiri swore under his breath.

He tucked the fuse under itself to shield its glow and drew his dagger. One fire pot would have to be enough. Gods curse the clumsy bastard who had ruined them already. Kaphiri crouched in the shadow of the ladder as another shadow climbed down.

Kaphiri waited until the sailor's feet hit the deck before he lashed out. The Tanite fell gurgling, a gaping wound in his neck as Kaphiri cut open his throat. A second sailor, then a third, followed the first, forcing Kaphiri back.

He lashed out at the second shadow, but the Tanite swayed back out of reach, falling into his comrade behind him and sending the third sailor reeling. The sailor hit the deck hard, falling onto the bags of linen and cracking the already lit clay pot beneath.

Kaphiri heard the sound and his blood froze. He turned and sprinted towards the bow, heedless of the debris in his path. He tripped and stumbled, hearing the shouts of surprise and anger behind him, and then a terrible whoosh as the oozing pitch spilled onto the lit fuse.

Kaphiri was thrown from his feet by the blast as the second of his pots exploded where he had left it beside the first. The scorching heat stole the air from his lungs and burned his skin. The two sailors at the base of the ladder were immolated instantly, the third man dancing aflame for several moments before he collapsed writhing and was lost from sight.

The fire lashed up through the hatchway, sending a geyser of flame onto the next deck. Kaphiri's ears rung with the sound, his wits scattered as he lashed out blindly at a shadow above him.

Heshka's terrified face swam into vision and Kaphiri held up an apologetic hand.

'We have to go,' Heshka screamed, gesturing forwards to where Uhman was already climbing the forward ladder.

Kaphiri nodded numbly, clambering to his feet and stumbling after them.

Cries of alarm came from the deck above, the greatest fear of sailors since mankind had taken to the water coming for the Tanites in the dead of night. More voices joined the terrified chorus, as cries of 'Fire! Seal the hatches!' reached the Thebans.

Somewhere another pot exploded, the fire lashing the roof and knocking the three Thebans down again. Uhman scrambled for the hatch, almost making it clear to the crew level before he fell back with a scream. His body tumbled back down to the keel, blood flowing freely from a mortal wound in his chest. He twitched twice and was then still.

Kaphiri clutched his dagger and made for the ladder himself but a shadow overhead gave him pause. Wild eyes peered down at him, and white teeth bared in a vicious snarl. The firelight exaggerated the shadows, giving the Tanite sailor a demonic visage.

Kaphiri glanced aft. The fire had reached halfway through the hold already, burning through linen and leather, grain and timber with equal ease.

'No,' he screamed, as the sailor above closed the hatch, locking it shut with dreadful finality. Heshka shoved past him, knocking his commander to the ground. He scaled the ladder, straining against the locked hatch but it did not budge.

The blood drained from Kaphiri's face as he looked back towards the wall of flame bearing down on him, the smoke cloying and acrid, filling his senses.

'Amun preserve me,' he whispered, as he clawed his way back to the ship's prow.

Kaphiri touched something sticky and he had a moment to consider Uhman's blood mixed with the pitch of his broken pot before the flames reached Heshka's abandoned fire pots. He had a moment to stare deep into the flames, the fire roaring up in a disturbingly crocodilian fashion, before he was immolated in a blistering detonation that tore the *Wrath of Tanis* apart and dragged the Tanite flagship down to a watery grave.

# Chapter Twenty-Seven

THE WRATH OF Thebes marched forth from the hilltop camp, coming down the plain in an inexorable tide. The fort had been emptied entirely, stripped down to its barest architecture. Anything of value had been sent south with a caravan of the wounded and lame. What little stores remained had been stowed for the journey back to Herakleopolis.

Takelot rode at the head of a vast column, the war crown upon his head and his flesh enveloped in bronze scales once more. No reserves had been left behind, for every man still able to hold a spear would be needed in this final midnight battle. The few chariots in working condition fanned out around their king as an honour guard, though they possessed little of the finery that often went with such a title.

Takelot smiled grimly at the sight of the burning Tanite fleet. Perhaps half the vessels were destroyed beyond salvage, the flagship among them. Alarm bells were still ringing, dulled to a faint chime with the distance, and the cries and screams of men in the water carried in the night-time breeze.

The march across the plains seemed to take both an eternity and yet no time at all. If the Tanites would not yield now, both sides faced oblivion. For the first time in his life, Takelot considered the very real possibility that he would not live to see the dawn. The thought brought none of the fear he was expecting. Instead, a gentle calm came over him, and he passed the march across the plains enjoying the sight of the constellations laid out before him in the heavens above.

The sound of mortal men brought him back to earth soon enough.

The Tanite camp was in uproar. Soldiers spilled from their tents like ants from a nest, hastily taking their positions in a long line of spears in front of the outer tents. Their formations were rushed and broken but those gaps were filling with remarkable alacrity, their discipline commendable in the face of the surprise assault.

Takelot raised his hand to signal the halt, searching for the Tanite commanders and their king, but there was no sign of Shoshenq. The front ranks broke open and a lone horseman rode out to meet him. In the rider's hand, the battle standard of the Tanite throne fluttered as he cantered forward.

Even in the dark, Takelot recognised Shoshenq's deputy, the Inspector of the Palace of Tanis. 'Ankherednefer, it is good to see you,' said Takelot.

Ankherednefer ignored the greeting. 'This way, please. Pharaoh wishes to speak with you.' He turned without waiting for a reply. Takelot watched him go before he decided that there was little to be gained from Shoshenq killing him inside his camp. The Thebans would charge and burn the Tanite camp to the ground if their king did not soon return.

The front lines stumbled over themselves to keep clear of Takelot's chariot, watching him pass with fascinated hatred. Takelot did not deign to look at them. He rode down the central thoroughfare, regarding the Tanite defences with reluctant admiration. Concentric walls of sharpened stakes would have made taking the camp costly in the extreme.

The royal tent could not be missed. Embroidered cloth and fine timbers from the Fertile Crescent made up Shoshenq's wartime residence, and the cloying smell of incense seeped into the surrounds.

Ankherednefer pushed through the tent flaps without a backward glance. The guards at the entrance eyed Takelot warily and he favoured them with a thin smile. So far, none had dared try relieving him of his weapons, and none tried now as he dismounted and marched towards the tent's entrance. Takelot followed through into a low-lit chamber, stifling hot and filled with conflicting scents.

To his right was a small altar, replete with fresh offerings and smouldering incense cones. Bronze statuettes of the Theban triad, father Amun, mother Mut and the holy child Khons, stood among offerings of food and wine. It was almost identical in shape to the statuettes Takelot had in his own tent, though the fashion of Karnak was far more gilded and elaborate in design

'If we both seek the gods' approval,' began Takelot, 'which of us do they listen to?'

Shoshenq sat behind his desk, a sheaf of papyrus paper before him. He looked every inch the scribe, not a king, and he massaged his writing hand as Takelot smiled down at him. Dark circles ringed his puffy eyes and his robes were spattered with ink.

'Have a seat.' For his dishevelment, his voice was clear and strong.

Takelot glanced in the direction of the guards outside and shook his head. 'I will stand.'

Shoshenq snorted and shook his head. 'As you wish. Why would you learn humility now of all times?' He rubbed his eyes and stood, pushing past Ankherednefer to pour himself a cup of wine. He took a long swallow and turned back to Takelot. 'I am withdrawing my army at dawn.'

'So soon?' asked Takelot, feigning surprise.

'Do not push me, traitor. There are matters I have to attend to that surpass even your pathetic insurrection.'

Takelot crossed his arms. 'Your terms?'

'You have them. I am leaving for Tanis tomorrow. I suggest you set course south. My men will not molest your passage, and I expect the same in return.'

'Ah, Shalmaneser, is it?' asked Takelot. The king of the Assyrian Empire had given Shoshenq's predecessor, Takelot's own grandfather, a great deal of trouble in Egypt's territories in the Levant. Perversely, Takelot now considered, Shalmaneser's own son and heir sought to hasten his inheritance and had begun a civil war. The empire had been broken and the war with Egypt seemingly forgotten, unless one side had finally triumphed.

'Shalmaneser is dead,' answered Ankherednefer, ignoring the withering look from his king. 'His son has restarted your grandfather's war. As if your family was not responsible for enough bloodshed.'

'Then I wish you the gods' favour. May you triumph there and your name echo for a million years,' said Takelot. 'While we are in truce, you may consider your southern border secured by a newfound ally, not a vassal. When you burn and sack the cities of Assyria, perhaps you might consider a gesture of goodwill to your friends in Thebes appropriate. It has cost me much to maintain hold of the south, after all.'

Shoshenq's face turned the colour of his wine. 'You burn my ships and you slaughter my men! You dare now to speak to of restitution?'

'You sit on my throne,' countered Takelot, calmly.

'Get out, Takelot, you spawn of Set's cursed loins. I regret the day I spoke in your favour. Your grandfather wanted to bring you to Tanis. To watch you closely. I told him it would be better to have blood kin in the south. Reliable blood,' spat Shoshenq.

Takelot raised an eyebrow. 'Reliable enough to rule the south, but not to sit on the throne? It seems your designs have reached fruition after all.'

The fire in Shoshenq's eyes guttered and died and he slumped back into his chair. 'Go, pull back to your city of priests. Go home, Takelot. If there is anything left of it.'

Takelot turned to leave but he paused at Shoshenq's final words. 'What do you mean?'

'You don't know?' Shoshenq looked up at Takelot, incredulous. 'I had thought you remained here out of sheer stubbornness. But you genuinely don't know, do you?' For the first time, Shoshenq's lips cracked into something resembling a smile.

'Speak plainly,' said Takelot, filled with a sudden need to be away from here.

Shoshenq sifted through the scrolls on his desk, plucking one of the smallest and passed it to Ankherednefer who handed it to Takelot.

'Thebes is in rebellion,' said Shoshenq. 'Not yours, by the way, but another one. It seems your priests disliked your decision to march north as much as I did. Karnak has taken control of the city.'

'Harsiese,' snapped Takelot. 'This is no trick?'

Shoshenq smiled in genuine mirth. 'Oh, it is. But not one of my making.'

Takelot read the missive once more, the words searing into his mind. *Vizier dead. Karnak in open rebellion. Hermopolis under siege. Nubia walks.* Takelot stepped forward and tossed the note back on Shoshenq's desk and left without looking back.

Shoshenq called after him. 'This is not over, Takelot.'

Takelot paused on the threshold as the guards swept aside the tent opening. 'It never is, Senneker.'

THE TEMPLE RESTORATIONS took far longer than Osorkon anticipated. Within a fortnight, the Temple of Thoth's structure had been shored up, but fires had blackened the priceless murals and bas reliefs. To make matters worse, artisans skilled enough to repair them were in short supply. Despite the setbacks, and there were many, Osorkon found a kind of peace in the work of raising monuments. He held the first service the morning after the sanctum doors were refitted, rededicating the sacred space in the god's name. The first offerings had been given that day and Osorkon had called on the God of Wisdom to guide his people along a better path than the one they now suffered. He took to spending long hours in the temple sanctum, conversing with the god and contemplating the road ahead.

He was not a priest of Thoth, but he was the closest servant of the divine within a league or more, and so temple duties both mundane and esoteric fell to him. To his chagrin, none of the priests of Hermopolis had survived the occupation. The rich and indolent temple staff had been among the first to succumb to Malkesh's predations. Fleshy bodies and shaved scalps, so often a mark of respect and learning among Egyptian society, had marked them for death as soon as the walls were taken, interrogated for their riches, both real and imagined.

They were not alone in their persecution.

Great piles of the dead filled the warehouses in the city's south side, which Osorkon had declared a quarantine zone, forbidden to all but the embalmers. Osorkon rewarded the priests of death well, offering them the finest of the remaining food and drink to sustain them through the gruelling process of preserving the legions of dead. Thousands had been slaughtered with impunity, and even the richest among the dead had to make do with the most basic of mortuary treatments in the name of efficiency.

The coppery stink of spilled blood never quite faded, and Osorkon lit twice the prescribed amount of incense, hoping to please Thoth with his devotion and so draw the god's attention to Hermopolis. The ruined sanctum had broken Osorkon's heart when he had first seen it, the desecration too devastating to even anger him. The altar had been torn down, the sacred barque smashed to kindling, and the holy reliefs scratched and burned away.

Only one blessing had come out the destruction; the cult statue of Thoth had been preserved. The living embodiment of the ibis god was shaped from black granite, not gold, and the horde had overlooked the inconspicuous statuette, helping themselves to the other treasures within.

Osorkon looked down at the statue, feeling the immense power within. The god's link to the mortal earth stood in front of him in his chosen city and Osorkon knelt before it, overcome with humility in the face of the heavenly presence.

'Sacred Thoth, Lord of Scribes and Bringer of Magic, I am Amun, the Father of the Heavens and the Lord of the Two Lands. Hear me, Thoth, that you may nourish yourself anew. The defilers of your sacred places, which I have sent into the hands of Anubis, await your divine judgement,' said Osorkon, identifying with his own patron god and so borrowing a measure of his deity's power.

Osorkon brought forth a platter of fruit and fish. It was a paltry offering, worthy for a frontier temple to a minor deity, but Osorkon prayed the god would understand.

'Eat now, Sacred One. Replenish your powers for I bring forth unto you the light of day.'

Osorkon rocked back on to his haunches and closed his eyes, smelling the scent of sacred incense and baked fish. Peace came over him and he lingered for a few moments more. Here, in this place, none of the outside world dared disturb him. Even Bakenptah was reluctant to intrude on the more sacred areas of the temples, and only another prophet would even consider entering a god's sanctum without express permission.

Osorkon waited for the god to eat and drink, before he took a mouthful of fish and a sip of wine himself. The fare was adequate to his taste and he rose to his feet and picked up the platters, bowing once more to the statue. He passed back through the portals, each layer of the temple walls bringing him one step closer to the business of being a prince once more.

'The god is content,' intoned Osorkon, bowing to the temple guardians as he passed the outermost wall. He handed them the foodstuffs, which they accepted gratefully. As always, after the god had drawn divine nourishment, the offerings were left to the priests and temple staff, but the smell was no longer enticing to Osorkon.

'Blessings upon you, Prince Osorkon,' they said together and stepped past him to secure the outer doors. Half a dozen of Malkesh's men, now slaves in chains to the Hermopolitans, watched the exchange sullenly. Osorkon stared back until they broke contact. He had not shied away from making an example of the least cooperative, and by now, none could be in doubt of their new station in life. They were grey and gaunt, their limbs covered in dust and scratches from long days of carrying stone. Those that fell in their work were simply thrown into the river, alive or dead, for supplies were few and pity was non-existent.

How many more would fall to prey to murders or attacks by the Hermopolitans would remain to be seen, though Osorkon had banned the slaves from being assaulted, at least for a non-disciplinary reason. They were far more useful being put to work undoing the damage they had done under Malkesh's leadership, though Osorkon could not blame the city's residents for lashing out. He might have done the same, for the fires of vengeance burned as brightly in his breast as any of them as he walked through the city towards the hospital warehouses where Akhetep remained indisposed.

Most of the Hermopolitans sought to return to a resemblance of normal life, though many yet lingered in the hospital under Amenmose's care. The healer of Deir el-Medina had as much, if not more, experience setting broken bones and tending infected scratches than Osorkon had swinging a sword, and he thanked any god that would listen for the man's presence. The prince visited when he could, though he had never been easy around the lame and the crippled. Without an intact body, the spirit would spend eternity carrying those injuries through the afterlife, unless a fine enough substitute was made and buried with him. Death held little fear for Osorkon, but being maiming or crippled was a terror as primal within him as a fear of heights or snakes.

Osorkon spied the familiar sight of Amenmose's hospital and stepped within, immediately overcome by the wave of healing incense that washed over him. In the god's sanctum within the temples, it covered the smell of ash and soot. Here it covered the sickly smell of rotting flesh.

Amenmose noticed him enter. 'My prince, you are just in time.'

Osorkon did not have time to ask what for. Amenmose turned and bid him follow to the far end of the warehouse and out through a small door. Osorkon blinked away the sunshine and so did not see the patient until he was nearly on top of him.

One of the Theban charioteers lay tied down on a low cot. His arms and legs were restrained, and leather straps wrapped around his forehead and chest. The patient was dazed, his eyes unfocused and thick saliva dripped from his lips, wetting a wadded linen gag that had been stuffed into his mouth.

'What have you done to him?' asked Osorkon in alarm.

'Given him something for the pain,' replied Amenmose, as he continued his hidden preparations.

Red and purple discolouration stained the charioteer's left knee and lower leg. In the centre, a patch of black, crusty skin oozed a dark yellow fluid. The veins from the wound out were dark and very visible. Even in the fresh air, Osorkon could smell the rot. He tore his eyes away from the wound at the sound of a blade being sharpened.

'No.'

Amenmose looked up from where he ran a whetstone over a serrated blade. The healer held it up to the light and then over the open flame that burned beside him. A pot of boiling water bubbled in the centre of the flames.

'The bone has not set well. It has become infected and soon his blood will turn to poison. I must remove the limb.'

Osorkon baulked in horror. 'You can't!'

'If I don't, he dies,' said Amenmose matter-of-factly, as he tied a rope tight around the man's thigh.

'Have you done this before?'

'Too many times,' replied Amenmose. 'Now, hold him still. The cut must be precise.'

Osorkon and three of Amenmose's assistants held the man down; one at each leg, one on the chest and another holding down his shoulders and head. The charioteer's eyes snapped open and he screamed through the gag as Amenmose began to saw. Skin and muscle parted like ripe fruit and blood flowed from the wound as the man thrashed against his bonds.

'Chisel,' said Amenmose, taking the implement from his assistant and holding a hammer in his other hand. Osorkon turned away. Chisel on bone sounded too much like chisel on stone until the last sickening crack.

The charioteer's muffled screams subsided as he at last slipped into blessed unconsciousness. Osorkon released the intact leg, the clammy skin now covered in a sheen of sweat. He looked out over the river, as Amenmose cut through the rest of the flesh. He only returned when he heard Amenmose begin stitch and bandage the stump.

'Have this taken to the embalmers and returned to him. He may wish to keep it,' said Amenmose, handing the offending limb to the man beside him. The healer bid his remaining assistants move the patient indoors and turned to Osorkon.

'Thank you for your assistance. You have come to see Lord Akhetep, I trust?'

'If you will permit me,' replied Osorkon

Amenmose smiled. 'Would that all men respect the healer's art as you do. I must warn you. He is strong enough for visitors but not for travel, much as he will try to convince you otherwise. I must keep him here for longer.'

'I understand.' Osorkon turned to go, but Amenmose caught him by the arm.

'You reopened the temples today?'

'I did,' said Osorkon, knowing full well what Amenmose meant.

The healer smiled. 'Then I wish you luck. Go forth with the blessings of all that you have saved here. May Amun guide you on the road to Thebes and beyond.'

Osorkon nodded and stepped back inside, taking the time to meet and inquire with some of the other wounded. The ones that were fit had already been discharged, and to his disappointment he found no more recruits for the voyage to Thebes. Perhaps one hundred and fifty among the charioteers were fighting fit, a meagre unit compared to the host three times that number he had left with.

Osorkon approached the cot of his chariot commander but Akhetep was motionless, apart from the steady rhythm of his chest rising and falling. Perhaps it was kinder to let him sleep. There would be time to talk when Thebes was retaken. He turned away, but Akhetep stirred.

'You are awake,' said Osorkon.

Akhetep's eyes fluttered open. 'A brother's screams will do that to a man.'

Osorkon smiled weakly. 'Sorry.' He sat on the cot's edge, looking out over the men he would be leaving behind. So few were returning home. The loss tore at him. 'We are leaving tomorrow.'

'I am coming with you.' Akhetep struggled to rise, the leather harness keeping him immobile. He grunted with pain, sweat breaking out from his temples at the effort.

Osorkon shook his head. 'You will stay here and rest. Oversee the reconstruction when you regain the strength to do so, but remain here until you are fully healed. I have given Amenmose my full authority in your care. You will obey him as you obey me, commander.'

Akhetep sagged, his breath coming ragged. 'My place is at your side.'

'It is, but until you are healed you are doing no-one any favours by jumping back into the fray,' said Osorkon, laying a gentle hand on Akhetep's shoulder and pushing him back down. It required no more effort than moving an infant. 'This is something Bakenptah and I must do. Alone.' He softened his tone at Akhetep's crestfallen expression. 'Even Karoadjet is staying here until I am certain that Thebes is under control. Amenmose tells me you have healing yet to do, and you have done enough already. The war is won. You have earned your rest, my friend.'

'As you say, my prince.' Akhetep closed his eyes. 'Just don't do anything stupid without me.'

# Chapter Twenty-Eight

THE VOYAGE TO Thebes passed with ease, though Karoadjet had not taken the news of her husband's departure with the same grace as Akhetep. She had railed against his decision to leave her behind with a venom that few knew she was capable of, but his word had been final. Hermopolis had suffered, true, but there was no further risk now that Malkesh was dead. Between the walking wounded and the citizen militia he had organised, Hermopolis was becoming as safe a place as any with Takelot's army guarding the north and Osorkon's meagre forces sailing south.

The *Sobek is Content* was a fine ship, but she had suffered under Malkesh's care and the sailors Osorkon employed lamented the tortured state of the vessel. Osorkon lay awake each night expecting one more test, but the gods were silent for the reckoning to come. Each night, he ordered the ship lamps extinguished and the captain to sail on the far side of the river, lest their arrival in the Theban harbour be seen by unfriendly eyes.

'We shall enter the city from the northern wall, but we must be swift,' he told his men. 'We will not last long undiscovered and we must hit the temple hard. We will secure the rest of the city when Karnak is ours.'

'Not from the harbour?' asked Bakenptah.

'It is too far. The temples of Mut and Khons are irrelevant, only the great Temple of Amun matters now. From the temple's south and west are the two Avenues. Both leave us dangerously exposed when we need to secure the inner precinct without raising an alarm.

No, we will take the gatehouse and come from the temple's quiet side. They will not see us coming.'

Osorkon reinforced his command more than once, until he was certain there would be no distractions. Most of the men had their families back in Hermopolis, but few among them did not have a sibling, cousin or parent within those city walls.

At first, the absence of trade caravans and merchant fleets was an oddity, but the further south they sailed the clearer the evidence of treachery became. Farmers and traders should have been bustling past one another for a prime position in the Theban marketplaces, but silence and dust greeted the new arrivals as they docked at a deserted port.

On the day they arrived in Thebes, the land was barren in its entirety, not a soul seen even in the light of midmorning. It was a strange and eerie sight.

'The land is dead,' said Bakenptah. 'We can only assume they know we are coming.' Every man in the company knew it to be true, but few could break through the unease to nod in agreement. Were it not for the thin fingers of smoke drifting beyond the city walls, Osorkon might have thought the city swallowed entirely by the realm of the dead.

His company numbered a mere one hundred and fifty warriors on foot, for there was barely enough room for each man aboard the ship, let alone their war machines and mounts. Few of them grumbled and those that did, did so out of boredom. Each of them was a veteran without peer, forged in the fires of successive conflicts and tempered in the blood of enemies and treacherous countrymen alike. They would fight however their prince needed them to.

'There is no glory in this,' muttered Captain Ikhet.

'We are not here for glory,' replied Osorkon. 'We are here to take back our home.'

The ship glided past the northern walls and every eye on board followed the city gates. From sunrise to sunset the gates should have been open, with a checkpoint admitting traffic in and out of the city. Now, just before noon, it was closed and silent as if thousands of men waited to besiege its walls. Osorkon shielded his eyes from the sun. If there were men guarding the wall at all, then they were very well hidden.

The *Sobek is Content* drifted to a berth north of the city boundary, a shallow stretch of sand that the ship easily navigated. The Thebans disembarked and marched towards the gate, arrows nocked and spears ready, though Osorkon saw no signs of life.

How many times had he passed these very doors, the gateway to a childhood that suddenly seemed so distant? Osorkon stepped right up to the doors, listening and hearing nothing beyond them. He pounded on the timbers and waited, certain that he could rush whoever opened the gates before they could raise the alarm. No answer was forthcoming. He kicked the door in frustration and stepped back, but the gatehouse itself seemed entirely empty.

'What do we do now?' asked Bakenptah, his gaze never wavering from the walls.

Osorkon swore. 'We wait. If there is no sign of life before tomorrow morning, we take the harbour and enter that way. Let us hope they surrender now. Pray that someone comes, brother, because if not, we will be fighting our way in and I am tired of the smell of blood.'

The company made camp in the abandoned sheds, none of them eager to return to the closed confines of the ship. Only the smallest cooking fires were allowed, for Osorkon wanted their passage hidden for now.

At nightfall, after they were rested and had eaten, Osorkon sent out his watch. 'Ghere, Ankhu, take five men each and establish a picket on the east and south-east walls. If you see anything move, bring word immediately. Now go.' Osorkon watched the soldiers disappear running in the night before he directed his remaining men to scavenge through the abandoned warehouses.

Looted fishing nets brought them the first fresh food they had eaten in a week, and there was enough scrap timber to burn for months on end. Most of the sheds were empty though, stripped of everything of value.

The moon rose well into the night, and still no sign of life came forth from Thebes. Osorkon gazed at the walls as the men talked and ate and drank. That Karnak had turned against him could no longer be in doubt. No other could challenge his sister's power, no other with the backing or political clout to even dream of upsetting the order. If the traitorous priests had truly spent all their military force in the Nubian horde, then perhaps even the warriors he had with him were enough to give them pause.

Every hour the pickets came in and with each negative report Osorkon's mood grew darker. It was almost midnight before the night stirred anew and one of the sentries emerged from among the warehouses, dragging a supine figure behind him.

'Found this one snooping around outside.' He tossed the struggling figure in front of the fire as the charioteers stood and circled him like a pack of hyenas around a wounded gazelle. Ikhet recognised him first.

'Traitor.' Ikhet leapt to his feet with sword in hand and closed in on the fallen man.

Osorkon blocked Ikhet's path and stood looming over the newcomer. The prince made no move to help the fallen man up. 'Harsiese.'

The prophet shuffled to his knees and grimaced up at Osorkon. Harsiese's features were swollen and contorted with pain, but otherwise little different to how he remembered them. His eyes though, beheld a darkness Osorkon had never seen in them before.

'So, you have come after all,' said Harsiese.

'Yes, to put an end to your treacherous order,' replied Osorkon, his hand straying to the sword strapped at his hip.

'Not me,' spat Harsiese. 'Senmut and his followers. They have taken control of the city.'

The charioteers bristled at the name of the former Third Prophet, now turncoat theocrat.

'What is the meaning of this? Why are the gates of my home closed to me?' asked Osorkon.

Harsiese grunted and showed them his hands. The scars of rope burn marked his wrists and minor cuts marked the flesh of his knuckles. The skin was pink with recent healing but the torment of his capture was clear enough. 'No traffic is allowed in or out of the city, by order of the priests of Karnak. I had to climb over the walls to find you.'

'I am a priest of Karnak. As are you. Where are the gate guards?'

Harsiese spat again and with some effort rose to his feet. 'Manning the walls of the temples instead. Senmut has made the Precinct of Amun his private domain.'

'Heretic,' snapped Bakenptah.

'Blasphemer,' hissed another charioteer.

Osorkon held up a hand for silence. 'If what you say is true, he is all of these things and he will be punished accordingly.'

'If what I say is true?' snapped Harsiese. 'You damned-'

'May I remind you that despite what has happened here, I am your prince and you will speak to me with the appropriate respect,' interrupted Osorkon. 'You got here readily enough. I assume you have a way back inside the walls?'

'I have men inside.'

'Then take us in.'

'I cannot. We must wait for a signal and I must return it. If I don't, you will never get in.' Harsiese saw the charioteers close in and hissed vehemently. 'I have faced many ordeals of late and my trust is in short supply.'

'As have all in this company.' Osorkon turned to his captain and pointed to the south. 'Ikhet, recall the others. Make it quick and quiet.' Osorkon pushed the wrathful captain towards his chariot and turned back to Harsiese. 'Come, sit and have a drink.' Osorkon led Harsiese to the makeshift seats around the fire and passed the prophet a wineskin. Harsiese drank deeply and a chuckle escaped his lips.

'One of mine,' he said wistfully.

'The very same,' confirmed Osorkon. 'Now explain why you are wearing the tattered robes of a lowly fish merchant.'

'I am a stranger in my own town,' replied Harsiese. 'As I said, my trials have not been easy.'

'Nor mine, now speak plainly and tell me what happened here.'

'Senmut has gone mad. He forced me out of the city and attacked me on the open road. He took me prisoner for a time,' said Harsiese grimacing.

Osorkon frowned. The visions he had seen under the influence of Chief Pediese's potion had been pushed to the back of his mind during the battle for Hermopolis, but now the details came flooding back with full force. 'I know. I saw it.'

'You… saw it? And you did nothing?'

'It is difficult to explain. Keep talking.'

Harsiese looked as though he would press the issue, but let it go. 'How many have you brought with you? Surely this is not all.'

'We had trouble in Hermopolis. One hundred and fifty of my charioteers are still in fighting condition.'

'So few? By the gods…' Harsiese gasped. 'Had you brought more we could have taken the city easily, but with your numbers it may still come to a fight. Senmut still has many followers. Your charioteers are skilled, but Senmut has five fanatics to every one of your warriors. Can you face that?'

As if on cue, the returning charioteers re-entered the camp, taking their places around the fires and eyeing the new arrival with no small suspicion. Osorkon rose to meet them for they were brothers in all things now, not merely master and servant. 'These men have followed me through the underworld all the way from the Crag of Amun, Great of Roaring. The others yet recover in Hermopolis, for the fight was a hard one. Every one of the warriors here is up to the task.'

'What of the army your father took with him?' asked Harsiese.

'I have had no word from my father in weeks. As I said, we have been elsewhere and difficult to reach.'

Harsiese passed back the wineskin. 'I am sorry to hear that. May the gods watch over him as our chosen son. He has Ukhesh and Kaphiri with him, yes? They fought with you at Dakhla, did they not?'

Osorkon nodded. 'They did, and I was glad for their presence then as I am for their allegiance now. What happened here, Harsiese? Truly. We entrusted you with the city and you lost it. Our people suffer because you could not see the viper at your back.'

Harsiese's eyes flashed in anger. 'Does this look like a man in power?' He dropped his robe, his shendyt falling to his ankles as he stood before the warriors of Osorkon completely naked. Without the covering of cloth, his injuries looked worse. Yellow bruises and contusions covered his body from chest and legs and raised, crusted wounds marked his tormenters had pressed hot irons to his flesh.

'Trust is in short supply in these times,' said Osorkon.

Harsiese's retort was cut off as the call of an eagle-owl sounded over the docks. It was a poor imitation for those trained in such things but passable enough to the casual observer. 'Trust that we will lose this city forever if we don't go now,' he said, fastening his robe.

Osorkon signalled to his men. With sword scabbards fastened, and shield and spear in hand, the last charioteers of the Crag jogged to the main gate. Osorkon caught up to Harsiese who was already halfway back to the walls. 'If this is so urgent, why did your friends wait?'

'I was right in needing time to convince you of my loyalty. My... friends feared you would kill me on sight.'

'Who else is helping you?'

Harsiese's eyes narrowed though he looked straight ahead. The gesture was not lost on Osorkon. 'Your sister and Pedubast. She is safe,' he added quickly, 'but she too has suffered through this crisis. The Vizier is dead, or so Pedubast tells me.'

'You don't trust him?' asked Bakenptah, as they stepped inside the shadow of the walls.

'He is a priest of Amun,' said Harsiese, with a small shrug. 'If we survive this, you will come to know him and make your own decision. We have been using his house as a base.'

'It may not be safe there when the fighting begins. Our plans must change,' said Osorkon, turning to his warriors. 'We will take the palace first. As Harsiese said, Senmut barely has the men to challenge us. Perhaps a symbolic victory might prevent further bloodshed.'

'When we are inside, go straight to the house of Pedubast. Bring my sister to the palace as quick as you are able. We will take the seat of power first and make our presence known. Any who wish to surrender then may do so.'

Osorkon rolled his shoulders and shared a glance with Bakenptah, as the gates were hauled open by unseen allies and the city beyond became visible. 'Any that don't will suffer the Sons of Takelot.'

IN THE YEARS to come, engraved on bas reliefs in the temple grounds and on the frontiers of empire, the battle for Thebes would be remembered as a glorious liberation. The princes of Thebes had returned, guided by the hand of Amun to defend their people against the insidious corruption that had bloomed in the cankerous heart of Karnak.

For now, though, Thebes was a city absent of light and life. Cooking fires only dully illuminated houses from within, and furtive shadows moved behind closed curtains. The streets were entirely vacant, with no sign of even a stray dog or cat to disturb the stillness. Market stalls were shuttered and the taverns were dark. There were no sounds of revelry, nothing of joy, or even of pain or sorrow. There was nothing at all.

'Senmut has imposed a curfew,' explained Harsiese. He walked at the head of the formation with Osorkon and Bakenptah, careful not to move too far ahead from the safety of the armed host at his back.

Osorkon paused in the middle of the street. The charioteers, now on foot, formed a loose wedge behind him. Osorkon closed his eyes and cocked his head. Nothing but the sound of his men breathing interrupted the stillness. 'And yet, there are no guards? How does Lord Senmut enforce his rule when his followers are absent?'

Harsiese grimaced. 'After the first few examples, none have dared risk it again.'

'The Vizier?'

Harsiese nodded once. 'Senmut conducts all of his business from the hall of Karnak. The palace guard still serve the palace as a show of force, but few enough are now stationed there after your sister escaped and the Vizier died. They guard the temples, though Senmut keeps them plied with wine and smoke,' said Harsiese.

Before Osorkon could stop him, his brother pushed past and seized Harsiese by the front of his robes. He was young still, barely twenty, but three years of fighting had made him lean and hard, while Harsiese's capture had left him emaciated. The prophet fell back, but Bakenptah kept him upright, lifting him onto his toes.

'You know all this and yet you let this viper take our city? Where were you when he was plotting behind our backs? While my brother and I fight to unite this country, you let what we have already won slip away?'

'Easy, Bakenptah.' Osorkon's voice cut the silence, the voice that had given commands in the midst of frenetic battle. Bakenptah released the priest and backed away, his eyes narrowing with unsuppressed anger.

Harsiese smoothed down his ragged robes and glance at Bakenptah warily. He looked as though he would say something, but the fire in Osorkon's eyes changed his mind. 'Senmut still believes Pedubast is in his confidence. It was difficult to learn more without arousing his suspicions,' said Harsiese.

Osorkon nodded. 'And where is your ally, Pedubast? I desire to meet with him.'

Harsiese clasped his hands together and bowed low, his eyes fixed on Osorkon's feet. 'He is organising in other areas of the city. You will meet him when the time comes, my prince.'

Osorkon looked away. Far beyond the skyline of slums and marketplaces, the highest points of the temple portals were visible. On the other side of the city, the great portal entrance to the Great Hypostyle Hall peaked above the houses of the people. To have traitors and heretics in control of such holy ground made his teeth itch. 'I have faced nothing but lies and treachery since I left this city. If I find you are keeping something from me, then my wrath will be Amun incarnate. Are we clear?'

'As clear the waters of the Sacred Lake,' said Harsiese with a bow.

'Good, then we make for the palace. Find Isetweret and bring her to the throne room.'

Passage through to the administrative quarter was without impediment. The jostle of armoured men running through the streets kept most of the city's occupants indoors, though once or twice Osorkon caught the curious face of a child peering out into the night-time world.

The buildings of governance surrounding the monolithic Vizier's palace were illuminated, for even treachery of the basest nature could not halt the wheels of bureaucracy entirely. If Senmut had styled himself king, he had not done so here. The vizier's palace was dark and quiet, the braziers unlit and the lavish rooms fallen into disuse.

A foul stench caught in Osorkon's throat as soon as he stood in the shadow of the building and his foot slid in something sticky. He gagged as he steadied himself, scraping the dark fluid against the road before he led his men upward. Two guards lounged in the entrance to the atrium, their spears discarded as they passed a clay pot of beer between them.

The sound of hundreds of feet roused them from their stupor. As one, they saw the force arrayed against them and tried to flee. Bakenptah charged after the first man, tackling him to the ground with his arm locked around the man's throat to stifle his cries.

Osorkon reversed his spear and rammed the butt into lower back of the second man. He overbalanced and fell forward, the beer slowing his reflexes just enough to send him crashing face first into the sandstone wall. His skull cracked onto the sandstone floor and he was still.

Osorkon paused at the threshold of the stairs. Bakenptah went to step past him, but Osorkon caught his shoulder. To fall to ambush now would be a jest worthy of Set, and so Osorkon led the way, spear held at the ready, Bakenptah a step behind him. The brothers thrust through the door, but the atrium was deserted. Osorkon nodded the all clear and the soldiers of the Crag followed their lords in, fanning out to cover every passage leading out.

'Ikhet, take fifty men and secure the east wing. Heret, take another fifty and secure the west. The rest of you are with me. We secure the throne.' Quickly and quietly, the teams peeled off. Osorkon led Bakenptah and his men straight ahead, through the corridor leading to the great hall, the site of the vizier's throne and the seat of power in Thebes.

Osorkon considered sending Bakenptah and a smaller team to cover more ground but decided against it. It was only right that his brother be at his side for this triumph.

Osorkon jogged ahead, setting the pace through the deserted halls and corridors, the palace possessing an inert lifelessness he had never seen here before. He stepped around the first corner, coming face-to-face with a patrol. They stopped dead, all twenty of them, surprised at the figure that had appeared in their midst. Osorkon raised his empty hands and went to speak but the first soldier lunged at him with a frightened shout.

The spear tip raked across Osorkon's ribs leaving a stinging gash under his armour. Osorkon snarled and drew his sword on the return stroke, slashing the blade through the spear's haft. Bakenptah leapt forward and buried his own spear into the guard's chest, pinning him gasping to the floor.

'Surrender,' roared Osorkon. The fifty warriors that had followed him spilled out into the hall, weapons bared and expressions murderous. The nineteen remaining soldiers dropped their weapons in a near-simultaneous clang, terrified as they listened to their comrade expire on the ground.

Osorkon's hand went to his ribs. The seeping cut stung, but it was superficial, irritating him more than it hurt. After his battle against Malkesh, his shirt of beaten scales had become more of a patchwork liability than the fine armour it had once been.

Osorkon strode up to the next man in line. 'You know who I am?'

The soldier nodded dumbly.

'Tell me, where is the Vizier Hory? Do you know of his fate?'

The soldier looked sideways at his comrades. He had gone quite pale.

'How many more of you are there? Speak, before I cut out your tongues and leave you to wander the Field of Reeds forever mute.' The soldiers flinched at the threat, but none went to answer. Whether it was misplaced loyalty that bound them or stark fear that stole their voice was unclear.

Osorkon laid the flat of his sword on the closest man's shoulder. 'I am not in the habit of asking twice.' The man looked as though he would be sick, and he mumbled something under his breath. The sword point pricked his throat before he found his voice.

'Three other patrols in the palace, no larger than ours. My prince,' he added hastily. Osorkon's lowered his sword and the man's legs gave out beneath them. 'Bind their hands,' he ordered. 'Bakenptah, on me.'

The brothers left half of their men to oversee the prisoners and ventured deeper into the palace, coming finally to the massive cedar doors of the throne room. They were firmly closed, and the brothers both had to push to open the way. Osorkon stepped through first into a room of pale light. The braziers were cold, the torches burned out long ago, and the heavy scent of dust and staleness settled in the air, the only illumination provided by the wan moonlight filtering through the high windows. Even in the darkness, the columns were beautiful, painted scenes that triggered a deep nostalgia in Osorkon. He saw they were having a similar effect on Bakenptah, and the brothers took a moment to walk down the main path, not as petitioners but as conquerors.

Apart from themselves, there was no sign of life. The soldiers hung back, guarding the entrance, instinctively sensing that their masters would walk these final steps alone.

The throne was just as Osorkon remembered it, but why, he thought, should it be anything other? A foul pretender had tried to wrest the city from him and had failed to do so, just as all who challenged him were destined to fall. The pretender's life was now measured in scant hours, a forgettable footnote of history that would mark just one of Osorkon's many victories.

Osorkon climbed the steps of the dais, running his hands over the carvings on the throne, feeling every ridge and bump as his eyes adjusted to the dull glint of gilding. He felt power swell within him at that touch, and he turned with a flourish of his sword in hand, to take in the whole chamber.

'Welcome home, dear brother,' said Osorkon. 'Thebes belongs to the House of Takelot once more. Could you imagine a more glorious site?'

Bakenptah climbed the first steps of the dais. 'Senmut's head on a pike, aye.'

Before Osorkon could reply, they heard a commotion at the door, and a single figure pushed through the soldiers standing guard there. Harsiese loped up, his expression creased with concern and no small amount of fear.

Osorkon was down the dais in a moment, meeting Harsiese halfway up the hall.

'Where is my sister? Where is Isetweret?' he demanded.

'She is outside. On the steps. I cannot rouse her,' replied Harsiese, out of breath.

Cold fear gripped Osorkon's heart and he sprinted back down the hall, dimly aware of Bakenptah's footsteps close behind him. The brothers ran back through past their captives, into the atrium and toward the palace steps, ignoring the entreaties and cries of confusion from their men.

They only stopped running as they reached the stairs and saw the streets around deserted but for a heavily pregnant woman on her knees at the lowest step, her features wracked with a terrible and all-consuming grief as she stared up at the sky. Osorkon's nose wrinkled at the smell again as he sheathed his sword and slowly approached his sister.

'Iset?' Osorkon asked, as he knelt beside her. Goosepimples covered every inch of exposed skin and she looked as haggard and drawn as any of them. Osorkon reached out to her, recoiling as Isetweret shrieked and lashed out at him. Rough nails raked his forearms and the screams seemed to go on without pause for breath until he clutched her forearms and held her still. She was gaunt and thin, the bones of her arms and shoulders wrapped in pale, blotched skin.

'It is us, sweet sister. Your brothers have come for you,' pressed Osorkon.

Her screams ended in a choke as she focused on the faces in front of her. A small gasp escaped her cracked lips and her eyes began to mist. Osorkon held her to him as great, heaving sobs wracked her thin frame.

'By the gods, what have they done to you?' he whispered as he held her close. Isetweret buried her face in the crook of his neck, her tears spilling down his armour like raindrops.

Bakenptah knelt beside them and laid a hand on her back, his expression hardening when his felt how pronounced her ribs were. Isetweret's hand lashed out and clutched his arm like a lifeline, her strength borne of desperation and relief in equal measure.

Outside the palace, the city of Thebes was beginning to stir as the children of Pharaoh clung together in the darkness.

They found Hory soon enough. He had died in torment, but one final injustice had been heaped upon him after death; he had been left to rot, a feast for flies and carrion birds.

The full force of Isetweret's grief suddenly became very apparent. How long had she been forced to hide away, knowing her kind-hearted beloved was slowly dying in agony, but entirely powerless to stop it?

Osorkon shivered at the thought. He left Bakenptah to coax Isetweret out of her despair, the only man in the city he dared leave her alone with, while he secured the rest of the palace himself. The other patrols, outnumbered by far, surrendered just as easily as the first, the captives herded into the throne room and tied together in long chains until the depth of their loyalty could be ascertained.

Osorkon waited below, the bulk of his forces arrayed on the street outside the palace, as a few of Ikhet's men cut Hory down. Harsiese stood alongside him, his nose and mouth covered by the hood of his robes. The stench of death was all around and neither man ventured to speak first. Dark stains streaked the palace façade where his vital fluids had leaked out after death, collecting in the foul-smelling pool Osorkon had stepped in on the way up.

'Watch out!' cried a voice sounded from above.

Osorkon leapt back as a flash of white plummeted towards them, swearing as it hit the ground. The skull burst open like a rotten egg and smelled worse. Writhing maggots and strips of rotting flesh splashed out over the road. The neck had decayed so much that the head had been held on by a few scant strips of sinew, tearing at the merest movement from above. Osorkon stared down at the broken skull of a man he once knew, and coldness banished any sense of mercy he had left in him. Beside him, Harsiese retched.

'Did you know of this?' said Osorkon, his voice low. Harsiese's silence was all the confirmation he needed. 'Why did you say nothing? Why did Pedubast not intervene?'

'I arrived in Thebes well afterward,' said Harsiese. 'As for our ally, ask yourself what manner of man does this and then ask yourself if you'd wish to get in his way.'

'I intend to do that and more,' said Osorkon, and gave the order to move out.

Harsiese shuffled after him. 'Then you are a braver man than I. Senmut is not the man I once knew. He is consumed by his own greed and lust for power.'

'Men do not change, Harsiese. Whatever he is now was always beneath the surface. We just did not see it. I will be more careful in future in whom I place my trust.'

The rest of the passage to Karnak passed in silence. At thoroughfares and marketplaces, warriors in groups of two or three peeled off to secure the city's gates and military stores. Osorkon gave each of them a token from the palace. All who marched under the banner of the Prince of Thebes did so in his name.

Before long, the houses and stores gave way to open spaces and beyond that, the Avenue of Rams that led to the great portals of Karnak. The first pylon reared up from the earth as though it were a mountain. A single monolith shaped by the hands of men. Great braziers burned at the entrance, and there could be no doubt that the lifelessness of the city would not extend here into the temples.

'Does Senmut now fear nightfall?' wondered Osorkon aloud.

'I suspect he fears a great many things,' replied Harsiese. 'The men here are those most loyal to him. They may not break like those at the palace.'

Osorkon smiled for the first time that night. The veterans at his back would welcome the challenge. The fervour in their eyes spoke of vengeance long overdue, ready to fight and die at their prince's word. Osorkon loved their blind devotion, even as it worried him. He ordered them to secret themselves in the houses and alleys beyond the temple boundary, bows held ready for what would come. It would be a much simpler thing to enter the temple without raising the alarm, and to be drawn into combat at the first pylon would risk a bloodbath in the confined space. No, if the guards would not surrender, they would have to die, quickly and cleanly.

Osorkon led Harsiese alone up the Avenue of Rams, feeling the judgemental eyes of the ram-headed god following him. 'Forgive me for the blood I must spill in your holy sanctuary,' he murmured, as Harsiese muttered aloud prayers of justice and protection.

Halfway up the avenue, Osorkon saw the outlines of men beyond the portal. Their movements were unhurried, and by some miracle the firelight dimmed their night sight until Osorkon was almost in the archway.

'State your business,' said the first guard. He was fresh-faced, his chin hairless with youth rather than the razor, but his tone spoke of unbridled arrogance beyond his years. Six others formed a barrier behind him, glaring at Osorkon and Harsiese like they were beggars.

'I am Prince Osorkon of Thebes, son of Pharaoh Takelot the second of that name, and heir apparent to the throne of Egypt. State your business in blocking my passage.'

The young guard simply stared, sharing a glance with his companions. He licked his lips nervously and stepped forward into the firelight. Osorkon was armed but Harsiese was not, and seven against one were odds the young guard was seemingly comfortable with.

'Whoever you are, you are mad to try to enter the temples,' said the guard, drawing his sword and holding the point to Osorkon's belly. 'You will surrender yourself into my custody.'

'My father is behind me with the Theban army,' Osorkon lied. 'Step aside or I will consider you implicit in this heresy for which the penalty is death.'

The guard's eyes flickered, but he stopped himself from looking to his comrades for support. 'Lord Senmut rules here now. I say again, surrender yourself, or die where you stand with my blade in your gut.'

Osorkon sighed. 'Very well, I submit to the will of the temples.' He knelt before the youth. Harsiese followed his lead. Osorkon had just a second to enjoy the confusion on the young guard's face before an arrow lanced through his throat.

The air hissed overhead and all seven were struck down by an invisible death. Each was a kill shot, as Osorkon had expected. The men in his company trained daily to hit moving targets in the heat of battle from a racing chariot. To hit stationary targets, silhouetting themselves in the firelight, was a laughably simple task.

Osorkon took a moment to savour their handiwork before he was up and through the First Pylon and into the temple grounds.

The grounds were alive with activity even at this midnight hour, though there was none of the solemness expected and an uncharacteristic revelry that infuriated Osorkon with its impiety. Oblations and offerings were essential services throughout night and day, keeping the gods nourished and content, but the priests here appeared drunk with wine, intoxicated with smoke and moving to song that had no place being played on temple grounds. Few priests looked up at the armed men in their midst. Evidently, Senmut's paranoia had made such a sight common of late.

'There, beyond the Sacred Lake. That is where Senmut has made his lair,' said Harsiese. The hall was a surprisingly austere accommodation for a theocrat, but as Osorkon got closer, the stink of conflicting incense and stale drink wafted out to greet them.

The main building was as hot as a tavern and smelled worse. Osorkon's lip curled at the sight of the debauchery as he stepped into the sanctum of heresy. Senmut had always been ruled by vice, but this was excess unbridled. Men and women lounged unconscious on gilded cushions and brightly coloured rugs. Spilled wine jugs lay scattered across the floor, and heady-smelling smoke drifted from abandoned clay pipes. Half-eaten wild game, fowl, and poached fish lay on silver platters beside a surfeit of roasted vegetables, sweet honey, and fresh bread.

Osorkon led his company through the naked, languid forms, careful not to tread on fingers or other outstretched appendages. A gaunt figure with a beaked nose and deep-set eyes stirred as shadows flickered over him. His eyes fluttered open, fixing on the warriors standing over him. Before he could draw breath to shout, an arrow lanced through the man's open mouth. The arrowhead punched through the back of the man's skull, the feathered shaft sticking out between his teeth. The man gasped once, before his eyes rolled back into his head and he fell back onto the cushions convulsing. Osorkon nodded at the archer behind him, who watched the dying man with cold amusement. Not one of Senmut's followers stirred as the man's lifeblood splashed over the floor.

Osorkon searched the floor for the familiar figure, toying with the idea of ordering everyone in the room to be put to death as they slept, but he pushed the idea of massacre from his mind as he saw a side passage and sprawling limbs within.

Senmut lay asleep and snoring in the next room, a private bedroom which should have been set aside for the supplies of the temple scribes. Chicken fat greased his chin, and crumbs and splashes of wine covered the bedsheets. He was not alone either. Three young women and one young man slept beside their new master, as unresponsive as the rest of them as armed men filled the space.

Osorkon snatched up a goblet inlaid with gold and held it out before him. He dropped the cup and it hit the floor with a clang. Senmut's eyes shot open and he bolted upright, a snarl on his lips. The anger died on his face as he realised who it was that stood before him.

Osorkon knelt on the bed next to him, his bloody sword held across his lap.

'Hello, Senmut. I am home.'

# Chapter Twenty-Nine

DAWN BROUGHT THEBES back to life. At first, the streets remained empty, its citizens fearful that the news of liberation was merely a new test of compliance from the priests of Karnak. None among the people were quick to forget the fates of those that had failed previous tests of fealty. Soon, though, as Osorkon made his presence more widely known, there could be no doubt that the Sons of Takelot had returned, any disquiet previously felt towards the Theban pharaoh put aside in the vanquishing of a greater evil.

With Senmut and the other conspirators in custody, the rest of the city fell into Osorkon's control in short order. Those of Senmut's guards that surrendered without a fight were temporarily disarmed but forgiven, plans already made to break up old units into new formations led by Osorkon's veterans. A detailed proscription would come later, but for now, the city was secure, and the walls fully manned once more under their rightful ruler.

As the sun first shone over the eastern horizon, Osorkon conducted the dawn prayers in the presence of every priest of Karnak, bar the ones under lock and key. The inner sanctum was, and always would be, reserved for the chosen prophets, but priests of all rank waited beyond the temple walls for news from the avenging prince.

'Great Amun,' he had said, once the god was nourished and clothed. 'How can you have let such blasphemy enter your most sacred spaces? I lay the blame at your feet, Great One. I charge you, in all your power, with failure to watch over your own. Your domain has been poisoned, and your followers humbled.'

Osorkon stared down at the cult statue of Amun, dressed, fed and standing accused by the god's most loyal and devoted follower.

'I, as your representative on earth, demand that you to bring down your punishment on those that have wronged you and your family. May the great mother Mut deny them nurture. May the divine son Khons hunt them endlessly in the beyond! For your failure as the god of this land, I call on you now. Let none be beyond your wrath.'

So spoken, Osorkon left the god to ruminate on his words and return to the awaiting priests. There were many among the conspirators that sadly did not surprise Osorkon, but many more that had wandered from the light, too weak-willed to protest their changing destiny. The priesthoods always drew the ambitious, but it drew also those that needed a firm hand to guide them, men who would always be followers and could be no more blamed for their desertion of duty than a goat wandering from its pen.

Others though, were all too culpable, all too knowing in their self-serving devotion to a new order. Names that once inspired devotion and piety were now watchwords for treason and heresy.

In the courts of Egypt, even those accused of the gravest crimes were permitted to protest their innocence, but there could be no doubt here of their guilt. Senmut had been all too eager to name his collaborators, and the list of names grew by the hour as frightened citizens too came forward to condemn the actions of those they had suffered under.

Within a day, a list of twenty names of the arch-traitors had been compiled, the very worst of the ringleaders for whom no punishment was severe enough. Twelve of those were present in the temples at the time of Osorkon's liberation. The others were judged guilty in absentia. Some tended to temple holdings outside the city, while others, like Sarasesh, were on expeditions elsewhere. Yet more, like Tasenhor, were already dead.

The naming of Harsiese, Pedubast, and his brother Iuput among the collaborators gave Osorkon pause. Were it not for his visions under Pediese's spiritual draught, he might have been swayed to

414

believe the scale of Harsiese's ambition and punish him among the guilty. The tortures inflicted on his body, however, proved his lack of guilt, if not his outright innocence. With Harsiese's freedom from blame and his vouching for Pedubast, Osorkon found he could not indict the latter either.

Osorkon met the brother priests in the early hours, distantly remembering two unremarkable faces, one with eyes of incredible focus and the other with eyes that never stopped moving.

'It seems I am in your debt, to both of you,' he said, greeting them by the shores of the Sacred Lake, the cool water still and clean of taint.

Pedubast had smiled and bowed, but there was little warmth in the gesture. Iuput just stared. 'There is no debt to be had, my prince,' said Pedubast. 'Entrust that the temples have been righted once more and that the balance of Ma'at is maintained.'

Osorkon had looked out over the temples then, the golden daylight suffusing the sandstone walls with a warmth that made his heart ache with relief and pride that he served the gods in such an immortal place. 'Even so, there must been some boon I can grant you for helping my sister, and for all that you have done turning the people against Senmut.'

Pedubast smiled again. 'We will consider your offer, my prince, but for now we are content in the service of Thebes. Until then, I will enjoy watching those that upset the balance of the land be struck down as they deserve.'

Osorkon had taken his leave soon after, struck by a disquiet he did not understand.

A SMALL DAIS had been erected at the entrance to the Avenue of Rams, a paltry homage to the platform constructed when Osorkon's grandfather Nimlot had been buried years before. It seemed all of Thebes had turned out to see the sentencing, and here and there stall vendors moved through the press of people selling fried fish and baked bread as thousands of eyes turned to witness the traitors' sentencing be carried out. The twelve heretics knelt on the dais bound at the wrists and ankles. One of Osorkon's veterans stood behind each of them, holding them firm.

Osorkon mounted the dais and walked past the prisoners, making eye contact with each until he reached the last. Senmut glared up at him, trying to look defiant, but beneath the twitching smirk there was very real fear.

Osorkon raised his hands for quiet and slowly the murmur of the crowd subsided, letting all eyes linger on him and know that his return was not mere hearsay. Upon his head was a nemes headdress of blue and gold, and a crisp white shendyt was wrapped around his waist. From his belt hung his sword and dagger, freshly cleaned, sharpened and oiled, and his skin shone with newfound health and glistening oils.

He would have preferred to wear his armour, but his cloak of bronze scales would need weeks in the artisan's workshop before it was serviceable again, and justice could not wait. He let the silence linger a moment longer as the crowd waited for him to speak.

'My father, Takelot, Pharaoh of Upper Egypt, fights the invader Shoshenq in the north and sends the cur back to his hole in Tanis. Herakleopolis stands with us. Hermopolis stands with us. The band of savages that these men bought with your coin have been defeated, scattered to the winds.' The crowd jeered at conspirators as Osorkon continued. 'Never again will my beloved city fall into the hands of the impious. While my family rules, Thebes will always be the heart of the south, where all men and women of this land are free in the sight of the gods.'

Osorkon drew his sword and held it up to catch the light.

'I have fought foreigners and my own kin to reach home again. I have slain the impious, the treacherous, and the deluded. I have ended all that sought to end me, and I vow in the sight of gods and men that my arm has never been stronger.' Every man, woman, and child were held captivated, and the cheers and jeers were isolated and quickly silenced. 'It is clear to me now that even the once-pious may fall. The supervision of the divine must always be maintained, lest the Rule of Ma'at become unbalanced. The prophets have been found wanting,' he said, pointing to the kneeling Senmut.

'While my father rules in his benevolence, I will be your High Priest of Amun. None shall escape my wrath, for I am Osorkon the Liberator, the Chosen of the Great God.' His thrust his sword higher, and this time the crowd roared at his pronouncement. To Osorkon, there was no more satisfying feeling. He savoured every moment of it, wringing every shred of devotion from them all. He was Osorkon and he was Amun, the god's instrument on earth. It seemed an age before the crowd quietened once more, and Osorkon's chest heaved with the exertion of his words.

'In front of the great portals of Karnak, let the gods witness justice be done,' he roared, his sword swinging around to point at the kneeling conspirators.

One by one, Osorkon's veterans stepped forward and plunged their swords downward into the soft flesh between neck and collarbone. The conspirators stiffened and vomited blood, and they died to a chorus of satisfied cheer from the thousands of witnesses.

After the first two, the others struggled, weeping and shrieking for mercy, but they were held tight in the grips of men that had lost their friends and brothers because of their heretical greed.

The swords pierced their hearts, an immortal mark of their blasphemy that Anubis would notice when he cast his judgement. Without an intact heart, their place in the afterlife would never be one of contentment, their spirits never truly at peace.

When it came to Naroleth, the priest screamed and thrashed, but his bonds and the strength of his captor held him fast. He frothed at the mouth as he bucked and twisted.

'No, it was Harsiese too. And Pedubast! Them too. I did nothing!' he screamed.

Osorkon turned and his eyes fell on Pedubast standing at the front of the crowd. For a moment, real fear spread over his face, but it was gone behind a mask of impassivity before the prince was sure he had seen it. Osorkon broke turn away, returning his attention to Naroleth's protests. His sword licked out and Naroleth's throat opened in a spray of crimson. The soldier behind him held him up a moment longer as his lifeblood spilled down his chest, only releasing the priest when his head slumped forth in death.

Within minutes, eleven bodies lay slumped on the dais, rivulets of blood running thick between the wooden boards to soak into the earth underneath.

Osorkon sheathed his sword and drew the *Tooth of Sobek*. The dagger, a gift from his father, had never left his side. It was a symbol of pharaonic power, of the strength to rule, and it was as precious to him as any object on this earth.

Senmut's face was deathly pale and he trembled with fear, but he glared at Osorkon with unconcealed hatred. Osorkon gestured to the veteran behind him and brought Senmut struggling to his feet. Tears glistened in the corners of his eyes, and his chin was wrinkled with terror.

'Your sister still lives because of me,' Senmut hissed. 'I could have had her killed.'

'What you have done to her is no life at all,' Osorkon replied.

Osorkon met the heretic priest's gaze a moment longer, his back to the roaring crowd.

'Know this before you die, Senmut. I am going to burn your body until the flesh and fat have melted from your bones. Then I will have a blacksmith grind them into powder. Then a dozen riders will carry what is left of you to the furthest reaches of the empire and bury the ashes in unmarked graves. You will wander the deserts neither here nor there, forever without form, forever lusting for the life you cast aside so casually the moment you betrayed me.'

Osorkon had a moment to savour the priest's look of abject horror before he sliced the blade up under the priest's lowest rib. Senmut screamed, the pitch of his agony heightening as terror was contorted with pain as Osorkon plunged a hand into the wound. The fallen priest sagged, his expression slack as the prince's arm sunk deeper and deeper into his body.

Senmut could feel the defiling limb probing deeper within him, and knew the very moment the prince found what he sought. Osorkon locked eyes with Senmut, as he wrapped his fingers around the priest's beating heart.

Senmut tried to scream, but all that emerged was a wet gurgle as Osorkon clenched and pulled. Blood vessels tore, muscles rent and Osorkon tore Senmut's treacherous heart out through his chest.

Senmut's eyes rolled back, his chest a wash of crimson before his legs gave out and he hit the dais hard. He twitched once, twice, and then was still. Osorkon looked over at his veterans and dropped the heart beside Senmut's corpse as the crowd roared behind him.

'Tear down the dais. Build a pyre. Burn the bodies.'

The messenger came late in the night. Too late in his campaign Takelot had learned that his sons planned to march on Thebes. Too late he had learned that Thebes had turned at all. How had Shoshenq known his rule already lay in ruin? What sort of king could not control his own city?

To mobilise an army many thousands strong was an unending battle of logistics, and the weeks of organising rations and planning the march home had seen Takelot send out a dozen of his most capable spies to ascertain the extent of this southern treachery.

An official missive had come from Osorkon almost a week ago, and a great weight had been lifted from his heart.

*Thebes retaken. Traitors dead. Rule of Takelot restored without challenge.*

That weight had returned when the first spies did, each one with grim news.

Hermopolis lay in ruin. The villages of the nome were charnel houses, and a trail of pillage and rapine led all the way to the heart of his new seat in Herakleopolis.

He kept this information secret as long as he could, but it was inevitable that knowledge of the war would filter through his command structure and spread at the speed of thought. Either way, the full impact would be revealed on their return to Thebes, whatever his will.

His sons had been victorious though, defeating an army that vastly outnumbered their own, and for that he was proud. Pride turned to ash when a little past midnight two nights before he was due to depart, his tent fluttered open and a guard gently awakened him.

'Beg your pardon, my king, but a messenger has returned.'

Takelot rubbed his eyes and beckoned him. Whatever little sleep he had already had would have to be enough tonight. He rose from bed and slipped on his robes. 'Send him in.'

A slender figure slipped through the opening and knelt before the king.

'You have news,' said Takelot. It was not a question.

The messenger nodded. 'Thebes is retaken. The city is at peace.'

'This I know, what else do you bring?'

'The princes and princess are healthy and well. The vizier is dead.' The messenger spoke without emotion and Takelot absorbed the fact as though he were hearing a report on grain. Hory was yet another name on an ever-growing tally of death. The messenger looked uncomfortable. It was the first time Takelot had seen him show any genuine expression at all.

'There is something else,' said Takelot. 'Speak plainly and without fear.'

'The priests that Prince Osorkon ordered executed. He had their bodies burned.'

Takelot closed his eyes. 'How many?'

'All of them, my king,' replied the messenger. 'Twelve priests were put to the torch on the first day. To my knowledge another five burnings have happened since then. Most were well-connected. Already, news of these punishments has spread far and wide.'

'You have seen this with your own eyes?'

'I have seen the pyres, though I regret I cannot confirm the bodies,' the messenger admitted with a small shrug, 'but it is the talk of the city, from fisherman to cloth merchant to prophet of the gods.'

Takelot nodded slowly. 'That will be all. Stay close. I may have need of you again. See that you have a hot meal and comfortable place to sleep. You have my gratitude.'

The messenger bowed and slipped out as quietly as he had come.

Takelot rose and poured himself a cup of wine, barely tasting it, the movements a habit that occupied his body while his mind was awhirl. He knew their youthful fervour for what it was, for he had once been the same, but this...

'Oh, my son,' whispered Takelot. 'What have you done?'

# Chapter Thirty

HARSIESE WALKED AMONG the bas reliefs as though in a dream. The Great Hypostyle Hall was replete with vistas of gods and men in the sacred places on earth and in heaven. Larger than life-size, great kings of the past offered incense to Amun and the sacred family. For a time, he had feared he would never see such exquisite craftsmanship again, nor ever gaze upon the vivid palette of colour that long dead artisans had used to bring the images to life.

The wounds to his body had healed until he suffered only the occasional ache, but the wounds to his spirit would take much longer to heal.

Of all the prophets, Senmut had been the only lowborn. Had that envy somehow twisted his ambitions? Could Harsiese have treated him differently, done something to avoid all this bloodshed? The questions were pointless now, but he found himself considering them more and more in his quieter moments. Regardless, he had survived. Not only that, but he had survived against a foe that wanted him to die in agony. And yet, somehow, he felt guilty.

And so, he wandered the precincts, seeking some meaning in the carvings that yet eluded him, some answer for the turmoil of emotion that plagued him each day. He heard the whispers from priests young and old that he had been changed irrevocably by his experiences. They were right, but he took no umbrage at their presumption.

He had changed. Amun had lifted him up again, reminding him of the fragility of this mortal life, and the meaning of his life as a prophet of the gods.

In recent days, the nagging idea of finding his father's tomb had returned, first as an itch and then as a burning, all-consuming need. In the turmoil of the civil war, the desire to relocate his ancestral tombs had been quite forgotten, but the war was now over and he was free to put the resources of Karnak at his own disposal.

With the smell of Senmut's ashes still in his nostrils, Osorkon had summoned Harsiese to the inner sanctum of the Temple of Amun. Together, they breathed deep of the sacred incense and cleansed themselves of the blood they had shed to be here.

It would take the prince much longer to expunge himself of his deeds though, Harsiese considered, even as Osorkon smiled as though his blasphemy had been entirely natural.

'There is much work yet to be done to secure the north. I will come south when my duties call, but until such a time as Shoshenq is confined permanently to the north, I will rule from the Crag of Amun. The ceremonies and dedications I will return for, but the day-to-day running I entrust to you, Harsiese.'

He had simply nodded, mumbling platitudes and assuring Osorkon he would do all within his power to restore Karnak's glory and bring the temples back into the public trust. To do the work without the glory of the title would be his fate for the time-being, but it kept his mind occupied and gave him the safety of prestige once more. It also gave him a chance to continue his own work without the scrutiny of a High Priest's position.

He could live with that. For now.

Harsiese started, glancing out of the corner of his eye for the source of his paranoia. For weeks now, the nagging sensation that he was being watched plagued him. He tried to put it down to his past trauma, but he could not entirely convince himself of the fact.

He passed through more of the pillars coming to the base of his favourite scene. Here, a High Priest that was the spitting image of his father, the elder Harsiese, was offering food and drink to Amun himself.

'I will find you again, father. I promise.'

Harsiese closed his eyes and laid a hand on the pillar. He felt the thrum of power in those stones. His fingers tingled at the touch, setting his mind at ease for the first time in months. He was home, he was alive, and the gods themselves ordained his mission. What man, mortal or otherwise, could stand before him now?

PEDUBAST LOST SIGHT of the wandering Harsiese and turned away. His newfound ally had lived as though in a trance since the death of the conspirators, his mind broken almost beyond repair. That was good. Pedubast had been right to change sides, good fortune had brought Harsiese to him. The prophet would make a valuable ally.

The stench of burning ash would take weeks to clear, and his colleagues complained of the blasphemy, protesting at the barbaric treatment of the temple hierarch. To Pedubast, the smell of Senmut's demise was a sickly-sweet stench laden with promise.

Already there were whispers that the sons of Takelot were touched by the gods of disorder and chaos. The heretics had been rotten to the core, true, but to burn the bodies of holy men invited retribution from beyond the grave. Without peace in the afterlife, even a novice priest knew that wandering shades would find a way to avenge themselves. The elder prince had marked himself as a target.

Osorkon was barbaric in his vengeance and Bakenptah was little better, though Pedubast admitted they were both their father's sons. To have come through what they had showed incredible fortitude that few, even among the nobility, would have managed.

The boys were touched by the divine. That much was clear. Descended from the bloodthirsty Libyan stock of the Meshwesh migration, they were as much nomadic savages as those they had fought.

More would need to be drawn into the web if order was to be maintained and the civil wars that plagued Egypt brought to a halt. The loss of Malkesh was a thorn, but Pedubast shed no tears for his loss. He was but one of many of the dispossessed that would fight for coin. His brother would find more.

Malkesh's incursion had destroyed, or severely depleted at the very least, many of the outposts and border towns at the southern edge of Egyptian land, paving the way for incursions and raids from the Nubian tribes of the northern Bagrawiyah at the First Cataract. What few people were left were driven northward, and without a sizable military to push them back, Pedubast had taken his own initiative and dispatched his brother to nudge the burgeoning disorder back in the direction best for Egypt.

Iuput did not possess the head for intrigue that Pedubast did, but he had a phenomenal memory and was able to absorb the languages and customs of foreign peoples with enviable ease. To meet with the Nubian tribes and persuade them that there were richer enemies to fight should be a simple enough task for the savant, more so if rich gifts from the city of Thebes could sway the chieftains in the belief that Pharaoh was a more generous master than their own Great King ruling from distant Napata.

Pedubast stepped out into the light and knelt by the Sacred Lake. Priests of Amun, and of Mut and Khonsu smiled at him as they completed their ablutions, and he smiled back.

'It is a glorious day. The blessings of the holy family upon you,' he said.

'And you, brother,' intoned the priest at his side.

Yes, there would be others to bring to the cause.

# Epilogue

THE LANDSCAPE WAS a rocky desert of spinifex and gnarled trees with roots that sank deep into the earth. This was Kush, a hard land that bred a hard people. Iuput climbed the next rise and looked out over the vast expanse. Somewhere, in this gods-forsaken place, were men that his brother needed. He heard the clank of pots and satisfied groans as his porters collapsed beneath the sparse shade of a lone tree.

Iuput's brow furrowed. 'We have gone no more than ten kilometres this morning. There is still much ground to cover.'

His porters grumbled but none would dare gainsay a priest of Amun. They hefted packs filled with food, water, and spare cloth as well as precious stones and fine linen, and trudged onward.

Sheref, the leader of the porters, came forward and bowed deeply. 'Perhaps giving the men a short rest might increase our distance by day's end? Happy men are productive men after all, lord,' he said. Sheref had tried talking to him of morale when they lost two men to asp bites in one night, but the topic seemed to confuse the priest and Sheref soon put it from his mind. They had a mission and they would see it through. That is all there was to it.

Iuput looked down at him unblinking. 'If you think that is best.' Iuput didn't see Sheref shiver as those pale eyes left him. Iuput's moods were unpredictable and his memory was infallible, but his brother's temper was a sight worse. When they returned, *if* they returned, Iuput would tell his brother the whole journey in exhaustive detail.

Iuput gestured to a ridge almost three leagues away. 'We need to make that rock line by dark. It is imperative that we find cover while the sun still shines.'

Sheref's expression was doubtful, but Iuput looked to be already plotting the course through the valley in his mind. The priest glanced back absently.

'You have something on you.'

Sheref glanced down at the beetle crawling up his leg and brushed it off with a start. 'Not Ra, not any of the gods have power here,' he grumbled as he climbed up after the priest. 'This is dangerous country.'

Iuput nodded as though Sheref had commented on the weather. 'My brother needs dangerous people.'

A trail of dust drifted high in the wind, a thin pillar of sand stretching into the heavens. At first, Iuput took it to be a dust devil, a tiny funnel of wind that sucked the debris from the earth, but then the dust came on directly towards them. As the minutes went by, the base of the dust column solidified into the shapes of camels, then men riding astride those camels.

'Excellent,' said Iuput. 'Here are some of them now.'

# CHARACTER LIST

(* indicates real historical figures)

AKHETEP: friend to Osorkon, Commander of the Royal Chariots

AMAKET: sole survivor of the attack on Khnefren

AMENMOSE: healer and snake charmer from Deir el-Medina

*ANKHEREDNEFER: Inspector of the Palace in Tanis

ASHRAFA: captain of Herakleopolis

*BAKENPTAH: Prince of Thebes, younger brother of Osorkon

HAMMA: chief architect of Herakleopolis

HARELOTHIS: Great Chief of the Meshwesh

*HARSIESE: prophet of Amun

HEKHENFER: royal charioteer

HERYTEP: Theban noble, father of Karoadjet

HESHKA: soldier of Thebes

HORY: son of Nakhtefmut, husband of Isetweret

IKHET: friend of Osorkon, officer of the Royal Charioteers

IRBEKH: royal charioteer

*ISETWERET: sister of Osorkon and Bakenptah, princess of Thebes

*IUPUT: priest of Amun, brother of Pedubast

KAPHIRI: General of Thebes

*KAROADJET: wife of Osorkon, princess of Thebes

*KAROMAMA MERYMUT: the 'Beloved of Mut', Great Royal Wife to Takelot II, mother of Osorkon, Bakenptah and Isetweret

*KHONSEFANKH: Nomarch of Herakleopolis, brother of Takelot and uncle of Osorkon

KHONTEF: accomplice of Senmut, captor of Harsiese

*LAMINTU: Royal Shieldbearer to Osorkon II

MALKESH: pirate warlord of the Red Sea.

NAKHTEFMUT: vizier of Thebes

NAROLETH: priest of Amun

NEFERADJET: mother of Karoadjet

*NESPERENNUB: Priest of Amun

*NIMLOT: High Priest of Amun. Son of Pharaoh Osorkon II and father of Takelot II [deceased]

OLEKH: charioteer, driver of Takelot II

*OSORKON II: Pharaoh of Egypt [deceased]

*OSORKON: Prince of Thebes, son of Takelot

*PAAMENY: Royal Physician to Osorkon II

*PEDUBAST: priest of Amun, brother of Iuput

PEREFTEP: Chancellor of Thebes

SENMUT: Prophet of Amun

SHEREF: chief porter of Iuput

*SHOSHENQ III: Pharaoh of Tanis and Lower Egypt

*TAKELOT II: Pharaoh of Thebes and Upper Egypt, son of Nimlot and grandson of Pharaoh Osorkon II

TASENHOR: priest of Amun

TIBEKH: cousin of Osorkon, son of Khonsefankh

UHMAN: soldier of Thebes

UKHESH: General of Hermopolis

# GLOSSARY

AKHET: one of the three seasons in Ancient Egypt. The time of inundation when the river swells and covers the floodplains with fertile silt and mud.

AMUN: the father and king of the gods and one of the most powerful deities in the Egyptian pantheon. Worshipped as part of the Theban triad.

BASTET: the cat goddess and a deity of protection and fertility. Her major cult centre was Bubastis.

BLUE CROWN: the crown worn by pharaohs in times of war.

CHARIOT: a two-wheeled vehicle drawn by a pair of horses and crewed by a driver and an archer. Favoured method of war for the pharaohs themselves and used in the army in place of cavalry.

HOUR PRIEST: a priest who specialises in astronomy and the heavens as well as the more practical task of making and keeping calendars.

KHONSU: the moon god of healing and a protector of travellers. Worshipped as part of the Theban triad with his father Amun and his mother Mut.

MESHWESH: often abbreviated in Ancient Egyptian as the Ma. A Libyan tribe of Berber origin, originating from what is now central-western Libya, they were in almost constant conflict with Egypt towards the end of the New Kingdom. Came to power and ruled Egypt during the early Third Intermediate Period.

MUT: the mother goddess, consort of Amun. Worshipped as part of the Theban triad.

NEMES: the striped cloth headdress traditionally worn by pharaohs. Often blue and gold in colour.

PERET: one of the three seasons in Ancient Egypt. The time when the water recedes and the planting of crops begins.

PROPHET: the four highest offices of a priesthood. The first prophet is also called the High Priest.

RED CROWN: the outer part of the twin crown, representing Lower Egypt.

RULE OF MA'AT: the concept of cosmic harmony, brought about by good and just actions. Represented by the example of Ma'at, the goddess who personifies truth, justice, order and righteousness.

SEKHMET: the lioness goddess, protector of pharaohs, the hunter goddess and embodying war and violence.

SHENDYT: a kilt-like garment made of cloth and worn around the waist.

SHOMU: one of the three seasons in Ancient Egypt. The time of dryness.

SOBEK: the crocodile god embodying Pharaonic protection, but also possessed of a fluid and sometimes violent nature.

TAWERET: the hippopotamus goddess of fertility and childbirth.

VIZIER: the highest-ranking officials of the state administration appointed by Pharaoh and responsible for running the country's judiciary and civil bureaucracy. From the New Kingdom. One rules in the north and one in the south.

WHITE CROWN: the inner part of the twin crown, representing Upper Egypt.

Ryan Pope is an Australian historical fiction author. Born in 1992 on a northern mountain inhabited by snakes, kangaroos and an echidna named Rex, his parents later saw sense and moved south. He grew up on the Sunshine Coast, a place deceptively named as it often rained. As such, he developed a love of books and reading early on. He has been fascinated by ancient cultures all his life and would visit more if they weren't all so far away.

Based in Brisbane, Ryan has worked as a magazine editor, curriculum editor and freelance writer/editor. At university, he studied Communication and Writing and completed a Master's thesis titled "Fictional Languages and Identity in Fantasy and Science Fiction".